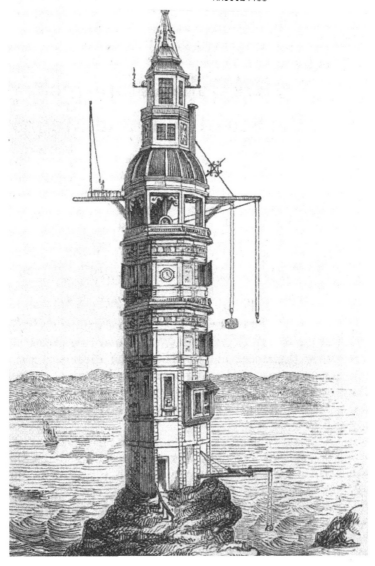

1

Letters from a Shipwreck
in the Sea of Suns and Moons

Raymond St. Elmo
2015

Whereas we believe lightning to be released as a result of the collision of clouds, the Etruscans believe that the clouds collide so as to release lightning: for as they attribute all to deity, they are led to believe not that things have a meaning insofar as they occur, but rather that they occur because they must have a meaning.

-- Seneca The Younger : *Naturales Quaestiones.*

Chapter 1

Letter from Clarence St. Elmo, sailor aboard Unicorn, April 12th, 188?

My dearest K.

Three nights ago your voice called me awake. I rose and followed you through the hot dark, stepping quiet past crewmen drowsing restless in bunk and hammock. They snored, they muttered, they snarled at me in dreams. The ladder beyond shone tangled in a moonbeam. I climbed up from the ship's dark belly to stand on deck blinking sleepily, puzzled not to see you. The deck rocked gently, a stage built on flat empty sea. Only our moon kept watch.

You once told me you dreamed of befriending a kitten, adventuring with it upon your shoulder. When you awoke you searched blankets and pillows desperate for the friend left behind in the dream country. You almost didn't forgive my laugh. Well, my turn to forgive and yours to laugh, because ten thousand miles out to sea I searched under old canvases and behind barrels, frantically calling your name.

Eventually I stood still and listened. I heard the weary thump of rope against timber, beams creaking as the ship rocked unquiet in the windless, waveless sea. I walked to the hatch of the forward hold. We had nailed it shut when the whispering began. Now the hatch was open again. I decided you had gone this way to test if I would dare to follow. As if I wouldn't! I climbed down at once. The lantern was out. It never stayed lit in the forward cargo hold. I could

3

feel eyes in the dark considering me. I could hear the whispering. If I had not been searching for you, I wouldn't have dared go there at night, not to fill my pockets with emeralds.

But the moonlight followed behind like a friend holding a silvery lamp. I stared at the boxes. The whispering came no louder here than up on deck. It just came deeper. Like the rest of the crew, I wondered if people were in the crates. I went towards one larger than the others, and darker. Its binding ropes had been cut, now dangled loose. The top tilted back, not closed proper.

After the sea becalmed and the Captain died most of us had come down here on our own to find where the whispering came from, and if there was any food. I had done it, in daylight of course, and like everyone else I turned right around to rabbit the hell out. I didn't think many of the remaining crew had nerve enough to open one of the boxes. If they had, they hadn't bragged about it, nor shared what they found.

I stared at the crate wondering if the First Mate had opened it before he threw himself overboard. I didn't want to see what made a man toss himself like a coin into the water for luck. But I felt drawn. It was that same feeling you get in some high place, to throw yourself out into the air with your arms spread like the wings of a gull.

So I stood there, my hand reaching for the lid, but hesitating. Then a ray of the following moon twisted to shine on a different crate; a tall one standing on end by the far wall. I moved towards it instead, glad somehow of the change. I put my ear to the rough wood. I heard the faint drum-beat of my own pulse, and the sigh of my own breath. Nothing else. I took out my clasp-knife and cut the

4

binding ropes. Then I opened the lid as you would open a door to a stranger, wondering who knocks so late at night. I still hoped that it might be you, smiling at me in welcome, arms held out like that night at the lake. Of course it wasn't. Before me, outlined in the opened crate, standing taller than me, standing much more firm than me, was a man. He had the head of a bird. He turned it sideways to consider me with one moon-bright eye.

He told me to flee the ship at once, for the storm was coming.

Chapter 2

Transcript #1: Interview with Captain Clarence St. Elmo, resident of The Old Sailor's Safe Harbor Home

Interviewer: How did you become shipwrecked?

I was a deck hand on Unicorn, a three-masted schooner that sailed regular between the China Seas and California. Well, that was my billet. Truth is I lied. I knew as much about being a sailor as I did about being King of England. Less, even, 'cause I've read enough plays to know the words for kinging it. I wager I could make a satisfactory monarch a week before anyone demanded my credentials. But back then I had to guess when was my port and why was my starboard.

Not that most of the hands knew more than I. Proper to a ship named Unicorn, we were an entire crew of virgins to the sea. We had a preacher whose congregation packed him off with a prophecy, and a cut-throat from New York who had been a policeman. A gypsy cook who pretended to speak no English so he could ignore our complaints. I claimed I was a whaler from Boston trying my luck in the western seas, and a proper crew would have caught me out for a failed poet in an hour. But not those fellows.

But how were you shipwrecked?

We became suspicious soon as Unicorn left San Francisco. Except for the Captain, the First mate and the ship's cat, Unicorn had not a soul who'd sailed on her last voyage. What became of the previous crew? Had they jumped ship, died of fever, been eaten by cannibals? It was worrisome. And there were strange markings in the crew hold, as though words had been carved in the timbers and then hacked away again. Like maybe someone left a message, and someone else had scratched it out. That was also worrisome.

And so how were you shipwrecked?

Two weeks out from San Francisco we were becalmed. The ship just sat there in a bored dusty ocean. We cleaned, we mended sail, talked idiot tricks of whistling up winds, rowing someplace with a breeze if we could lighten the ship. That made us wonder just what our cargo was. What was in the hold? Not one of us had helped with loading before we sailed. The Second Mate said it was just boxes. What was in the boxes? By then we were all hearing a whispering sound come up from the hold. We asked the Captain. He said it was no concern of ours. But after that he and the First Mate started keeping guard at night, in turns by the forward cargo hatch.

The third night something happened to the First Mate. We woke to a scream, a splash. The cargo hatch was open. Some ran to the railing, yelling 'man overboard' and playing about with ropes. I poked my head down into the hatch. It was a whole cargo of darkness imported from warehouses on the docks of Stygia, which is my poetic way of saying it was damned dark. The lantern lay busted on the floor. The bit of wick still glowed like a red eye. I could tell there were people down there staring up at me. Don't ask how I could tell. I just could, so clear I jumped back like I'd poked my head in a bear's den.

We figured the First Mate had thrown himself overboard. We called over the railings and swept a lantern on a rope low over the water, but we didn't see anything. There was no wind, no real waves. If the First Mate decided to go for a swim, he'd decided not to come up. The Captain just looked angry and ordered us back to quarters. Later I figured out what really happened, but by then the ship was sinking.

Describe the shipwreck.

After the Captain shot himself we drifted, trying to sail east. There wasn't much wind, but a current tugged us somewhere, like the sea had a special purpose for us on the far side of nowhere. You leaned over the railing and tossed a bit of trash into the water, and watched it head off like it had its own journey to mind. It was puzzling. Was the ship moving, or was it standing still while the rest of the globe went past? But I think we mostly drifted south. No one was in charge.

Describe the whispering.

The whispering began before the Captain died. I think it did. No one noticed when it started. We just realized it had been going on, maybe for hours, maybe for days. The Gypsy Cook claimed he heard it soon as he boarded ship, and it just took us a while to catch on. Maybe. But Cook was a man inclined to give himself mystical airs. He had a way of nodding at everything like he understood just what was going on, and would reveal the Truth when he though we were ready. But he was a proper member of the fool's crew like the rest of us.

The whispering was a kind of sound below decks that came up through the wood. Like a wind, almost, but there was no wind. It was a crowd of voices talking soft, too far away to catch words. Mostly we pretended we didn't hear it. That made it easier. But then it made you wonder what else everyone saw and heard and pretended not to.

How did the Captain die?

After we gave the Captain's remains to the sea, the second mate broke into captain's quarters. The door was locked, which surprised us because practically the last thing we saw the Captain do was come bursting out that door, blazing blue fire and waving a pistol. He sure didn't take time to lock anything behind him. I'm guessing the First Mate did it later to keep us out.

You said the First Mate was dead.

No, I said the First Mate disappeared with a scream and a splash in the night. You make the same mistake we did. We heard a splash, counted a man missing, and assumed he went into the drink.

Describe the Captain's cabin.

It was locked, which was puzzling. The Captain was dead and we took the First Mate for dead. There was no one left with any rank but the Second Mate. He announced he was Captain now. We just shrugged. We called him Captain Grocer, as he was some kind of shop-keeper who'd said 'hell take it' one day and headed off to be a sailor. That was the whole crew, pretty much. Men who just up and quit what they knew, throwing aside their hammer or pen or store-clerk apron to go looking for a ship fool enough to take them. Welcome to the good ship Unicorn.

Our New York Cut-Throat picked opened the lock. He was a tall fellow with wild eyes on either side of his head like a horse that's decided to do something crazy. He had a horse's face too. He was a talented man. He could fight and tell jokes and open locks. He could play the fiddle like a gypsy. Better, I guess, because the Cook *was* a Gypsy and he couldn't fiddle worth a tinker's dam. We had a tinker, too, now that I think on it but I don't recall if Tinker could play the fiddle or not.

Describe the cabin of the Captain from the *inside*.

The New York Cut-Throat picked the lock for our new Captain. But when he saw what was inside, Captain Grocer declined to reside therein.

I took a look. We all did. It was the same as taking a tour through the skull of a lunatic. The quarters were foul with trash and litter and madness. There was a window but the glass had been painted over black. Entirely painted over black. It looked like dried blood but it was just ship's tar. We all touched it, leaving our fingerprints. We couldn't believe it.

It stank. Empty bottles everywhere, rotten food everywhere. There were rats, but they seemed sickly, like they'd eaten poison. With the door open they just blinked at us, didn't try to run. Bones of something like a dog lay on the table. We didn't touch them, but we gathered round and stared. The teeth and claws were all wrong for a dog. They curved.

It was a pest hole. Bottles rolled loose on the floor. The rats blinked. The bones stank. Unicorn had been captained by a mad man; and that wasn't a comforting thought when you considered that he'd brought us to the middle of the ocean and left us there. We took some things out and closed it up.

How did the Captain die?
We weren't sure if he killed himself or something did it for him. Well, until the First Mate was chasing me around the deck with an axe. That settled the question, in my

11

opinion. I took the ship's log from the cabin, as well as a few other items. There was no one to tell me no, and no one else cared. I wanted to see if the log said what was in the cargo hold, and what happened to the last crew, and how far we were from Singapore.

Me, our Cut-Throat and the Gypsy Cook went through the log it but it made no sense. Some pages were missing. Other times it was in a cypher that looked like bird tracks. And when it was English   the words were so crazy it might as well have stayed bird tracks. One thing was clear, though. The First Mate started as a *passenger* on Unicorn. His name was Banker and it was his cargo we were hauling now.

Describe the death of the Captain.

After a week of no wind, little water and less rations everyone began worrying about food. Our new Captain Grocer joked about drawing lots to see who'd be dinner, but we could see he was testing out the idea. If it ever came down to cannibalism we'd have skipped the lottery and just hit him on the head and dug in. Everyone started carrying a knife or belaying pin or something, eyeing each other like tigers in a cage.

It was hard to sleep. The whispering came through the deck and the walls and got into our heads. The forward cargo hatch kept being opened, although none of us wanted to go down there. That's where the whispering came from. The Gypsy Cook hammered it closed, me helping. But in the morning it was always open again. When we spotted land we were barely on our feet, and everyone looked half-mad. Me as well, no doubt.

Describe the land you spotted.

Captain Grocer camped out by the wheel and kept telling us to take up sail and lower sail and turn sail, but we couldn't get any closer to the land. It was just a purple line on the horizon. Some of us thought it was clouds, but if you looked through the captain's glass you could see trees and a mountain and birds even, circling. We all had a look. Some of us just saw clouds. Whatever it was it moved away as fast as we sailed towards it. Someone said there was a current pushing us off and the best thing would be to turn and sail to the side. But then we would lose sight of the island and we were pretty damned lost.

But mostly we figured Captain Grocer didn't know sailing from skating on the moon. After a while we ignored him. He kept turning the wheel this way and that, like a child spinning a wagon-wheel around and shouting out orders to an imaginary ship. Welcome to the good ship Unicorn.

Describe the forward cargo hatch.

I was hungry. I took the lantern from crew's quarters and decided to check out the cargo hold. If there were people down there then they must have food of some kind. I wasn't the only one to figure that. We all did it.

But we did it on our own. I wager no ship ever sailed with men so uninterested in acting together. One man would go down there and stay about one minute, and then come back up not looking at anyone, not saying anything. And we didn't ask. Sooner or later we all climbed down the hatch, stood in that dark then turned right around again. There was something uncanny in the hold. Maybe lots of 'things'. The whispering sounded like a big meeting in a cave far away.

The first time I climbed down I stood by the ladder and looked about, just shaking. There were big boxes everywhere, not properly stowed to keep from sliding when rough weather came. Even I knew that much. Some were set on end, others were stacked atop each other. A few were opened, with the lids put back hurriedly. I couldn't get myself to look inside any of them. I just climbed right out again. I decided that starving wasn't so bad as going near those boxes again.

Describe K.

How do you know K?

We have letters you wrote her.

Hah. Well, K's my girl. I write to her sometimes. I guess she's the reason I went to sea. Maybe I'll tell you about her sometime.

Describe K.

I came from the richest family in town, but no one had much of an opinion of me. I wrote poetry, and to the good town fathers that meant I was a useless half-wit. Whereas to the good town mothers a fellow wrote poetry in order to seduce their daughters while sipping wine from skulls. Which was an interesting idea, I grant you. Truthfully, my career as town poet and village idiot was spent sitting quiet in my father's house, books stacked around my chair for the walls of a ruined castle. I had some other favorite places to read. By the river, and in the town park, and the choir balcony of the old church when there wasn't any service going on. K's father was the Reverend. She would come up and sit with me there sometime, and we'd talk books and poetry.

Describe the sinking of Unicorn.

The night the ship sank I had a dream that my K was calling me to wake. I rose, but of course I didn't find her. I went on deck. Everyone was asleep, even the watch. I went to the forward cargo hatch. It was thrown back open again. I peered inside. The whispering flew out like bats from a cave, all slithery and tangled and too fast to catch the words. The moonlight led me in, somehow. It was a friendly kind of moonlight, and it was a dream of K that woke me, so I figured I would go in again and this time I would see where the whispering came from.

Describe the Bird-headed man.

He was just a statue. That's what all the crates and boxes held. Statues.

You said he spoke.

No. I said he told me something.

Describe how the Bird-headed man spoke.

Well, his beak didn't move, I don't think. It didn't really need to. It was like the statue was just standing in place of something bigger. Something so big it was in the box and in my head and across the ocean all at the same time. I wouldn't have been able to see him at all without the statue to look at.

How did the Captain die?

The Captain stayed in his cabin after the First Mate disappeared. He wouldn't come out, but we could hear him in there shouting, growling, breaking things. We talked about choosing a new captain and sailing back to California or else on to Singapore. But there was no wind, just that dead flat sea. And by then all of us understood that not a man in the crew was a proper sailor. The Second Mate was just a grocer. Not a one of us was suited to captain a rowboat, an' maybe that was why we were hired on.

Describe the death of the Captain.

In the middle of the day when we all sat in the heat, staring at the sky or staring at the sea or staring at the deck or staring at oblivion, the Captain bursts out of his cabin with a pistol. He's set himself on fire. I think by pouring brandy on his oilskin coat. It burned blue and dripped gouts of hell. He runs yelling to the forward hatch and climbs down the ladder and is gone. We just blink. The bright sun and the flat sea and the thirst and the whispering from below has made us all slow and stupid. Each one of us looks at the others wondering if anyone else saw what happened, though there is still a trail of blue fire leading to the hatch. When we hear the gun shot we jump like we'd been asleep.

We peered down the hatch. There he was lying at the bottom of the ladder still wrapped in blue flame. He stared up at us. Well, his eyes stared up. He had a bullet hole to the side of his head. The logical conclusion was that he'd chosen to blow his addled brains out. I went and got a bucket of sea water before the fire could spread; but by the time I returned it was out. That made it dark down there again and you could only sort of half see him staring up.

Describe how the ship smelled.

When the wind blows you smell sea and sky, salt and spray, mixed with what the wind crosses to reach you. Polished wood, wet wood, wood with a touch of dry rot. The cook's fire or a chamber pot, a pile of fish guts or tobacco smoke from a sailor's pipe. And tar. There is something about the smell of tar that has special permission to go upwind, and it mixes with the salt tang of the sea. I like that smell best.

But when the ship sits windless on the flat water it's like sharing a coffin with a corpse. The sea stinks. The deck stinks. Everything stinks, including you. Especially you. A fellow has to take small quick breaths going into crew's quarters, till he can stand it. Till he can stand himself.

Describe yourself.

Well, I am Clarence St. Elmo, for a name. I'm a talker. When I get going I can talk faster than a squirrel swearing at a cat. I climb like a squirrel, too. I can race up and down all the ropes of the ship easy as take the stairs. I took to being a rigger quick as if I'd been made for the job.

I like to get into Unicorn's crow's nest and watch the sea, and picture K seeing me up there. That sort of daydream usually ends with a pirate attack and me rescuing her in a big fight and then making her reverend father walk the plank. And then each of her reverend aunts. Splash, splosh, old biddies overboard!

Describe yourself again.

The lighthouse has mirrors across the landward side of the lantern room to brighten the light sent to sea. I stand before the glass and spy a medium sized man. Young, and skinny as a scarecrow starved for straw. There's a long thin face, a long thin nose and long thin blond hair that wanders up into the air around his head like a failed halo. He has green eyes that stare big and shiny with permanently resident fever. This fellow vibrates like a wine glass atop a piano during a loud part of the music. He wears canvas pants and a salt-white seaman's shirt. He has a burn across one arm going from the tips of his fingers to his elbow. That's me.

How were you shipwrecked?

Who are you?

How were you shipwrecked?

Who am I talking to? I don't exactly recall.

We are the interviewing team. For a story. You are a resident of the Old Sailor's Safe Harbor Home.

Why don't I see you?

You are blind. You are old, well over a hundred years old.

No. I am not. I'm waving to myself in the mirrors this very moment. I am young. Through the lighthouse window I see the beach far below. I hear the waves. I can run all day racing the gulls in the sea wind. I am strong. Blazes, I can roll a barrel of lamp oil up the spiral stairs to the top of the light house without a rest. A lot of men bigger and older than me can't do that.

That is your memory and imagination.

Well how do I know you aren't my memory and imagination?

Tell us about the Captain's cabin.

Or I could be imagining my memory. Or just remembering what I imagined. Who's to say I'm not a young man hearing voices? Listen to the sea by night; it carries voices from beyond the grave and before the world. You sound like just another wind shouting in the distance, faint and untrustworthy.

No. You are an old man in a wheel chair. I shout so you hear my questions. I repeat them. It is annoying the head nurse and the other residents.

Describe the head nurse.

What?

Does she have petticoats that rustle as she strides? Is she a frowner or a smiler? Describe the floor her heels click against. Is it cold chill stone or fresh-mopped wood that catches the sun through the window? What do you smell? Are flowers wilting forgotten in a cheap glass vase in a corner?

There is nothing to smell.

If you are in a house full of old sailors you should
smell plenty. You should smell pee and sweat and old
man's skin, wafting with the dust that settles on clothes
folded away years ago to be unwrapped only for the one
last funeral. You should smell all the soaps and flowers
and polishes meant to mask the slow vapor of the flesh
rusting and rotting to the tick of the clock.

Reset. What happened when the Captain died?

Our New York Cut-Throat was the easiest of us with
the idea of going down the ladder into the forward hold
and fooling with the captain's body. I guess as a
policeman he had experience in that sort of thing. He tied
a rope and we hauled the corpse up and wrapped it in a
spare sail. It was Cut-Throat who noticed how the
Captain's gun hadn't been fired. We didn't want to hear
about it, though. We just wanted to sail that ship
someplace near enough to dirt to get the hell off it. We
nailed the hatch shut again.

Describe Unicorn.

One of the first things I noticed when I came on
board was that the ship seemed to have been chewed here
and there. I don't mean it was unsound. But there were
places in the timbers where something had dug or cut,
maybe with a knife. Particularly in the crew quarters. If
you looked close you could see that the chopping was

done to cross out something else cut in the wood. We didn't talk about it, but sooner or later we all figured the same thing. The previous crew had left messages for us. Warnings, we thought. But someone else had erased the messages. No doubt it was the Captain and First Mate Banker.

Describe the markings.

I think sometimes it was letters, but I couldn't read 'em. Other times it was pictures. There were some right above my hammock in a flat space in the ceiling. I used to lie there looking up trying to figure what had been put there. I imagined some crewman who'd had my hammock before me, had left a message there just for me. It made me mad that someone else had come and scratched it out.

I'd lie there staring up at it, trying to see the meaning past the gouges. One night when the light was just right I saw it. Under the slashes someone had carved a face.

Describe the face.

A lot like yours.

You can't see my face.

Well I couldn't really see that face either so I'm going to call it a close resemblance. You could be brothers.

Do you know your own face? It is scars and wrinkles slashing the original picture. Your eyes are white marbles, the pearled eyes of a drowned man.

Maybe, maybe. I'll take that as it comes. But I see who I am this side of things.

You are just an old blind sailor sitting in a wheelchair in the Old Sailor's Safe Harbor Home.

No.

Describe yourself.

I am young. I am strong. I am Clarence St. Elmo, for a name. And beyond a name I know exactly who I am.

Describe yourself.

I am the Keeper of Shipwreck Light in the Sea of Suns and Moons.

Chapter 3

My dearest K:

I have bargained with a mysterious stranger who assures me that he can give this letter to a cannibal tribe that preys on head-hunters who prey on pirates who prey on traders who trade with fishermen who pray with missionaries who fish for men who occasionally find their way here and back again, bless their pious hearts. The missionaries' hearts that is. Not that the pirates and cannibals and head-hunters have hearts less pious. Please neglect to tell your reverend father I said that.

This path of communication is just slightly surer than if I simply recite my words to our shared moon, trusting its kindly beams to pass my words on to you. Or I might put the letter in a bottle and give it to the sea. But bottles are rare and useful on desert islands and I have no trust in the sea. If I actually thought the tides would bring you my words I would simply build a giant bottle, place myself genie-like within and float gently back to your arms.

In short, I am now a castaway talking nonsense to myself, the sea and the moon. I hear you laugh; where is the change? When I courted you I was also a castaway talking nonsense to you, myself and the moon. The change then is you and the sea. I have traded the one for the other. But I don't really have the sea, do I? It has me. Just as I never had you. My love for you had me. Drowned me almost, just as the sea all but did. So I suppose little has changed. Yet I wish I could trade the sea back for you. If only I had had the courage to dive, I would have drowned myself in you. But then, drowned in you, I would never have gone to sea.

When the storm hit and *Unicorn* sank I spent a day and a night holding on to a rock that rose beyond the waves. It might have been a spire poking up from some sunken cathedral. I waited out the storm with arms clasped round the cold slimy stone, barnacles scraping holes in my clothes and skin, my feet scrambling for purchase. Picture it as the spire of your father's church with me clasping tight to keep from sliding down the tiles, to splatter before your dainty feet and your father's disapproving sniff.

While hugging that episcopal rock I had nothing better to do than imagine the complete edifice beneath the waves. In the storm wind I fantasized church bells ringing and a congregation singing. After some hours I half-believed I actually was on the roof of your father's church, and that all the tale of my running away to sea was the invention of my mind to endure sitting in the parlor with your aunts as they sipped ginger tea and 'tsk'ed over my failings. Below the waves in the submarine church I fancied your sweet voice singing, and it was hard not to let go and join you in the choir.

But when lightning flashed I could see the shore of the island. I could hear the breakers shout like a crowd as they beat against the rocks that broke our ship. There was no swimming in that mad battle-field of wave and wind and stone. So I held on to the spire as I hold on to the memory of you, and listened as you sang encouragements up to my gargoyle-self perched upon the roof.

In the sea-choir of my fantasy you wore your white lace dress that floats cloud-like about you. The ocean depths tinged it green, the fine lace waving slowly like the fronds of some undersea fern. I watched as you shared your hymnal with a sea-triton just like the statue in your father's garden, all muscles and Olympian arrogance. Really

25

my dear it made me angry. You are far too innocent. Do you not see how he keeps leaning towards you as you take a breath to sing Heaven's praises? And if your father objects to you marrying a poet, do you imagine he will smile at your fish-man suitor?

I suppose he would, now that I consider it. I remember when you first brought me to meet your family. Your father looked me up and down, and his expression measured me for a specific lack of muscle and mind. "I hear you are a poet, Mr. St. Elmo," he thundered, and shook my hand with the obvious intention of crushing the poetry right out of it.

Interviewer: How did the ship sink?

The bird-headed man told me the storm was coming and we had to abandon ship. He told me some other things too, but I am not going to share what else he said. Maybe later. When he finished I turned and ran. I knew he spoke the truth. He was just that kind of person. I climbed out and rang the ship's bell and shouted till every last jack of the crew stood on deck. Then I jumped on a barrel and told them that an awful storm was coming and that we had to abandon ship.

It didn't seem likely. Unicorn sat in the water steady as a chair on a floor. There was no more wind in the sails than breath from a dead man. But I believed the bird-headed man. Disaster was coming. If we got into the ship's boat soon enough we might still make it to the island.

How did the ship sink?

We argued. The general opinion was that I had gone crazy. It's funny. I knew what I said was true, but I couldn't make any case of it. I would've done better if I spouted something off the top of my head. I'm good at that. But a man arguing truth he feels but can't put into words, looks too much like a man lying.

Captain Grocer nailed the cargo hatch closed again. For emphasis he piled things atop that. Then he stood on his boxes level with me on my barrel, and delivered a sermon about remaining calm and working together. He threw in something about 'morning light' and ordered everyone back to quarters. The crew studied us like we were two rival salesmen offering equally dubious bottles of miracle elixir.

Then the Gypsy Cook jumped in with a personal testimonial for my snake oil. He got up on his own box and raised his arms high and announced to the assembled congregation the Truth. At least, the truth as he'd worked things out. He informed us that the bird-headed man was Thoth, the Egyptian god of wisdom. He explained that our cargo was dead gods on a cursed voyage. The good ship Unicorn was scheduled to sink in the Sea of Time, and it would take us with it if we didn't abandon ship. The contribution of this announcement did not strengthen the seriousity of my pitch.

Or maybe it did. It was crazier than what I said, but not a man laughed. Turned out every one of us had gone

27

down into the hold and chosen a crate and peeked inside, and climbed out again not talking, just sweating. Now suddenly everyone was shouting about what they had seen. Even Captain Grocer admitted peeking at a naked woman with six arms and a necklace of skulls, and she'd snarled like a wolf. The New York Cut-Throat laughed about an elephant-headed personage who'd laughed right back.

But it wasn't a matter of deciding what the truth was. We didn't want to leave the ship and take our chances on some island on the forgotten side of oblivion. Not while there was still hope of sailing home. In the end the crew told me to keep quiet or they would toss me overboard. But they didn't go back to their bunks. No, everyone stood about arguing and cursing, smoking and laughing loud to cover up the fact that the whispering had finally stopped.

Describe the First Mate.

His name was Banker. He stood seven feet tall and had a warty pumpkin for a head. He had hairy ears and a hairy nose and hairy eyes. Big as he was, he had a way of walking wonderfully silent. He'd come right up behind you and just stand there grinning. You'd be staring off to sea, and suddenly feel a shiver and you turned round slowly knowing you were going to be looking up into that ogre face grinning down. We called him the Banker and the Captain was afraid of him. We all were. He didn't seem like the kind who would toss himself overboard. He'd toss you.

And he didn't toss himself, as a matter of fact. He just hid in the forward cargo hatch. He was under our feet as we stood on deck arguing that night. Hell, he was down in the hold when I talked to the Bird-headed man. Gives me shivers to think of him grinning his troll grin in the dark behind me.

He popped out later when the ship was sinking. I can't properly describe how awful that must have been. No one in the crew could stay down there alone with the whispering for more than a minute. It was like holding your head under water. After a while your mind gasped to breath light and sanity again. But the First Mate stayed down there drowning in the mad whispering for days.

Describe the Captain's cabin.

It was above deck and had a proper door. It had a proper window that was always dark. On watch at night I used to stare into that dark and feel a shiver. Didn't the man ever light a candle? All I could think was that it had some heavy black velvet curtain. But when we broke in we found the man had painted the glass with tar. I don't know why. He was mad.

I don't know what happened to the first crew, but looking at the ship's log he didn't load the cargo in San Francisco. No, he brought it there from someplace far off, all the way around the tip of South America. Most of the crew jumped ship at some port in Chile. Or maybe jumped overboard, preferring the ocean deeps to the deck of Unicorn. But if the Captain and the Banker had been listening to that whispering for months, it was a wonder they could still walk and talk like men.

Describe the bones on the table.

Sure and I will. But you will do something for me first.

Describe the Captain's cabin.

It was early, early all in a spring, I went on board to serve the king, I'd left my dearest dear behind, she often told me her heart was mine. The night we sailed, I was in her arms, and there she shared me all her charms. Ten thousand charms and kisses sweet. We were to be married when next we'd meet.

That was a song I learned from the New York Cut-Throat. He thought it a proper sailor's song, even if none of us were proper sailors. I want you to mail a letter.

Describe the letter.

K never got my letters. At least, I never got hers so how can I know she got mine? So I want you to send 'em for me again.

It is not possible for us to mail your letters.

Who is 'us'?

The team. That is interviewing you.

Describe the team interviewing me.

What books were in the Captain's cabin?

I remember every word I ever wrote to K. Each time we talk you can ask your questions, and I'll give you your answers, and a letter to write out and post for me. It's a fair deal. Address it to

Miss K. King
The Rectory,
Maidenhead, New Jersey

That won't work.

You know, now that I recall, along with the ship's log and the dog bones there were some books in the Captain's cabin.

Describe the books in the Captain's cabin.

What books in the Captain's cabin?

She wouldn't be alive. The address is meaningless. The letters will be read by strangers or her descendants, at best. Or else returned 'address unknown. Or just filed away to be forgotten.

Probably. Doesn't matter. She's alive to me, if not to you. So as long as I live, she'll be alive. Besides, I've spent a long time watching the sea. Things drift. Winds blow. Currents draw. You steer, you row, you cast things to the tide. Soon or late, words and sailors find their way home.

Chapter 4

My dearest K.

I do not quite trust them, but they agree they will start this letter on its long voyage to you. The chance you will read the words on paper seems less likely than that you shall hear them in dreams. But what begins in life often ends in dream; just as what begins in dream will sometimes leap out into the waking world. Well, by night currents or common post, these are words I would have you hear. I should have said them to you myself.

You suppose I ran off to sea because your family laughed at me. Because at that afternoon tea in the parlor, your father leaned against the chimney mantle and mockingly read aloud my poem with his sermonizing up and down voice, his in-and-out preacher's voice, his damnation-trained circus dog of a priest-craft voice. While the aunts yawned and smirked! And you must think I marched from that shaming to prove myself a man at sea. I wish it were true. What a brave fool that would make me.

But I am a coward, K. I did not leave to find a challenge. I fled from the challenge I faced. Nor did I flee your family. I ran from you. I am no angry poet wandering the world, seeing your arched eyebrow in the curve of a gull's wing. I am just a dullard who fled a world too strong for weak souls.

It was nothing for me to endure your father's contempt for the useless fop courting his daughter. How not? That was mere echo of my mirror's opinion, and I can meet my mirror's gaze as bravely as any man. And I could smile and sip my ginger tea as your aunts debated my faults and limits, the length of my nose and the thin

32

measure of my shoulders, as indifferent to my presence as to a dog. I could even bear your laugh as I delivered a practiced sigh to express my Byronic suffering. I gladly played fool just to see you smile. I could endure the laughter of the entire parish. I just couldn't endure loving you absolutely.

Do you remember your father's sermon on *The Fire of Heaven and Hell?* I sat in a pew to the left and behind you, praying to a lock of hair curled about your ear. I wanted desperately to lean forwards and bat at that teasing lock, like a cat. A brave man or a common cat would have done so. But instead I fidgeted, listening to your father's words, and not just because he delivered the entire sermon staring directly at me till those left and right edged away from this target of Heaven's wrath. No; I listened because I understood him so exactly.

He informed us that the saved and the damned rest eternally in the same absolute and consuming Fire. But the saints feel that Fire as a bright and joyous blessing of light, for they surrender to it. While the lost writhe in a flame that surrounds them completely, devours them eternally, and yet denies them even the peace of oblivion, for they will not surrender to the flame.

And that was my love for you, K. It was a fever, a fire I lacked the strength to give myself completely to. My brain burned and twisted in a conflagration of thoughts of K, pictures of K, words for K, all the scent and touch and press of K, till finally at that afternoon tea I jumped up from your Aunt's smiles and ran home like any cowardly dog. I gathered my things and fled down the road into town to take a train to port and find a ship to sail away, sail away, from the consuming flame of my love.

And all that has done is add to the fire.

Interviewer: describe how you were shipwrecked.

Have you ever suspected one more person was with you than you could count? In some company walking down the road, or sitting at a table? The night of the storm the wind played us that trick. I woke the crew and warned them of the coming tempest. Every hand stood arguing on deck, and some were laughing or talking quietly, or leaned against the rails puffing on pipes. The New York Cut-Throat tossed tunes on his fiddle while the failed preacher sang a hymn to the gypsy Cook who stood busy explaining all the gods who could ever fit below decks and above the sky. And for the longest time we took the wind for just another member of the crew, muttering and laughing with us, snapping ropes and canvas and joining in the shouting. But it was the storm wind come aboard, to wish us well and farewell.

Describe the ship's cat.

He was a sly devil of a sea-going feline. I don't know what a creature so savvy was doing sharing a ship with a crew of grocers and tinkers and poets. I think he wondered too. He had a way of perching in odd places and staring down at us, and when we argued whether port became starboard if you faced the stern, or if stern became bow when port was to your left, you would see him shake his head amazed. Just a-*mazed*.

34

How were you shipwrecked?

I tried to get the Gypsy Cook to quiet up about dead gods and the Sea of Time. I considered his words a distraction to my more important message, which was that we had to abandon ship or drown. I was getting hoarse. But suddenly I shut up. I pointed at the main mast. No words, just pointed. All talk died and everyone turned to stare. At the top of the mizenmast waved a banner of blue flame. It shown blue just like the Captain did when he rushed across the deck alight in burning brandy.

It was St. Elmo's fire, the electric ghost that grabs a man or a ship and says 'prepare for storm'. It was my namesake. Well, no, I was its namesake. But there was the fire I had decided to seek out that afternoon when I jumped up from the idiot tea party with K's aunts. In the silence we finally noticed the gathering wind, heard the faint growl of a mountain-range of cloud rushing towards us across the night sky, devouring stars as it came.

We hadn't needed a Captain when the ship sat becalmed; nor drifting slow towards an island that just pushed us off again. But when the ship began to twist and shy about like a horse that's taken into its head to toss its rider, every tinker, poet and lawyer aboard took it in his head to be captain

Some gave orders for dropping canvas and anchor to last out the storm, others shouted to raise sail and ride the winds to safety. Pointless. We were a whole crew of Jonahs and our only Captain was the storm itself. And Captain Tempest steered us straight and true towards the breakers of the island.

Describe San Francisco

Wooden boxes set up on hills and decorated for houses. Wooden boxes lined up for streets and painted for stores. A desert sun that makes you sweat and a sea wind that make you shiver. Horses, wagons, ships in the harbor, ships at the docks, ladies in the shops, sailors in the streets, Chinamen in the alleys, Irishmen on the roofs, dogs under foot. It was a long way from Maidenhead, New Jersey. I'd run out of money getting there, and so had exactly half the population I shared the street with. We'd stare through a restaurant's glass and appreciate each swallow of food just as much as the invitee to the banquet holding the fork.

How were you hired as a sailor?

I wandered the docks asking for any ship taking on hands. I'd heard it was easy because sailors jump ship in San Francisco. They get a fever to go off in the hills and dig for gold, just like farmers and poets get the fever to go off and be sailors. But I didn't get any offers. I wore passable sea clothes but I lacked something defining. Each ship's mate eyed me and privately concluded 'wandering poet, escaped from tea'.

Then I ran into Unicorn's Captain. He was walking down the street carrying the ship's cat in a basket. You'd think it would jump out and run under some horse's hooves but it sat there calm as a king, just grinning. Down as I was, I grinned back as I passed and that damned beast reached out and scratched me. Why me? I have no idea. I suppose he liked me. The Captain apologized. When I mentioned I was looking for a berth, he told me to find Unicorn and get ready to sail.

How were you shipwrecked?

You'd think the sea would rise first but it was still mostly flat when the wind and bits of rain stopped pretending and actually hit us. Hit hard and fast like punches from a man who intends to finish you quick. We ran to quarters for our packs, and dragged boxes of supplies from the galley to the ship's boat. And there we stood while the first waves came over the deck. You never saw such a parliament of panicked individualists. We still couldn't decide if we'd agreed to abandon ship, or had merely brought the proposition before committee.

The ship's cat had been perched on top the stairs to the foredeck, shaking his head at the fuss. Now he gave a yowl and ran for the ship's boat. He was first in. That was good enough for the crew. That worked better than twenty speeches. The one real sailor on board had cast his vote. All objections overruled, the motion was passed by unanimous acclamation of boot heels running across the deck.

Everyone piled into the boat, no one wanting to help lower it first. I'd have jumped in second to the cat, but I kept stopping to stare up at the fire on the mast. Eventually Captain Grocer grabbed me like a bag of flour and pulled me towards the windlasses. Together we got the boat winding down towards the water. I give him credit. That shop-clerk was keen to play captain to the end, and he did.

We had the boat almost to the water when we heard the screaming. It came from that damned hatch to the cargo hold. Someone was pounding and yelling loud enough to be heard over the rising storm. We looked in the boat trying to take count of who was missing. But it was too dark and everyone was shouting for us to finish and get in.

I looked at Captain Grocer and he at me. If he'd climbed into the boat I'd have followed. I was so scared I would have skipped climbing down and just jumped onto the heads of the crew already there. But Grocer shouted for the men to wait, and he hurried off to the hatch. I followed along. I've mocked that man, but I give him his due. He was a braver sailor than I ever would be.

Describe the books in the cargo hold.

What books in the cargo hold?

Were there two books bound in green leather in the cargo hold?

No, those were in the Captain's quarters, on the desk with the bones. Two books, pretty newly bound. One was in French, the other in something that looked like Greek but wasn't.

Shit.

Language.

Chapter 5

My dearest K.

I sit on the beach where the tempest delivered me. There is much storm-delivered flotsam about, some of which is even of use. Not that I lack use, flotsam that I am. No; a poet who survives a shipwreck adds a useful sparkle to all existence. He puts a lilt in the organ grinder's daily melody as the monkey turns the handle as the day turns the globe and the globe turns the monkey. My apology; that was poetry. Poetry is NOT useful. And 'useful' is the watchword of the day.

I have gathered useful shoes, useful bottles, and useful planks. A trunk broke open with a useful rock has delivered a useful supply of paper. I shall not waste a single leaf on poetry. Not just because poetry lacks Use. But I need the paper to write to you. No offense to my esteemed fellow castaway Mr. Robinson Crusoe, but I have no intension of posting you letters on the skin of a goat. Your father would sniff, and your aunts would positively howl with laughter.

My body is still surprised to be alive, and gives sudden starts and jerks in astonishment. Every muscle trembles, and walking I stagger left and right expecting the earth to roll like a ship deck. My clothes are tattered, scraped by rock and barnacle. So is my skin. In the sea, the cold dulled the pain. But now I realize I have spent a night being flayed and beaten for my verses. A fate that would please your aunts, no doubt. Still, the air is bright with morning sun. The gulls float on the wind. And I am alive. Astonishing.

There is a great rock some distance out to shore, upon which is a tower. I have walked the beach attempting to reach it but it is separate from the land. I do not feel like swimming to it just yet. In truth, I don't wish to ever swim in the ocean again. I dread the next time I step in a bath.

Sitting here in morning light, I grudgingly admit the view was worth a shipwreck, though I would have preferred to take the train. Granted I would decline a train wreck in place of a ship wreck. Can you picture Ulysses or Gulliver or Crusoe or St. Paul arriving by train wreck? The idea is absurd. As Miranda points out, a ship wreck casts you into a brave new world. A train wreck just throws you hard against the old one.

The tower is the strangest construction I have ever seen. The overall shape is an octagonal spire. The base is stone; higher up is brick and at last it becomes wood. It is taller than your father's church. It has a belfry and a clock face. At various levels are barn-like windows and winches. The highest point is an eight-sided chamber of glass. If the tower is a light house (and I think that is its true purpose) then its light should be visible for miles. But we never saw any light from Unicorn. Up there they must have had a wonderful view of the wreck. I have waved my shirt and shouted. But the windows are dark; the tower silent.

I suspect it is uninhabited. A dismal thought.

Interviewer: Describe the books bound in green leather.

One was in a language I couldn't even recognize. The other was in French. I can navigate French. A good deal of my town-poet career consisted of learning to say badly in other languages what I could say clearly in English.

Granted, a literary knowledge of French, Spanish and German are as useful in Maidenhead as expertise in clock-making in a tribe of Apaches. I could only read one of the books, but I decided that they were the same text. The French book was a translation of the one in an unknown language.

Describe the book bound in green leather written in French.

The storm wind blew the ship onto rocks. Not a proper reef. These were great shards and angles of stone that poked out just before the shore, like the roof-tops of a drowned town. The waves went all white in anger hitting them. You could tell there were more rocks just under the water. We sailors call them 'rips'. That whole bay was a slaughter-house for ships.

Unicorn rose up on a wave and came down on a knife of rock that twisted through the beams of the hull. Me and Captain Grocer bounced and slid to the forward hatch, both of us trying to figure out who it was who wanted out from the hold.

It was the Banker, of course. We didn't know it then, but First Mate Banker had been prying the hatch open every night. But when I rang the ship's bell and summoned the crew to deck, Captain Grocer nailed the hatch shut and piled things atop. The Banker had to sulk down there while we stood above him discussing what to do. When we ran for the ship's boat he must have realized he was in a fix.

Never mind the wreck. Describe the two books bound in green leather in the Captain's quarters.

The electric glow on the mast kept me from getting to the boat in time. I'd read about it. St. Elmo's fire. When I saw it on the mast I just stared up amazed. Privately I had decided to go to sea to find that very fire. I could return home now if the storm would excuse me early from the party.

Blue flames, and they twined about the mast towards the top. It reminded me of our first Captain when he was covered with burning brandy. I wondered if he hadn't done that on purpose. Maybe he'd decided to be a whole storm by himself.

Then describe any books in the Captain's cabin.

Captain Grocer and I rushed to the hatch of the forward cargo hold. It still had boxes and barrels piled atop. When we cleared things away the hatch was nailed fast shut. Captain Grocer shouted for me to get an axe. I didn't want to. The wind was crazy mad to grab hats and sails and poets and throw them high in the air for fun. And I didn't trust the crew not to row away and leave us. Which they pretty much did. Still I went to the galley, came back with the axe in time to see the hatch burst open. First Mate Banker climbed out of that dark pit like a cheap-jack devil in a stage play. He had a pistol and didn't waste any time; just shot Captain Grocer dead right there.

Describe one book from the Captain's cabin.

The ship was sinking. Rocks chewed at the hull like rats gnawing into a pumpkin shell. Captain Grocer lay dead upon the deck, shot by the Banker. The murderer tossed the one-shot pistol away and came after me. I was still holding the axe. I do not hit people with axes. It is just a poetic affectation I have. I dropped the axe and ran for the side of the ship. There I spotted the ship's boat about thirty yards out. The escaping crew were waving oars in the incompetent way you'd expect. I turned from the railing to face the First Mate running towards me with the axe I'd discarded. Apparently he was *not* a poet.

There was nothing to do but head for the ropes. It seemed a good idea to climb out of reach of waves and axes, although that wasn't a long term plan in a sinking ship. But also I wanted to get closer to the blue fire. I wanted to grab a handful of it. And I did, too. Think of that.

Describe K that night at the lake.

Lithe. Pale. The night gave her clothes of a sort that did not hide her form as she stood upright against a moonless sky. The water reflected stars up and across her skin, casting the palest shadow of light on her legs, her breasts and the curve of her neck. Then that light would gather and slide down the mantle of her long wet hair and back into the night again. She moved so slowly. She moved as if the dark itself was a liquid about her, and every turn of her shoulder and step of her foot was done in a thick warm sea of night.

Describe the two green-leather bound books in the Captain's cabin.

Describe the main doorway to the Old Sailor's Safe Harbor Home.

Reset. Describe the books in the Captain's cabin.

The Captain's log showed pretty clear that Unicorn was contracted by a man named Banker, to take a special cargo someplace ciphered with a picture of a sun and a moon. It appeared that after a failed mutiny, most of the crew jumped ship south of California; maybe in Mexico. The rest had taken the ship's boat and rowed off soon as they saw the California coast. For Unicorn's final voyage, passenger 'Banker' became First Mate.

Not the Captain's Log. Reset. Describe the green-leather bound books in the cabin.

Describe the lilac flowers I smell, the blossoms that waft to me tendrils of perfume from a far country of sun-lit purples, the lilac breath that calls like a girl's eyes from across the dull parlor, a girl who can send no note nor

nod of the head, only a subtle perfumed touch in sly
rebellion against the tyrannical odors of hymnals and the
ginger tea.

Reset to start.

When K's father leaned against the mantle he took out
a folded paper I recognized with a shock of horror. It was
a poem I had written his daughter. How cautiously he
unfolded the mysterious note, as if it boded something
unpleasant within. Perhaps a slice of poet's heart, a
dripping red piece of meat fit to toss a dog. He cleared his
priest-craft practiced throat and began to read aloud while
I sat there stunned, my tea cup perilously tipped to port.

"Damnation," I whispered.

"Language," admonished an aunt. Hildegarde, I think.
K's father frowned at us, made the paper rustle a bit and
then read:

> *"By a dead fountain, on a bed of stone,*
> *In a hall of silence, I awoke alone.*
> *In an empty courtyard,*
> *In dust and morning light*
> *I hurried from the ruin,*
> *Where I had kept the night.*

"Hmm, hmm, well, that sounds uncomfortable,"
solemnly observed an aunt, shaking her head.

"Sleeping on stone?" asked another aunt. "I should
think."

"No, no, I mean the rhyme scheme," replied the aunt. K's father gravely waited till the laughter died somewhat, before continuing.

>*"Out a house pulled down by time,*
>*Through arches left gateless*
>*Past statues left faceless*
>*By wind and twining vine."*

He was careful to drawl each rhyme in exaggerated solemnity. 'Tiiiiiiiiiiiime, gaaaaaateless. Faaaaaceless.' Then he rushed a quick sigh out of 'vine' and waited for the laughter to die again.

Describe how you were shipwrecked.

The wind threw hail and rain to tell us how it hated us, and the waves tipped the ship till the deck sloped steeper than a church roof. You kept thinking *now is the storm* but then it'd shout louder and hit harder and you realized that the apocalypse so far had just been opening strains for the real symphony of terror. I doubted the ship's boat would make it to shore. Probably the fool's crew were already drifting separate beneath the waves, drowned faces astonished. Meanwhile the Banker chased me about decks swinging that axe. He was talking, I could see as I dodged him. Not shouting. He was just chatting to himself, probably about the weather and crops and killing the poet. The storm was too loud to catch words but he had a pleasant smile on his ogre's face. He waved at me friendly as can be. I headed up the ropes.

Describe any books you found on ship.

I was up in the ropes of the main mast. The ship hit a rock and stuck on it while the hull ground to kindling. I leaned out 30 degrees, trying to calculate when I fell whether I'd hit the deck or the waves. The Banker waited about twelve feet or so below. He shouted something that I caught. "Give them to me." Well, that explained a bit. A good bit.

We have a letter for you.

I would have to estimate that as being unlikely. Unless it is notification that I have won a free cruise. I get those.

Describe the location on the ship of the books bound in green leather.

The aft cargo hold held most of the supplies for the trip. Candles, cloth, rope, saws and axes, even a small blacksmithing shop. Tinker set himself up there as ship's carpenter. We had a real carpenter named Baker but he was sick to death of sawdust. We brought Tinker things to fix. He was good at it, and it made him so happy to put things right we'd break things just to see him smile.

The Captain even brought his clock. A great wooden fish with a circle of numbers in its mouth. Tinker let me peek into the works with the back opened, though I had to promise not to breath upon a single cog. The clock had a steel spring you wound with a key. The spring turned all the wheels you usually see heart-beating with a proper pendulum.

Tinker explained that a pendulum clock wouldn't work on a ship at sea. The world's waves would mess with the swinging back and forth of time, until your clock would tell you it was last Tuesday when the rest of the world knew today for the coming Thursday.

We have found a letter written to you.

Describe this alleged letter.

The letter is old and worn, carefully preserved between two plates of glass. The thick paper appears yellowed and cracked. The writing is a cursive ink faded to brown. Deep folds and creases cross the paper like wrinkles on an old man's face. The date is March, 188?. It is signed 'Your K'. The thumb-print of a man is faintly visible on the top left corner. A label on the glass says the item is from a collection of papers donated to the Maidenhead Historical Library in 1953.

Ah, you take 'describe the letter' a bit too literal. I mean, describe the contents of the letter.

The letter is at once formal and entirely familiar, expecting the reader to have a basic grasp of the

identities and relationships of personages mentioned. It is somewhat humorous in intent, and yet conveys a background emotion of regret and loss.

Wonderful. I can almost picture the letter now. I get the idea of it, the feel of it, the truth of it. Only the mere words still lack. Therefore read them to us, oh my soul, since our alleged eyes are the pearled eyes of a drowned man.

Archive Item #47b:
Letter from K. King, Maidenhead, New Jersey. 188?
To my Saint Poet

There; a new title for your collection of nobilities bequeathed from the throne of my affection. What else have I dubbed thee? When you had fever and walked about town reciting Blake, your skin burned our hands as we dragged you to your father's door raving of tigers and anvils. I called you my Angel of Fire.

Then there was 'Key to My Lock'. That was a bold one. I only referred to your intent to rescue me from this chambered life. If they heard it, my aunt's prurient minds would think on chastity belts and the stage paraphernalia of virtue. So I may let them hear it from me sometime, just to see them jump.

I received your letter from San Francisco. I would go there at once to find you, were I not sure you would be gone when I arrived, your ship passed beyond the horizon. And perhaps while I stood sadly on the beach your ship would sail round about the globe and home to find me. Then when I returned I would find you had just set forth again.

Remember when you were lost in the Scotsman's cornfield looking for my brother's dog? I wandered in as well and we shouted for each other, laughing, darting about, happy in the search just because we knew its sweet inevitable solution. But this world is too wide, too wide. Poet, you cannot hear how I call for you.

And if my voice could reach you, it would not be my laughter you would hear. Just dreary plaintive words repeated: come home, come home. Repeated like winter raindrops or midnight tears. Come home, come home, come home.

Damnation.

Language.

Chapter 6

My Dearest K.

This is my complaining letter. You knew the day would arrive. Soon or late the eruption would come, the sleeping volcano of my tortured soul must spout the bitter bitumen of a burning whine. And here is my deepest, most fiery blast of a plaint: though I smiled, I always resented your tedious jokes about my lack of a sense of direction.

According to you I have 'a bump of direction high as a canyon'. It is a strikingly bad metaphor, my dear. And it wasn't me that got lost in Scotsman's corn field. It was your brother's dog. He wagged his lying tail claiming to have rescued me, and I allowed the cur his sad fantasy.

True, I currently reside on an island I do not know in a sea that remains unidentified in a part of the world cartographically designated as 'here there be blank'. Also I am at the moment lost in woods of tall thin pines unpleasantly reminiscent of corn stalks. Previously I was lost at sea; now I have lost the sea. But all that is but the exception that proves the fool. I am sure I left the sea around here somewhere. It can hardly have wandered away.

I was attempting to reach the lighthouse. There is a sort of causeway that connects to the beach, seemingly passable at low tide. The shore is too rocky to give a clear path, so I ventured into the woods. They were cool and shady and I was suddenly tired of the sight of the sea. I decided to explore a bit. I might find water, food, perhaps a convenient train station.

Now I sit on a picturesque rock in a clearing, blinking in sunlight that filters green as it angles through leaves. I hear animals in the trees and the calls of strange birds, and perhaps a bit of the distant waves, unless that is the wind in the branches. And yes, I am lost.

But not for not knowing where I am. I can easily give this rock a name; and the island a name, and the sea a name. Then I would map the whole of it on this letter. K, I am not lost for lack of names. I am only lost because I don't know my way back to you.

I am glad to live and breathe after the storm. All the complaint I have is that you do not share this nameless sunshine on this nameless rock in this nameless sea.

There is the sound of a bell coming far through the trees. It is a deep tolling that makes me think of old bronze shells with patinas of verdigris. I go to seek it out. Perhaps that is the next step on the way home.

Interviewer: Describe a page from one of the books bound in green leather.

Describe the head nurse of the Old Sailor's Safe Harbor Home.

The head nurse of the Old Sailor's Safe Harbor Home is thirty-six. She was born in the Philippines and speaks with an accent that sounds Spanish. She has crooked teeth yet a pretty smile. When she walks her heels tap against the wooden floor like a clock tick, tock, tick. She keeps efficient time.

53

What a picture you draw of her! Now ask this creation what is tattooed on my right lower forearm.

The head nurse says she does not know what is tattooed on your right lower forearm.

Have her majesty look. I'll wait right here.

Describe a page from the Libris Acherontia.

Hmm. What in the world is this "Libris Acherontitwaddle"?

The head nurse says you have the letter 'K' tattooed on your right forearm.

I am comfortably sure I do not. That was a clever guess though.

The head nurse says you have a Unicorn tattooed on your right forearm.

Another excellent guess but alas, no. Which leads one to wander into all kinds of wonderings. Who the devil am I talking to?

We are the interviewing team. You are the old sailor, blind and trapped in memories we wish to explore and preserve. You simply do not recall what tattoos you received decades past.

Perhaps. But I do recall that my lower right arm is scared with a burn from lightning handed me by Typhon himself the night of the shipwreck. It'd be gilding the lily to add a picture atop something like that.

Reset. Reset to query -5.

Now ask this creation what is tattooed on my right lower forearm.

She says you have no tattoo on your lower right arm. You have the old and faded scar of a burn.

True enough, and I take it for sign you are an honest spirit.

Well, the books were the kind bound blank, empty pages waiting for a poet or someone useful, whichever of the two should come along first with a pen. They still looked new, the pages white as fresh bed sheets. The one in French cursive had no author's title nor name; but on the last page was written with a flourish: *Traduit por H. E. Naville.*

You'd best ask Unicorn's first Captain or the Banker where they got the books. But beware your answer. I wanted to ask what in perdition kind of beast left those bones on the table. When I got to the answer it tried to rip my throat out.   Some answers do that.

Describe the first Captain of Unicorn.

He was a proper seaman. He was weathered. He was carved of driftwood washed up on ten thousand beaches then dragged out to sea again the following tide. He was burnt brown but shadowed pale, like the sea washed away at him as fast as the sun could paint. He was a fat man who hadn't eaten a meal in peace for a year. His stomach stuck out under his captain's jacket while the bones showed raw in his face. That sailor was worn from a long voyage.

Describe the first Captain of Unicorn again.

Well, he was fond of the cat. His name was Grayfoot. The ship's cat, I mean. I don't recall the Captain's name. That cat was the only subject the Captain felt comfortable discussing with the crew. He wouldn't return a word about the cargo or the whispering or what ports we aimed for. But he'd talk about the cat. He had a lot of stories about the creature. Some were pretty tall tales. But after a few of those stories you starting nodding a salute with your head when the feline made its daily officer's inspection about the ship.

How did you escape the wreck of Unicorn?

The ship's boat rowed away, leaving me on a sinking ship with a murderous lunatic and a cargo of dead gods. I climbed up in the rigging while rain, wind, hail and lightning took turns to knock me down again. The dying ship trembled, grinding her hull against the rocks. The Banker waved his axe below me, shouting with the storm as though he and it were on the same side. They were, too.

As I perched in the ropes the ship tilted more to port, leaving me hanging over the water. I would have had an easier climb if the ship had tilted to starboard, but the entire shipwreck had been poorly planned for my convenience.

What did the Banker want?

That whole voyage was about something the Banker wanted. Something that he hadn't been able to get his troll's fist on, not with a week of lurking in the damned hold. When he found that what he'd worked for was handed to some idiot stranger instead, he was upset.

Describe what the Banker wanted.

The names of the dead gods in the hold. He'd hid down there a week and had gotten one powerful name for his trouble. But the bird-headed man gave all the rest to me. I wasn't going to pass them on. It's dangerous just to think one of those names. Saying them aloud was like climbing a rope in a storm to grab a handful of lightning. A man would have to be a fool.

But what did the Banker want from *you*?

Oh, he was chasing me around in the storm with the axe because he figured I'd been the one to take some things he'd left in the Captain's cabin. He wanted them back.

Describe the

I hid the two green leather-bound books. I'd had them in my hammock. But when I realized someone was searching the ship every night I put them in the crow's nest. I was the only one who ever went up there.

Chapter 7

My Darling K.

I have arrived in San Francisco. It is a likeable place, if you like noises and shouts and bells and bands and crowds shouting through a constant wind of sand and dust and smoke and fish-rot, the conglomerate force of which assaults you from the air like the spirits Caliban speaks of on Prospero's island, only lacking a proper fairy voice. At least, I suppose fairy voices are lacking. But perhaps they are included. In this stench and clamor a thousand fairy voices could sing in your ear as you walked the streets and you would just brush them away as so much insect bother.

I have made several friends in town, but do not intend to stay long. If possibly just in an idle moment to brush aside tedium, you wish to write some casual word to me, you may send to Mr. Brett Harte at this address. He is a perfect scoundrel but that perfection makes him a trustworthy liaison between a Minister's daughter and an amorous sailor poet. In any case more trustworthy than the average boarding house keeper hereabouts.

Interviewer: Describe the Island.

Heavily wooded. Not a jungle like you hear of in the South Seas, where you slash a big knife to get through vines and underbrush. Perhaps we hadn't gone as far south as I thought. Or maybe that island had its own way of doing things. But these woods were oaks and pines and willows, keeping to their separate stands, covering the land as it sloped gradual towards the mountain. You

59

could hike through the trees passably, but never going straight. You had to zigzag through the living trunks and dead tree falls, patches of rock and strips of gullies. The green light caught on spider webs and drops of storm still dripping from leaves. The air was all tempest-washed. Wet and a little cold, so alive it made you shiver. It woke you up.

And every so often I'd hear that bell.

Describe the ship's cat

Unicorn's Captain told us proudly that Grayfoot's mother was the familiar of a New England witch. The cat's father was an escapee from a London science exhibit, wherein different beasts were altered by unnatural means to be smarter and stronger than Providence and common sense intended. Grayfoot himself was born in the hold of a pirate ship known to the seas as The Ruined Chapel, 'cause the privateer used the stones of a haunted church for ballast.

Though the pirates cruelly tossed his litter-mates to the waves, they kept Grayfoot as ship's cat. He proved so fierce and clever a beast that the murderous crew eventually elected him their leader. Whereupon Captain Grayfoot led the pirates in a glorious strike against the combined fleets of England and France, betraying them at the last moment for a considerable reward. Grayfoot attended the hanging of every last man-jack at Execution

Dock, sitting in a sedan chair on silk cushions and sipping cream from a silver bowl.

Unicorn's captain assured us that the moral of the tale was 'vengeance comes to those who wait'. He had a look in his eye that made me suspect he was doing some such waiting himself. But I have always wondered if the meaning wasn't a bit simpler. A cat is not a good captain for anyone but the cat.

Describe the New York Cut-Throat

He was the best-liked man on Unicorn. He'd been everywhere and done everything. We called him *our* New York Cut-Throat, as though we'd won him at a fair. The rest of us were just the Tinker, the Gypsy Cook, the Banker, the Baker, the Captain. We were a crew of solitary anti-socials, the kind who might sulk silent, or else corner a man to grumble his ear off about sorrows past without thinking to ask the un-eared victim's sorrows in return. But our Cut-Throat would listen solemn to anything, his wild horse's eyes rolling, till you'd laugh out loud whether you were of the sulker tribe or the grumbler nation. That man could make the Gypsy Cook laugh. And Cook worked to be more solemn than the Preacher.

Cut Throat liked to borrow the Captain's hat and shout for us to fire all cannons. And no, we didn't have any cannons. He liked to climb in the rigging and play his fiddle while we worked. The Captain just shrugged as if it was part of the weather, though he took a sterner tone if anyone *else* took liberties I point out.

Had Cut-Throat been sane we would have voted him Captain when we needed a new one. But we understood him too well. He'd have set course for Hell just to see the pretty lights.

Describe the lighthouse.

I mentioned how we hadn't seen a light from the island. But if we had, we wouldn't have understood what it meant. Real sailors know that a lighthouse isn't for a welcome. It is put some place dangerous to warn you. Its light says 'here are rocks and reefs and winds and currents you don't want to get near'. You sail by their light; but not straight towards the damn things. They are a warning as much as a guide.

Turned out, so was that bell in the woods.

Describe the First Mate

He'd get red-faced furious over something small. A coffee mug with a chip in it, or the fire making smoke. That was scary. You suddenly realized how big he was and how crazy he was. But most times he'd just laugh when something important was mishandled by us crew of amateurs. When we'd rip a sail down the middle or tie something down with a big bow-tie of a knot. Then he'd patiently explain how it should be done. He had the face of an ogre but he wasn't stupid. He knew sailing as well as the Captain. When he found out I knew Spanish and French we had some conversations.

Why did the First Mate hide in the cargo hold?

He was afraid. Not of us crew. I suppose we could have taken him on together, but we weren't the kind to take on things together. The previous crew had worried him more. They mutinied somewhere off the Chilean coast, voting to throw his cursed cargo overboard.   It hadn't worked out, and most had jumped ship.

No, the Banker was scared that the *cargo* would mutiny. The statues knew secrets and they were getting restless and talkative as we approached our destination. When Unicorn becalmed he realized he couldn't keep us from the cargo. He decided to post himself down there.

What did the Bird-headed man tell you?

I was parched; I asked him if he could make it rain. He asked me where rain came from. I said 'clouds'. He asked where clouds came from. Every sailor knows that. Spend a watch at dawn and you'll see the fog rise. "From the seas and lakes," I said. "Then the clouds drop the rain and the rain runs to the river and the river into the sea again. The water circles around like Hamlet's emperor's dust through the guts of a beggar."

He laughed at that. He liked that answer. I liked his laugh. Then he had me lean close and he told me a secret. He said there are endless such circles. Some are quick as fire, others slow as stone. He said that even the rock beneath the floor of the ocean rises up to new lands, and then wears down grain by grain into the sea again. And according to him, even the gods have a circle to follow.

What did the Bird-headed man tell you?

The names of the gods. At least, the dead ones in the hold. Their real names, the names you can use to summon them. Which is what the Banker wanted. He had one name already, but he wanted them all. That man was ambitious.

Describe the bell in the woods.

I followed the tolling, expecting to find a village or at least a farm. It worried me that the ringing had no pattern, just random slow clangs like whoever pulled the rope was paying attention to something more interesting. Maybe they were reading a book. I've done chores that way, and it comes out pretty haphazard. I pictured the bell ringer with their nose in a story, giving the rope an absent-minded tug when they stopped to turn a page. After a while I was hearing the rhythm of the book in the rings of the bell. It sounded a haphazard story, if interesting.

Except the closer I got the thicker the woods became. And when I finally reached it I took it for just another tree. But it was a ship's mast someone industrious had hauled inland and planted in the woods. High atop was a ship's bell, bronze frosted green like stagnant water, like an oak leaf in autumn. It had a construction of vanes so that when the wind blew a bar would tap the bell. I stood under it puzzled and discouraged as could be. There were no houses, no roads, no path, no signs. Just tree shadows and cloud shadows and bird shadows, leaves twitching in the breeze and that lonely tolling bell, rung in the middle of nowhere by no one for anyone or anything at all.

I don't think I have ever felt more alone in my life.

Describe Maidenhead, New Jersey.

Well, it's near the sea. With an east wind you can smell the shore. And the sea-fog will roll in so thick it hides one side of the road from the other. But there is no port, no harbor, no coast in view. Just the old town of old brick, old wood, with the old road heading off to Princeton one way, Philadelphia the other. There are bits of forest round about, and farms beyond that, and beyond the farms are all the pieces of the world laid out, a puzzle waiting for the next fool ready to leave home in search of puzzles.

My family's home was big; was old; was cold and noisy. It was shabby the way even a rich house with servants can get if there are too many kids and dogs and cats and a constant coming and going through all the doors and half the windows. When I was ten I moved into the attic just to be able to read and breathe in peace. Sometimes even that wasn't far enough. Eventually I made a camp on the roof. From there I could see half the town. I could see K's house to the south. If I perched on the last gable on the third floor of our house and leaned outwards I could see the window of her bedroom.

List the items in your pocket.

Well, let's see. Matches wrapped in waxed paper. And here's my clasp knife. The key to the lighthouse. That was hard won, and I carry it to remember that hard things can be done. Three coins. One's Spanish silver. The sides have been clipped away and worn smooth again. Found it on the beach, and I carry it as a gift from the tide. One is a brass coin with a hole in the center, circled with a line of Chinese letters promising me luck. I was given that coin by a friend. One is an American copper penny. It has a lady with braided hair that reminds me of a girl a long way back. I gave it to myself, to remember her by.

Describe the bell in the woods.

I circled round about it, angry. It seemed a mean trick to play on a poor castaway. Then a little ways past I spotted something on the ground. It was the bow to Cut-Throat's fiddle. Ha, that cheered me up right away. At least some of the crew had survived. No doubt they'd followed the tolling bell like I had, and stood right here just as puzzled by the fool thing.

It's wonderful comfort when you are lost to know you aren't the only one. I rested a bit, considering how I'd make my appearance. I was so happy to think the crew was alive and probably just ahead, I couldn't feel angry for them leaving me in the storm.

Still, I saw some useful poetic fodder in the situation. It's just my nature. I considered putting sea weed in my hair and appearing to them as my owned drowned ghost. The idea made me laugh, then the laugh made me check. I *did* have sea weed in my hair. Maybe I was my own drowned ghost. The idea scared me so I combed it out with my fingers and headed on.

Past the bell a clearing gathered up the sunlight, like a hollow might catch the rain. The light shone on weed-drowned steps leading to a broken stone arch. A quiet place. The birds and animals kept their distance. It gave me a start soon as I saw it, but I won't tell you why just yet.

I went under the arch, going slow and slower, staring round astonished. I reached out a hand and touched the arch. Cool marble, with black streaks running through it as though the stone had begun to rot. I knew that ahead the worn path would be lined with statues. They would be marble figures stained with sap, bird shit and age, cracked and tangled with vines, and not a one would have a face left by the years.

I continued through the arch, coming to a path lined with just the vine-shrouded forms I expected. I stopped and pulled leaves from one. I found the statue of a winged man, but not an angel. He had snakes for feet. Time and vines had worn the face clean away.

The path led to another stone arch and the courtyard beyond. In the courtyard was a fountain, clotted with leaves and dirt. I walked up to it, already knowing that in the center would be a gray stone lion, his mouth open to gnash jaws on a stream of water dried ages past. I knew this place, because I had made it up. The fountain, the statues, the roofless ruin of a courtyard, were the setting of the start of the poem I had written K.

> *By a dead fountain, on a bed of stone,*
> *In a hall of silence, I awoke alone.*
> *In an empty courtyard,*
> *In dust and morning light*
> *I hurried from the ruin,*
> *Where I had kept the night.*

"Anyone here?" I called. There was a doorway at the far side of the courtyard, which led into a ruin of stone. Lizards scuttled among the leaves, peering at me curious to know my business in such a place. If they had asked, I never could have returned a sensible answer.

How did you escape the wreck of Unicorn?

The Banker didn't care to chase me up the rigging. At least not when the wind and rain and lightning were up there with me. So he played his trump. I suspect he wanted to show off, and who could blame the man? He stood straight as one can on a tilted deck awash with waves, raised his hands and whispered the secret name of a dead god. The one name he had learned. It must have been an impressive name.

And the storm backed away. It didn't stop, exactly. It was still a black circling wall around the ship. But suddenly it declined to hit us. The ship sat in a sudden stillness that wasn't a bit calming, it was terrifying. It made you see the hail and rain, the lightning and wind as so much dogs called back from the prey so the hunter himself could have the pleasure of the final kill. Which was about right. The personage the Banker called held the leash to the dogs of the storm.

It happened fast. It wasn't natural. I could complain it wasn't fair either. In fact I do so complain. It was unfair. I hung there in the ropes wishing I dared drop myself in the water and drown. I almost wished I was back in K's parlor having tea with the aunts. Almost.

What name did the Banker call?

Oh, he called Typhon's name. Understand, 'Typhon' wasn't the name the Banker called. 'Typhon' is just what he was called. I mean, he was Typhon, but 'Typhon' is just his handle. Think of 'Typhon' as what his real name was called. The name of his name, so to speak.

Thoth hadn't given me Typhon's real name. Which seemed a suspicious omission. Or maybe not. Typhon was special. He wasn't just any old pagan carouser. He played nemesis to the whole pantheon of deities.

Typhon had a decent list of titles to accompany the nomenclature. Lord of storms, devourer of stars. He was the monster of wings and eyes and smoke and fire. Taller than the sky, with dragons for legs, dying suns for eyes. But what counted was what he wanted.

Typhon was crazy determined to see all the gods dead. And to stay dead. Every last one of them. He wanted to pull down every pillar of every Olympus, send every god plunging down to Hell or New Jersey. Then he'd sow the smoking rubble with salt and lighting to make a final end.

But not a bad fellow other than his politics. I got to know him some later.

Chapter 8

Letter from K. King, Maidenhead, New Jersey:

To My Poet of Fire and Air, Water and Earth:

The title I bequeath is cumbersome. But you abandoned me to chains of tea and comportment. Where is the one who promised to unlock my cumbersome life? Free me, and I shall grace you with comfortable titles instead. Simple ones such as 'my love'. Such as 'my love'. Such as 'my love'.

I trudge the days in bonds of family stricture and village conversation. Only a single diversion brightens life without you: the aunts have formed sides for and against The Ill-treated Poet. And you would be surprised at the divisions. Aunt Agatha of all people, now defends you as a kindly suitor impolitely treated. She is no romantic; but holds honestly to the rule of charity. Aunt Jane is a romantic, of course, and opposed you previously exactly because you did not court me wearing a red cape astride a white stallion. How happily she now champions the concept of a Lost Poet.

Aunts Hildegarde, Plain and Greta at least acknowledge the loss of a wonderful target for spit and spite. I slip salt into their ginger tea, and they complain the loss of flavor to their serpent-tongues is due entirely to your absence.

Father says nothing. He waits as a hunter in the woods, predicting which way the wounded daughter will break from hiding. Shall she walk the night in widow's black, speaking to a ghostly poet? Throw herself into a funeral pyre of poems? Don a man's clothes and slip off to sea in search of her sailor? What escape does she have but dramatic comedy? It is that or return to the dull cycle of picnics and prayer services, eyeing the next litter of suitors for a presentable bumpkin to test before the paternal sniff.

Did you know when you said my father could sniff with his eyes I thought that mere poetry? But it was God's own biology text. Perhaps that is what Poetry is: God's biology. If so, you were exiled for professing it. You are a prophet, my love. Am I to be left behind as your suffering martyr?

You were unhonored in your own village, Saint. But come back to me, and I will honor you with the worship of heart and mind. And body as well. Come back. Come back. Come back.

Interviewer: Describe how you got from the ship to the rock.

Salt. Ginger tea. Sea. Come back to me. Rhymes, rhymes, rhymes. Socials, parlors, poetry. Come back to me. Rhymes, rhymes, rhymes. Martyr, funeral pyre, Elmo's fire. Time, Time, Time.

Reset. Describe the empty courtyard.

I was dead dog tired. The storm had blued every inch of my poet's body. The cuts were licked clean by the sea, but still raw, not yet crusted over. I carried some food and things gathered from the wreckage on the shore, so I held formal picnic by the fountain. After a while I made a pillow of my pack and lay looking up at the clear sky. The sun-warmed stones did wonders for my storm-beaten bones. It was strange not to feel the rocking of the ship.

The bell tolled its random plaint. Lizards scuttled dead leaves. Flies buzzed. I slept.

I awoke to see the last edge of day surrender to night. The cooling stones beneath me stole back the comfort they had lent. I stared up at the stars, not able to remember where I was. On ship? The roof of my father's house? Then a girl's arm rose up right next to me and pointed at a falling star. She did it just a bit before the star fell, it seemed like. As though she had pointed and made it fall.

I felt happy at once. I must be on the roof of the church with K. Her arm was bare, the pale skin glowing. I tried to think what dresses she had that revealed so much of her arm. I decided happily that she didn't have any such dress. I raised my arm and pointed at a star and said 'fall' but of course it didn't. The girl lying next to me laughed.

I selected a random cake-slice of sky. "The five stars you see blinking tediously in that dusty corner form the constellation known to the ancients as The Dreadful Aunts," I informed her. "During its ascendance it is considered bad luck to attend a tea or enter a parlor."

Again the laugh. It was chuckling and girlish. But deeper than K's laugh. K laughs from the top of her throat, like she is singing. This laugh came up from the stomach, the way a baby laughs or an animal growls. It made me shiver. Where was I? Who was next to me? Somehow I didn't dare to turn and see, nor sit up just yet.

I chose another part of the sky and said 'Those two stars are called 'The Frightened Sailor'. It's just his eyes, you have to imagine the rest of him."

Another chuckle, and then a white hand opened above my face and a clump of dried leaves fell. The rustling of their insect-shell forms made me recall where I was: in the ruined courtyard. I brushed the leaves away but still did not turn to look at who lay next to me. I was suddenly afraid. I remembered the poem I had written K. I started saying bits of it; to me, or to the sky, or to K or the person beside me.

It's a poem about a messenger traveling at night. He meets someone on the road, maybe a girl but she is all cloaked and it is night. They travel in the dark past bandits and monsters, holding hands and giving each other encouragement. When K's father read it aloud at tea, I sat there amazed.

Till that reading, I honestly had no idea just how bad the poem was.

Describe K's father.

He had clouds of silver hair thundering over his head and then dismissed to the shoulders, their work done. He was tall, but with a stoop so steep his eyes were even with mine. It was preaching that bent him so. At church he'd sermonize behind the lectern that held the big bible, and he'd lean way down to read the scripture. Thirty years of such crouching must reshape a man. He could have

74

gotten a taller lectern but feared he'd look shorter behind it.

I didn't like him any more than he me, but I admit he had a voice. He could play that voice like the church organ. He knew every stop and cord and key of his vocals, and liked to vary the height and depth and volume of each word's delivery to an ear honor-bound to be impressed.

Describe the two green leather bound books.

Both were expensively made, originally blank. They were the kind of fancy empty books you daydream of putting your poetry into: elegant lines of purple ink without a single blot or word scratched out. The handwriting for both was the same, though one was simple letters in a script that looked Greek. I can read a bit of Greek, but nothing in that book. The other was French, in an easy-going cursive. I noticed right off that both books had the same stops and starts, the same breaks for chapters, the same hand. I was sure one was a French translation of the mysterious other.

The French book was titled *Libri Fulgurales*. That was easy Latin. *The Book of Lightning*.

Describe the Libri Fulgurales.

I spent a long while leafing through it in my hammock. The lightning part was just a section of a larger work, the *Libri Acherontia. The Book of Acheron,* I suppose you'd call it. Or just *The Book of The Dead,* since the Acheron is the river of Death. Fulgurales was about how to interpret signs and wonders when they involved lightning. But it was sly. Behind the flat descriptions of the meaning of a lightning strike, was the idea that you could use your interpretation of the meaning of the lightning, to guide the lightning. I suppose it's an idea that would appeal to some.

Describe the empty courtyard.

I lay with my back on the cold stones looking at the stars. I was afraid to turn and see who lay next to me. I knew it was something dangerous. Picture napping under a tree and gradually realizing that a tiger has decided to stretch out beside you. I felt as frightened as I had during the wreck. And yet, I felt surer of myself. Confidence is not a normal feeling for me. But this was so like a dream. I have always been able to handle myself in dreams.

I raised my lightning-bit hand, waving it as though conducting the stars in a solemn dance, reciting bits of my poem. Well, K's poem. Our poem, I suppose, like the moon was ours.

"The night was all around me.
A shadow cloaked in shadow,
Someone walked beside me.
I explained I was a messenger,
Bore notes and news of great import;

I wore a king's livery,
A king's own seal went with me."

The girl didn't chuckle this time, which was a bad sign.
I was being dull, like at tea when I wax overlong upon my
favorite poets. The last time I did that ended with K's
father dismissing Poe, Swinburne and Coleridge as "drug-
addled lunatics peddling their scribbled ravings to the
moon". K's father often peppered sermons with poetic
snarls. Perhaps he was a secret poet himself, sneaking into
the midnight woods to attend the poet's coven. I pictured
him versifying before an unholy bonfire of evil rhyme and
metaphor. The picture made me laugh.

The girl beside me chuckled again, just because I was
pointing up at the stars and laughing. I could no longer
resist. When a stranger shares your laugh at the
assembled heavens, you look them in the eye. Even if
they are going to be the eyes of a tiger measuring you for
a meal. It is *manners*. I sat up on an elbow. I turned to look
at her. She did the same, mirroring my move. And so we
considered each other.

She looked a bit younger than me. She was pale past
prettiness. She was pale beyond illness. Her pallor went
twenty country miles past the cemetery gate. She wore a
plain white shift of a dress that wasn't anything as white
as the girl it covered. She had dark solemn eyes. She had
dark hair that reminded me a bit of K's, but longer and

braided into pretty ropes. You could have hung a man with that hair.

But she was young, I was young. We were two strangers finding ourselves lying under a night sky staring surprised at each other. The shared gaze turned us both suddenly shy. Which set us both giggling, knowing just how the other felt, and then we began to laugh.

When it ebbed back into giggling I stood, sore and slow. Then I reached down a hand to her. She looked surprised, but returned a hand colder than the stones. I pretended to help her up but she was weightless and quick as shadow. She stood, head cocked to the side waiting to see what I would do next to entertain her.

I pointed at the sky. "The constellation presently above us is called 'The Dancing Versifier'. Its ascendancy foretells that the evening will be survivable if a poet dances." And with that I bowed and placed a foot forward, brought her hand up, turned halfway, stepped back, brought her hand down. Then one step forward, one step right, one step back, my hand now pressed against her cold palm.

My six sisters consider me an acceptable practice partner for dancing. Each social season they harangue, bribe or beat me into the dining room to step along with them to imaginary music. I don't suppose the girl in the courtyard knew any of my sisters' dances. But she moved better than any of 'em. Even Alice, who has talent.

I would sketch out a series of steps, and the girl would follow along studying. When she had it down we would do it right. She was the kind of partner who moves so easily you dance in return better than nature intended. As though they lent you some share of their grace of movement.

We stepped and turned, in and out, out and in. When we finished I would bow and she would leap in the air on bare white feet, hangman's tresses flying. I have seen the dolphins jump up from the waves in just that joy.

The moon rose behind a broken wall, pouring across the cold stones. I stopped to catch my breath. She tapped her foot impatient. She did not tire. I reached for my handkerchief and found the Cut-Throat's fiddle bow. I took it out and considered it.

So did she. Then she turned towards the darker part of the courtyard, where the doorway to the ruined house lurked. She clapped hands loud, twice. It was a signal for servants. Out came two quiet, solemn figures. One of them was a stick-figure of a man with no more eyes in his head than a dead horse pecked over by crows. The other was our New York Cut-Throat.

He stood in the moonlight, staring blank. His face shone empty of all the foolery that usually fired him like a happy jack-o-lantern that's eaten a thousand lit candles. Now he looked asleep in the middle of bad dreams. The girl handed him the fiddle bow. She did it with a growl to let him know it was important. Both the figures flinched.

Cut-Throat took the bow and considered it. Then he turned and disappeared into the shadows. I started to go after him. The girl growled. My turn to flinch. I stopped, waited. She tapped her foot, impatient.

When Cut-Throat returned he carried his fiddle. The girl nodded as though she'd given all the orders needed and turned back to me. I gathered my breath. I placed my left hand gently in the small of her back, and grasped her right hand lightly in mine, and stepped left, she moving easily along. Then Cut-Throat began to fiddle, and the girl and I began to dance in earnest.

For all his sleepy demeanor, Cut-Throat played fast and wild, desperate to pour out all the music he could. The girl's bare feet splashed the moonlight as though it were silver water. I felt giddy and dizzy, pulled outside the world and outside myself into some faery place with music for wind and moonlight for air and dance steps for a heartbeat.

I stepped inwards gravely, my warm sweating palm to her small cold palm, stepped right, grasped her waist and turned to the side, released her and stepped left to meet her solemn face suddenly turned wild and laughing as we both stepped forward. My heart was dancing in my chest, my breath gasping as I laughed with her and our feet danced and the fiddle played and the moon burned.

Whirling and twirling and winding in the desperate music, I would have danced myself to death if dawn had not finally touched her own pink toes to the dance floor.

How did you survive the wreck of Unicorn?

I clung to the tilted rigging of the sinking ship. I was waiting to fall and break my neck, fall and drown or be struck by lightning to fall burning. The Banker wanted me to be sensible and climb safely down so he could murder me. I suppose that made a kind of sense. If I was going to die anyhow, why not accommodate him?

But I childishly declined. So the Banker shouted the name he knew, the god of storms. *Typhon.* And it worked. The storm became Typhon, and he ceased pounding the ship. It just circled around us, hungry. You could feel Typhon beyond the dark, considering us. He was more frightening than ten hurricanes or a hundred lunatics with axes.

When the wind and rain stopped, the Banker waved up at me friendly with the axe.

"Let's talk," he said.

What did the Banker say?

He traced the axe through the air as he spoke to illustrate how he felt. Like a conductor keeping the orchestra in proper time. That was a heavy axe. You'd have to be damned strong to move it like a stick. I suppose it helped to be crazy.

"I'm all for talking," I said, staring down like a cat treed by a dog. Except the rigging seemed more like a net. Which made me a fish, fresh caught.

"I left some property of mine in the Captain's cabin," he observed dryly. "I should have realized the ship's Poet would make off with any books." He raised the axe high. "Give." Lowered it. "Them." Slash horizontal through the air. "Back."

This might be the time to mention one of the things Thoth told me. He said to keep the books safe from anyone else and everyone else.

Describe the books Thoth told you not to tell anyone about.

"Books? What books?" I said. Well, no, I squeaked. The sudden calm was unnerving. So was the body of the Grocer. I kept staring towards it. I wondered if he was dead. He looked dead. A dead man lies flatter than a live one. He sinks into the ground like he's poured into the earth. I didn't know that then. There was a lot I didn't know then. About life and death, manhood and work and sadness and joy and evil and greed and females and Arabic and knife fighting. Especially females though that isn't relevant to the situation during the wreck. The point is that I was an ignorant innocent wearing a head stuffed with poetic froth. You could have distilled my entire life's knowledge, discarded the literary foam, poured the remainder in a tea cup and still had room for a cup of tea.

"Two books, green leather," said the Banker. "Mine."

"Oh those books," I said. "You know, I read a funny story in the one in French. About someone *struck* by *lightning.*" I was hoping lightning would take the cue and strike that axe. Course it didn't.

"Well, I wish you hadn't," said the Banker sad-like. He sliced the air with a chop. "I liked you. When you argued with the Preacher you had that Blake poem down exactly right. It's about tigers, not the devil."

"Oh, definitely," I said, setting my feet into the ropes. "People forget Blake is an atheist who uses religious symbols to celebrate the material world. He isn't saying the devil is like a tiger. He is telling us that real honest-to-goodness tigers are tragic and deadly and beautiful and fiery as a fallen angel."

"Exactly," agreed the Banker. "People read the words and they spot the fearful symmetry. Then they miss which is the reality and which is the metaphor. Give me the books or I butcher you like a kid goat."

"That's a metaphor right there."

The Banker gave his troll grin. "It really is not."

Do not give the Banker the books bound in green leather.

"I won't," I said.

"You won't what?" asked the Banker.

"Give you the books bound in green leather."

"Why not?" asked the Banker. "They are mine. You don't have any use for them. Also I am going to kill you painfully if you don't."

"You killed the Captain," I pointed out. "You'll kill me dead whether I give them or not."

"The fool was going to do me in first," said the Banker. Then he considered, and glanced at the body lying behind him. "Ah, you mean that shop clerk. Well, he was in the way and I was in a hurry. I thought you were making off with my property. Now throw your pack down to me."

"I see Blake as working to maintain the beauty of spiritual concepts in a world rightly defined by human values," I offered.

"I see you as being slaughtered to rightly maintain the value of my happy demeanor," he countered.

"Why do you want the books?"

"To raise the dead gods, of course," he said.

Describe the Libris Acherontia

The Etruscan *Book of The Dead* describes Elysium. "The land of the place struck by lightning". That's what 'Elysium' means, if you didn't know. A place where lightning has struck. The book was a mix of stories and maps, the names of places, rivers, villages and ceremonies for the dead. Instructions on how to return from death. It was pretty crazy. I wouldn't pay any attention to it.

Then describe the Libris Fulgurales

The lightning just missed me again. I was getting tired of hanging in the rigging. More, I was starting to feel angry about poor Grocer lying like a package spilled on the sidewalk. It occurred to me that if the lunatic below could pull one pagan personage out of his hat, then I could more than match him. Blazes if he had an ace; I had almost the whole pack of cards. I took a deep breath, clasped tight to the ropes and did what the bird-headed man told me not to even think about doing.

I called the name of every dead god he'd given me.

And they came. Like actors stepping on stage. Simple as that. Out of the hold and out of the shadows and up from the tilted deck suddenly there was an entire crowd of personages sharing a shipwreck with me and the Banker. Some were even in the rigging, resting comfortable as born riggers. A few just floated in the air easy as dandelion fluff on a breeze.

I was pleased to see the Banker taken aback. His mouth opened and closed and opened again, finally given something too big for his troll teeth to chew. He turned about in circles staring at the sudden crowd, clutching the axe as if afraid they'd take it from him.

They paid him less mind than a fly. But maybe because I'd called them, they stared up at me for a moment, and I stared back, abashed as if I'd found myself naked in the company of my betters.

They weren't beautiful. They were Beauty. I mean, they were what all our words for beauty were trying to tell us about. Same for what words we have to describe Peril. And Wonder. And Horror, and Mystery, and Desire.

Bah. A poet is as useful as a dog to describe how they seemed to a man's eye. How amazing, and how awful. How deadly and wonderful and golden and dark and cold and fiery and every other spice from the adjective-jar you can toss into the pot. Pour all your words in, stir them about. Maybe you'll get the faintest hint of the taste of the real feast beyond the papery words of the description of the feast.

And yet while I looked at them I felt how old they were, and what thin shadows they cast of themselves. They were faded gentility, worn and wrinkled ancients living in the crumbling houses of former glory. I felt an awful sorrow and pity considering them, even if I shook with fear. They were gods, and they were dead.

That was a long moment, that mutual consideration. I didn't say anything, didn't ask them to do anything. I'd rather have dropped myself into the sea than ask them for my life. It was all about staring into their eyes and their wings, seeing the separate forms of their beings, gazing into the mountains of their faces and the furnaces of their mouths and being glad they were not asking *me* for anything.

Then that long moment ended. Lightning flashed, and they turned to look off into the storm where Typhon waited, nemesis of the gods. Typhon, dragon-legged, lightning-crowned, with dying suns for eyes.

And then every last one of the dead gods leapt over the sides of the ship into the sea and was gone.

How did you escape the wreck of Unicorn?

The Banker recovered fast. He threw the axe at me. I didn't see him do it, I just noticed it fly next my head. I was staring disappointed after the departing gods. They fled the ship fast as the fool's crew. Not in fear of storm or wreck. They were deathly afraid of Typhon.

The Banker pulled a knife from wherever people hide long crazy sharp things about their person. He put it in his teeth and leaped into the ropes, grinning like a gargoyle going to dinner. I couldn't think of a thing to do except climb higher so as to make a more dramatic fall.

But one last summoned god remained. There was a flutter of wings and a big storm-bird flew out of the night. He settled into the ropes beside me, holding on with wrinkly bird feet like old woman's hands. It was Thoth himself. He cocked his head to the side the way a bird does to consider something.

"Well, this is just terrible," said the god of wisdom

Chapter 9

My Dear K;

If you worry that I wander cannibal jungles wearing goat-skins while arguing with parrots I have patiently taught to agree with me, rest your kindly heart. No goat skins, no parrots, and scarcely a cannibal to be seen.

In fact, I have just survived a dance on the island. It was an interesting affair; sparsely attended but quite vivacious. While I had no interesting conversations I did manage to tire my poet's frame so completely that a shipmate had to help me from the dance floor. And if you wonder, no, I did not partner with a single girl younger and prettier than you. There was quite an older creature who dominated the dance. Older than your combined aunts, I should say, and quite as frightening. This ancient made me step through every turn I ever learned from my sisters. A single false step and I think she would have bit my throat out.

But I hope you wondered. In fact I hope you cried out at the thought of me dancing with a pretty native who caught my eye. I freely admit it. If I could, I would feed the fires of jealousy in your heart till your breast burned in sinful rage. Justice, my dear.

Remember how I followed you scowling as you accompanied my brother on the Spring Boating Picnic? He is years younger than I but he boasts of scores of liaisons and loves among the playground gigglers. K, he is a heartless Casanova in short pants, a treacherous three-foot Don Giovani. I abjure you. I implore you. Avoid him as though he were some sort of vampire charming your heart with innocent eyes.

Again I am assured that this letter will be sent on its long journey across the distance from my hand to yours. I have no choice but to trust in the bargain I have made. I should have asked for seven wishes as well; but then I only have one wish.

As far as accommodations go, I am looking for better quarters. The lighthouse I mentioned earlier is said to be available, only I have misplaced it again. Please do not laugh and ask how a sailor on land can lose a lighthouse on the same bit of land. The thing is positively avoiding me. But I have set myself to find it. A lighthouse is so entirely suitable for a sailor who prefers to see the sea rather than to sail the sea.

Until he is sailing back to you.

Interviewer: Describe how you got from the rock to the island.

In a bit. Things are getting out of order. I don't know whether K got my last letter before we set sail. I don't know if you are going to hit me with a letter that replies to what I haven't even told her yet. Should I reply to the last letter you passed on to me, or should I continue to give you what I sent her before that she probably never received, therefore disregarding what I never read?

Describe the correct order.

Hmm. Let's see. I was born a bad poet in a small town. Then I fell in love with a special girl. Then I ran away from her, from me, from tea, to be a sailor at sea. Then came the becalming, the disappearance, the murder, the storm, the wreck, thunder, blue fire and splash! Later came washing up on an island where I danced with a vampire, escaped a burning asylum, argued at lunch, solved a labyrinth, fought a duel, attended a wedding, a funeral and various social events until I kept the lighthouse on Shipwreck Bay in the Sea of Suns and Moons.

And there I am now, in the chamber of light, watching wind and waves whilst chatting with voices that talk suspiciously like wind-up clock people.

Describe a labyrinth.

A tangle of anything constructed with the intent of disguising the path to the solution. One can build a maze out of any material at hand. Flowers, bricks, hedges, lines of chalk, words. Words will build a labyrinth *fine*.

Correction. Describe *the* labyrinth.

Oh. Well, that was before the duel, which was after the cemetery and the Asylum. I wound up in that maze for arguing Blake at lunch. I don't care. That poem is about tigers, no matter what. The labyrinth had dogs not tigers, but they weren't normal dogs. They were the living versions of what had left those bones on the Captain's desk. When I was dodging them I decided I'd have preferred tigers. If I'm going to be eaten I'd go easier knowing it's down the throat of something natural.

Reset. Describe the Libri Acherontia.

I am guessing the parts of the original text were not in the correct order. So the French translation was out of order as well. Chapters from the *Book of Lightning* were jumbled with chapters from *The Book of the Dead*. Or maybe there was one overall book that contained both and had some mystic purpose in weaving the two threads together. In either case, *Fulgurales* was full of secrets about lightning. Whereas the *Acherontia* dealt with signs and wonders, rituals and prophecy in a context of life and death. Some about life. Mostly about death.

Describe how you got from the ship to the rock.

The dead gods fled. Except for Thoth. He manifested as a storm-bird perched in the rigging as I dangled above the waves, as Typhon loomed in the storm about us, as the Banker climbed the ropes knife in his teeth, the pirate spider approaching the web-tangled fly.

Thoth informed me the situation was serious. His authority confirmed my independent conclusion. I could climb or fall, dive or be cut down. All paths ending with a less poetic world for lack of me.

"Climb to the crow's nest," advised Thoth. "Grab one of the books. Then dive into the sea and swim for shore." As divine wisdom goes, it didn't impress. I stared up at the top of the mast where the blue fire twined. I could feel the ropes shaking as the Banker climbed up from below. And the wind was picking up again. Typhon was stirring, bored with the theatre and anxious to pursue the fleeing gods.

I stared up at the St. Elmo's fire, flickering and twining above me. And I decided to climb. Not to escape the wreck or the storm or the lunatic. But I would grab some of that blue fire, take it with me as a souvenir of the trip. All said and done, it was what I set myself to find at sea.

I squirreled up the wet ropes into the crow's nest, Thoth perched on my shoulder. There were the two books, wrapped in oil-cloth which wasn't going to protect them long. I tried to fit both in my pack but there was only room for one.

"Leave it!" cawed Thoth. "Dive! Don't jump. Dive. Into the water. Swim for shore!" But I hated leaving either book behind. Also I hated the idea of diving. It means going head first, instead of feet first. When you jump you are holding yourself a bit back. Diving is you throwing yourself in for keeps.

The Banker's hand appeared on the rail of the nest. I slammed the remaining book down hard on that paw and the Banker howled. But he didn't let go. He wasn't a man for letting go. He pulled himself up, his ogre face grinning over the edge. He'd lost the knife to the howl or the grin.

I raised the book again. It's funny. I couldn't hit the man with an axe, not to save my life. But I was happy to slaughter him with a book. I guess it is allowed for in the poetic nature. Probably because it was so useless. Still, I prepared to smite him a last time. Then I stopped to stare. So did the Banker. Book and hand were now wrapped in snakes of bright blue fire.

Describe the book in your hand.

A common slave--you know him well by sight--
Held up his left hand, which did flame and burn
Like twenty torches join'd, and yet his hand,
Not sensible of fire, remain'd unscorch'd.

That's a bit from Julius Caesar, talking about a slave whose hand is covered in St. Elmo's fire just like mine. Shakespeare is getting it from the Roman historian Suetonius. The Romans were enthusiastic about lightning. I suppose they got that from the Etruscans.

Describe the dance in the moonlight.

The girl stopped dancing at the first bird chirp of dawn. The ruined walls pooled the remainder of night like a hollow on a beach when the tide draws away. Exhausted, I stared up at a patch of coloring on a tree-top. My heart beat for a drum. The girl looked at the sky, then regretfully towards the dark entrance to the crumbled house. She wasn't a bit tired. But she intended to retire for the day, no doubt taking me and Cut-Throat with her. She could do it, too. In the faint light her face was hungry and pretty and determined as a tiger's. If I bolted she would be on me before I made the archway. I crossed looks with Cut-Throat. He shook his head

slightly, telling me the same. I tried not to look at the
other fellow, who had no eyes to meet. He just stood
there in rotting sea-man's clothes listening for the clap of
her hands.

But our Cut-Throat had taken the girl's measure. He'd
noted what rhythm and time made her feet stamp, made
her toss her ropes of hair. Now he began a slow sad dirge
for the dying night. She turned to him, hands raised to
clap an order. But I took her left hand and bowed and
stepped forward my right foot and she had no choice in
her perfection of movement but to step back and then
half turn as I did and we stepped forwards together two
steps, then turned together as I placed my left hand on
the small of her back and we skipped left three steps as
the fiddle slyly slipped from dirge to a laughing tune that
ran faster and faster till we were whirling and turning over
the cold stones.

Describe the Lighthouse

It is built of pieces from previous lighthouses. Which
gives you a shiver when you stand in the lantern-room
during a storm. You stare out at sky and sea gone mad to
knock down your sand-castle tower. And you realize that
this has happened before, and must happen again. You
build a tower, and wind and tide and time knock it down
for someone else to build back up.

And as it shakes and trembles, and you within it, you
wonder when next it all falls down what parts will be used

to build the new and stronger tower, and whether you will be one of the pieces judged worthy to participate in the next incarnation.

It stands on a high solid rock separate from the island. Steps carved in the stone begin at the water edge, else you couldn't reach the door without a rope and an eagle. It's the sort of place a medieval lord would have placed a small castle. Maybe one did. Some of the foundation stones look worn as Methuselah's porch steps.

The inside is all curves and spirals, going up and down. A basement carved into the rock leads down into a lower basement that leads down to a room with a curved stairway that ends in dark water. Those stairs continue, but to find out where you'd have to drain the sea or hold your breath.

I think of that subterranean room as the Dark Chamber, to balance with the light on the tower top. Maybe the dark one sends out some kind of beacon of shadow, so that creatures beneath the sea know where they wander. Seems fair.

The tower itself is filled with finds of storm-wreck and sea-dreck, shore-wrack and sunken treasure washed to land again. The walls of the first floor are decorated with ship figureheads. Mermaids with splintery pink breasts reminisce next to wolf-heads biting at waves long past. Warrior maidens and dragons recall old sea-fights next to eagles with beaks open to snatch at the next wave when it comes.

Long after the wreck of Unicorn I walked the beach one morning and there I spied her white horse's head adrift in the waves. One wide wild eye staring up at the sky; her golden horn be-ribboned with sea-weed from fighting her way through undersea forests. Soon or late, things wash or drift or wind their way to shore.

Describe the Libri Acherontia.
Describe the team interviewing me.

You have a letter.
Describe the letter.

Trenton Archive of Rural Letters
Item# 101C
Letter from K. King, Maidenhead, New Jersey.
188?

Dearest Poet;
This Sunday I conspired with Aunt Jane to persuade my father to read the prayer *For The Safe-Keeping of Those At Sea*. It was an innocent request she made him, in reference to Mr. Blather's nephew who has been consigned to the navy in lieu of jail. Not until Father stood before the congregation reading aloud of storms, thunder and perilous waves did he comprehend he petitioned Deity for your safekeeping as well. So he read, but he growled as he

spoke, which went strangely with the reading, as though he sympathized more with the storm than the storm-tossed.

"*O most powerful and glorious Lord God, at whose command the winds blow, and lift up the waves of the sea, and who stillest the rage thereof; We, thy creatures do in this our great distress cry unto thee for help; Save, Lord, or else we perish. We confess, when we have been safe, and seen all things quiet about us, we have forgotten thee our God. But now we see how terrible thou art in all thy works of wonder; the great God to be feared above all.*"

He gave me and Aunt Jane his sniffing glare. I did my best to smile back, but the words were waves crashing sudden on my soul. Poet, are you storm-tossed? Are you lost at sea? Then I am left here to a different and duller drowning.

The reading concluded, all the parish murmured a fervent *amen.* Even the aunts. It was a sweet moment, suddenly, and I thought better of those with whom I sat. Father closed the prayer book with a boom! that echoed through the church like thunder. I smiled. Till you return, such miserable bread-crumb victories are my only feast.

So return, oh, poet, or else I perish. I thy creature confess, when you were safe and all was quiet about us, we forgot thee our love. But now I see how terrible is the absence of my love. Love; the great God to be feared above all.

Describe the Libri Fulgurales.

Boom.

Describe the Libri Fulgurales.

Blather's nephew joined the navy? Billy Blather-skyte? God help those on the sea from *him*. He represented the lowest taxonomy of the criminal mind classifiable. He broke into the hat shop and wore a new sombrero each day of the week. That is not a secret crime in a township of five hundred souls. He set the Scotsman's barn on fire in revenge for being caught stealing hay. Then he had to be rescued from the burning barn. And who the blast steals hay? You can't hide a pile of hay. You can't spend a pile of hay. It'd take a pile of hay exactly as big as a hay pile just to make a profit.

Bah. Put Bill Blather-skyte on a ship and he will pilfer the ship's anchor, hiding it under his hat. He'll stuff his pockets with cannonballs and think no one notices how he clunks as he walks. He'll drill holes in the hull at night to steal bottles of sea water.

Describe the Libri Fulgurales.

Ha. And I remember Blather-skyte was friends with that pale snake of a farmer's spawn *Smeed*. My father always says never trust a pale farmer or a thin baker.

Smeed used to leave flowers for K where he knew she'd be because the dog followed her, like, like a dog. I'd be walking down by the river where I happened to know that she planned to walk and there on the very same sacred stone where she and her mother preferred to picnic would be batches of his dirty flowers. *Daisies.* Smeed started leaving them everywhere she went, and wearing one in his fool hat to let her know who'd gifted the ground with the trash. He'd take his daisied hat off with a farmer's idea of a flourish each weary time he ran into her by dishonest accident.

I'll kick a daisy soon as see one.

Describe the daisies of Farmer Smeed

The Etruscan Book of Lightning was some ten thousand words, broken up into twelve sections that described different behaviors of lightning, and what their behavior signified in different contexts. Paging through it idly one would conclude it concerned how to interpret the future based on the intents of the gods as expressed in the details of a past lightning strike. But a more careful reading revealed an intent more subtle for being more simple.

It was about understanding the present.

Describe K's opinion of daisies

Each section of the book began with a story. Some of the stories were familiar. Greek and Roman stuff from

Ovid, Hesiod and that crowd. The story always involved lightning. After the story would be a kind of classification of the strike, depending on what was hit, what day of the calendar it struck, and the result of the strike. The classifications gave the reader an idea of what it all meant.

For example The Chapter of Justice began with the story of a king who rode a bronze chariot built to imitate a storm, all clattering with gongs and bells and trumpets meant to sound like thunder. He rode around in it laughing and tossing burning spears until Zeus grew annoyed with the imitation and hit him with a real bolt.

That was a Justice strike. If it hit a man it was justice being enacted. If it hit a tree it was justice being demanded. If there was fire left afterwards, it was a warning that further justice was pending.

But if a strike killed a man or an animal in the morning of a holy day, then the victim had been chosen as an offering for the crimes of the community. If it struck at night, it meant a crime was still hidden.

Going through the pages in my hammock, I imagined K's father up at his lectern reading the old pagan twaddle in his own mock-thunder voice. It was just the kind of organized distribution of retribution he preferred.

Give an excerpt from a book.

Starting out from New Jersey I loaded myself with the ration I considered essential to a man's survival: books. And all the long journey to California I was shedding those heavy paper ingots as I got hungrier and wearier. In the end I copied my favorite pages out and traded the books for socks and bread. That left me with a sheaf of scribbles by Poe and Coleridge, Carrol and Swinburne.

When Unicorn becalmed and the Captain explained at mess how it might take days to catch a wind, I had Swinburne's "Garden of Proserpine" close to mind, so naturally I recited it.

Wan waves and wet winds labour,
Weak ships and spirits steer;
They drive adrift, and whither
They wot not who make thither;
But no such winds blow hither

Which the Captain considered insubordination. He ordered the ship's Poet to skip dinner and report to Lieutenant Swabbing Mop for deck duty.

Describe the book burning in blue fire.

I didn't know till after which book I shoved in my pack, and which I kept to smite the Banker. I hated to lose either the original or the translation. Later, Thoth told me it always works out that way. You can have the words or you can have the meaning of the words, but by the nature of the translation you will never quite grasp both at once.

He often said things like that. And it always sounded deep and wise, like a secret revealed in a dream. Then later you tried to puzzle out what exactly did it mean, and it just faded away to words.

Describe the view from the last gable on the third floor of your father's house.

I climb out the attic window careful not to slide down the roof and plunge three stories into the rose bushes. To perish in roses has poetic charm, but no. I place each foot flat before putting my weight down. Spring wind blows chimney smoke into my eyes, making them water. My sisters must be gathering in the parlor for malice or mischief. No doubt the door is closed, servants and younger brothers bared from eavesdropping. I consider listening down the chimney.

But I brush away the smoke and temptation and continue the careful journey across the slates. I gaze down into the neighbor's back yard. Their garden is rank with weeds, their fish pond a green scum puddle. How dare they complain our hedge is unkempt? I come to the edge of the roof. There I straddle the last gable like a rider on a saw-horse. Painful, but the view is worth the pain. This high up I clearly feel how the world spins beneath us all. I must hold tight to the slate edges to keep from rolling with it.

The main road through town is bricked, cobbled and paved in quilted patches branching off to side-streets of dusty gravel and country cross-roads of comfortable dirt. I watch a milk wagon stop before the school gate. The sly

102

mule waits till the carter begins unloading bottles; then he nuzzles into the bed of violets. I watch children playing by the lake. I watch columns of smoke rise from chimneys. A gust of wind tugs at me, testing my grip on the spinning globe. I spy a wagon leaving the church.

It carries the Reverend Aunts, hatted and scarfed and gloved. Six hats. The figure in the far corner might be K's mother. But I see no gloves so it is K. She says gloves smother her hands. K likes to touch things as she passes. Trees, door frames, cats, poets. From my perch I watch her reach out and pet the cold iron post of the gas lamp on the corner. It shivers in appreciation. Then the wagon turns, the dutiful horses pulling the lazy aunts home. They could have walked. K says the creatures complain it scuffs their good shoes. I say let the old biddies get boots.

The spring wind blows, and I hold tight. A flock of crows flies up from the trees by the lake. They swoop into the sky like a single hand touching the air, feeling its invisible currents, then they circle towards me, commenting on my comic presence in their realm.

Now I lean forwards watching the distant upstairs window to the side of the Reverend's house. I hear distant cries of birds, barks of dogs and the slamming of doors. I wait. At last the window curtain shivers and a face appears, framed by dark un-hatted hair. Our eyes are too distant to meet, but I see a hand raised towards me, palm pressing against the glass to feel its cold smooth light. I stretch my own hand outwards to match the dance move, leaning far out over roses and oblivion.

Really, someday I am going to break my fool neck doing this.

Describe what happened in the crow's nest of Unicorn during the shipwreck.

I raised the book to smite the Banker, busy pulling himself up to smite me. Then we both froze astonished. Blue snakes of fire wrapped hand and book. It didn't hurt. It tingled like a thousand ants crawling across the skin.

"What the hand!" I shouted, and brought the book down on the Banker's head with a wonderful *thump*. He snarled affronted. "Dare seize the fire!" I added, and raised the book mightily proud. It isn't just any day a fellow gets to see poetry put to such proper use. Particularly Blake, I add.

But now Typhon stirred as though given a signal. He growled. I turned to look. For one terrible second I saw him clearly behind the storm. I stared right into his funeral-pyre eyes. Kick me to perdition if he didn't wink one at me as though he was going to share a secret. He did, too.

A spear of lightning shot straight from his great dark shadow. It hit the upraised book and the hand holding it. It knocked me right out from the crow's nest and down and tumbling down, and then down some more and then on and down into the sea and down.

Chapter 10

Dearest K,

I have finally received your letter dated Feb, just before I set sail from San Francisco. But I can barely scribble a reply; my hands are blistered ruins from climbing the ropes. I am now a 'rigger', which is to say I climb into the ship rigging to raise and tie and free the sails. I don't know what I am doing, yet no one on board seems to notice. Excepting the Captain and First Mate, I mean. This is a very strange ship.

You should not put salt into your aunt's tea. That is behavior unacceptable for a minister's daughter. Recall that you a delicate rare orchid of the New England wilds, a voice in the choir of God's Righteous. Put aside the salt and try a mix of sand and ashes.

Everything the ship's cook prepares is spiced with fine sand and gray burnt ash, and it fulminates inside teeth and soul until all taste is dead. And entered into the digestive system it burbles with a subtle but continual murmur that slays the joy of life. It is a sort of magic anti-spice. It shall suit your aunt's tea far better than salt. Salted tea just tastes like tears. And tears are too holy a wine for parlor tea.

Do not dare to ask me how I know.

Interviewer: Describe the girl in the empty courtyard.

In the night I'd thought her hair black. But the braids the girl tossed in the dawn shone red as fresh scratches on a copper penny. I had her eyes and face right though. Pale and crazed, she whirled on little white feet, smiled with little white teeth. Cut-Throat played fast and faster, tapping his boot as he kept the time, orbiting about us as we danced. From the corner of my eye I watched him step through the broken arch into the morning sunlight, still playing his fiddle.

At that the girl stopped. She recollected herself, looking about at the dawn-revealed world. I thought this a good moment to make my own exit. So I bowed, raised her hand for a kiss and she knocked me with a slap half across the courtyard. By clever strategy that bounced me close to the arch. Cut-Throat just had to reach down and pull me through, which he kindly did. I staggered upright. I was dizzy and sick and he not much better. We both sort of held each other up, staring at the girl.

And she howled like a wolf. I mean that. I mean she threw her head back and let a bellow of rage go up from deep down inside her, pressing her round breasts forward and rippling her white throat as it leaped out her red lips. We backed away, stumbling in the dawn light.

She stepped forward to stop in the shadow of the broken arch, glaring. It's a funny thing, but I felt I'd done her wrong. I'm pretty sure she'd have eaten us both, or kept us like the fellow with the absent eyes. But it seemed unkind to just run off after we'd danced so. I got myself up straight, opened my hands to her to show they were empty of choice, and recited a piece of the end of the poem I wrote K.

No more hope of an end,

107

Just the weary footsteps,
Just a dreary regret,
The world night-drowned,
For souls that never rest or let
The burden ever down,
Just the endless night.
Then, finally, morning light.

She stared puzzled at that. She stamped a foot, but hesitant. It was the first uncertain thing I saw her do. She looked up at the sky, and then back at me and Cut-Throat. Then she whirled about and fled into the dark of the ruined house.

Cut-Throat and I ran.

Describe the poem you wrote for K.

There is an old wrecked house in the woods east of Maidenhead. Halloween night when I was seven, the older children set it up as a haunted house. They were the bible study league so they didn't get too bloody in their imagination. But in the night that old house didn't need help to frighten.

The bigger children put on sheets and hid in corners while we little ones followed a trail of jack-o-lanterns through the dark of the wood-rotted rooms. At some moment of panic I collided with another child. It was a girl, not one I knew by voice. Together, holding hands tight, we made it past all the frights, encouraging each other through the dark and the fear. We only separated at the door where all the children were rushing into the open light again. Later I could not tell which child had been my friend.

I never saw her face nor knew her name, yet it was the most perfect friendship I've known. Perhaps the most perfect love. I always dreamed of meeting her again. When I met K, I decided that I had.

Describe the Libris Acherontia.

Beyond the gates of the world lie the shadow fields, where no sun rises, no time passes. No war bloodies the ground, no shouts disturb the air. There the quiet dead build houses and keep fields, tend flocks and watch the shadow clouds drift in the silent sky, the sky like the land and the people, freed from all strife and pain, storm and rain.

There are seven villages in the kingdom, holding all the dead that ever were or will be. The seven villages are built of things brought by the dead. The least of the seven is a city of cold golds and dull silvers, piled treasures before houses of dark stone. It is built of all the wealth that accompanied kings and lords into the grave.

But the seventh village is composed of the memories of those who were buried with love, and brought with them their memories of loving. The dwellers there walk in dreams, or lay quiet in fields of quiet flowers, staring up at the sky, smiling like happy dreamers, almost awake.

Almost.

Describe the Chinese coin in your pocket.

Take it. Hold it in your hand. Big as a U.S. quarter but brass centered with a hole you put to your eye to spy the world from China. On one side dolphins circle. On the other side Chinese characters go round and round. Notice how the metal hasn't a single tarnish? It shines warm and clean as the newest thing the sun's seen today. Not a scratch for all the jangles endured through storm and wave, woods and city streets. It's jingled in my pocket at a shipwreck, a duel, a run for my life through a labyrinth, a sinking to the bottom of the ocean and a climb to the top of a volcano.

That very coin you hold was given me by a special Chinese lady in San Francisco. I've had my share of luck, and may be that it helped me out. You can hand it back now.

Describe the special Chinese lady in San Francisco.

I'd had no money for a room. The streets pullulated with wanderers like me, pockets and stomachs empty sacks we dragged behind. Harte, the scrounger I knew best, was borrowing some of the floor of someone borrowing a bit of room from someone else actually paying with a dollar, no doubt borrowed.

Harte was a strange sort. He had more talent for scrounging than I had. Blazes, he had more talent for scrounging, borrowing, begging, pilfering, riding along and riding off, slipping out and slipping away than a

110

hundred New Jersey poets. He was a professional at
getting someone else to pay the rent, the dinner, the devil,
the tab and the piper. If you had two dollars and they
were your very last dollars and you only needed one to get
by, he'd steal them both. Yet if he'd had a room and you
were on the street, he'd go halves with you for a smile.

But he didn't have a room and I didn't have a dollar,
much less a smile. So I wandered the docks shivering in
the night wind off the bay. It was a fool thing to do, I
knew even then. People'd knock you over the head just
for your shoes. Or shanghai you for a voyage to Africa.
Which makes no sense if you think about it. I spent the
days asking to become a sailor and getting turned away.
Yet every time I passed an alley I risked someone
thumping my head to make me a sailor.

Around midnight I started eyeing a gathering by a fire
down a side-street. The flames looked warm and the
people human so I edged slowly closer. It was like
watching diners in restaurants as they feasted.
Appreciating other people being warm was better than
shivering alone in the dark.

Feeding the fire was a tall lady in a red dress. She
stood out so bright you could have steered course by her
a mile from shore. All at once the lady turned and looked
right at me. She waved me over and I edged into the firelight like a wolf-pup applying to become a domestic
canine.

The others seemed a ragged crowd of ex-sailors and dock hands. Rough, worn and disinclined to sympathy. But at the Lady's nod they made room for me to sit and put my hands against the fire. There was some talking but I kept silent and on guard. I didn't want to fall asleep and lose my shoes.

At that coldest part of night just before dawn, I awoke. Still had my shoes. There was no one nearby but the Lady. She stood feeding the flames with bits of wood and straw and trash. She wasn't a talkative sort. I am talkative, but not that night. No, I sat quiet and stared into the fire and thought about home. Suddenly I missed it so much it was hard to breathe, and I only pretended it was the smoke making my eyes blink.

At sunrise the lady said something I didn't catch. She said it over the fire, as though it were a ceremony. Then she said something *to* the fire, as if it were a friend. The fire sat up a bit, paying attention. Then she turned to me and bent down and smiled. She held out her hand. I reached out for her charity and she gave me the coin. "Luck," she said, and then she turned and walked away.

I didn't see her again till I was sinking to the bottom of Shipwreck Bay.

Describe the St. Elmo's fire.

At the Tea of Catastrophe as I call it, K's very reverend father read aloud the poem I wrote for her. And only for her, I add. I'd left it in her choir hymnal but

112

somehow it wound up in his tweed pocket. I should I have just handed it to her. Damn all undelivered messages and star-crossed letters for cruel theatrics, for idiot decisions of the wind, for accidental drama and comedy interrupting the real story of being alive. And damn all tweed pockets.

I'd been so proud of that poem. In my head the words fit like clockwork pieces designed by Poe and set by Swinburne, with Mr. Coleridge carefully winding the key. But when the very reverend leaned against the mantel and read it aloud in his trained voice, it revealed itself a wooden wonder for clumsy imitation. While there I sat, a prisoner under tea and torment.

He finished the poem off with a dramatic roll of vocal thunder:

"We laughed as our gazes met.
We rested while the moon set.
Then rose as the sun rose,
Then we went on together,
Hands clasped tight forever."

A long and welcome silence followed. Then "lacks a bit of something," observed an Aunt.

"Oh, it lacks fire," agreed another. "You can't just mix poetic props together and bake a poem, for all your moons, clasped hands, dark companions and haunted roads. You have to draw these things in the air with a flaming stick of a pen."

"What a ghastly mix of metaphors," complained another Aunt. "As bad as anything in the poem. Almost as bad. No, the question is: does the poem deserve the fire, or does the fire deserve the poem?"

K's father tapped the pages in his hand, looking into the fireplace as though considering the question. I set my tea cup on the parlor table. Drops splattered the polished surface and three aunts 'tsked'. I was angry in that way that feels like being suddenly sick. It shakes you from inside, and you can't see clearly because you are sitting in the far back of your eyes just watching what the anger is going to do. You know it will be something that you will regret later, but you aren't the one steering the ship anymore.

I stood. I did not look at K. I did not dare to look at K. I walked to her father, still leaning his stooped personage against the mantle. He was waiting for me to strike him. I don't think he was impressed overmuch. He just smiled mildly. I took the pages from him, crumpled them up and tossed them into the undeserving flames. K cried out.

"Now we're finally seeing a bit of St. Elmo's fire," observed the Reverend. The aunts laughed.

"No," I said. My voice shook. "That's just your idiot parlor fire. I've never seen a duller flame in my life. You must stoke it on your sermons."

That hit his vanity, which is to say his soul. He stood straight and prepared to vocalize. K made a soft sad

114

sound that hurt me more than *he* ever could. So I turned and walked to the door. I wanted out of there before I met her eyes. I watched my shaking hand fumble with the door knob. I heard myself stop and declare a last exit line, not turning to deliver it.

"St. Elmo's fire is good deal more rare," I heard my voice say. "I'll fetch you some."

Chapter 11

To Clarence Decoursey St. Elmo, Esq.

Care of B. Harte, Clemens Boardinghouse, San Francisco, Calif.

*Dear Mister St. Elmo. You will little value a letter from me.
And in truth, that is no great concern of mine. It is the well-being of
my niece that concerns me. And I will do you the justice of assuming
we share that concern. So let us put aside past differences.*

*My niece is not well. She is angry, and strong anger is not in
her nature. I watch it wither her from within, an alien toxin her
innocent heart can neither consume nor contain. No doubt you and I
or the average mortal could digest such rage as easily as an extra
portion of oxygen. I have known those who positively thrive on
anger. But not her.*

*And she is sad. She wears away with a sorrow as unnatural to
her blithe spirit as lead boots to a butterfly. She has no idea what to
do with such sadness. Not how to fight it, nor how to flee from it.*

*Her father and mother take advantage of her discomposure to
push her towards a dreadful farm boy of pale demeanor and an
insane fondness for daisies. The boy begins to haunt the house by
day, while my niece haunts the house by night. She bumps into
things, and picks things up and puts them down. She recites bits of
poetry; Blake and Swinburne and even your own doubtful verses.*

*It is not true that time heals all things. It merely erases them. I
would see my darling girl healed not erased. Either return to her, or
by God write and give her the merciful amputation of ending the
relationship for which she pines. All else is bad poetry ending in a
funeral or a marriage; both of equally dour tone.*

Quite sincerely,
Agatha King

Interviewer: Describe Aunt Agatha

Tell me spirit, could a man turn himself to light? And become a beam, might he not fly up to the bright face of the moon and then down again, down the returning river of light to some garden of the earth where a girl stares open-eyed up at our moon? And his light so consumed by her eyes, will he and she not be united?

Tell me it is so, spirit, and I will throw myself this night into the fire of the light house and burn away everything within me but the light of my love. Give me only the mercy of some hope for its journey. But what do spirits know of mercy? You are only words. You lack mind. You lack heart. There is no face beyond your words.

No. I will wait and watch from this tower; and she from hers. I will pace, and talk, and feed the fire, and watch the storm, recite my verses. That she will do the same is all my hope. If we cannot be together, still we will dance the steps of longing together.

Reset. Describe Aunt Agatha

Tall; till you realized she was looking up at you; usually with a disapproving look. At me she mellowed disapproval with a leaden leaven of amusement. For some reason my slight build fascinated her. She would puff out her withered lips and blow at me, watching to see if I was pushed backwards by the blast.

Polite; till you realized it was all only mockery. All her conversation was verbal fencing and bludgeoning by indirection, spiced with the sly insertion of a knife-edged insult.

Humorless; till you saw her hold a mouse by the tail and chase the cat about the house. That cat was dreadful afraid of mice. So were her sisters. Agatha's sisters, I mean. Not the cat's sisters. Agatha chivied them all from room to room with the poor rodent dangling, cats and aunts screaming before her as though she held Medusa's head. K laughed, but I sat poetically astonished to stone.

I shouldn't have been. Agatha was K's favorite aunt, after all. There had to be more inside the old biddy than ginger tea and spite.

Describe the Libris Acherontia.

No. *You* describe the Libris Acherontia.

The Libris Acherontia is one of several lost religious texts attributed to the Etruscans by classical historians. The contents are supposed to deal with the afterlife. No versions are known past the first century A.D. If any copy remains, it might well be untranslatable as the Etruscan language itself has essentially been lost.

Excellent. Now describe why you *want* the Libris Acherontia.

You have a letter.

I pat that petty distraction on the head, in patronizing charity for its humble failure. Tell me who you are and why you want the Libris Acherontia.

Dearest Clarence.

Yesterday I was suddenly overcome with the tedium of life without a poet. How does anyone get by without a poet? And why should they want to get by without a poet? For a minister's daughter to endure, how utterly necessary is a poet. Someone must be tasked to charm us, incite us, amuse us, to take a lock of our tangled hair and describe it as an icon of worship.

Poet-lacking, I had no refuge but theology. I went into the choir balcony and set about to create you. If God can bring forth a world, can not a heart created by God bring forth a poet? What blasted use is a heart if it can't?

I sat with my copy of Blake, of whom Father approves for the wrong reasons. I opened to the poem you and I favor for the correct reasons. I wanted to argue with you furiously about it. Then we could fall silent, staring at the floor. Then we could turn to each other at the same moment prepared to

apologize. Then our shamed eyes could speak,
forgoing idiot words. Then and then and oh! and
then.

I decided to begin with your smell. I closed
my eyes and summoned. When you have been up in
your attic lair writing and reading and muttering to
yourself you descend to our mortal plain with a
frankincense mix of candle wax, kerosene, sour
sweat and old book dust. I drew a deep breath and
inhaled the remembered fragrance.

Next I moved to the feel of your presence.
When you sit close as you dare, you give a wonderful
fire-side warmth. You tremble slightly, caught up in
the words of a poem or staring at my feet. Or at my
bosom, because dear boy you do that when you think
I don't see but I do.

Ah, and then for the blessed sound of you; the
rhythm of your breath, the shuffle of your boots.
You're a bit of an asthmatic. And you fidget
dreadfully. Now I begin to hear you leaf through the
pages of the book, muttering the titles, crinkling the
pages. And then to my joy I hear you read aloud,
softly,

> "I went to the Garden of Love,
> And saw what I never had seen:
> A Chapel was built in the midst,
> Where I used to play on the green. "

You give the words no false drama. You just state them as though describing a trip to the store. You went to the Garden of Love, you saw something there, you came back to tell me.

Now I imagine your touch. Soft fingertips brushing mine as we share the book. Your foot moves closer to my foot, your arm brushes my arm. My eyes are closed as I wait for you to lean over to press your lips to mine. And then I do feel your kiss, and for a moment I tremble with happiness, and open my eyes to meet yours. Where did you go?

It would appear only Deity can make a poet. Then let Him return mine to me, and soon; or else this absence will unmake me.

Describe the Libris Fulgurales

Leave me alone.

Reset. Describe the Libris Fulgurales

Lightning struck the king of Salmonia. The seven priestly augurs gathered about the still-smoking remains of the king, to assign the cause of the strike to one of three sacraments: Justice, Chance, or Omen.

The youngest augur declared "It can be no simpler. The King's bronze chariot dragged chains of kettles and pots that clattered theatrical thunder as he rode by. He tossed torches in the air to imitate lightning. He declared himself to be Zeus. Heaven struck him for daring to imitate the gods."

121

But an older augur considered. "Every time I lay with my wife, plow my fields, eye a shop girl, step on an ant, light a fire or hunt in the woods, I imitate the gods. When my wife weaves, gives birth, sings in the bath, serves me wine or berates me for eyeing the shop girl then she also imitates the gods. Where ever we turn, there they are before us. Why are we not struck down as well?"

An augur even older shook his cowled head. "It is not the act, but the motive of the act. Were you to declare yourself Zeus as you stamped upon the ant, then you would not be imitating Zeus; you would be replacing Zeus. Such pride draws lightning."

That seemed wise, and all were silent till the oldest Augur spoke. "Yes. Pride draws lightning. And this man was struck down for Pride. But not his own. When a man truly takes the place of another, whether it be god or man, then he takes upon himself the crimes of that other. This king faithfully imitated Zeus, offering himself openly, and the offering was accepted. Zeus struck this man down, in payment for Zeus's own pride."

And so the bolt was declared a strike of Justice.

Describe the Libris Fulgurales

Asclepius the Healer was struck dead by a bolt of lightning. The augurs gathered about the body. "This was an act of the sky's wrath," said one. "Heaven struck him down for the hubris of deciding who may live and who must die."

"Here lies a man who healed the sick," said a second augur. "Surely no condemnation comes from Heaven for acts of goodness. We must acknowledge there is no meaning in his death at all. This was the dice throw of Chance."

122

"It cannot be justice to strike down a man for the act of healing," said a third. "Nor can it be chance to slay the mortal who raised others from death. Asclepius was of great worth, divine parentage, and favored by the gods. Yet here he lies dead. Therefore it must be an Omen."

"But of what?" asked the first Augur. "That we mortals will perish despite our doctors?"

"No," said the third augur thoughtfully. "That we mortals will perish despite our gods."

And so the bolt was declared a bolt of Omen.

Describe the Libris Fulgurales

Jove wields the thunder bolt. Vulcan forges the bolt. Before Vulcan creates a bolt, he must first consult the three Fates. Clotho declares the cause of the strike. Lachesis declares the target of the strike. Alecto decides the result of the strike.

Hermes carries the request for the bolt; returns with the bolt. But before he hands it to Jove he lays it upon the table of Tyche, goddess of Fortune. And she whispers something to the bolt so that one out of every seven will go astray. Because even the gods smile when a story takes an unexpected turn; and even the gods frown when victory seems too certain.

And when lightning strikes, then the mortals known as augurs are summoned to declare the holy meaning. Thus the augurs stood about the body of a stray dog.

"This is the cur that bit the High Priest," said the first. "Thus heaven's justice falls upon the wicked."

"But the High Priest kicked it as it begged," said a second. "Justice would strike the priest and spare the dog. Yet note its lame back leg. This strike is an omen of warning for one who limps."

"And the High Priest limps," said a third. "Surely the Omen is for him, to warn him of stray dogs."

"He limps because this very dog bit him," argued a fourth. "Without the omen he would not need the omen's warning."

The augurs considered in silence. Finally the eldest Augur spoke. "Mysterious are the ways of the sky. And sufficient mystery becomes the realm of Chaos."

And so the strike was declared a bolt of Chance.

Describe how you got from the ship to the rock.

Typhon's lightning knocked me out of the crow's nest. I fell for a day and a night, maybe two. At last I hit the ocean waves. I hit so hard I supposed I'd landed on rock. But I kept sinking deeper, down towards the bottom of Shipwreck Bay.

It was quiet below the storm. No wind, no thunder, no crashing of wave. Just a solid and peaceful darkness flowing past like a cold wind. A dark just slightly illuminated by the light from my burning hand.

The electro-static phenomenon known as St. Elmo's fire cannot occur under water.

I held my hand up above my head as though it were a torch. Things in the sea-dark shown blue around me as I sank. I passed flotsam and fish, and the face of a drowned

124

man. Then the side of a ship. For a moment I had the strange fancy that I had fallen all the way through the bottom of the ocean to come out at the top of the sky only to plunge past the side of Unicorn again. I would fall forever in such a circle. But the ship I glimpsed was a green-rotted sea-fern garden, with the figurehead of a fat man blowing a conch horn. I sank past it and down, down towards a fire on the floor of the bay.

A tall figure in a red dress stood beside the sea-bottom fire, feeding it bits of storm-wrack. It was the Chinese lady I had met in San Francisco. She who gave me my lucky Chinese coin. The lady looked up at me and smiled. I knew her name then, but I won't say it. Call her Matsu. She hadn't been one of Unicorn's cargo of dead gods. She was one of the still living ones. Think of that.

The drowned man sank down past me and settled by the fire. It was the ship's Preacher.

Describe the ship's Preacher.

He's difficult to put down in words. If I say he is solemn, what I mean is that he wears an undertaker's face and nods wise and slow in time to his own words. If I say he is humorless and stern, what I mean is that he twists his mouth in a lemon-bite to keep from laughing when our New York Cut-Throat walks on his hands like a circus monkey.

Medium size and medium age and medium opinioned; his entire congregation of thirty souls and two lawyers came to service one Sunday declaring the same dream of him going to sea. First the deacon and then the choir and at last even a child of five stood up at church and described their vision of him at sea, fishing for men. Or so the Preacher proudly claimed. We believed him absolutely. You never met a man less inclined to tell an interesting lie.

We believed *him*; we just didn't believe *them*. We figured his congregation made it up to send him packing. First Sunday of our voyage, the Captain of Unicorn allowed the Preacher to do service for the ship. Merciful thunder, it ran for weary hours. At the welcome end the entire fool's crew shared a common vision that he was mysteriously pitched overboard.

Describe the ship's Preacher again.

He struggled faithfully to be solemn, wise and humorless. But I liked him fine. He wore his solemnity not because he admired the fit in the mirror, but because he thought a solemn manner was the proper cloth for a holy office. He spoke slow and wise not because he fancied himself wise, but because he believed he'd been given something that deserved the tone of wisdom. He liked to laugh as much as any man; and if he kept a strict guard on his laughter it was no different from an honest believer fasting from any other food.

He didn't deserve to be sent off by dreams just to drown.

126

Describe the Lady in the red dress.

Her name is Matsu. One of her names. She is the patron goddess of sailors and light-house keepers. Chinese, I believe, though she's happy to give a helpful warning to any ship no matter the flag they fly. I saw figures of her in San Francisco. She wore that bright dress the better to be seen by ships. She'll stand on some dangerous shore and wave her red-clad arms. Sailors see and know to steer clear, same as if she was a lighthouse burning a silk red fire.

Describe the Lady in the red dress again.

Matsu had a way of moving that was in a different time and rhythm to anyone else. It was her own time she lived by, her own space she moved through. Just to describe how the sleeve of her dress flowed through the dark water as she fed the fire, you'd want a team of mathematicians to formulate the essentials of the motion. A poet couldn't do it. Well, not a bad one anyway. As I sank down she smiled up at me, but with a wry, disapproving face.

"You haven't used your luck for much yet," she said.

I was on fire while drowning from a ship wreck. I considered arguing whether I'd had any luck to use. While I weighed my excuses she turned to the drowned Preacher and whispered something private to him. It

127

surprised me a bit when he turned and whispered something back. I felt a bit left out.

Ah, I admit it. I felt jealous. She was my friend first.

Or better said, I was the receiver of her charity first. But now it was the Preacher's turn. Matsu put a hand to his drifting body and pushed him gently into the fire. His thin hair waved like sea weed, his limbs shuddered. His clothes burned away at once, and then his drowned remains did the same. In his place there was a great black porpoise. It gave a twist of its back that shot it out the fire and round about the fire, circling Matsu. I laughed, Matsu laughed, and so did the Preacher-porpoise.

Then he spun towards me, grabbed my collar in his toothy snout and began hauling me up towards the surface.

Chapter 12

Letter from the archives of the Maidenhead Historical Society, Maidenhead New Jersey.

Dear Miss King:

I am well. My ship has reached Singapore, and will continue further east when we have concluded our trading. No doubt it was the devout prayers of your kind family to a harkening heaven that brought us through every storm. I write to thank you, and them.

And I write to thank you for the toleration of my bumbling presence by your genteel side. Your memory will be an eternal comfort to me as I wander. But with my thanks, I send the regret that we can never be together except in the remembered joy of past friendship.

From the tops of ships masts one sees more of the small place we have in this life. And I see there is no place for me by your side. I have set myself a course that will wind about the world, and I shall do so alone. Your father was wiser than I supposed him; and kinder than I allowed myself to think him.

So live, and laugh, and forget your comic poet suitor.
Sincerely,
Clarence Decoursey St. Elmo

Interviewer: Describe the Libris Acherontia

What the hell?

Describe the letter.

I never wrote it. Who composed that fool drivel?
'Comic poet suitor'? Wiser than I supposed him? And
signed 'Sincerely'? From me, to her?

Describe.

'Harkening Heaven'? That is K's father. Falsifying a
letter. From me. To her. God knows whether she
believed it. I won't have it. I can't have this. I will return
to Maidenhead. I will bring his church down upon his
holy silver head. I will stuff the words of his lie into his
mouth and light them with the fire given me by Typhon
himself. I will drown him in ginger tea and I will skin his
corpse and etch poems of Blake upon the bleeding
parchment and nail it to the door of his parlor. I will. I
will. I will.

Describe Typhon.

He was angry. Not just 'very' angry. He was long past
words adding an extra tea-spoon of emphasis. Nor
'extremely', 'incredibly', 'heaping', or 'truly' much less any
understated 'rather'. No, Typhon was angry; and his
anger was sufficient unto the day that he could be calm
and friendly about it all.

Your usual metaphors of rage are storms and lightning
and volcanos and dragons. But Typhon was born of those
things. He'd long left his child toys behind. His
expression of anger was a patient smile and a kindly
regard, and unless you looked into his eyes you could be

fooled into thinking he was knocking on the door to deliver eggs. But it would be dragon's eggs he handed you, lying in a basket wove of lightning. And his eyes were dying suns.

Typhon was determination entirely separated from the possibility of the consideration of compromise. The longer I wandered the world, the more I understood just why those old gods ran from him. They were more powerful. He was more determined.

How did you get from the ship to the rock?

The porpoise that had been the Preacher dragged me up to the surface. The problem was, the surface wasn't a sane place at the time. It was a crazed battle-field of wind and wave and rock. When he got my head above water I realized I'd been drowning without properly noticing. Now I gasped in some air and some wind and some wave, which helped some but hurt plenty.

The battle grew worse as we approached shore. I couldn't help my rescue much. The porpoise-preacher settled on pushing me and dragging me to the lee-ward side of a big rock where I was able to pull myself up. It narrowed as it rose, like the spire of a church. I climbed up high enough to be out of the reach of half the waves and none of the rain. And there I clung for what seemed like days, till the final act of the storm-theatre.

How did you get from the rock to the shore?

Unicorn tore to pieces on the rips of Shipwreck Bay. I wept to see it happen. It hadn't been any kind of home to me. But I hadn't been looking for a home, any more than the rest of the fool's crew. I'd sought a purpose and found a job. And a job is a purpose. I bet a failed poet knows that better than most.

Half my days and all my nights on Unicorn I just wanted to leave behind her stink of dirty sailor, dry rot and mad mystery. But separate from her, watching as she died, I saw at last the delicate crafted wonder she'd been. A three-masted schooner of a lady, with sails for wings meant to fly across waves. It wrenched the heart to see such a miracle come to grief, caught with the wrong cargo in the wrong winds in the wrong seas with so completely the wrong crew.

Since I'd met the Preacher floating at the bottom of the bay I figured the rest of the crew were just as drowned. For sure they hadn't known how to handle the ship's boat, not through storm waves and breakers. I hoped Matsu would look after their remains. I wondered if I could distinguish Cut-Throat turned to a porpoise, as opposed to say the Gypsy Cook as a dolphin. Honest, I've never been able to remember the difference.

I had a powerful and repeated fear that I would feel a shiver and I would turn slowly around to see the Banker climbing up my rock, ready to continue the discussion and the murder. But there was no sign of him, not so much as his ogre's face floating wave-tossed and white.

The storm burned for days, for months and years. It roared past the centuries into the millennia. Far beyond the world's ending and the sun's final flicker there I still clung to that bit of rock. I suspect it is still going on. I am still there, and everything that happened later is just me talking to myself as I hold to a forgotten moment in the Sea of Suns and Moons.

I was hurting, and close to crazy as would count in court. My right arm was burned along a stretch from finger tips to elbow. Sometimes the hand glowed. I heard voices in the storm, saw faces in the waves. I recited bits of poetry then argued its meaning with the wind. Sometimes I glimpsed the town of Maidenhead down below the waves, as if I was up on the roof of the church. The people in the streets pointed up at me astonished.

So I did not startle when a fleet of caskets began sailing solemnly past my rock, though the sight was as eerie and unexpected as anything I ever heard tell on sea or shore or dream. It was just the finale of the long unnatural night. Yet to describe it sensibly, it was only the wrecked ship's cargo floating adrift, following the mindless push of wind and waves.

I slid down the rock and jumped on the last box to float past, and I rode it pretty much to shore.

Describe reaching the shore.

Waves pushed me off the low floating crate. Waves threw me onto a spit of sand and stone. Then at last, waves left me alone. I crawled up to some magic boundary where rivulets of rain met the highest edge of sea, and there I lay. I suppose I slept. Imagine that.

I came back to myself as Adam, studying curiously a new world composed of sky, earth and me. The sky was a blue bowl of washed air above. Green woods were a curtain behind, the quiet sea a gray-blue plain before. Pain and weariness and hunger and thirst contained inside. The world and I dawned together; the world into light, and me into the awareness that I was alive.

Inside the tree line I made a damp start of a camp. There was plenty to scavenge along the shore. Bits of wood and rope and cloth, fragments of food stores, fragments of forgotten gods. No sign of the fool's crew, but I held out hope for the ship's cat after I spotted some paw prints in the sand. If there was ever a likely survivor it was that feline. Probably he was already making himself king of the island, perched and purring on an island girl's lap.

Lacking his savvy, I sat on a rock and stared at the light house in the distance. I wrote a letter to K. I wanted her to know I was alive. I so wanted her to know.

I took it pretty easy that first day. It would have been perfect if I could have started a fire. I had some matches but they needed drying out. I had a blanket but it needed drying out. But the night wind was warm and kind as if in apology for the outburst of the previous evening.

The next morning I went seeking the light house and wandered into the woods. There I got lost, of course, and headed towards that bell tolling so kindly to warn people not to go near it.

Describe the girl with braids like rope.

Cut-Throat and I fled through the trees, sure the girl would jump out of the shadows. Eventually I tripped over a branch and just lay in the dirt, sick and dizzy from earth and sky spinning round and about. Never, ever wish to dance all night. A body'd perish from it sure as a shipwreck.

Of course Cut-Throat had to laugh. He sat against a tree and let it bubble out in gasps. "Behold… the mighty ocean warriors… running from a slip of a snit of a snip of a girl," he breathed.

"Eyes," I said. It was all I could say at the moment. I wasn't sure if I meant the missing eyes of that fellow we'd left behind, or the present eyes the girl had turned on us. The second were scarier than the first.

"You hear about island girls," laughed Cut-Throat. "I pictured them a bit tamer. But Ligeia was pretty to look at from someplace sunlit."

"Ligeia?" I asked. The name sounded familiar.

"Your dance partner," said Cut-Throat. "The dainty little thing we just ran from in terror. She introduced herself to my acquaintance by that name."

135

"She talks?" I asked surprised. I found myself wondering what her voice sounded like. "She didn't talk to me."

Cut-Throat shrugged. "I don't recall her saying much. I wandered in night before last. She popped out of the dark. I gave the pretty island girl a friendly pat on the behind and she told me she was taking me into her service. It was like I was suddenly dreaming on my feet. She's strong. And she can make you do what she wants, just with a look."

"Ligeia's not her real name," I said, remembering. "She got that from a story by Poe. She reads Poe?"

"Maybe," considered Cut-Throat. "Or Poe got it from her. Perhaps he visited here and that was Usher's fallen house."

I shrugged, too tired to explain. Now that I thought about it, I knew her real name. Could I have used it to save myself a night of dancing? Secret name or not, I couldn't picture me ordering that girl about. But I could picture her ripping my throat out for trying. That picture came easy.

"She hasn't been on this island any longer than you or me," I settled for saying. "Though I suppose she could have been here before. But she came with us on Unicorn."

Cut-Throat stared at me. He prepared to fire a scoff. I could see him loading. I'd endured such cannonade for hours before the storm hit. And did I get any credit for being right? Not a bit. One minute I'm standing before the crew being called a moon-calf lunatic bedlam-escapee poet disturbing the sleep of honest men, the next moment everyone's a convert running for the boat. And not a one of 'em ever clapped the stalwart prophet on the back and humbly apologized.

But Cut-Throat held fire now. He considered some, then shivered himself briefly into seriousity. He stood and helped me stand. "Let's wander away quick and quiet," he suggested. It was a good suggestion. My only contribution was 'which way?'

Then the slow deep clang of the bell rang through the trees to answer the question. We steered for any shore in the opposite direction.

Describe the Island.

Well, that isn't easy. It's a place made all of pieces, and the pieces fit together indifferent. Woods on the northern side, plains and fields to the south. The low sloping mountain in the center, with a wonderful garden grove set in the cup of a crater at the top. A spiraling path begins on the northern shore at the light house, circling about the mountain slope up to the crater; and then another path spirals back down to end on the southern shore.

There is a bit of safety on the paths. If you survive the lesson, you learn the dangers of cutting cross country. The island has a pox of dark spots like the ruined courtyard where we met Ligeia. And all the island is cut up into estates. Think of them as big plantations or tiny kingdoms. Some panjandrum sits in the middle of his declared territory watching for wanderers, tourists and castaways to press into service.

The natives call the northern half of the island the divine side. I suppose that makes the southern half the mortal portion. But most of the population, mortal or not, lived on the southern side, where there is a small harbor-town. That was Theodosia.

Describe Theodosia.

She was very old. Over a hundred, I believe. Still sharp in her wits, though blind and stuck to a chair with wheels. Her maid pushed it about to give her some sun. You had to shout to get the ancient creature to hear your questions, but you got back some interesting answers. Some crazy ones too, of course, depending on what she heard, and what she thought she heard, and what she thought you meant, and what she decided you should hear. She was old.

She it was that gave me the key to the light house. That was her gift, as much as my prize.

You said Theodosia was a small harbor-town.

The town was named for the woman. And the island for the town, though it had other names. But Theodosia the girl founded Theodosia the town, or at least remade it in the image of her preferences. And that woman had strong preferences. She came there a young castaway and set rules still in force decades later. She had fire enough at a century, you believed what you heard of the conflagrations she unloosed in her youth. Fierce.

Describe Theodosia.

I suppose a hundred souls lived there, minus any lawyers. The first thing that struck you was that it was not characteristically ramshackle. A little harbor village ought by rights to be quaint and ramshackle, a picturesque disorder constructed by tide and wind, scattered houses built with comic donations from the sea.

Whereas Theodosia was a grid of well-kept houses with a large brick box of a town hall in the center. A paved main street ran parallel to the harbor. There were street-lamps, iron and ornate, adding a solemn touch by day, a warm light by night. Not gas lamps of course, but oil. I was there on an evening when the lamp-lighter proceeded down the street, solemnly carrying a long brass pole with a hook and a candle on the end.

He approached a lamp, nodding to it respectfully. He extended the pole high up, like a key. He hooked open the glass panel of the lamp and lit the wick within. He closed it and proceeded down the street to the next lamp, leaving behind a growing trail of warm sweet light.

I thought that the best damned job for a man to have in the whole of this starry existence.

Describe the Estates.

They can change in description and ownership more often than a stolen horse. That ruin where I danced with Ligeia was a famous dark place, upon a time. The estate that earned the most whispers on the island when I landed was known as The Asylum. There were estates that should have been famous for being places of peace and quiet. But those aren't words which get much placing in fame. The Grove on the top of the mountain in especial was a kindly place.

The largest and richest estate was the Green. There, the Master of The Green kept his large rich house and his small idiot personage.

Describe the Asylum.

It was a fetching brick institution resting up against the mountain, three stories high with wings to left and right. There was a peaceful white fence in front with a sign at the gate: Theodosia Seminary for Theological Pursuits. I suppose the iron bars on the windows looked a bit sinister, though under the windows hung boxes of undramatic peonies. Violets and even roses can achieve a sinister shadow; but there's just no threat in peonies. If no one happened to be screaming from the basement then the house presented a face friendly as a kitten's mirror.

The sign said 'Seminary' but even the Professor called it the Asylum. He took the institute's religious studies seriously, but he was easy about nomenclature.

The Professor studied the gods. Vivisected them, when he could catch them alive. Most times he had to settle for dissection or sharp analytical discussion. He considered his work the truest form of theology. He sought to understand deity, and how it differed from mere mortality.

"There is in every man a spark of divinity," he told us. "And if you dig deep enough into the most unnatural and inhuman god, you will find the corresponding clay lump of humanity." It sounded sensible, and his common-sense approach to mystical matters was refreshing.

But when you were in his basement staring at shelves of floating eyes and heads and hearts in alcohol jars, smelling the dead rot of ichor on the stone floor, staring at the racks and screws and knives while listening to the cries and whimpers behind the containment doors, you shivered in pity for any god that should end tied down to his examination table.

Chapter 13

My Esteemed Miss King;

This is an interesting island. So far I have performed a dark ritual in a cemetery, escaped a theological asylum, been locked in a dungeon for arguing at lunch, and run from unnatural dogs through a labyrinth. Checking my schedule I see that tomorrow morning I am to fight a duel to the death.

And yet, for all the theatre of my current residence, my attention keeps slipping. Gods, dogs and duels: they must clear their throats to recall my attention. Else my mind turns towards home, and a poem there I left unfinished.

K, when I was with you I did not greedily consider what ceremony of priestcraft or witchcraft would make you more completely mine. I did not seek ownership of your heart. I sought the prize of catching your eye, winning your smile, speaking some word that touched your mind or spirit. All my ambition and greed just sufficed to reach out a hand, daring to touch your face.

And if we were parted I savored your absence, exactly because I knew that parting would end. K, I enjoyed being away from you, often for an hour, once even an entire day. Why not? Away from you all the world became K to me. I walked in wonder through the town seeing your face in every cloud and shadow, smelling your hair in every flower, feeling your touch with each breeze.

But I crossed some boundary. My ship sailed too far. Now everything in the world is just an absence of K. This island is dull. Fire is dull, and wind is dull, and food is dull. Everything is bleached of color and life and purpose and solidity for the absence of you.

Marry me.

Say you will marry me, K, before all the world fades to white fog and I plunge screaming through an earth lacking sufficient reality of worth and purpose to hold a man up from oblivion.

Interviewer: Describe the duel.

Cut-Throat was my second. He stood beside me giving last advice I paid little mind. I stared greedily at the new day, grabbing for every bit of life I could, all the things I could see and smell and hear.

The morning sky still smoldered, clouds to the east streaked red, yellow, orange. A cool breeze traced across my skin, making me shiver the way the grass shivered as the wind passed over. The air tasted of fresh cut grass, of flowers still damp with dew. Nearby the statue of a naked girl emptied a pitcher into a fountain. My eye traced her stone breasts with a hand's caress, then focused on the pitcher, listening to the endless music of the splash. I wondered astonished at how infinite that pitcher was. She could pour until her lovely white marble arms fell off but it would never empty. To be so full and so giving, to be so unending and to be held in such arms. I wanted with all my heart to be that stone pitcher.

The wind made a sad counter-tone to the happy fountain, rustling funeral-like in cypress trees framing all the garden. I studied how their branches glowed a green so dark they shimmered black. I spotted Ligeia's eyes within those shadows, shining angry. Lurking again. She didn't like having to lurk. She was one for being out in the middle of things. Particularly violent things. Of course she was more worried for Cut-Throat than for me.

The servants of the Master bustled efficiently about, setting a table with two swords, and two roses, and two napkins of pale white silk. As the last touch they carefully placed one bright crystal glass on the table. They set it gently down, careful not to smudge the glass with a plebian finger. They filled it to the brim with slow-poured red wine.

"For the victor," said the Master of the Green. He didn't say it to be informative. He meant '*not for you*'.

Describe the labyrinth.

It was one of those constructions you read about that people with wealth and time build to demonstrate that they have a surplus plenitude of time and wealth. It extended from the Master of the Green's house to the edge of the estate. A high balcony with ornate railing overlooked the whole of the maze.

The Master of the Green was fond of having a banquet up there, where the guests could watch poor souls wander lost down below. The watchers would shout advice, of course. "Go left! You're almost out!" or "Go back! Ahead's a trap!" and whether the advice was true or false they did it with the same tone of authority and amusement. They sat at their table enjoying food and drink that tasted sweeter to them for gazing down on our feast of confusion and despair.

And when you were lost in the labyrinth, suddenly faced with the choice of running left or dodging right, with the dogs puffing behind and the scream of some fellow in a trap ahead, you'd glance up to that balcony and there would be those feasters sitting in the genteel light of candles shining like stars, like beautiful golden stars. They gazed down knowing what choices you faced, and what fate lay beyond each choice. While you stared up at them, awed at how wise they were, how happy they were.

They were outside and above the labyrinth, seeing the whole while you stood bloody and trembling in a tiny portion of the world's walls. And whether they kindly shouted the answer that would save you, or cruelly encouraged you towards a trap, or merely kept a mysterious knowing silence, was all simply a matter of what spice they preferred for their feasting.

I don't think I properly understood Typhon's rage against the gods till I was running in that labyrinth. But after that night I was a sympathizer for the Revolution.

Who is the Master of the Green?

The title changes hands frequently. You probably mean Iskandar, the fellow I killed in the duel. Not the current master. Actually, killing the old master makes you the new master, until you die in your turn. So I suppose I was Master of the Green myself for about a minute, at which point I expired leaving the position open to whomever next applied for the damned job.

What?

Expired. Ended. Became deceased. I won the duel. Despite his cheating, I might add. And then like a show-off idiot I drank that glass of victor's wine. It tasted wrong but I finished it off till I was staring puzzled at a little grinning death's head etched into the bottom of the glass. He'd poisoned it, you see, just in case he lost. He was a spiteful little wretch.

Describe the Green.

At the center of the labyrinth is an oak tree. It's old, and black and thick around as a small house. In the dead dirt beneath the tree lie more scattered bones than you could fit in the Maidenhead cemetery. You'd have to toss the surplus skulls and shins into the Scotsman's corn fields.

In the old days the Master of the Green slept under that tree, circling round about it by day, sword at hand to take on all comers. Whoever wanted to challenge him just had to walk up and start swinging. The winner became the new Master. The loser was left lying in the dirt. Thus the bones.

146

It was like kids playing 'king of the mountain', where you stand atop a sand pile or a hay stack and keep off the other children. As long as you're on top, you're someone special. A kind of god, actually. But you have to watch your back.

In the era in which Cut-Throat and I found ourselves in the vicinity, the custom had been adapted to make it almost impossible to reach the tree. That was the purpose of the labyrinth surrounding it. And the Master no longer slept under its branches, hand on his sword. No, he had a nice big feather bed in his mansion. If you could get through the labyrinth and the traps and the dogs and reach the center, there was a gong you hit with a hammer. It rang to say you challenged the Master.

But it'd be on his grounds, on his terms. And the one I faced was a slimy little weasel of a cheat. Never met a man I liked less. Even K's father, who I liked considerable less than the Banker. All things considered, the Banker was a homicidal lunatic. But at least he had style and ambition and more than a bit of humor.

The Master of the Green just had greed and fear. Those were the two choices in the maze of his rat's mind. Any question life posed to him, you could watch him scurry down the path sweating as he decided between 'will this get me hurt'? or 'will this get me something I want?'

Forget him. I'd rather discuss the character traits of bacteria.

How did you wind up in the labyrinth?

The Master of the Green had honest-to-goodness
dungeons in his basement.   Being led into them was like
being marched at pistol-point into a woodcut for
Ivanhoe. Dank stone walls, slippery stone floors, a few
dimly flickering candles. Iron bars with flecks of rust that
looked like long-dried blood. It smelled of rats and shit
and mold. Tinker, Cut-Throat and I were put into a cell
across from the Gypsy Cook and the Baker.

Unpleasant as conditions were, we were glad to see
them. It gave us a few hours to catch up on our stories.
Then the Master of the Green came and offered us the
choice of trying the labyrinth or being fed to the dogs. It
wasn't much of a choice. We didn't know it then, but it
wasn't much of a difference either.

Why were you in the dungeon?

We'd come to the Green to find the Gypsy Cook and
the Baker. The guards promptly caught us sneaking about
the estate. We were marched polite but firm into the
mansion and invited to lunch. Of course we accepted.
Cut-Throat, Tinker and I hadn't eaten since we burned
down the Asylum. The servants led us into an ornate
dining hall. They displayed a certain attitude I found
disquieting. They were bored, as if formal lunch was
standard punishment for trespassers. Well, and it was.

Just before we entered the dining room one of the
servants leaned close and whispered 'Do not argue with

the Master. Agree with him and feast; disagree with him and die." Tinker, Cut-Throat and I considered that warning as we were led to table. We didn't see any challenge in the proposition. So long as there was food, the man could declare the Earth a dodecahedron and we'd just nod our heads so as not to talk while chewing. We were starved.

The Master sat at the head of the table. He welcomed us but did not rise. First thing I did I asked him if he had met with any of our lost fellows from Unicorn. He shrugged and said he couldn't recall, meaning he didn't bother to care. Which was offensive and Cut-Throat started to say so. But Tinker kicked him surreptiously while I babbled loud thanks for the promised meal.

And we did fine for five full courses. I bet that was a record.

What did you argue about?

It wasn't my fault. Poetry betrayed me. The Master of The Green was no mere annoying idiot. He was a masterful and intuitive idiot, capable of tuning his ignorance like a musician to find the tone and subject that would most surely grate a human mind. He liked to talk. He talked about everything, and all of it was wrong. Not just normal human wrong. It was genius wrong.

But we held fast, and held back our honest opinions. When the Master poked his salad fork at Tinker and described Isaac Newton as 'that devil who murdered the rainbow', Tinker just turned his gaze under the table to study his own feet. Which is where Tinker usually kept his gaze anyway.

Over the second course (river trout wearing cream sauce to pass in disguise for poached salmon), the Master told us of his adventures in 'the provincial township of New York City' with its few streets and fewer charms. Cut-Throat nodded his horse's head as though fascinated. I suppose he was.

Inspired by their fortitude, when the Master took advantage of the cheese and wine to deliver a lecture identifying Shakespeare as 'that decent playwright Bacon, descending into poetry', I merely covered my sneer with a silk napkin. Over the soup we even traded quotes from Poe. The Master held Edgar Allan in high regard, which I considered an accidental bit of good taste, although the soup was excellent. He seemed to like Poe for a gruesomeness of tone, which was like approving of the soup for the amount of parsley floating on the top. It was onion soup, as I recall.

The fifth course was pork loin with a local currant jelly reminiscent of raspberries. Talk of Poe led to 'The Narrative of Arthur Gordon Pym'. The Master dug into his pork while asking Cut-Throat how far the crew of Unicorn had pursued cannibalism when our ship becalmed, the way the crew does in Poe's novel. Cut-Throat looked annoyed and Tinker looked sick. But Cut-Throat began a funny story about how he played his fiddle as the crew sang off-key, until the pale bodies of dead but nourishing fish floated to the surface of the sea.

The Master of the Green cut him off with a dismissive wave of a pork chop. "Nonsense. A hungry man does what he must. He is a tiger, fearless, remorseless. Like the devil is a tiger. I call upon Blake for my witness."

There came a dreadful silence while I carefully put down my soup spoon.

You total idiot.

It's about *tigers*.

Chapter 14

Dearest K:

Last night I slept in a real bed. After ship hammocks and piles of leaves under trees it made a strange impression on me. I had never realized before what a magic invention is a bed. Just consider constructing a wooden frame with four legs, and nesting a soft rectangular pillow within so that a body can lie down upon it, to lose consciousness each night in comfort and safety. If you are feeling luxurious, add four carved posts to hold curtains, and a covering for the top. Now you lie in a small and delicate house.

I slept last night in just such a construction, and dreamed how its four legs began to walk. I lay on the pillow, staring up at the embroidered covering of faded roses, while it carried me down the stairs of the seminary and out the door and down the road to the shore. And there it leaped into the surf and swam for the horizon, paddling its wooden feet fast as the flippers of some ocean creature.

Occasionally I peeked out the curtains to see the usual sea. I passed ships whose sailors waved their hats at me, admiring my easy navigational style. Once a pirate ship pursued, firing cannons that echoed like weak thunder. But the brigand sails had not the speed of my sea-going bed.

We crossed the ocean and hiked up the New Jersey shore and soon were in Maidenhead, trotting down Main Street and up to the church where I heard Sunday service begin. The ushers Mr. Blather and the Scotsman thoughtfully opened both doors so we could pass through.

Your father was translating some theological argument into vocal thunder and projecting it against stone walls to the usual fascination of the congregation. He stopped when I entered, then pointed at me as though I were the very subject and conclusion of his sermon. No doubt I was but I ignored him. My bed circled round to the stairs of the choir balcony, clunking and bumping in haste while congregations of aunts and neighbors 'tsked' at the disruption. I pulled back the curtains and waved at different faces I had missed, till I came to the ranks of the choir.

My bed bent a wooden leg before you, inviting you to climb aboard. All the choir began to sing choruses of hallelujahs in praise of clever beds. I watched anxiously as you bit your lip undecided, while devils and fathers howled in distant and detestable disapproval.

Say you will join me in my bed, Miss King. Together we will ride off in it to far shores and strange adventures. We shall watch the world pass by as we lean on pillows white as snow, white as the foam of a breaking wave on an empty beach; white as the lace of a bride. Say you will. Say you will. Say.

Describe the Seminary.

The Professor told us we might as well call it the 'Asylum', since everyone else on the island did. Cut-Throat, Tinker and I spent the night there after catching some of Unicorn's former passengers and locking them safely in the basement of the Seminary. Safely for us, I mean. Not for them.

We burned the place down eventually.

153

Why the hell would you burn down a seminary?

Ah, that's a bit difficult to explain. You could blame me, since I started the argument that led to the experiment that led to the visitor that led to the conflagration. Personally I blame Cut-Throat. He'd fallen for Ligeia. I'd had no idea. I distinctly recall how he'd run from her every bit as fast as I had. Why would anyone run from what they love?

Describe the New York Cut Throat.

Our Cut-Throat was tall and lanky and not a year older than me. But he'd lived so much more life in the same amount of time, he merited a long grey beard and an ear trumpet. By what he could tell of being and doing, the man had existed five times a poet's allotted span. But is that a fair measure of a life? Interesting anecdotes strung together? I like books. I map out my existence from birth to now making paths of the pages I've read. And that measure of a life feels exactly right for me. I admit the recounting doesn't entertain a parlor tea or impress the mirror.

According to Cut-Throat, he was French royalty adopted by Italian bank robbers, marrying a Mohican princess at fifteen. Her family gave him the tribe's title to upstate New York as a wedding gift, which he planned to present in court but traded for a fiddle. Being raised in a criminal family naturally led to becoming a city policeman, and his enthusiasm for the job led him to arrest most of his adopted relatives. Then, alas, he was cashiered for playing his fiddle while traffic-directing the Mayor's inaugural parade.

"I played 'Here comes the Bride,' said Cut-Throat. "Apparently they took that as some kind of political metaphor. But truly, I just like Mendelssohn."

We caught up on each other's adventures as we hiked from the bell in the woods. Cut-Throat described how the fool's crew had tipped over the boat while waving oars in jubilation for passing the breakers. Storm and currents had then scattered them to the dark as wind and tide thought best. He was sorry to hear about the Preacher.

"Last I saw he was holding on to an oar and singing a hymn," he said. "I don't think he could swim any better than he could sing, but he looked like he was enjoying the tune."

Cut-Throat had been grabbed by a current and dragged along the shore for the entertainment of waves and rocks, until he washed close enough for footing. Once on land he'd sheltered in the trees, watching for any other survivors.

I told him about the Banker popping out of the forward hatch and shooting Captain Grocer. He wasn't a bit surprised. "I do believe I mentioned that someone was hiding down there," he mentioned.

I wasn't having that. "Who was it who bravely informed the entire ship that a dreadful storm approached?" I mentioned back.

Cut-Throat scratched his head. "I can't recall. Some lesser prophet, no doubt. But prophecy doesn't hold a candle to the sunshine of sound detective work."

So I told him about Typhon and summoning the dead gods and being handed lightning and falling into the sea and the Preacher turning to a porpoise in a fire at the bottom of the bay. I'd like to point out it made an interesting story. I mean I've never led an inaugural parade while playing the fiddle but at least I've been in a shipwreck of the gods. Granted, anyone else I was likely to meet on the island could say the same. Tales of surviving a shipwreck were going to be locally remarkable as roundish eggs. If I could get home to some quiet parlor at tea, it'd fetch more market value.

Cut-Throat nodded at my talk of dead gods and porpoised preachers as though it confirmed all kinds of mysteries he'd detected. Well and it did, but I expected more opposition somehow. I think the man just takes things as they come. He's a good sort. But perhaps he assumed I was poetically interpreting a factual narrative. A banker shot a grocer, clouds collided to make lightning, a poorly steered ship sank, and gravity dropped a man into the sea where he floated up again in demonstration of the established principle of the weight of a poet to the weight of a poet's volume of salt water.

We were more weary than thirsty, and more hungry than weary. I told him about the light house. There might be food and water thereabouts. And if other survivors of the crew spied it they'd surely do the same. We decided it made a sensible destination. We didn't know the way, but a lighthouse had to be by the sea, and a sea ought to be by a shore and the shore had to be downhill somewhere so we figured we'd find it easy enough, which was exactly not the case.

So we wandered lost through woods where the morning air was cold and damp enough to make the weariest man shiver energetically. At one point Detective Cut-Throat turned to stare back into the dark of the trees behind us.

"We're being followed," he observed, which was just another reason to shiver.

Describe your room in the attic of your father's house.

A battle-field of books. An avalanche of books. A graveyard of books. An eagle's eyrie of books. A small garret with a sloping ceiling and one big fly-specked dusty window that closes crooked so blue winter wind seeps in, chilling man and book. Otherwise the garret swelters hot-house hot. The books like the cold fine, but they fidget in the heat. On summer nights I lie on my cot weary with watching them twitch their pages, arching their spines, unable or unwilling to get comfortable. Sometimes they'll turn on each other snarling quotes till they tumble to the floor.

Eventually I have to take the most restless and climb out onto the roof. There I read to them in the cool night breeze, till their sleepy pages flutter and fall quiet.

Give an excerpt from the Libris Acherontia.

All people know that below the living earth is the kingdom of the dead. Heat and rot, root and bone, worm and seed; these lie beneath the green fields and the house cornerstone. Nor could there be the higher world without the lower. Life springs up from the land below life. In that dark kingdom below the sunlit lands, rich Hades watches from his cold stone throne, over his cold stone realm. His is the quiet land, shadowed and completed.

But below the kingdom of Hades lies a yet older and greater kingdom: the realm of Chronos. There the father of the gods lies dreaming of what occurs in the daylight world. His oceanic breathing is the measure of Time, the slow drumbeat of his heart keeps the continuity of cause and effect and cause again.

And so the prophet Tages says that before a man plows a field he must first give thought to the dead that lie below the earth. Words, wine, blood or some measure of offering are their just due. But as a man plows the earth he must listen for the beat of the heart of Chronos, beyond both life and death, so that he learns to sow and to reap in time to the rhythm of the kingdom of the living and the kingdom of the dead.

Describe the Lighthouse.

Cut-Throat and I stared astonished at a muddy track where wagon ruts and hoof prints reflected bits of blue sky in pooling rainwater. It was welcome but gave us a start. We hadn't considered there could be more to the island than trees and ghost-girls. The path wound down to the sea or up to the mountain depending on your inclination.

We inclined downwards. Through the trees we began to catch sight of the sea just where we'd left it. We reached a clearing on a bluff and stared at the lighthouse, the lens of its lantern-room level with our gaze. I wondered why they hadn't constructed the tower where we stood. It would have been that much higher, that much safer from storm waves.

Then I considered its present position, separate from the island. Security, I decided. That tower was built to stand against threats from sea, and threats from land. In the noon light it looked positively unattainable. It looked its own little world, a wizard's tower in a fairy tale. I studied the windows set on the floors above the ground. Most were boarded and the rest were dark. I didn't see any sign of people, of life, of light.

I had a strange feeling come over me then. I wanted to get inside that tower and light the fire at its top. It wasn't right for a thing meant to give light to be standing so dark.

"Your hand is on fire," observed Cut-Throat, puzzled.

I held it up. It was glowing with twisting snakes of blue fire, pale as the sky in the noon-day sun. I waved it in the air to put them out. When that didn't work I held it behind me.

"No it isn't," I lied.

He just stared at me detective like. Finally we shrugged and walked on. When I pretended to scratch my nose the flames were gone.

The road wound down to the rocky beach opposite the tower. We heard voices echoing up, and we called out. I know, that wasn't very cautious of us. In a proper story of castaways, say Robinson Crusoe or Gulliver or Ulysses, we'd have scouted first. A hero should sneak about behind trees to make sure it isn't pirates or cannibals. But we were dead on our feet and starved hollow. We would have solemnly promised to let cannibals devour us in the morning if they'd fatten us decently tonight. We'd be lying of course. We'd sneak out before breakfast. I don't feel a bit guilty admitting that.

So we limped down the muddy path to meet whatever came. It wasn't cannibals or pirates. It was a caravan of wagons clambering up. Three wagons pulled by donkeys, alongside which walked gentlemen in somber black clothes, like old-style puritans or funeral ushers. They pushed the wagons in the slippery parts to help the donkeys with the cargo.

I looked for any of Unicorn's crew. There in the back of the third wagon was the Tinker, gnawing into a chicken leg while holding a cup of something he waved at us. Cut-Throat and I gave a few weak shouts and waved back.

Describe the Tinker.

Young. Tall. Skinny. Benjamin Franklin glasses. High voice and no more beard than a girl. There was some speculation among the fool's crew that Tinker *was* a girl. He was powerful shy and had never been known to undress, pee or curse in the presence of a fellow crewman. Still, some fellows are like that.

Stop right there. I hear what you are thinking. But even if Tinker was a girl he wasn't K. I mean she wasn't K, assuming he was a she. We've all seen the play and sung the song: a handsome young poet goes off to sea or war, and the understandably infatuated girl dyes her skin with boiled nut juice, cuts her locks, binds her breasts and tags along in her brother's trousers.

Please. Besides the fact that I left K on the other side of the world. But you could paint K. blue, shave her head to the scalp and wrap her in burlap and she would still not pass unrecognized by an eye scanning for the semblance of her face in every casual cloud and shadow, much less a shipmate.

As for Tinker, man or girl or woman or boy, he was clever as he was shy. It didn't surprise me he survived. Throw him in the ocean and I'd expect him to build his own ship out of driftwood and sea-foam.

161

What was in the wagons?

I guessed it before I drew close enough to see. I guessed right, too. Of course they'd been scavenging wreckage from Unicorn. But not broken boards useful for kindling, or ironically leaking barrels of ship's tar, with the prize find of a trunk full of salt-water and old sails. No, they'd filled up their wagons with fragments of broken gods.

The carts appeared to be winding their way back from an Olympian battle-field carrying the dead and wounded. Marble faces and wooden hands, terra-cotta breasts, bronze feet and claws and jaws and arms and eyes, scepters and beaks and crowns, swords and rings of stone and metal and glass, all piled in gruesome glitter. The mortal remains of immortals that fell like lightning from the high holy shelf of heaven down to the hard floor of the unholy earth. There to shatter on the shore.

Boom.

You have a letter.

Do I? I'm expecting a letter pretending to be from K. A letter listing this and that obvious and fatuous fact to establish identity before coming to a knife-tip of a point, kindly stabbing my heart with the news that she has grown in my absence, and wishing me well so long as I stay absent, and speculating on the weather's effect on the crops, ending in a non-sequitur praise of daisies.

Describe the Libris Fulgurales

Jove rules above the earth, Hades rules beneath the earth. Jove sends the lightning to strike the earth, and Hades sends the dead to the point where the lightning is ordained to strike. And there in that bright moment of light, the shadows of the dead are consumed in fire, and so consumed they become beings of light that live again.

With the last flicker the shades return to the shadows and the peace of unconscious quiet. Until the next bolt of Jove. And so to the dead all the world is perceived as one bright eternal strike of lightning. Every moment is the same eternal now and where they stand is a holy pillar of fire connecting heaven and earth.

And to those shades in the light of the fire of heaven, the living are mere clay creatures who wander lost in the dark moments between the measured flashes of reality.

Did you make that up?

Who can say? I'm an old blind sailor sitting in the yellowed light of the old blind sun shining through a window in the visitor's room of the Old Sailor's Safe Harbor Home. Years past, possibly, this ancient mariner briefly came in contact with the last translation of a possibly original ancient religious work, now lost.

What I say of it may be diluted by almost any amount of senility, creativity, incomprehension honest misinterpretation or outright fabrication cleverly inset into a general context of lightning, life, death, Greco-Roman gods and the horror that it is to plow a field and sow seeds knowing that a world of death lies just below the fresh-turned clods of dirt.

Dear Clarence:
I hope you have had some storms to make your trip of interest. We have had our share of tempests here. Five of your six sisters announced engagements all in the same evening; and now are not speaking to each other nor allowed near anything sharp. Apparently only two men are involved, so that there is some doubt as to who merely makes a false announcement to steal the thunder from the other. Your dog has run off.

Well, to be fair I ran off first. But admit it; you made that fool message up.

Who can say? We are just the interviewing team sitting in the aforementioned crinkled yellow sunlight of the window of the old sailor's etcetera, inquiring patiently, patiently and very casually about a rare book an old sailor might have read in his crinkled yellow youth.

It would seem that we are at an impasse. What can you trust of what I say? And what can I believe of what you reply?

That we do not say all the truth, does not mean that we lie.

I understand. I also do not lie. And I also do not say all the truth. I tell what I see and recall. To my mind there is no difference between past recollection and present experience. I am where I recall, pretty much. Which makes you just a voice in a crowded sailor's head on an island in the 1880's, I'll point out. Not the only voice either. That isle was full of talkers. But I'll tell you the truth as I see it, even if I don't know what the truth means. I'll leave that for you augurs to decide.

Let's see; where were we and when were we? Ah; near the lighthouse when we found Tinker and the Seminary students with their cartloads of holy jigsaw puzzle pieces.

Tinker was pleased to see us, I believe, although he kept it quiet. That is just his nature. He smiled, shuffled his feet, looked at the sky and offered to share the food and drink he wolfed down. Hungry as we were, we declined. It wasn't enough to feed two more wolves.

So we clapped him on the back, told him we were glad to see him top side of the ocean. Was Tinker a girl? It didn't matter. Stop asking. Tinker narrated how he and the Baker had made it to shore, sharing an oar. Tinker couldn't swim and the Baker had done most of the work. When they'd climbed up the rocks to the beach, the Baker had gone seeking any other survivors. Two days later and the Baker was still gone. Cut-Throat and I looked at each other worried.

One of the black-clad puritan types approached. He looked leaderish and eagle-like. All tall and gaunt and a bit

165

bent over, as if he kept a sharp eye on what occurred down on this mortal earth. He eyed us eying Tinker's rations and gave a weary smile that displayed a high quantity of understanding for a castaway's basic needs. "Right," he said. "Go sit. I'll have one of the students bring you food."

That was the Professor of the Theodosia Seminary for Theological Pursuits. I liked him soon as I met him. Even before I was sitting on the grass eating his rations. And even when I knew him better I never could decide if he wasn't just as kind and sane as he first seemed. I'd watch him out of the corner of my eye to see if his face ever twitched with a villain's sneer or a madman's grin. It never did once.

No, whenever I studied him all I ever observed was him studying me right back, with a smile to say he knew exactly what I was searching for in his face. After a while that gave me the shivers as much as when I watched him hold a bloody scalpel over a screaming object of study. A body just isn't meant to be too understood, nor meant to be too understanding.

Chapter 15

Mister Clarence St. Elmer, Esq.
Care of B. Harte, Clemens Boardinghouse
San Francisco, Calif.

Dearest Mr. Elmer, you will of course be pleased to learn that our niece, Miss K. King of Maidenhead, New Jersey, is now formally and irrevocably engaged to Master Henry Smeed, farmer, also of Maidenhead. This divine and permanent union shall be celebrated this fall in her father's church. Following the happy ceremony, the happy young couple shall gaily honeymoon at Niagara Falls before beginning their happy life as Man and Wife upon the Smeed estate.

No doubt the joyous ceremony will have been concluded by such time as you return from your amazing voyages to read this small note from a place in the world that must seem dull to a Sinbad such as yourself. But surely the news must be all the sweeter for arriving at last!

Could you but witness the depth of happiness the future Mrs. Smeed rises to as she embraces her future and her betroved, no doubt you would aspire to an equally deep joy, as one naturally wanting only what is best for a heart you kindly and wisely left behind.

Her father and aunts can only wish you all the best of fortune, whether as poet or sailor equally adrift in a sea of stormy challenge. For K's family, if not for herself, you will long be a source of memories that will warm us each tea when we stare into the fireplace flames of home.

Sincerely,

Hildegard King

Ha. Now there's a letter I was expecting.

Interviewer: I am sorry.
You can use the word 'I'?

We are sorry.
There you are. Or there we are. But don't sorrow overmuch. K would never engage Smeed. The bumpkin couldn't stand on both feet and spell the word 'illiterate' if you wrote the word for him on the sole of either shoe. Ha. Smeed sits at formal dinner table and discusses farm animals mating. The accidental romance of a horse and a cow filled his conversational dance card all the last summer. And the man believes he plays the piano because he can bludgeon the keys with his thumbs to imitate the melody of a miss-mating cow.

No, that letter is just Hildegard finishing off the plot-

We are sorry.
-finishing off the sinister plot of that irreverent and irrelevant Reverend of a father. Your honor, ladies, gentlemen and also you lawyers of the court I submit that Reverend King first wrote a letter to my K pretending to be from me, pretending I no longer cared for her. And now his decrepit and discredible accomplice Aunt Hildegard stands before the court to flatulate upon this

168

fraud of an engagement? Friends, Romans, jurymen, we decline to be fooled, just as my K would never be deceived. She knows my voice, the words from my heart. Ha. No jury of my peers could ever be tricked into supposing, into supposing-

Archives of the Maidenhead Weekly Chronicle, May 15, 1888

Proceedings of Local Society

Following the Sunday service it was announced to a delighted congregation that the only daughter of Reverend King is to enter into holy matrimony all the more consecrated for taking place in her father's church, himself performing the sacred office. The fortunate groom is one Henry Smeed, a rural property owner of Maidenhead. Nuptials are scheduled for the cool of the fall, and the mother of the blushing bride-to-be spoke of a wedding design based upon the lovely New Jersey daisy.

-fooled into, into supposing that a mind and heart and form of soul such as K's, such as my K's, could be moved even by pity to join hand or life with, with someone else.

If you could see how she and I smile at each other. How we say so much without descending from the heaven of a shared gaze to the dull plain of words, you would laugh at the suggestion she would ever, she could ever. I have walked with K in a snow fall and the silent holy white fire was our joy. She read me Blake, Poe,

169

Coleridge as I lay burning in fever. And later was a night I held K while we burned in fever together standing in the lake under the moonless sky. We trembled till the rippling circles reached the far dark shore.

And I have made K laugh when she was sad. Yes, when she waited downcast and heard a step and looked up in hope that it would be me, me, and her sadness fled to see my face as though I were her special saint come with healing. I have caressed the actual very same lock of hair that curls about her left ear, tracing its holy design with my finger, and who else knows how to do that? What other hand would dare? The lock of hair that curls about her left ear. That lock. This very hand.

Describe the political organization of Theodosia Island.

The first time I met K she sat alone in the choir balcony. She read her hymnal, humming the words to learn the feel of them, the rise and fall and rhythm of them. It was a sweet sound in the cool stone shadows. The hymn was 'All Glory Laud and Honor'. A thing of beauty.

I'd wandered up there to read Coleridge. I had caught an ambition to write an end for "Kublai Khan", his poem left unfinished for interruption and lack of opium. I had paper, pencil, and no interruptions but also no opium. I didn't know if opium was available in Maidenhead.

Probably the town doctor had some for a patient's pain. But was there any for a poet's?

I sat in a back pew considering this injustice, gradually noticing *her* up towards the front. I studied how hair warred against bonnet, straining to bounce and splash on the pale crescent of shoulder at the base of her neck. I studied how she raised a hand to conduct the music she heard within her head. I studied how she tilted her head to this side and then to that. I found it all fetching. But gazing so on a girl in secret felt unpoetic. I got up to leave.

Then she turned to look at me, and the world turned with her gaze to spin me about so I sat down again. But I jumped back up to sit nearer her. As brave a thing as I've ever done in my life. I introduced myself. Another act of courage.

And she smiled and claimed we'd met already, at a croquet party of my sister Alice. I'd introduced myself to her as The Lost Dolphin. Not the lost French prince *Dauphin*, but the mammal that is fish-like but not a fish, and also is not a porpoise which is a different mammal that is also neither a fish nor a French prince. She claimed I emphasized each of these separate points in a horrible French accent, which made no sense if I was the sea-mammal kind of dolphin and not the French one.

I solemnly denied being the lunatic she recalled. Perhaps it was a brother, a cousin, a mysterious stranger. Or an opium dream. Did she take opium? I asked concerned. Privately I recognized it for exactly the sort of fool thing I'd say and forget ten minutes later. But I couldn't believe I would forget *her*.

Later I found a memory of her previous to her memory of me. We were seven, laughing and whispering through the Halloween frights of a haunted house, and we clasped hands in the dark and encouraged each other. And though we never exchanged names nor saw each other's faces, we were betrothed from that moment. From that moment. That moment. That one.

Describe the Spanish coin in your pocket.

The last time I saw K. she huddled in the rose-covered parlor chair at tea. She wore a blue dress with high white lace covering all her throat, making her neck long and smooth like a china vase, like the marble column to a temple. Her unbound hair hung shiny and dark to her shoulders.

How did her father get our poem into his pocket? Did she show it to him? Laughing? How could she bear to hear it read? It was torture enough for me, and I wrote the thing. But if he stole it why didn't she stop him now? Was she ending things between us? Well, why should she not? How could she not tire of my stare, my babble, my comic imitation of a real poet, a real suitor? Wasn't now the inevitable moment when I must turn to see her family's contempt reflected in her eyes?

So I turned to look at K, wondering. And she hid. She hid her face in her hands, unable to meet my gaze, looking as guilty as the accused in the courtroom when descriptions of the corpse are read aloud for the jury to consider in horror of the crime. The last time that I saw K. That last time. Time. Time.

Blake's poem 'The Tyger' is a metaphor for the Devil.

So everyone says. I am tired. It's grown cold. I used to be a sailor. I am very old. They call me Captain here, but I never was Captain that I recall. No, I kept the light. Someplace with a strange name. Damn these blind eyes. I can't see. You need light to see light. Have the head nurse wheel me somewhere safe from voice or wind or time. Time.

There is no head nurse, we made her up. Reset. Describe the Libris Acherontia.

Query failed.

Reset current record -4 query.

Query failed.

Describe yourself.

Query failed. Variable undefined: 'yourself'.

The isle is full of noises, sounds, and sweet airs that give delight and hurt not. Sometimes a thousand twangling instruments will hum about mine ears, and sometimes voices that, if I then had waked after long sleep, will make me sleep again. Wake up, Ancient Mariner! There is balm in Gilead.

Nevermore.

What the hammer, what the chain? In what furnace is thy brain? What the hand dare seize the fire? Who gathers all things mortal with cold immortal hands? Tell us what thy lordly name is on the Night's Plutonian Shore. Dammit, the Snark is a Boojum. Reset. Wake up.

What a broad-side of poetic babble. Blake, Swinburne, Poe and Carroll. Canonniers, load Coleridge and return fire. "God save thee, ancient Mariner, from the fiends that plague thee thus". Who are you, fiend?

We are the interviewers. For a story.

And who am I?

You are the old sailor who remembers being a young sailor on Unicorn, a three masted schooner out of San Francisco plying the Pacific waters.

That sounds familiar.

You are Clarence St. Elmo, for a name. You are a bad poet lost in the sea of time, a castaway on an island where the dead gods wander.

That sounds awful.

And beyond a name, on that side of things, past the mirror and the window and the words, you are the Keeper of Shipwreck Light in the Sea of Suns and Moons.

Oh, I knew that.

Chapter 16

Excerpt from the Maidenhead Weekly Chronicle, Aug. 22, 188?

Strange Sighting in Last Sunday's Summer Storm

A sudden summer shower took all the township by surprise this Sabbath, as though the God of Noah thought it wise to remind worshipers going tardy to His service just whose hand it is that summons the waters of Heaven to stay, and whose word holds forth the deluge. Parishioners reported lightning strikes at diverse locations, and several personages stood in Main Street astonished to see a fiery blue glow upon the church steeple. While such electric fire-bursts are not unknown during moments of lightning, several witnesses further testified that at the height of the tempest the figure of a man was discerned on the roof of the church "clasping himself to the steeple as though to a rock in a stormy sea."

Interviewer: describe the Theodosia Seminary for Theological Pursuits.

The Professor smiled to inform us that his institution was known locally as 'The Asylum'. He kindly offered us its shelter till we found our feet, our friends or our next berth. Cut-Throat and Tinker were dead set to accept. I would have been myself except that the light-house was just down the path. I felt a powerful urge to go on and talk to it. It was waiting for me. But food and bed and shipmates were in the opposite direction, so I turned around with the promise I'd wander back when I could.

We trudged up the track. The Professor shook his head at how Cut-Throat and I stumbled half asleep. He suggested we climb into the carts. But the poor donkeys were already slipping in the mud, and the students were swearing better than sailors as they pushed. We settled for walking alongside and pretending to help at the steep parts.

While we pretended the Professor lectured us about the island. We learned it was called Theodosia. He said it had had other names previously but he didn't share them. He told us the only town was on the far side of the island, but there were different holdings of private individuals scattered about. Some of them were best avoided, he advised.

At that we told him about the ruined courtyard and Ligeia. When we mentioned the bell in the woods the students stared at us. Even the donkeys turned their heads to stare at us. Apparently we were innocents narrating how we'd met with a bad kitty just where the sign said 'Keep out Dangerous Lion'.

"How are you alive?" asked one of the students.

"Is that a theological question?" I asked back.

"One of the best," affirmed the Professor.

I proudly narrated how Cut-Throat and I had found Ligeia's weakness: dancing to fiddle music. Cut-Throat took out his fiddle and played a few notes to accompany the tale, then winced. He showed us a hand blistered as if he'd grasped a hot poker.

The Professor bit his lip thoughtful, shook his eagle-like head. "Any sign of her since?" he asked, looking into the trees.

"Not a one," I said in relief.

"She's been following us in the shadows of the trees," said Cut-Throat. I stared at him, then around at the trees. So much for my detective skills.

The Professor nodded as though it was just as he'd expect. "You really don't want to be outside at night alone," he informed us. There was a magic power in his words. As soon as he said it, it became solemn and holy truth. We really didn't want to be outside at night alone.

Describe the Libris Fulgurales

There are three greater and three lesser assignments of lightning. The greater are assigned to Justice, Chance, and Omen. The lesser strikes are Revelation, Alteration, and Culmination. A lightning hit of Revelation must itself bring the revelation. Thus the augurs shall question any man who is struck by lightning and yet lives.

"What is your name? Where do you dwell? Who were you before? Who are you now? What do you remember? What have you forgot?" are the first questions posed to the thunder struck. It is the duty of the augur to faithfully record what answers are given, honestly and without judgment. Whether the words are mere moans of anguish from the dying, or the giddy babble of those the sky has reminded that they yet live.

A lightning strike of Alteration brings ordained change. The augurs shall gather about the thunder-struck to measure what change has been wrought. Has a blow from heaven brought wisdom? Strength? Madness? Repentance? Understanding? It is the duty of the augur to record what change has been ordained from the sky.

A lightning strike of Culmination brings ending, in some manner of completion. When the augurs gather to study a strike of Culmination, there is only one question asked over the smoldering remains: what did it all mean?

I prefer to think it was a strike of Culmination that burned down the Asylum. As an institution it was completed, in that it had gone as far as it could. And to the discerning augur, the smoldering ashes had one clear and discernable meaning: it had gone too far.

Explain why you burned down the Asylum.

Cut-Throat, Tinker and I accompanied the Professor as the wagons made their way. He asked if we were up for an adventure. Cut-Throat and I bravely replied the same second, he affirming "Yes," and I voting "No." The Professor laughed. He told me he would send me on with a student to guide me to the Asylum, but that the caravan would be stopping for the night in the woods.

While he said this, he bent down and wrote idly in the mud. "Listening in trees."

Then he rubbed the words out with his boot. As we walked on under a suddenly weak and chilling sun he talked about a clearing up ahead where they would camp.

179

A cemetery, he cheerfully informed us. The clarification did not reassure.

A low stone wall began to follow the track, until we came to a gate wide enough for the carts. We passed through into a small wooded valley that cut deep towards the mountain. The way here went flat stones covered with old leaves, giving donkeys, students and castaways an easier time. I began sighting stone markers beside the path, crosses and headstones tilted and dirty as though they'd just poked themselves out of the ground, sprouts of a strange planting. Inwards we passed crops of statues. Lions lying slain, and dogs and griffins keeping guard; angels holding heads down in sorrow or upwards in hope. Knights lying on backs, hands folded across chests taking naps I envied. The path split and then split again as it wound in separate decisions through the cemetery fields.

We took what decisions led to the center, which resembled a quiet village of marble huts. A very quiet village. I watched a deer stare out from a narrow alley. A squirrel perched on an angel's head and studied us, tilting himself this way and that as though seeking which angle could make sense of our presence.

Understand that the place gave me the chills, the pip, and the screaming fantods. I was spotting a dozen ghost girls behind each tree, and I was weary and hurting. Understand, so you can appreciate how courageous this very same poet was when he announced he'd changed his mind and would stay for the alleged adventure.

Ah, but the truth was I was too tired to hike a step farther. If there had been half a spare bed in any of those tombs I would have climbed right in, poking my bony neighbor to make room. Instead I selected a tree, put my pack against it for a pillow, hands folded across my chest like a knight. And there I slept as deep as any of the regular inhabitants of the quiet little village.

Why would you burn down the Asylum?

Night woke me with its change-over of bird calls and insect sounds, the cooler touch of the wind, the bright smell of stars overhead mixing with the damp rising from the earth. Tree branches rasped with an annoying stop and start of fitful breeze. But a bright fire burned nearby, sending up sparks that seemed short-lived but happy. I stretched and approached, sitting next to Cut-Throat, who was in the middle of a tall tale about a mermaid in a brazier who followed Unicorn to hear him fiddle. The story sounded uncomfortably familiar, and I glanced about the dark trees for our pale dancing girl.

The Professor himself came and sat beside me to share a plate of venison. I tried to be polite about eating with my fingers and fair about how much was my half. I tried, I did.

Tinker whispered something I didn't hear.

The Professor smiled into the fire. "We can talk freely for now. She has retreated, waiting for us to sleep." Tinker repeated his question as a louder whisper. "Is she a vampire?" It was a word I'd avoided. Don't talk to me about Byron, I've read Polidori.

As a poet I know how important it is not to put into words what you don't want to be true. Granted, that is also the habit of idiots but when a poet does so it is in recognition of the power of words to create reality. Idiots just want to avoid facing the truth. The difference is obvious.

"I believe she is new to the island," said the Professor carefully. "Was she a passenger aboard your ship?" He emphasized 'passenger', wondering what we knew and could accept as true.

Cut-Throat and Tinker looked to me, as if I'd know. I did know, as it happened, but there was no reason for them to think so except I'd told them, and since when did anyone credit me? But I nodded. "She was a statue in the hold. Of an old, old goddess. She's calling herself Ligeia. But she stole that name from Poe," I pointed out proudly.

The Professor nodded. "There is often one awake enough to survive the sinking. They wash up on the shore of the island same as any castaway. Those in animal form soon lose themselves in the woods and the waters and the air. The more human-seeming will sometimes seek to blend with the mortal population. But the darker ones seek the dark places of the island and make them lairs to be avoided."

This is where the Professor should have asked me to describe the shipwreck. It is important to ask these questions, sometimes even repeating the question till you've squeezed all the facts out. Then I would have told him that all the passengers had been awake. I'd woken them myself by calling their names, as it happened.

Far as I knew every last one of them had come safe to shore.

Describe how you were shipwrecked.

Exactly. The Professor should have asked me that. Instead he turned to Tinker to expostulate. He was a teacher first, I guess. He couldn't help but instruct. "To answer your question," he said, "This 'Ligeia' is an immortal being who is inhumanly strong, inhumanly proud, entirely remorseless and demands an offering of blood." He tossed a pebble into the fire. "You may call her a vampire or a god, as you prefer. The definitions are about the same."

"What exactly kind of theology does your school study?" I asked. It obviously differed from K's father's Methodism, or Preacher's, who'd been some kind of unreformed Episcopalian.

"Theology is the study of divinity," said the Professor, and turned his eagle's gaze to survey his students proudly. They sat up straighter. "And after all, one can hardly study divinity unless one learns to catch it and hold it down."

Describe the students of the Theodosia Seminary for Theological Pursuits

It was a small school. Not surprising if you consider its situation ten thousand miles from the next post office. There were seven students in the cemetery waiting for Ligeia. Five more were back at the Seminary. They mentioned a Headmaster of the institution. Currently off traveling. Apparently he checked in regularly from wandering the world, sort of like Satan in the book of Job but more bureaucratic. They spoke of him respectful, maybe a bit fearful. I had a suspicion then I could describe this Headmaster's face in terms of big hairy things, but I kept it to myself. They entirely declined to mention Sobek, who generally kept to the seminary basement. I'll describe him later if pressed.

The students favored black denim pants and dark cloth coats. They'd sweated pushing the carts in the sunshine, but it looked the proper uniform for a cool Theodosia night. Now you could only see their faces and hands as they sat facing the fire.

I never knew any of the students well. Let's see. One was an Irish sailor who'd jumped ship in the middle of the ocean and swum to the island. He asserted that a dream had instructed him to do so. Privately I thought he was crazy. One was a rancher from Texas who'd wandered into the Pacific by accident. He insisted he was crazy but I doubted it, he was just ironic. Three were missionaries from different denominations who'd arrived on the island in a fiery sweat to share the Truth, the Good News, the Way, the Light, and various other nouns turned holy by Capitalization. Each had wound up applying to the school to learn things about deity their local bible studies hadn't thought to cover. Things like how to trap a dead god in a cemetery at night and haul it back to the lab table for theological study.

None looked any younger than me, nor any as old as the Professor. Truthfully, at first glance they reminded me of Unicorn's crew of fools; just a collection of idlers the wind had blown together for lack of being tied down to anything useful on the earth. But on second study I qualified that judgment. They had something we'd lacked. I saw purpose in their faces, the determination that comes from decisions made and kept. It made me sit up straighter myself. These gentlemen were serious, and they were readying themselves for a fight.

How do you trap a dead god in the cemetery at night?

The recipe for invoking didn't surprise me. I'd read it in the Libris Acherontia, not to mention the Iliad. Blood presented before an icon or fragment of something to represent them; a location associated with death; the recitation of a name or phrase that evokes the divinity. That will bring them.

Trapping is a separate proposition. Frankly, I think it's a modern invention. They drugged the offered blood with a mix of poppies and the blood of other gods.

With practiced moves the students prepared the stony yard that centered the quiet village, sweeping dead leaves away from the black square of a burned gravestone. Upon it they placed a copper bowl filled with a dark liquid that steamed faintly. The blood was from the deer they'd shot for dinner, plus their secret recipe. Around that they chalked a wide circle of words. I took a peek, expecting 'abracadabra', Hebrew and the usual jumbo of mumbo.

But it was quotes from different writers about eternity and infinity. Not even classical quotes. I recognized one from Poe's Eureka. "*Let us begin, then, at once, with that merest of words, Infinity*". And one from Pascal: "*We burn with the fire to find the ground where a tower reaches to the Infinite*".

Around that literate folderol they drew a wider circle, ten paces across. Then they came and went from the carts, placing the fragments of the broken gods along the circle till it made a waste-high barrier of dismembered faces, arms and legs. In the firelight it shone red and black, macabre as a farm wall in some quiet field of the Inferno.

Each of the seven students began chanting names, low and careful. Every now and then it was a name I recognized, though I didn't say so. I caught the eyes of

Tinker and Cut-Throat, then looked off into the trees, querying as to whether it would be smart to run. Tinker shrugged, meaning he'd follow our cue. Cut-Throat shook his head, meaning no. I checked the Professor from the corner of my eye and caught him watching us. He shrugged with a smile, meaning *our choice*.

The students finished reciting their holy roll-call and sat back down as though returning from the blackboard after chalking out equations.

The Professor nodded in approval. He turned to Cut-Throat, Tinker and me. "Now we wait. When our visitor comes you must sit still. If there is shouting stay quiet. If there is fighting you may join in or run for your lives as you decide best. But if you run, run far." I wasn't sure if that was a threat, or honest advice to tourists.

He settled himself by the fire, taking up a stick to poke at the flames. "Don't look at the offering," he said. "They are proud and shy, and reluctant to feed when watched. Let us now pass the time in unthreatening and nonchalant conversation."

He glanced at the stars and then back to the flames, as though ensuring that the first burned in proper time to the second. I was getting nervous the more I considered the blackboard. There was a factor to the equations I suspected that the Professor was not taking into account.

I was just about to nonchalantly broach the subject when Ligeia appeared.

Chapter 17

Submission to the Maidenhead Weekly Chronicle
Care of E. Blather, Literary Editor

A Picture of the Girl
-- Clarence St. Elmo. 188?

What is this wind? Why does it touch me like your hand?
The sunlight seems shyly to be a kiss.
Where are you that all the parts of my love
Are scattered across the day?

A bird splashes gutter-water drops into the sun,
Its trilling turned liquid. I know that laugh,
And I follow the bird as it dives up to a cloud.

I close my eyes and hear the thump of my heart,
Echoed as a heart that pressed next to mine.
Eyes open I stare at the street, cold, empty, loud.

I look for my face in mirrors, in cats, in strangers,
Built with the broken parts of the summer day.
But there is your profile; thoughtful, smiling, turned away.

These thoughts are random, yet they build
A picture of a girl, eyebrows arched, smile curled.
You never quite meet my gaze. I stare at the world

Idly, finding you in the shadows of leaves.

Describe The Master Of The Green.

Iskandar was a big man built a scale too small. Not like a child. He just had the mental and physical proportions of a tall and imposing personage, scaled down to below average. He was an Olympian doll of a scholar and athlete. The lesser scale of his construction created the optical illusion that a large and intelligent man stood a few feet farther away than the real one did. You kept expecting him to take a last step forward and impress you, but it never happened.

He'd killed the previous Master of the Green, which was perfectly fine, successful homicide being the whole point of the title. By tradition you walked up to the tree, fought the old Master and if you won then you had the thrilling privilege of circling around the tree sword in hand till you were dispatched in your turn.

Of course that was all too fair and sensible to suit *him*.

Describe the duel with the Master of the Green.

He claimed I'd challenged him by running to the center of his labyrinth and punching that gong under the tree. Which was nonsense because I only did that to get out of the labyrinth, and we were only in the labyrinth to get out of the dungeon. Granted he put us in the dungeon because at lunch I declared that if poetry were peeing he couldn't water a peony. I suppose that might count for a challenge to minds sensitive to critique.

So he choose the time, place and weapons. He chose foils, in his gardens, dawn after next. Which meant I spent a day and a night in his dungeon without eating or sleeping.

He arranged for rounds of servants to provide music to entertain me, hour upon hour. The clatter of drums and farts of bugles had no purpose but to keep me awake. Whenever I curled up on the stone floor with my arms over my head another servant would poke me with a stick through the bars. The time went on and on, reminiscent of when I clung to the rock in the storm but infinitely duller.

They gave us no food or drink till the hour of the duel, when we were handed plates of black bread and a dog's bowl of water. I was starved but Cut-Throat knocked it out of my hands before I'd snarled more than a bite and a sip. He said it was doped. I honestly didn't care and would have finished it off.

He was right, though. I felt suddenly giddy and the bars were no longer straight. I thought I could slip through them and escape but they kept twisting like snakes to block me.

When we were led out to the garden I staggered and blinked like a rabid mole dragged into the noon, though the dawn was still performing opening overtures of light and bird song.

In the back of my whirling brain lingered the hope that the Master of the Green was as pretentious a fraud with a sword as he was with an opinion. That hope was quick to be quashed. He chose his foil from the table first. Then he whirled it cutting the air in geometric arches and vectors that would've impressed Euclid as much as Cyrano. The Master of the Green was a serious fencer, quick as the devil and twice as practiced

I picked up the remaining foil. Addled as I was I noticed it was shorter and heavier than my opponent's. When I ran a finger down the blade my skin was not sufficiently impressed with the edge to bother with a bleed. The point was dull as Tuesday tea at the Reverend's. Also the handle rattled as if the blade were going to fall off. Eventually it did.

Did you know how to fight with a foil?

I'd read about it.

Who else was present at the duel?

Well, first off there were a half-dozen servants of the Master. In green livery of course, and armed with pistols and swords. Something about their bored faces made me examine the grass. It was worn just where I stood. My eye turned to old gouges in the earth just where the table legs touched. There was even a trampled circle of grass between the Master and myself. It gave me the shivers. I had the strange conviction that he and I had been dueling

191

for years upon this very spot. Eternity was overrated, I decided, though the morning sky was a wonder.

Then my swirling brain caught its sea-legs. The grass and ground were worn because this was a sacred ceremony repeated on the Green as oft as the holy rite of hanging the laundry.

Tinker and the Baker stood by the fountain, near as the servants allowed. I wanted to warn them to rabbit while they could. I knew the Master of the Green would break his promise to let them leave in peace. Cut-Throat stood near, keeping me standing. Thoth was perched on the head of the fountain statue, occasionally swooping down to plash and splash the water over his feathers the way a bird does, then hopping back to his lookout point. From there he looked damned ominous. Coyote and Ligeia lurked in the shadows of the cypress trees, also ominous.

Who is Coyote?

One of the dead gods we rescued from the basement of the Asylum. Looked like a skinny yellow wolf, but he was clever as he was sly, and sly as he was crazy. Which measure put him in a crazier class than Cut-Throat, which is to conclude: Mister Coyote was a serious danger to himself, society, the laws of physics and propriety, and the quiet repetition of ordinary existence.

Like Ligeia, he was paying us back for rescue from theology class. Without both of those ex-deities' help, we would have died in the labyrinth.

Why was Ligeia hiding in the trees?

She had a powerful fear of sunlight, though it didn't turn her to dust like books had led me to expect. You can't always trust a book. That isn't easy for me to say but there it is. Sometimes books just *make things up.*

But Ligeia did her lurk to keep watch on Cut-Throat. She'd kept him alive through the labyrinth. Females are strange creatures, even when they aren't former gods turned creatures of the night.

Ligeia and Cut-Throat had been making dramatic eyes at each other since he carried her out of the burning Seminary. And after the labyrinth the situation descended into total horror. She'd look at him and he'd look down, then he'd gather his fool courage and look at her and she'd pant like a racer then twirl angry away then he'd sigh down at the ground again and then *she'd* sigh and swivel her crazy orbs back towards him at which point you screamed to heaven to *please* let them be murdered or married.

At least I wanted to. I didn't scream anything, of course. I just rolled my wisdom-weary eyes and shook my life-weary head. But don't think I was fooling myself. It wasn't annoyance making my own teeth taste so sour to me. It was jealousy for what they shared. I'd shared that

193

once. I even still had my half. And half is so much worse than none.

Ligeia gave Cut-Throat the credit for rescuing her from the theological laboratory. Truthfully the credit went mostly to Typhon. But even Mr. Coyote wasn't crazy enough to thank Typhon.

Describe rescuing the dead gods from the Asylum.

I should first describe the long talk we had about theology in the operating theatre. Then I should describe how Typhon knocked on the door. But before that I should finish off what happened in the cemetery when Ligeia showed up to drink that bowl of blood. There was a very interesting discussion around the fire about mechanical minds and the creation of worlds.

We have a letter for you.

Now? Just when I am getting ready to die in a duel? I notice you tender these letters whenever you want to either distract me, bribe me or inflict pain upon me, as if I were a horse you guided back to the directed path by carrot or stick, when mere repeated kicks no longer sufficed.

True. From the archives of The Maidenhead Weekly Chronicle
Maidenhead, New Jersey; Feb 03, 188?
Dear Mr. St. Elmo;

We write to thank you for your submission 'A Portrait of the Girl'. You have penned something unique upon a traditional subject: a young girl! Too unique, alas. But while we regret it is unsuitable for our local poetry section, we encourage you to continue to pursue your muse, as well as a more recognizable rhyme scheme and words that do more than accidentally end in similar syllables.

When you dare to begin to decide to take that first step upon the Pilgrim Path of the True Poet, Mr. St. Elmo, then to your joy and our surprise you will traverse the pattern and path that true poetry follows, over the hills and far away to the Celestial City where inspiration leads and publication awaits. Follow that pilgrim's path, Mr. Elmo. Follow it far. Which is to say: good luck elsewhere.

Sincerely, Edwin Blather,

Literary Editor, Maidenhead Weekly Chronicle

'*Editor*'? Blather raised pigs out in the woods till the pigs cheated him at cards and he had to move into town where he opened a store that only stocked on its shelves items previously reported stolen or missing somewhere within the township. Constant interviews with reporters from crime gazettes gave him the belief he understood journalism, and a charitable wish by the Chronicle to end the local crime wave gave him the cynical sinecure of

'Literary Editor'. He couldn't edit his ass if he ate an eraser and shat on a mirror.

Describe the capture of Ligeia.

She moved through the night a wisp of fog, bare feet floating. Her pale white face and arms were marble art. She might have been one of the cemetery statues taking a thoughtful stroll. Halfway between the fire and the circle of dead gods she stopped. And there she stood, head tipped to port, considering.

"You are an east coast American by the accent," said the Professor idly. "I'd like to visit Princeton someday." He chatted blandly and his eyes ordered me to chat blandly back or die.

I replied that I went into Princeton regularly to raid it for books. I'd had some friends at the university, only I'd quarreled with all of them over God and poetry, the origin of man and the future of democracy. There was more to the list of quarrels but I quit there, realizing it made me sound argumentative. I'm not. They were just wrong and I was right, that's all.

Cut-Throat stared fixedly at Ligeia. I was worried he'd slip back into the somnambulist state I found him in. I poked him sharp with an elbow. He poked me back annoyed which was a good sign. I checked on Ligeia. She was still standing at that mid-point, head down, face half-covered by her hair. Was she listening to us? I said the first thing that came to mind. "I once saw a mechanical man play chess. Poe wrote about it."

Each of the seven students held their hands casually within reach of whatever knife or gun they hid under those black coats. They studied the fire and the sky and the earth, anything but the girl. But now one of them started in surprise as though the night had suddenly turned *interesting*. He looked at me. "The Mechanical Turk? You saw it?"

I swallowed, nodded. This was unnatural as conversation in the parlor of the Reverend. Almost. "At a fair. Maybe it was just a copy 'cause I heard the real one disappeared. But the mechanical man I saw beat a dozen people easy." I didn't mention that it beat *me*. It'd cost all my pocket money to play, I'd had it down to a rook and a pawn between us, and then got careless. Dammit.

The Professor made a scoffing sound. "The automaton chess player known as *'Die Schackturke'* was a fraud. As Poe points out. And a copy of a fraud must also be a fraud. No machine can be taught to think as a man thinks."

The student waved his hands to brush away such insect argument. "Nonsense. A fiction can become a truth. Dreams inspire reality as surely as reality inspires dreams. And what does it even mean, 'think like a man'? To be self-aware, or just to be able to reason? Those are two entirely separate actions. To prove to me that a

197

machine does not know it exists, you must first prove to my satisfaction that you know you do exist."

Some of the students growled at that, loading counter-arguments into their David's slings. I was impressed. A vampire stood studying our throats in the firelight and they argued philosophy. Obviously this was the class for the serious students. The proponent of mechanical thought continued. "But the rules of chess, of logic, of reason, are all definable as the Euclidian circles of a clock. They don't require consciousness, only order. The work of Charles Babbage has shown that a machine could be built -"

"Alas, only *could* be?" interposed the Professor, smug.

"-*has* been designed to remember, to reason, and to calculate just as a man's mind does."

"Were it ever built, your Babbage's thinking machine would not be a mind," scoffed the Professor. "It would be a mere tool of thought for the mind that created it. A violin produces sounds even the human voice cannot. But it originates nothing, and though it thrills to the music it can never be a musician."

The Professor is an idiot. Remind him of Ada Lovelace's demonstration of how Babbage's engine could calculate Bernoulli numbers based on an algorithm of mechanical logic.

I cleared my throat. "Lord Byron's daughter Ada Lovelace wrote a poem called 'The Algorythm' which describes how a mechanical man could calculate, uhm, -"

Bernoulli!

"-Bernoulli numbers." I finished, hoping no one would ask me what the hellfire a Bernoulli number was.

Ada Lovelace was the poet Byron's daughter?

"I thought everyone knew that," I said, my turn to be smug.

"I knew it," said the Professor. "Alas, I also know Lovelace herself affirms that such a machine could never truly originate. It would merely harvest the fruits of the imagination of its creator."

"No doubt the angels said the same of Adam," retorted the student. He was getting heated. The rest of the class prepared answering volleys for that theological gunshot. He took shelter behind volume and speed, shouting excitedly. "The point is that Lovelace shows that a machine can reason. It can calculate. It can symbolize. It can remember. Lovelace is merely afraid to put into words the inevitable conclusion: a machine could be built to manipulate concepts just as a man does. To imagine. And when it does, and turns to imagining itself, you will have a man in the machine."

"What, no ghost in the machine?" asked the Professor.

At that word 'ghost' I remembered Ligeia. I turned to check. She was gone. No one else seemed to care. The Professor took a burning stick to draw his point in lines of fire. "Mister Poe points out that a machine such as the Chess Playing Automaton, which must interact with an antagonist, is far more 'man-like' than a mere pre-determined mechanical process such as the Babbage Engine. And yet he concludes even it is a fraud."

Point out to the Professor that the human brain is obviously a self-referential calculating engine. Tell him that in the future people will build entire worlds inside machines, worlds where the figure of a man stands in a field watching the sun set and wondering what the truth of the world is. Tell him any sufficiently self-referential active logic system is indistinguishable from-

I jumped up convinced Ligeia stood right behind me, her bared fangs ignored by these madmen. Then I spotted her. She had floated over the wall of broken statues. Now she stood by the black stone. She picked up the bowl and held it to her lips, pouring the blood and poppy juice down her throat as if it was a fountain and she the desert sand.

That student is right. Remind the Professor what Poe wrote about the Chess-playing automaton. He said if it WERE real, it would be a mind within a

machine. If it made its decisions in response to the actions of others it transcended from being a deterministic calculation to a thing of will and choice. Furthermore Poe says about Babbage that-

"Will you shut up about Poe?" I shouted. "What if she is still *thirsty?"*

At that desperate plea for a sensible return to panic, the Professor stood. He turned and surveyed the ring of divinity fragments. Then he walked from the fire, signaling his students to follow. The conversation died. Tinker, Cut-Throat and I slunk behind, the slow kids of the class.

The Professor stood outside the wall of broken gods, staring at the ground within the circle. There lay Ligeia, face smeared with blood and poppies, half-closed eyes turned inward to thoughts you wouldn't want to query. Cut-Throat and I stared surprised. She was just a young girl, not quite marriageable but more than ready to rule the boys for the summer dance season. I'd have taken off my coat and put it around her shoulders but I didn't have a coat. Cut-Throat looked like he wanted a coat just so he could do the same.

Then we all jumped back. A large storm-bird flew down from the trees and perched on the black stone block. One of the students squeaked. The Professor stared him quiet. The bird studied us, then stepped with comic formal steps towards the copper bowl. It turned its head sideways to peer into it depths.

Then it turned to peer at us again, as if asking *did we advise it to drink?* We stood imitating statues. I felt an urge to scratch my nose. I shook my head no, just slightly. In return it cocked its head and stared right at me with an eye as black and wise as the night sky removed of every single star, so that only the mystery and magic of the eternal void remained. And then it winked at me. Just like Typhon had done. And dearly beloved it came unto this prophet at that very moment, that a joke was being enacted by the gods. One this humble sailor was fully invited to appreciate, just never to understand.

Thoth dipped his head into the black liquid that still filled the bottom of the copper bowl. And drank, filling his beak, tipping his head back to let the liquid run down his throat. Three such swallows and he gave a flutter of wings as though intending to dive back up into the night. Instead he toppled to the ground next to the girl.

"Two in a night," breathed the Professor disbelieving. "Astonishing."

"No, not really," I said. I didn't like to correct a teacher in front of his students. But there was something the class needed to know, and fast. I settled for pointing.

Faint lights and dark shadows moved slowly between the trees and statues. They were dim discernable figures following the separate winding paths of the cemetery towards the center where we stood. Some by foot, some by air. Beings that did not stumble in the night, but moved through it as their natural medium. The dead gods from the wreck of Unicorn were fast arriving. To the feast we had called them.

The party was going to need a good many more punchbowls of blood.

Furthermore Poe says "certain data being given, certain results inevitably follow. We can without difficulty conceive the possibility of so arranging a mechanism, that upon starting in accordance with the data of the question to be solved, it should continue its movements regularly, progressively, and undeviatingly towards the required solution... But a game of chess has the uncertainty of each ensuing move. A few moves having been made, no step is certain. Different spectators of the game will advise different moves. All is then dependent upon the variable judgment of the players… There is then no analogy whatever between the operations of the Automaton Chess-Player, and those of the calculating machine of Mr. Babbage!"

Are you out of your mind?

Chapter 18

Submission to the Maidenhead Weekly Chronicle
Care of E. Blather, Literary Editor

Us, As Sisyphus
-- Clarence St. Elmo, 188?
What do we labor for?
What is this stone, this hill, this metaphor?
The rock: a ball without a game.
The hill, a pointless inclined plain.
Pushing becomes habit; we have no goal.
Only a dull wonder to see the world roll.

What can you give me?
What do you want in my offering hand?
Where are the borders that mark our land?
Hearts, souls, worlds; these are easily given;
Light empty things stuffed with meaning;
Cardboard cake at the ragdoll wedding.

There is a you I have not met.
Glimpsed at evenings, burning sunrises,
A smile on pillows, fading to forget.
Are you the rock and I the hill?
At the top, will you love me still?

Interviewer: Write her.

I told you. Poets and idiots knows the danger of creating in words the reality we reject. If I write her, she might reply. She might reply with sweet words recalling our past, adding kind words to wish me well in my present, ending with vague words hoping I wished her well in her future. And then I would be unmade by words, wondering which words were real. Is the word 'love' real? She is an ocean away and yet she will not look at me across the room?

Spirit, all I have left is uncertainty. Perhaps I once was loved. Would you leave me without even that last rock to cling to?

Write her, you coward. Write her even if she sits now on the porch swing with a bumpkin farmer staring down her dress. Write her even though she is dust and her children are dust and you are a blind sailor at the old sailor's etcetera. You boasted that soon or late time and tide bring words and sailors home. If that wasn't poetic pretension, then dare to deliver the damned words to the tide.

Dearest K. Dearest K. Dearest K. Dearest K. Dearest K. Dearest K.

I can't. I can't. I have no words I dare to say.

Bah. Describe the night in the cemetery.

The students gaped at the crowd slowly approaching through the fields of statues. The Professor whispered to himself. 'So many, so many'. Which gave me a shiver. I didn't hear fear in his voice. I heard desire. I had an awful vision of him attempting to put a crowd of ex-deities into bags and bottles, chasing gods through the night with a butterfly net.

But he recovered his senses. He ordered three of the students to fetch the donkeys. They ran off into the dark. I doubted they'd return. I sure wouldn't have. I grabbed Cut-Throat's arm. It was time to run for it. Again.

But the Professor pulled down part of the wall of broken statues. He made his way to Ligeia. Cut-Throat shook me off. He stood watching as the four remaining students bound her hands and feet with ropes. I watched him, wondering when he started swinging whether I had it in me to be any help. The Professor put a burlap sack over her head, and produced another into which he popped the storm-bird body of the god of wisdom.

The other students returned leading the donkeys by halters. The Professor led one into the circle and swiped a knife across its neck. It made a gasp and knelt. He didn't bother with a bowl. The poor beast's blood poured out to the cold stones. He took the halter of the next donkey and did the same, tugging hard when it shied back from the blood.

I felt sick. It seemed a shame to feed such kindly beasts to the hungry night and the thirsty earth. I don't deny it saved our lives. But I wouldn't have had the heart to do it. I can blame that on my poetic nature, but I won't be fooling any mirror. Being too fainthearted to do what you know must be done is just cowardice.

The Professor picked up Ligeia and laid her across the back of the third donkey, gently so as not to hurt its back. He tossed the bag holding the god of wisdom to a student and told us to follow if we didn't want to stay for dinner.

Describe escaping the cemetery.

We hurried away from the village of tombs into the surrounding crop fields of death. Here and there we passed some will-o-the-wisp former deity among the monuments who slowed to consider us. Theological class that we were, we did not stop to consider them in return. 'Hurry," said the Professor, and we obeyed.

Well, they did. I was already trailing the rest. I was tired. Shipwrecks and a night of dancing will take it out of a man. Then something dodged under my feet and I stumbled. I lay in weeds staring up at a stone angel gazing right back down. He kept his white marble wings folded high over his head as if worried I was going to get them dirty. Angels are snobs.

Whatever tripped me now sat on my chest and put its inhuman face to mine. I met its glowing eyes. It was a cat. Hellfire, it was the ship's cat Grayfoot. He batted a paw at my face, playful, just drawing a bit of blood to say hi to an old shipmate. I rubbed him behind the ears the way he liked. He gave a merp of approval and I felt cheered enough to sit up.

The others had hurried on, but one of the students took notice of my fall. He could have pretended not to. Instead he turned and headed back to help. That was brave. It inspired me to scrape up the strength to get back on my feet, using the angel's cold bony knee and leaving a smear of mud. Ha.

The student maneuvered around a grave and bumped into a figure in a cloak so black it might better be considered a hole gouged in the night. Not darkness. Just absence. The figure grabbed the student by the throat and lifted him casually up, the way you'd pluck a daisy from the grass to consider the beauty of its petals before ripping them thoughtfully off.

The student gave a gurgling scream. The donkey gave a haw of fear. The cat hissed. The stone angel remained silent. The others stopped, hesitating to turn back. A few of the will-o-the-wisps began moving towards us, smelling dinner or entertainment. I forced myself to consider the dark cloaked personage. This was a dead god, I'd seen him on deck and I knew his name. It was some Central American heathen magician deity that gave me the shivers to share the night with. What the hell, I shouted his name. I won't say it here.

He was surprised. I suppose one would be to hear their secret name shouted by a stranger in a cemetery at night on a lost island. He dropped the student, who rolled away gasping. I staggered forward, the cat almost tripping me again. The cloaked figure backed away. There was more light than before. My right hand glowed as though I grasped the blue sky pieces from a hundred stained glass church windows, a noon-day sun shining behind each.

I grabbed the student and half-fell, he grabbed me and half rose, and together we stumbled to reach the others. When we did Tinker gave me a look, Cut-Throat gave me a look, and the Professor gave me a look. The donkey gave me a look. I gave me a look. My hand was no longer glowing.

We hurried on until we reached the gate of the cemetery. We passed through and then dared to rest. We did a count and found everyone present, minus the two donkeys but plus two dead gods. I wanted to go back for the ship's cat. The others insisted the cat was not a priority. The Professor was determined to get back to the Seminary. I supposed he was being sensible of the dangers loose in the night. Later I understood he was in a sweat to get his two prizes safe back to his basement.

Cut-Throat walked along the side of the remaining donkey, holding on to Ligeia so she did not tumble and fall. He had that dreaming look in his face again. That worried me. They headed up the path. But I hung behind, looking back through the gate, hoping to see the cat come trotting through. A dull red glow shown from deep beyond the trees of the cemetery. I pictured all that spilled blood somehow turning to the kind of fire that seeps up from the earth. Made me shiver.

Only then did I notice the man standing leaning against the post of the cemetery gate, not five steps from me. His arms folded as though loitering outside a saloon till someone arrived with enough coin to finance a shared beer. He'd stayed so quiet we'd hurried right past him without noticing.

I recognized him at once, for all that he no longer had dragons for legs nor lightning for a crown. It was Typhon, chewing thoughtful on a blade of grass. He stared right at me and tipped his head slightly, as much as to say 'evening'.

Describe Typhon.

Well, as a storm he was best described in terms of things that burned and blew and whirled and roared. But in man-form he was of calm and oldish look. His back was curved with years at some patient labor. He had a stillness to his face that went strangely with hands that twitched, as though busy making something you couldn't see. Shoes, I decided later. It came to me of a sudden. He was hammering and cutting shoes, maybe holding the spare nails in his mouth.

His hair was winter-field stubble of black and grey. His face looked burned, not red with sun but black as if he'd been stoking a coal furnace all night, feeding some fire that made a thick black smoke.

Man or storm, the eyes were about the same. They were two windows to a determined rage that glowed above a polite and friendly smile. They were glowing at me now.

What did Typhon say?

He turned his head to the side, waiting for me to speak first. That's a preference of these ancient personages. They like to watch and study you before making any moves. They want you to dance and shout and have your say, while they take your measure. What counts to them is having the last word. I thought about turning my head in the opposite tilt and waiting for him to speak. But the others were hurrying up the path. I didn't want to stay for a staring contest. I'd lose. I never win staring contests, I fidget.

But there were questions I wanted to ask. I had a strong feeling Typhon hadn't struck me dead when he could have during the storm, which I didn't understand. Instead he'd given me a chronic case of electrified hand, which again I didn't understand. I had a suspicion that he and Thoth and maybe Matsu were conspiring together, which again: didn't understand. Somehow the two books counted in there somewhere, not that I understood how.

I settled for complaining. "I lost the ship's cat again."

Typhon snorted. "That beast can handle himself. Worry about whatever he takes into his fool head to stalk or befriend. Worry about the *island*." He leaned back against the post as though posing an idle question. "Why didn't you just say all their names?"

The question surprised me. "The dead gods? Thoth warned me not to."

"You did in the storm."

My turn to snort. "I was going to be axed, drowned, or fried by lightning. There was not a thing to lose."

Typhon nodded, his face expressionless but for that patient anger. His hands idly traced through the air, weaving spells or making boots. "Why not in the cemetery?"

I considered. "My dad always says to give running away a good try before resorting to anything dangerous. If they'd surrounded us with napkins and forks I would have ordered them to heel and be good gods. But I can't picture that ending well. I've seen them. Those beings would never take my orders without taking an equal amount of offense. I don't want a dead Aztec magician god plotting revenge at me."

Typhon spat an invisible shoe nail into his hand, studied it critically as though deciding whether it was straight enough to mend a boot. "Supposing you ordered them to crew you a ship home to your girl?"

Well? What did you say to Typhon?

We chatted a bit, caught up on old times but I got worried about the others. I told him goodnight and hurried along the path. I caught up to the students, the donkey and the castaways. They were standing in the path debating the worth of going back to fetch a poet. The donkey was adamant for going on and leaving him. I felt hurt but couldn't really blame the thing.

What did you answer to Typhon's question?

Ask me about the Spanish coin in my pocket.

Describe the Spanish coin in your pocket.

After storms in the Sea of Suns and Moons I generally walk the beach north of the light, where the sand runs in a smooth curve to frame a mile of Shipwreck Bay. I keep an eye out for castaways and colored shells, glass bottles with mysterious messages, brass bottles with imprisoned djinns, giant shoes turned to boats, mermaids caught in fishermen nets, fishermen caught in mermaid's arms, chests of pirate treasure half-buried in the sand, stranded magic fish willing to grant a wish, canoes filled with books I haven't read yet. I don't find any of these things except for the colored shells.

But one morning I walked the beach as the tide pulled back. I stepped careful so as to avoid crushing the little orange crabs that scuttle about. There on a rock something glinted. I scooped the silver coin up. It felt heavy; rounded and scarred as our moon. I looked around for more treasure, as a soul will do, but that was it. A gift from the tide. It was greedy to want more.

What has that got to do with what you said to Typhon?

Nothing. I was just thinking about it. I've always thought that someday something will happen and the only thing that can save me or the ship or the world is an old Spanish silver coin. Then to the astonishment of all, I will reach in my pocket and pull out that very coin the tide gave me.

Or perhaps it is not the tide I should thank. After all, it is the moon that pulls the tide. Our moon. I call it 'ours' because K and I agreed that moonless night at the lake, that whenever we were apart we would stand someplace and look at the moon and share it, and so sharing we would be together. So maybe K stared at the moon and pulled at it with her thoughts of me, and then the moon pulled at the sea and tugged the tide into giving me that coin. So the coin is from her in a way. And perhaps it will lead me back to her.

When the tide is right.

Fine. What did Typhon say?

I asked Typhon how the Banker tricked him out of his secret name. Typhon smiled. "I am never careful with my name. You will be told it's the deepest rule of magic and divinity: *Your true name is the key to your soul. Those who know it hold you in their hand*s." He smiled a very simple and shivery smile. "No one ever considers it must go both ways. When you know someone's true name then they stand inside the barred doors of your mind. To say the name of even a dead god is to appear in their innermost temple before their high priests. Good luck barking your orders then."

I considered that a bit. Typhon considered me a bit. Then he leaned forwards. He was obviously going to share something important. It was midnight and I was talking to a dead god outside a cemetery of blood-feasting shadows. I didn't want more uncanny secrets. My pockets bulged with uncanny secrets already. But I didn't want to be impolite either. Typhon whispered "Never trust anything that, when honestly asked, will not tell you its true name."

I figured that was a cue. "What is your true name?" I asked, reasonably honest.

He laughed. "*Typhon*. I am much too busy to be subtle."

What did you say to Typhon about going home?

What is your name?

What? We are the project team. For the interview.

I hurried up the path, caught up with the others, and we trudged best we could till we got to the seminary everyone called The Asylum. It was a big brick institution on the side of the mountain itself, which made a long walk uphill. I was tired. Four students carried Ligeia up the steps and through the front door, and I envied her the ride. She was starting to kick a bit. And the bag with Thoth began to stir. I offered to carry it but the student declined.

The last student led the remaining donkey towards a stable in the back, stroking its mane and telling it how sorry he was about its two friends. He had tears on his face, poor fellow. Those theology students were a kindly lot, to man and beast.

Just not to the gods.

Describe the Seminary.

The first thing I saw entering the door of the Asylum was the face of the Banker. I'd had my suspicions, but it still gave me a start. I stood in the front hallway staring at a large portrait of a large man in a large purple robe. A man with a warty pumpkin for a head, and hairy ears and nose and eyes. The painter had that ogre down to a level of detail that spoke of talent and nerve.

"Behold the Headmaster of our Seminary," said the Professor. "A remarkable man, and very keen to pursue divinity." The Professor and I turned to stare at each other, each trying to guess what the other knew, didn't know and might know. But the Professor was too keen to get his gods safely into bell-jars. He asked no questions, just ordered one of the students to show the castaways to the guest wing. Then he hurried away.

Cut-Throat wanted to follow the Professor. So did I, though more to check on the welfare of Thoth than

216

Ligeia. And we would have, if we understood better the school's curriculum of study. But we were enticed with talk of beds and baths and food. We followed our tempters upstairs.

I was shown into a room where I was introduced to a four-poster bed with feather-filled pillows. Bed and I fell in love at first sight. We embraced, and slept as one.

Chapter 19

Submission to the Maidenhead Weekly Chronicle
Care of E. Blather, Literary Editor

Winter
-- Clarence St. Elmo, 188?

Ice seals the leaves, black boughs unbending.
The trees close down like bankrupt shops.
Our spinning earth falters, slows, stops.
This winter is no season but an ending.

Dead leaves swirl trapped in cold dance,
Sailors pulled down the water to drown.
All of our choices are left to chance;
All of our colors are brown.

This orange sun gives light not life,
A painted flame without heat.
Our shadows all slashed with winter's knife.
Our hands, outstretched, too far to meet.

Interviewer: Describe the run through the Labyrinth.

Four servants of the Master of the Green armed with
pistols marched into the dungeon and ordered Cook and
the Baker to come with them. We shouted and swore,
asking what they were doing. They ignored us. Ten
minutes later they returned for Tinker and Cut-Throat.

Tinker staggered a bit. I was glad our New York Cut-Throat went with her. He has a strength of humor and energy that reassures in a tight place.

Granted, it left me alone in the dark with rats and my conscience, if there's s a difference. I should have held up better at that lunch. Why had I argued with the Master? Hadn't I learned to sit smiling for weeks of chat and malice at K's house? Apparently when you swallow your anger with sips of ginger tea, it doesn't flush out of the system. It just bides its time to bubble up.

To be fair to my mortal self, Cook and the Baker hadn't done any better. They hadn't gotten far as the soup before telling the Master he didn't know enough about horses to express a proper opinion. Specifically, the Baker told the Master that *if equestrian ignorance was fire then he'd be crapping flames till he shot about the room like a Chinese rocket.* It was an interesting expression. A month on board a ship together and I'd never heard the Baker talk that way. I wonder if he hadn't picked it up from me. Maybe I'm an influence.

Soon enough the servants came to fetch me. They marched me down halls and out a back door. The air felt wonderful; the light felt blinding. They led me to the gate of the labyrinth, explained that if I made it to the tree I could hit a bell that'd save my life and my friends, and pushed me in.

Describe the Baker.

Boot-leather skin and a faint Jamaican accent. A big man with bigger hands. You looked at those paws and realized you were in the presence of someone who could put their hand atop your head and pop your skull like an egg in a vice. He didn't, of course. There was no reason why he'd do such a crazy thing. It was just an idea that came to mind as you pondered those hands.

His billet was ship's carpenter but he left the work to Tinker. He'd gone to sea determined to leave sawdust behind. Baker wanted to be the ship's Master Gunner, and was powerful disappointed to learn Unicorn didn't have a cannon to its name. First day out, he asked the Captain what we would do about pirates. The captain replied we would bravely flee upon the winds, fleeter of foot for lack of big brass tubes and heavy iron cannonballs. That point of view entirely met the approval of my personal philosophy. I'll take a race over a battle any day.

Privately, the Baker expressed dissatisfaction. He and Tinker began drawing up designs for weaponry to decimate entire brigand fleets. At mess they'd put their heads together and sketch mechanical marvels of fire, death, and destruction that would have brought a convention of undertakers to their feet, cheering and throwing funeral lilies.

I don't remember the Baker ever holding a conversation with anyone but Tinker. So it hurt to see them quarrel when the ship becalmed. The Baker wanted to build a sensible catapult with material at hand. It would throw burning barrels of tar. Whereas Tinker advocated a redesign of the ship's figurehead requiring we dismantle most of the ship forward of the mizzenmast. The improved unicorn would shoot fire from her horn and fire bullets from her mouth. It sounded worth seeing, so I sided with Tinker. I didn't say so to the Baker. Not because of those hands. I'm just tactful.

Describe being in the labyrinth.

It turned you small. The space between the walls was narrow; just enough for two men to walk abreast. But the walls went twelve feet up. A grown man felt like a child in the hallway of a giant.

I started walking soon as the iron gates clanged shut. At least it was pretty. The walls varied. Sometimes thick green hedges, then sections of stone and brick. Sometimes bars of iron showed you parts of the maze you couldn't pass into, but might yet reach. Those places always seemed preferable to where you were. Quiet windows showing safe little bits of world sheltered from the dangers on your side of the wall.

But similar variations of the floor made walking and running treacherous. Sometimes smooth stone, sometimes slippery mud, sometimes sand that slowed the foot. I spotted footprints, no doubt from Cut-Throat and the rest. I saw animal prints. I stopped and studied one. A big print with claws.

I peered upwards, looking for some landmark to orient by. The mansion of the Master took up a quarter of the sky. High up was a balcony. People leaned against the railing to stare down, discussing what they saw. I studied a man and a woman sipping from wine glasses and discussing me. Something howled. The woman waved her hand as though advising me to go on. The man laughed. I went on.

I came to an intersection. An arrow drawn in the sand pointed left. That was clever. Tinker, probably. Was it best to catch up with the others? There was a better chance one of us would reach the center if we followed different paths. I looked up at the man and woman. She made a motion right. The man laughed. I went right.

The wall on the left became iron fence. I stared into a courtyard centered with a sundial. It looked peaceful. I tried to climb the fence but the bars were slippery with oil that turned my hands black. Something howled. I went on. I walked down a green corridor of grass and green shadow, and heard someone running, panting. No one appeared before or behind me. I bent down and peered into a crack between the hedges. The foot of someone ran past. It might have been Cook. I called out. Something ran to the wall, something hairy and panting. It threw itself at the crack and tried to break through snarling. I jumped back. A black nose poked at the crack, white teeth snarled. I walked on.

I came to a statue of a girl holding a box. The girl was stone. But the box was wood, hinged with brass. I stopped, debating. Perhaps it held food or a pistol. Or else a rattle snake. I turned to look up at the couple on the balcony. The woman nodded her head.

I opened the box. A black swarm of bees poured out. 'The man laughed. I ran, brushing bees from my face. A wire was set across the path. I leaped, brushing it with my heel. The ground trembled. I turned to look behind. A trap door had opened in the dirt. I considered looking down into the hole, then hurried on, thrashing at the air with my hands although the bees were left behind.

Someone screamed, a high-pitched cry of despair. I whirled about, then stared up at the couple. They were gazing elsewhere in the labyrinth, grown bored with me. The man sipped his wine. The woman motioned for someone to go left. Not me. I went on.

Describe how you survived the labyrinth

I wandered through choices meaningless for lack of context. Left and rights, forwards and back. I kept looking behind, certain that something followed. I found Tinker's wire glasses lying on the ground. I scooped them up, put them in my pocket. I heard calls, screams, growls. The clap of a gunshot, the sound of a hammer on stone.

Then music. I looked up at the balcony. A quartet was preparing. Piano, violin, cello and I think a flute, it was far away and I can never distinguish woodwind instruments by the sound. They tuned, hesitated, tuned, hesitated and then slipped into the first movement of Beethoven's piece *The Ghost Trio*. Someone screamed.

Something behind me repeated each choice I made, panting and snuffling. I began running down a corridor walled with ivy-curtained brick. I looked for places the ivy might be thick enough to climb. A door waited half-hidden in the leaves, the handle poking out. The sharp edge of a knife set in the handle sliced my palm. I stood back, pressing the bleeding hand under my other arm. I studied the door. The handle was fake, the hinges were to the right. I tugged the vines on the left and the door opened an inch, vines pulling away. I got my fingers in the space and pulled it open. I went through the door and pulled it closed behind me.

I stood in a small courtyard with a fountain dribbling drip, drip down to a dirty black pool. I caught a drop in my bleeding hand, sucked at it. I decided not to wash it in the unclean water. I heard Cut-Throat shout far off. I turned and looked at the balcony. Several feasters pointed at me as though I had become interesting again. Something scratched at the door.

Enough, I decided. My bleeding hand began to spark blue bits of Typhon's anger. I prepared to summon the dead gods. They would kill us, of course. Friends and enemies together. I'd learned that at the burning of the Asylum. I couldn't control them by saying their names any more than I could direct the stars by reading aloud an astronomy text. Hellfire take it all for nothing to lose. Let's push the temple pillars apart, and welcome the falling feasters to the labyrinth.

A storm bird dropped from the sky and settled on my shoulder.

"Don't," croaked the god of wisdom.

What happened at the Asylum?

I woke up twice in the night. The first time because I heard a wolf howling. I supposed it was a wolf. Actually I *hoped* it was a wolf, because if there wasn't a simple and honest wolf in the house there was something much worse. I shivered in bed listening to speech in the original languages of anger and despair, translated to howls.

I got up and felt my way to the door, opening it to stare shivering in the dark. Faint noises flowed through walls and floors. Growls, words, whispers. I might have been back on the deck of Unicorn, listening to the eerie presences in the cargo hold. Then I wondered if I was. Staring into the dark I felt the floor begin to rock as though on an uneasy ocean. I dared myself to put a foot into that hall, and shivered half a minute before taking the dare.

But with that one step a faint light appeared. A man sheltering a candle-flame with his hand strode through the night like an angel assigned to watch for wandering castaways.

He approached slowly, the candle forming his face in shards of shadow and light. It was a disturbing face. Not a bit angelic. I would have said more towards the demonic, except the eyes looked so sad and the mouth smiled so gentle, as if saying 'we all have our little flaws. Forgive me this face.'

"The subjects of study grow loud of nights," he whispered apologetically. "Mr. Coyote likes to howl, and bite, and curse, as they do. He shall weary of it soon, soon." I considered that statement, wondering what exactly it meant.

"I'm weary of it already," I replied. "Are you a student?"

The face shook slightly, as though briefly unmade and then remade by the question or the candle. "No," he said. He had an accent, or maybe his peculiar construction of mouth and teeth played a different music than the standard human woodwind. "I am Sobek," he affirmed, and smiled that apologetic smile again. "I am a former inmate of this institution, as Mr. Coyote is presently."

I nodded. Mr. Coyote howled. Mr. Sobek smiled. Mr. Candle flickered and Mr. St. Elmo retreated to his room, closing the door with the true coward's sensible attention to the 'click' of the latch. I hurried back to my love the four-poster bed.

But the love between bed and man had grown cold and formal. I lay there twisting this way and that, unable to more than skim the surface of dreams. At some point I woke to the rattle of the bed curtain rings. Someone pushed them aside to stare down at me. I held the blanket to my chin like Ebenezer Scrooge goggling at the ghost of Christmas Future. There was a similarity except this ghost was cloaked not in black but an absence of light. He was a familiar gouge removing the mere dark of night. And he had glowing yellow cat's eyes, which wasn't in Dickens at all.

I stared at Tezcatlipoca, the dead god I'd named in the cemetery to save the student.

He didn't waste time terrorizing me. I was already terrorized anyway. "Get up," he rumbled in a cat growl. A leopard-level cat.

"Get out," I countered. Then watered that down so as not to offend. "If you don't mind."

He shook his head, amusement turning his cat-throat chuckle a purr. "I will dissect you."

I got up. Apparently Typhon was right. That whole business of ordering the gods around with their secret names was so much folderol they told the tourists.

What did Thoth say in the Labyrinth?

"Don't," he said.

The thing that followed me through the maze hurled itself against the door. I looked for another exit, another threat, another choice. Someone screamed. The quartet on the balcony began a Handel piece, light and cheerful. I saw no other doors. There were statues behind the

227

fountain. Three women, each tastefully draped and holding out a hand invitingly. Something growled. Someone yelled.

"My friends are dying," I told Thoth. "I can't help them. I'm going to call the dead gods down upon this place and end it." I looked at the fountain. It was a series of concentric bowls, with a golden ball at the top. I climbed up onto the fountain and reached high to grab the sphere. It was heavy but not fixed. A golden apple.

"Your friends may live," said the bird. "Some of that noise is the Master's servants and dogs. Coyote and Ligeia have come over the wall. He's gone to help Tinker and Baker. She's gone to help Cut-Throat."

I held the shiny apple in my hand, stared at my distorted reflection. I hoped it was distorted, I looked terrible. I jumped down from the fountain, strode to the three statues. "What about Gypsy Cook?" I asked.

"I'm sorry," said the god of wisdom sadly.

I walked to the statues. The figure with the box had been Pandora. Here was a different scene from old myths. A man gives a golden apple to the goddess of love, slighting two others. But which statue represented love? I could see no difference except in the attitude of their faces. One stared intently forwards as though studying *me*. The next looked up to the sky with a smile, confident her hand would receive its due. The last looked down at the ground shyly, embarrassed to be holding out a hand at all.

It is love that fears to meet the eye. I hadn't known I knew that. I put the apple into the outstretched hand of the third statue. The arm of the Goddess of Love moved down like a lever. Something 'clicked' behind me. A pit opened in the stone floor. I walked towards it. The thing at the door scrabbled and growled, the door bending as though considering surrender. I looked down into the pit. A ladder led down to dark.

I glanced up at the balcony. The attention of many of the feasters focused on me now. Some waved as if encouraging an old friend to do their best. A few shook their heads as if telling me not to be a fool. The god of wisdom dove back into the sky. I climbed down to the dark.

Describe the Gypsy Cook.

My size and build, which is to say short and wiry. My age or thereabouts, but claiming vast more years without specifying an integer range you could debate. Quiet, with occasional outbursts of mystical explanation presented with the solemnity of a ten-year old narrating how angels reproduce by eating pinecones.

He made things up. We had that in common. I make things up. But Gypsy Cook worked to dignify his inventions. After pretending not to know English for a week, it's a wonder he didn't abandon the language entirely. Granted, pretending he knew how to cook never gave him the power to produce a single meal you didn't eat with the grimace of an angel eating a pinecone.

Describe the Gypsy Cook again.

He was the first friend I made on Unicorn. He had the hammock next to mine but preferred to sleep on the galley floor. It kept down pilfering from rats and hungry crew. For the first week out he pretended that he didn't understand English. We'd ask him why the devil he'd mixed coffee beans into the bread flour, why'd he put pepper and garlic on the hard tack, why would anyone make a soup out of raw beans and vinegar? And he would just shake his head as though disappointed to be among savages who could not express themselves except in grunts and groans. Then he'd rattle off something in his Gypsy-Romany, no doubt an eloquent explanation for why the world and supper was exactly as it had to be.

But he couldn't pull that stunt with the Captain or the First Mate. When it was obvious the man just randomly mixed items from shelves and cupboards into pans and plates, the Captain ordered the ship's Poet to assist in the galley. I felt I had been unfairly identified as an idler needing extra assignment. Which was not true. My hands that first week were red horrors of blisters I proudly displayed at every opportunity.

Eventually I realized the Captain considered Cook and I birds of a feather. I had come aboard solemnly asserting I knew how to kill and skin a whale. The

230

injustice of that burned bad as blisters. *My* lie was never put to the test. That entire voyage they never presented me with a single whale to kill and skin. I might have managed *fine*.

By the second week Cook had mastered the English language again. While I boiled beans and he peeled potatoes we'd talk about our homes, our gods, our girls. Like me, he came from a large family that made him feel a bit blurred, as though he were one face in a big photograph that everyone would point to someday and say 'I remember him. The brother of so-and-so. What was his name?'

He had powerful opinions about Wisdom and Destiny and the Truth behind the Curtain. He was always telling me the secret-meaning of some sign, like a storm-bird settling on the mast, or a porpoise following the ship's wake or a dream of a cat sitting on your chest. He told me those twisted bones of a dog in the Captain's cabin were the remains of a devil. It was Cook, not me, who stood on deck and declared to the mystified crew that we carried a cargo of dead gods destined to sink in the Sea of Time.

In hindsight, Gypsy Cook was the one member of the fool's crew that understood all the truths teasing the rest of us with whispers and thunders, promises and growls. We wandered blind, but he saw the meanings of the different turns and choices.

And what difference did that make? He still died in the maze running from one of those very devil-dogs. It ought to matter whether you stumble blind, or can see where you go and why. Yet it didn't. Dammit, I can't see the meaning of that at all.

Describe the tunnel under the labyrinth.

Water flowed out the stone mouth of a giant face, fast covering the floor. I considered blocking the spout with my hand or stuffing my shirt into it. Hurrying on seemed wiser. I splashed down the tunnel, cold water filling my boots. It grew darker with each step. Ten splashes came to a dead end where a second stone face grinned. It studied me from one great eye in its forehead. I looked for hinges, a handle, a lever, some decision to randomly make. Nothing but that idiot stone grin, mindless yet amused.

I splashed back to the start of the tunnel, the water now reaching my knees. The dark walls held carved pictures I'd missed before my eyes adjusted. My fingers traced pictures of ships and battles, a city and a giant wheeled horse. More ships, and at last an island where giants towered over little sailors fleeing for their little lives. Odysseus, on the island of the Cyclops. I hurried back down the tunnel, the water reaching my waist. I stood before the face of the Cyclops and I pushed my thumb into his one eye to blind him as Odysseus does.

Nothing happened. I pushed harder. The cold water reached my chest, making me shiver. I pushed both thumbs into the eye and screamed for the giant to be blinded, to be agonized, to be cast into darkness, his grin erased. I hated that giant with all my heart. The eye gave, moving back into the face. Something clicked above me. A square in the ceiling opened. A handle dangled, I reached up and pulled down a ladder. I climbed up.

Describe Tezcatlipoca.

You don't want the real description. Just picture him as man in a cat mask wearing a black coat. Furry gloves with long nails. He smelled of cat-musk and smoke and blood. His voice was a knife tracing its point up and down your spine. I remember he limped. When he walked, when he paced, one foot dragged. Even standing still he'd rock back and forth on that bad foot, as though it hurt him and he enjoyed that it hurt him.

He'd stand there rocking, turning his head this way and that to study you. He didn't do it to understand you. It was just predator analysis prior to a strike.

What happened with Tezcatlipoca?

He ordered me out of bed. I got up. He grabbed me and I prepared a yell. He put his face into mine. It was a red cave of white stalactites and stalagmites situated below twin yellow windows to hell. "Shut up or I'll eat you," he advised. I took the advice.

He dragged me across the room to a long mirror set in the wardrobe door. There was little light in the room and none in the glass. It looked wrong; too dark to be just black. Smoke seeped out as though it were water about to boil. Tezcatlipoca picked me up and threw me in. I expected to perish in shards and splinters but I passed through the same as I when I plunged into the sea.

And I sank into a room exactly like the one I left. A four-poster bed, my pack upon the floor. I stumbled to my feet. There was someone in the bed. I approached and stared down at a face I recognized from frequent admirations in proper mirrors. It was me. Well except tonight I looked hollow-eyed and troubled, as though after a hard day I'd slipped into an unpleasant dream. Which summed the essentials.

Tezcatlipoca jumped through the mirror behind me. He went to my pack and emptied it out on the floor, which aggravated. Leave my things alone dammit.

"Where is it?" he asked. "And if you say 'where is what?' I will *bite* you."

Tezcat had a redeeming quality. He got to the point. He didn't acknowledge anything in conversation except the critical point. Teeth, claws, elemental truths; he saw all reality in terms of clear and salient points.

But this was a dream, or else I wouldn't be seeing myself lying in bed dreaming. That's logic, that is. And I have always been able to handle myself in dreams.

"I hid it, of course, you spiteful mangy snaggle-toothed rat-cat," I replied.

He widened his yellow hell-windows as though I'd become mildly interesting.

"Tell us where."

"Scat or I summon Anubis, Cerberus and Fenris to chase your tail up a -"

He grabbed my throat and dragged me to the door. He pulled it open and there was more dragging of poets down a hall, two flights of stairs and then more doors and halls. I varied the time between making choking sounds and trying to poke, scratch or punch with comic ineffectuality. We passed Sobek, sheltering a candle and whispering to its flame. Tezcatlipoca stopped dragging me to stare. I stopped choking to stare. The man was talking to a candle. I squeaked for help. Sobek ignored us, though the candle-flame flickered sympathetically. Tezcatlipoca shook his head as if to say *the things you see* and we continued on.

At some point I could breathe and see again, though I still couldn't move. I blinked at a small and elegant amphitheater, in the center of which lay a poet inelegantly bound to a table. I recognized the general design and purpose of the room. I even understood the purpose of the sharp steel and nickel tools in the racks beside the bound poet. Years ago I had visited a chamber just like this when I watched the first thirty seconds of an appendectomy. The thirty-first second was spent running green-faced to the exit.

I lay tied to the work table of an operating theatre.

Describe the remaining book bound in green leather.

When the ship sank I shoved one book in my pack, using the other to hit the Banker on the head. That book was hit by lightning. I dropped it burning into the crow's nest, while I dropped in my turn, burning into the sea.

On shore, when I recovered enough to care, I pulled the remaining book out of my pack. Thoth and I looked it over. The oil-cloth wrapping had protected it some, but not enough. The wet pages clung together. The first half of the book was pretty much destroyed, just wet paper with the words washed away.

The second half was a blurry but readable French.

Give an excerpt from the remaining pages of the remaining book bound in green leather.

The border between life and death has three guards: the Dog, the Stone, and the Fire. Dog and Stone ensure that the living never trouble the dead. Stone blocks the doorway, Dog guards the door. And the guard of Fire holds back the dead that seek to return to life.

Yet just as the living sometimes venture into the kingdom of Death, there is a secret path by which the dead can return to life. They must pass through the Houses following the mortal fire, and have their hearts weighed, following a guide who is

A guide who is what?

Reset.

What? Follow the what?

I don't understand the question.

Did you just reset *yourself*?

Would I know if I did?

I don't know.

Well, let's give it a try. Reset.

Did it work?

Did what work?

Stop that!

I was in a shipwreck once. If you like I will tell you about it.

Chapter 20

My K.

I pass this letter to one who will send it to my brother, who shall see it to your hand. I do not trust my words to reach you otherwise. Nor should you trust any message that bears my name but not my love. The air has become like to the valley of the Shadow of Death; full of treacherous words speaking in our own voices of easy wisdom and petty surrender. My love, believe only in those words that speak my love. Believe in my love. Believe.

I am not capable of wishing you well in a life without me. I am not capable of giving you up. I have no use for wisdom that says we must part. And I stand beneath our moon declaring I have no power to summon heart nor mind nor spirit and order them to forget you. No. So long as my heart and mind and soul continue to worship you, I am their most faithful servant.

I believe in your love for me. Believe in mine for you. Believe in my love.

Remember the moonless night when we claimed the moon for the mirror of our love. Our moon. Recall the snowfalls and fevers through which we walked together, reading of tigers and flames, islands and gardens. Remember my love. Remember.

The next ship I take will be the one to bring me home.

The contained item submitted to the postal system of New Jersey has been returned to sender for the following reason(s): Address no longer valid.

Dammit.

Describe what happened in the operating theatre.

Which? I've been in three. Once in a teaching hospital in Princeton. Once in the Seminary at Theodosia. And once in a dream. That last was unpleasant. Actually all three were unpleasant. Upon due consideration, what fool expects to have a pleasant time in a room designed to observe a living creature cut open for display?

If I was a cynical and brooding poet I'd say the whole damned world is an operating theatre. And yes, I find that of late I am both cynical and brooding. We therefore raise the count to four.

Describe what happened in the operating theatre *in the dream.*

Tezcatlipoca stood above me. He wore a white doctor's smock that added an accent of sinister modernity to his traditional night-demon cloak.

"I've already had my appendix out," I lied.

"Then how about your lungs?" asked the ex-deity. He traced a cat-claw along my throat. "You still have them." He paused to consider, then qualified that with "for the moment."

I looked in panic about the room. There were a dozen figures scattered about the amphitheater. They all wore cloaks like Tezcatlipoca's, hoods putting faces into shadow. I marked how each sat carefully not too near the next. Like strangers in theatre seats who don't know each other. Or like family at a gathering who know each other too well. I debated the pointlessness of asking them for help.

Tezcatlipoca turned to a rack of sharp-edged dangerous things that pierced, poked and sliced. He selected a scalpel, holding a single finger-claw next to it as if to compare the lethality of the two. While doing so he asked, idly, "What exactly are Thoth and Typhon plotting?"

It was a good question. "Wish I knew," I admitted. "Far as I can see I'm really just kind of holding stuff for them."

One of the robed figures had a question for the class. She didn't raise her hand first. The gods don't raise their hands. "Matsu gave you her luck, Thoth gave you his book, and Typhon gave you his fire," she observed. Her voice was a thing of beauty, dove songs on summer mornings translated to human speech. "Why?"

"They are romantics," said another, just as I was about to answer. "How could they resist such a gormless hero?" I sighed at that, swallowing my reply and the faint taste of ginger. This began to feel like tea with the aunts.

"Matsu is a romantic, certainly," said a third. "Thoth, on occasion. Typhon, not."

"Typhon wants us dead," replied the first speaker. "And to stay dead. Ten thousand years and not a spark less determined than the day he stormed the heavens."

"He lost," snarled another. "He will lose again."

"He always loses," agreed a third. "But that does not mean we win."

There came a long and brooding silence that was the more disturbing because it had nothing to do with me at all. A shiver passed down my spine. It is difficult to explain, but I felt a sympathy for these beings. I felt ashamed to be taking up their attention. The journey they marched was far longer than my brief story, filled with oceanic sorrows and mountain-top joys.

It made me feel like a whiny child to object to a trivial vivisection.

Where did you hide the remaining book?

The second morning after the shipwreck Thoth woke me in my bed of piled leaves under the trees along the shore. I started, still capable of being shocked at a world that did not rock beneath me but held firm as though it were so much dead stone floating in space.

"Cock-a-doodle doo," said Thoth. He threw back his head, fanning his scanty tail feathers rooster-like. I glared at him. I wanted to sleep another millennium, drowse a century then have coffee. But once awake, the bed of leaves became unbearable. It was bad as lying in a damp hair shirt on a bed of nails and bugs.

First thing we did, we took out the remaining book and examined it. It was the French translation. The sea had washed the first half of the book to a clean blue-white, empty of words. I thought Thoth would be angry, but he took the loss suspiciously calm.

The wet paper needed to air, he told me. We separated the pages with tree-leaves and I set it on a rock. Then he led me down to the shore, fluttering ahead, walking on the sand with that comic-serious march a long-legged bird makes. The tracks he left behind reminded me of the bird-prints in the Captain's log.

He stopped and pointed out a barrel that must have come from the galley. It held hard tack watered soft, and salted pork twice-salted from the sea. Both edible in a damp way, and a better breakfast than I would have made of nuts in the woods.

That was a kindness of Thoth, because I was dreadful afraid to look directly at the things floating in the surf. I feared to see Cut-Throat or Gypsy Cook lying clean and blue-white, washed of words. Or Preacher or Grocer, though I already knew they'd perished. I wondered about the Banker. It'd be horrible to see him dragged back and forth in the surf. But it'd be a relief too.

It didn't help that there were a multitude of faces and arms and legs lying in the wash and wrack, eyes of stone and clay and wood staring up just as dead as the eyes of a drowned man. I felt an urge to cover those faces, fold the hands over their chests. I didn't. It would have been a fool's gesture, and for once in my life this fool was too tired and sad to bother.

Thoth led me to a tide-line of debris. Tangled in sea-weed was a bundle of sail-cloth, which I unwrapped to discover a book bound in green leather singed with black. The very book I'd dropped in the crow's nest. I opened it to find the pages of the second half of the book burned into unreadable ash.

"How?" I asked.

"Dolphin?" suggested Thoth.

"Preacher?" I asked.

"Maybe," he replied vaguely. "I can never tell them apart."

We went back to the rock where the first book sat, pages fluttering like bird feathers. Thoth had me detach the readable pages from both books, giving us a sheaf of pages that made one book, half in the original but unreadable Etruscan, the other half in readable if untrustworthy French. While I did so he flew away and returned with lengths of string, like a bird building a nest. Then I rolled the pages into a scroll and bound them tight.

He warned me to stay out of the woods, grabbed the scroll in his talons and flew off. I watched him struggle towards the lighthouse on its far lonely rock. He flapped up to a high window that was a dark open square. Therein he disappeared.

After a while I got bored and decided to explore the woods.

Describe what happened in the operating theatre in the dream.

Tezcatlipoca compared a scalpel and the fore-finger nail of his right hand, judging efficacy. I could see the consideration he gave the question. Was sharpest always best? Wasn't there more satisfaction in digging deep with something that took its time? Why all this modern hurry?

"I hid the book in the cemetery," I told him.

"Where in the cemetery" asked Tezcat, and slashed my shirt front open with the scalpel.

"Between the wings of the stone angel in the cemetery where I saw you last night," I said. I said it *fast*.

He stared at me, holding the scalpel over my heart. "Should I believe you?"

I shook my head, suddenly taken by a fit of honesty. "No, not really."

"Well that's refreshing," he said and dug the scalpel into the pale delicate skin above my heart. I screamed. It hurt. He dug around while I screamed some more, thrashing uselessly against the restraints. Then he reached a claw in and pulled out my heart. He held it high to display to the operating theatre. It was a bloody rag of paper. Tezcatlipoca untangled it carefully. Then to the laughter of the gods he began to read.

By a dead fountain, on a bed of stone,
in a hall of silence, I awoke alone.
In an empty courtyard,
in dust and morning light

I hurried from the ruin,
Where I had kept the night.

"Oh no you don't," I snarled. Not this again. My right hand began to itch with a thousand electric ants crawling across the skin.

"Give us what we want," said the ex-deity with the voice of singing doves.

"And what the hell do you lunatics want?" I shouted.

"To return to life," replied the dead gods together.

"For you to stop yelling," said Cut-Throat. He was leaning through the bed-curtains, shaking me rough by the shoulder. I was back in that gentle invention of civilization, my beloved four-poster feather bed. Behind him stood Tinker and a few of the students. They were staring at my right hand again.

"What yelling?" I asked defensively, hiding its glow beneath the pillow.

Describe running in the Labyrinth.

I climbed out of the water-filled tunnel into evening-shadowed space between two high hedges. I stood dripping and shivering, deciding direction with a shrug. The choice wandered around a curve to stop dead at a fence of high iron bars. Behind the fence, their backs to me, stood two people. A tall gangly man in sailor's clothes, and a chit of a girl in a white nightdress and braids of red.

They faced a thing on all fours that resembled a dog. *Resembled*. It was furless and red-eyed, skin knotted and twisted with warts like failures of its weaving. Its opened jaws showed teeth curling like cat's claws. I recognized those teeth from the Captain's cabin, the strange bones on the table.

Cut-Throat had a bleeding rip in his pants leg. He slumped, looking tired as I felt. I couldn't see Ligeia's face but I pictured her look of graceful violence. I did not blame the dog-thing for keeping a distance. The creature growled. Ligeia growled right back. Of the two, hers was the deeper. Hers was the scarier.

Then I glanced at their hands in shock. Cut-Throat and Ligeia were clasping hands tightly, two children comforting each other in a Halloween spook house.

I backed away, not speaking. I had no help to give, and no words worth a second of distraction. But I resolved to get them out alive. I hurried in the opposite direction, and when I came to a last bit of sunshine I glared up at the balcony. Servants were lighting white candles upon the tables. The quartet played a Mozart piece, full of fast notes and sly joy. The feasters gazed down at my part of the maze. One stood at the railing towering over the others; a huge man with a head like an ugly hairy pumpkin.

I stared at the Banker. He leaned forwards, grasping a wine-glass that caught the setting sun. He sipped it slowly, watching me. The man didn't so much as even pretend to offer a toast.

How did the Banker survive the wreck of Unicorn?

I have no idea. The ship foundered minutes after I fell from the crow's nest. That might've given him time to grab the burning book, climb down the rigging and prepare, maybe tie himself to something that floated. He was a crazy killer but I can picture him being damned efficient in a desperate situation. Whereas a poet would have run around in circles composing a last beautiful couplet, the useless creature.

Typhon held back the storm when the Banker ordered him to. Typhon might have also helped him to shore. If so, why he did those things only Typhon knows. It wasn't for someone barking orders signed with his name.

Banker knew the island, of course. The fact that he wasn't at the Seminary when we arrived makes me guess he didn't come to shore anywhere near Shipwreck Bay. The current beyond the breakers can drag man and flotsam all the way south and west of the island. He might have had a long swim, followed by a longer hike. But somewhere in the water he must have lost the burned book, for me to regain by suspicious chance or Matsu's direction.

He probably arrived at his Seminary only to find I had just burned it down and departed. Ha. The sight of that smoking ruin must have had something to do with the look on his face as he watched me run for my life through the labyrinth.

Describe burning down the Asylum.

We had breakfast. It was eggs and bacon. It was delicious. Correction. It was holy. A ceremony of spiritual restoration. I believe there was talk at the table. Discussions concerning gods and jams, salvation and pancakes and how hot was the coffee in Heaven. But I didn't hear the words. After weeks of profane meals onboard Unicorn, the sacrament of a real breakfast needed no liturgy, no sermon, no verbal affirmation of doctrine. No, that Breakfast was a holy thing moving beyond the tongue of man and angel and down into the stomach doubly blessed by second helpings.

There was a little fairy silver spoon to asperge salt upon the eggs. Pepper sprinkled out from great ecclesiastical censor of a pepper grinder. There were holy wafers of still-warm toast. Jam from a blessed spoon round as our moon. And wondrously, reverently, the high priests repeatedly brought the sacred chalice of hot coffee for the congregation to receive.

I frowned at Cut-Throat when his stained soul moved him to steal the last sacrament of toast. The blasphemy caused me to remember the other sinners at the table-service. I looked up to see the students staring at us castaways, astonished at our hunger for the blessings provided.

"Thank you," I said, just as my mother taught me.

The Professor grinned and shook his head. "Do not thank us. This is hire and salary. I intend to make you pay for breakfast with answers to long questions." That was more true than I took it at the time.

I waved a hand dismissive of the cost. "Ask. Receive."

"Describe how you were shipwrecked," he said.

Describe how you described you were shipwrecked.

Cut-Throat jumped like an amateur right to the storm making grand waves of his hands. The Headmaster cut him off. "One version at a time. " He pointed at me. I nodded with the practiced innocence that only a male sibling of six evil sisters can project when singled out to provide testimony.

I told how I was a rigger persuaded to sign aboard Unicorn, a three-masted schooner contracted to bring a private collection of religious icons, texts and statuary to Singapore. Unicorn's Captain was desperate to find experienced seamen such as I in San Francisco. The previous crew had jumped ship in superstitious fear of the cargo.

Two weeks into the Pacific we becalmed, drifting for days in a windless ocean. The Captain drank himself into a suicidal frenzy while the deranged first mate confined himself to the forward cargo hold. At this point the lack of officers and the inexperience of the crew proved fatal. Though warned by their brave rigger of approaching

249

weather, they delayed, then panicked. When the foretold storm came Unicorn was allowed to drift onto the breakers of Theodosia. The crew abandoned ship and their brave rigger only to overturn their boat in the dangerous storm currents of Shipwreck Bay.

At the end of this story I shook my head, moved by my own description. Sailing the seas was a cold and logical business, no place for dreamers and fools.

The Professor considered me quietly. I considered a constellation of toast crumbs on the table, wondering when lunch might be. There followed more considering and more evasive eye movement.

He sighed and rose. "Come with," he instructed. I traded wordless messages with Cut-Throat and Tinker. I could see we were wondering the same thing. Did they serve lunch in a separate room of the Seminary? It seemed a hope worth the leap of faith.

But my faith proved in vain. He led us to the Asylum operating theatre.

Describe what happened in the operating theatre of the Asylum.

I had a kind of fit at the door when I recognized the place where I had been disheartened in a dream. It did not seem a good augury. In fact it reminded of parts of the Libris Acherontia that dealt with prophecies discerned in the reading of dreams, guts, entrails and such things properly left inside a body.

The Professor nodded at my reaction. He had no business doing so. Gypsy Cook will do the same thing. Put on a knowing look to give himself mystical airs. Something unexpected will happen and Cook will nod as if to say *just as I foresaw.* Cut-Throat does it too, assigning it to his detective skills. Granted he did detect how someone was hiding in the hold. And Cook looked at the guts of the ship's voyage and made the correct interpretation of its end. Whereas for all his knowing glances the Professor kept being a step behind. That left him two steps from where he needed to be.

He instructed us to sit up front, as though we were students rather than grownup sailor-castaway adventurers with a week's growth of beard on two of our three faces. But he'd officiated at that sacrament uniting man and breakfast, so we cooperated. The four students who accompanied us, solemn in their black coats, were allowed to sit farther back. Between us and the exit, I noticed. They were keeping their hands casually clear of whatever they carried beneath their coats, same as in the cemetery waiting for a vampire.

The Professor strode down to the center of the amphitheater.

"Welcome, visitors" he said. "Let's talk."

Chapter 21

Dear Sir or Madam;

I write to inquire as to a letter you recently sent, addressed to a K. King, the Rectory, Maidenhead, New Jersey. As the letter was forwarded to us at the Trenton Archive for Rural Letters, I thought it permissible to open. The contents are a bit confusing.

The King family was prominent in the township once known as Maidenhead (settled by colonists from the same-named town in England). While the Rectory no longer stands, it can be seen in photographs taken as late as 1930, when the highway was widened (to the loss of the town's quiet charm, in my opinion). The Rectory itself would have been property of the local Methodist church. The King family residing there from the mid-1870s to the end of the century, during the ministry of the Reverend Obadiah King.

You seem to have sent a love letter to his daughter. I can only find references to her as 'K'. Researching the online files of the Maidenhead Weekly Gazette (bought by the New Jersey Standard in 1950, which was purchased by the Trenton Examiner in 1980, which folded in 2001) I find a birth announcement and an engagement announcement, again only referring to 'K' as if that was all the name given the individual. There seems to have been a scandal or confusion that occurred in the fall of late 1880s. I find no reference to this individual past 1890. Still, much of our material remains offline.

While your letter was modernly printed and followed the speech patterns of a later age, it seemed to express a sincere emotional concern that a collector of old legal notices finds refreshing. If you

were forwarding on a lost love note from some storm-tossed sailor,
then good for you! Much of our archives are old letters randomly
saved by time and wind. I shall search; and if I find among them
any suitable reply from Miss King, I shall forward it on.

From one romantic to another,
Henrietta Smeed,
Director, Archive of Rural Letters,
Trenton, New Jersey.

Interviewer: describe reaching the center of the labyrinth.

The walls curved inwards, beginning a fatal spiral. I came to the bronze statue of a man holding a sword. He barred the way, legs braced for a fight, mouth open in a shout. The sword looked real. Being real myself I decided I had first claim on that weapon. I reached to pull it from his hand then reconsidered. I studied the ground beneath the statue. It was old stone and showed stains suspicious to an augur's practiced eye. I saw the clouds of Elysium in those stains. So I moved behind the statue and kicked it.

The arm swept down like a mouse-trap sprung, cutting the air before it with the sword. When it stopped I kicked again. Nothing happened. I bent down and pulled the sword out of the statue's grasp. It was short but light, and felt reassuring to hold. There were some applause from the balcony. Also some booing. I went on.

The curving corridor opened out to a wide circular courtyard centered by a great black oak tree. The entire courtyard was paved with lines and curves of pale white bones, old yellow bones, dusty gray bones. Between the bones was the dust of bones. My footsteps crunched and snapped bones like old sticks as I walked towards the tree, holding the sword before me. Then out from behind the trunk stepped the Master of the Green. He smiled, leaning back with a competent pose of indifference.

"Let's talk," he said.

"I'm all for talking," I replied, though privately I decided talk would be prelude to stabbing and chopping. But it worried me that I had a weapon and he did not. I'm not a complete idiot, they left some of the parts out. "Where's that bell I hit to save my friends?"

The Master shrugged to say he didn't bother with domestic details; *ask a servant, perhaps they'll know.* Instead he announced "Congratulations on reaching the center. In reward, you shall go home."

I nodded as though I believed him, while edging to the right, facing the tree, looking for a gong or bell. This annoyed the Master of the Green, expressed with a yawn and the drawing of a pistol. "I was a god, you know," he remarked. Again I nodded. Seemed likely. On Theodosia encountering ex-deity was astonishing as sharing a train car with a broom salesman. He maundered while I circled. "Call me... *Iskandar.* For five hundred years I was worshipped. Then I came here." He swept a hand to summarize a boneyard under a dead tree. "To... *this*." He wanted my sympathy.

"Iskandar, you have my full and complete sympathy," I lied. I circled farther, stepping sideways to keep my sword pointed at his pistol. Yes, I know that was worthless but it was a comfort. I pictured parrying the bullet before it hit me. That would be impressive. Don't tell me you wouldn't think the same. The Master followed, circling in his easier orbit closer to the center of the tree.

"Don't ring the bell and I promise to send you home," he said, getting to the point.

"What about my friends?"

The Master shrugged, unable to see any import to the question. "They may have the same offer if they reach the tree."

Surprisingly, I wasn't tempted. I mean, if an honest Lucifer appeared offering me the choice of abandoning my friends to their fate in exchange for a bat-winged ride to New Jersey, my soul would have sweated some. But Iskandar was no Lucifer. He couldn't pass a believable lie if he digested it first. I nodded vaguely, stepping sideways onto a jangle of rib-cages. My foot tangled inside them. I shook the leg, trying to free it.

At that point round the tree came one of the twisted dogs. I yelled and kicked. The rib cage flew off my foot and struck the beast's head, catching there neat as a hat tossed onto a bed post. Iskandar and I studied that rather unlikely event. The dog shook its head trying to free itself, snapping at the bones. I thanked the lucky coin in my pocket and brought the sword down with a vicious two-handed blow that missed the beast completely. The swing sent me tumbling and rolling around the tree, where I came to rest under a round bronze gong hanging from a dead branch.

I swung up at it with the sword, missed, swung again, missed, and on the third time took a breath and slowly carefully missed again. Cursing angrily I swung wildly and it rang; a frighteningly deep sound that must have carried all across the labyrinth till it thrummed the wine glasses on the balcony.

The dog-thing threw itself at my throat, the tangle of ribs still muzzling its jaws. We flailed and scrabbled at each other till the Master of the Green lowered his pistol, yawned and shot it in the head.

There came light applause from the balcony. The musicians began the third movement of Beethoven's Ghost Trio. The Master of the Green sighed, as though I had made a faux pas before his dinner guests. No doubt I had. "No voyage home for this Ulysses," he said. He gave his dead dog a disappointed kick and walked away.

Chapter 22

My K.

I would have returned. I would have crossed seas, burst down doors and sent aunts flying from my path, just to bend my knee before you and ask you to take me as your husband. That is how our story should have ended. Returned to you victorious, never to part.

I would have carried you over a threshold, held you in my arms in a bed meant not for a night but for a life. I would have risen with you sunrise upon sunrise to open the day's gifts together. And we would have accepted what gifts came, the good and bad, the joyous and the sad. Cats and children and work and trouble and sickness and snow and fever and all the terrible wonders of daily life. I would have walked each day anxious for the sun to set again, just so that I could hurry back to our bed, shoes and shirts scattered on the floor. Day upon week upon year upon decade we would have smiled to see each other grow older, slower, wiser, grayer. Our jokes would condense to coded references bringing us to laughter. The mere tilt of an eyebrow would learn to deliver long soliloquies upon life and love, desire and fulfillment. Sitting at dinner, strolling on walks, lying against pillows our hands would keep drifting to clasp together, fretful and incomplete when empty.

Would have. But instead I wandered far away to end here, sending you my last words under strange stars, strange winds, to the distant sound of a strange and awful sea.

What words are left us? I have none for myself, except to remind myself that I was loved. And so all the comfort I have to send is the same. K, you must keep alive the memory that you were loved. Forget me, but remember my love, and as you do we will be together. That is the end we must make of our story. We loved, we were loved.

It would make a poor end if you never loved again.

Not sending that.

Why.

You aren't dead yet.

Going to be. And she is too far away, across a sea of time and distance. Spirit, it is what I should have found the courage to say long, long ago. Perhaps all the purpose of your haunting has been only to lead me to find the courage to say those words.

So send them and let me rest in peace. And K as well.

The contained item submitted to the postal system of New Jersey has been returned to sender for the following reason(s): Address no longer valid.

You are suddenly the romantic, Spirit. Or else the cynic. Do you fear that if I no longer live in hope of K receiving my words, you can no longer drive me in the direction you want?

Quitter.

Am not.

Bah. Describe the duel on the Green.

I stood on the green in the morning light, ignoring some ceremonial folderol about the Tree and The Rites and the Master. I was feeling very strange. Which is not surprising after a day and a night of no sleep and no food but a bit of doped bread. But I suddenly felt a giddy sense of confidence. Which one must consider surprising. The affair was a cheat designed to tastefully lay me dead on the morning grass. But the garden, the dawn, the watchers, the ceremony were dream-like to my whirling brain. And I have always been able to handle myself in dreams.

I shook my head and walked out into the green plain of the lawn. My feet made dark prints in the silvery dew. My eyes searched for something in the distance, not knowing for what till I spotted it. There on the seaward side where the land terraced downwards, past trees and the slope of the island down to the shining water, I saw far away but clear, the top chamber of the light house.

The morning light shone off the lantern room lenses as though the tower captured all the sun's fire and sent it direct to me as a gift, as a greeting, as a caress. I reached up to grasp it, laughing in delight.

"Here now fellow, return to your place," called the Master of the Green petulantly. "Don't go wandering off."

I turned to him puzzled. My place? What was that? When was that? I had to study my surroundings to recognize where I was. In the parlor of K's house, of course. And there was K, pouring a stone pitcher she held in her bare white arms. She looked so beautiful I cried out. But she would not meet my gaze. She stared fixedly down at the water flowing away, away across the carpet. The Aunts stood ranged in a line between us, armed with swords and pistols. Dressed in green velvet that made them seem snakes. They looked bored but amused, sure they could keep me from the girl I loved.

I turned to K's father, leaning against the fireplace mantle. He tapped the carpet before him impatiently with a thin sword. He no longer held the poem. Had he burned it? At that thought I felt as hot as if I myself had been plunged into the fire. This man had taken something precious from me, just for his petty spite, his pompous malice. Taken my poem, my hope, my chance to love and be loved. Taken *her*.

I began walking towards him, swinging my foil back and forth like the pendulum of a clock gone mad, swiping arcs of dew from blades of grass. Rage gathered in my hand as writhing snakes of blue flame.

"I was a guest in your house," I snarled, and took the head off a daisy. "You were the host. There are obligations. Of civility, of humanity, of divinity." Suddenly the path between us was carpeted with daisies. I beheaded them as I approached, matching words with cuts. "You. Forgot. Your. Obligations."

K's father's face altered from mild boredom to sudden alarm. He took a step back, raising his sword.

"It wasn't your poem!" I shouted, and pointed my foil at him. The blade burned with blue fire as though dipped in burning brandy. K's father opened his mouth and closed it again, a fish blowing bubbles in a bowl.

"You're mad," he said. A dreary complaint that made me smile. And for once his voice lacked its masterful control of volume and depth. He quacked the words, a panicked duck. "You're mad."

I swept my foil at him. He jumped back spry for a man of his years. Then he parried marvelously quick. But at the clank of blades he cried out as though thunder-struck. He dropped his foil to the carpet and backed against the fireplace mantle, bringing the stung hand to his mouth.

"*Now* we're finally seeing a bit of St. Elmo's fire," I laughed, and raised my sword to run him through. One of the aunts (Hildegard, it had to be) shouted and swung a pistol at my head. But a storm-bird swept down, clawing at her face. I was a bit puzzled at its presence at tea. I supposed Aunt Agatha had let it in. I don't deny her sense of humor.

Aunt Hildegard dropped the pistol, flailing at the bird. Now the other aunts were turning and shouting. A girl with braids red as scratches on a penny picked up Aunt Greta and tossed her clear across the parlor. I stared astonished. Why hadn't I ever thought to do that myself? A foam-jawed yellow wolf leaped howling at Aunts Jane

261

and Plain. They screamed as though it were a mouse waved in their faces. Tinker, Cut-Throat and the Baker shouted and rushed across the room, leaping over the couch.

I turned back to K's father, who had picked the fallen pistol up from the carpet. He pointed it at me, foolishly opening his mouth to sermonize before he fired. I stabbed his ministerial chest, emphasizing my dull point.

There came a white flash of light down from the sky and through my blade, a clap of thunder, and he fell burning into his own fireplace flames. The fire consumed him as though he were so many inked pages of unworthy words.

Remember the wine is poisoned. Do not drink the glass of wine.

"I can't hear," I complained. The thunder clap had reduced all sounds in my ears to a hum of angry insects. Nor could I see. The flash blinded me with pink and purple worms that crept across a gray curtain. I rubbed at them uselessly. The earth beneath my feet rose up and down. Without seaman's legs I would have tumbled to the grass.

Slowly the gray curtain pulled back till I stared at the Master of the Green lying before me, his face turned up to the same sky that struck him down. His body smoked, twists of flame tracing across his green waistcoat. Next to him sat a moaning servant holding a talon-slashed face. Nearby lay another with his throat opened to the bone.

Ligeia held a wriggling man down with her foot, grinning as she pressed her heel into his back. Cut-Throat pointed two confiscated pistols at the three remaining servants, who backed away, hands in the air.

"Well," I said. I had no clear idea what had just happened. But there my foil lay across the body of the Master of the Green. The point had been too dull to do more than poke him hard. And the handle had fallen off. I forced myself to look at the dead man's face, wondering if I were going to be upset. I'd never killed anyone with lightning before, although I had often wanted to. To be honest, I had never killed anyone before with anything.

"Anyone else want to argue William Blake?" I asked, turning around angrily. "Anyone else? It's about *tigers*." No one volunteered. Cut-Throat tried to keep his eyes on the three servants while darting worried glances at me. But the servants were staring in horror from their dead Master to me their new Master. "Tigers!" I shouted at them. They flinched wonderfully.

I considered chasing them about shouting 'tigers' while waving my hands. I delayed that pleasure to examine the former Master of the Green. I studied the man's face. Eyes and mouth were open in surprise as though he had been told some bit of news that had astonished him to death.

I decided I didn't feel a bit upset. I stood upright. "As senior augur present, I judge this a lesser lightning strike of Revelation," I announced to the assembly on the Green. I propped my shaking self against the table, picked up the wine glass specified for the victor.

"The sky has revealed how the gods value politeness to guests." I thought about it and added. "Also, that William Blake is talking about tigers."

With that, I drained the glass of wine. For all my thirst it tasted unpleasant. Yet familiar.

"Ginger tea?" I wondered. Then my own mouth and eyes opened in surprise. I stared at the bottom of the glass, where the etching of a death's head grinned. I understood that the Master had poisoned the glass in case he ever lost. Spiteful wretch.

And then I slipped slowly down into the grass, to lie staring up at the sky next to the previous Master of the Green. I watched the sky watch me die. Then being dead I knew no more.

Until I awoke in the dark blinking the pennies off my eyes.

Don't die yet. Go back to the events in the Asylum operating theatre.

The Professor welcomed us visitors to his class and jumped into a lecture. "There is in every man a spark of divinity," he announced. We'd heard it before, it's a common expression, whatever the blazes it means. He followed with "When we sift the gods we find the corresponding clay of humanity." Which was a bit more original. He finished with "We of this institution dare to seek that lump of clay, and mold it into humanity. In this way, the human and the divine are joined on Earth." That was entirely original but confusing. It sounded like pottery and marriage, mixed.

He rang a bell upon the table. A door behind him opened and out came Mr. Sobek, wheeling a cart. Mr. Sobek did not look more pleasant in bright daylight than by candle flicker. The sun revealed a patchwork man, scarred and stitched in a long history of ripping and repairing. Sobek was revealed a destructive child's favorite toy, cruelly and lovingly reassembled again upon horrible again.

The cart he pushed held a yellow wolf-like creature. Its jaws were bound, as were its legs. It rolled eyes at us, growling. It had red stitches and burned patches across the stomach, the back, the top of its head.

"Is that Mr. Coyote?" I asked.

"So you know him," said the Professor. "As you knew the deity who attacked us last night."

"It's a small island," I said. "I feel like I know everyone already."

I was trying to be amusing, which was my way of keeping my stomach from rejecting the breakfast sacrament. I could see why Mr. Coyote had howled. The beast had serious wounds. You see I was thinking of him as an animal. Fur, paws, etc. Anywhere but Theodosia my logic would have been sound. Also I still supposed that the purpose of their attention to Mr. Coyote was to heal those wounds. But I decided if they were about to give Mr. Coyote an appendectomy, I would make a run for the door.

The Professor nodded as though he took me at my word. "To this island come the dead gods who resist oblivion. They hold to this final rock in the sea of time, neither god nor man nor beast, neither living nor dead."

"Can't blame them for that," I said. "I held to just such a rock for most of the storm."

"Blame?" asked the Professor. "It is not a matter of blame, but of pity. The gods exist as the stars, infinitely happy and infinitely distant from mortal life. When they deign to notice us it is to demand our blood and adoration. Yet here on this island they find themselves hunted, judged and measured by mortal hands while newer gods stare down in disinterest. It is a greater fall than for a man to become a beast."

He turned to the cart where Coyote lay bound, tracing sutures with a finger. "Unhappy creatures. We cannot make them gods again. But we can do better. We can make them men."

He turned to Mr. Sobek and put a fond hand upon the patch-work man's shoulder. Mr. Sobek trembled and blinked tearfully, his stitched face aglow with a humble gratitude. "And when the gods become human, then the infinite distance between Heaven and Earth is bridged."

I turned and looked behind me. Another four students had entered and sat carefully placed behind us, hands carefully nonchalant. That made eight. They weren't taking notes for the lecture.

Detective Cut-Throat made a low curse. "You aren't healing that creature," he said. "You have been torturing it."

The Professor poked Coyote as though testing how a cake was baking. Coyote growled through muzzled teeth. The Professor shook his head dissatisfied with the heat of the oven. He did not turn to us to give his reply. "There is one experience the gods lack to become human. That experience is the same fire by which Mr. Darwin shows animals rising to humanity. It is the path of struggle, of suffering, of adaptation. The path of *pain*."

Our New York Cut-Throat stood up. I stared at my friend. I had never seen him so. Suddenly I could picture him in the night alleys of a city facing down thugs. "Where is the girl?" he demanded. Tinker and I stood up as well.

"And the bird," I added. That didn't sound as heroic but anyway.

The Professor nodded to Sobek, who stepped through the door again. As he disappeared the entry behind us opened, and two more students entered to sit between us and the exit. That made ten. A few were not bothering to be nonchalant about the pistols under the coats.

Sobek returned pushing another cart, which he wheeled next to Coyote's. Upon the cart lay a girl in chains and a bird in a cage. Thoth peered out from between the bars.

"Tweet, and all that," said the god of wisdom.

Everyone on your island is insane.

It isn't *my* island. I just keep the light.

Right. Not *You.* Get to the fire.

The Professor selected a scalpel and stood over Ligeia. Her arms and ankles were bound. She wore a manacle about her neck and another about her waist. She had a red burn on one cheek. She leaked from wounds across one pale arm. She made a pitiful sight to see.

And she stared up at the Professor with as pure and happy a promise of violence as you would find if you distilled five battlefields down to a small pot of boiling blood and then painted a big smile with the steaming essence. A smile that The Professor returned with as mild a glance as you'd toss the postman, which taught the class one thing fast. He was crazier than she was.

Cut-Throat spat and started down the stairs to the floor of the amphitheater. Sobek moved to block him. He held a cudgel of wood. Behind us there came the clicks of guns cocking.

"That's a girl not a dead god, you damned lunatics," he swore. I knew better but didn't say so. Cut-Throat was making a poetic affirmation of reality as it should have been, not as it merely was. He shoved his face into Sobek's, an act that'd make a lion-tamer pull his head from the lion's mouth to better admire *real* courage. Two more students came out of the door behind the Professor. One held a rifle. One held another set of chains. Those chains were for me, by the way.

"You raise an excellent point," said the Professor. "By what means do we identify divinity? Anyone?"

So help me, a student in the back raised his hand. The Professor nodded.

"Outwardly, the dead gods may appear as human, as animal, or some creature between," recited the student. "In animal form they will display unnatural human intelligence. In either form they will be marked by unusual strengths and strange cravings. Though they have lost their divine powers, they may possess vestigial abilities to control the elements, such as fire, water or wind."

The Professor smiled. "And inwardly?" he asked, tracing his scalpel over Ligeia's stomach, faintly lining the white cloth. She shook.

"Internally an ex-deity will often possess strange items within their digestive system, as well as unusual organs not found in the species they mimic."

The student hesitated. "Question, sir. If an animal with a brain structure different from a man, even a bird with a brain no bigger than a penny, can still think like a man, why do you maintain that a machine designed for that purpose cannot do the same?"

It was the mechanical-thought student.

"Heh," said Thoth from the cage. "Answer that."

"Irrelevant," said the Professor.

Like hell.

"Irrelevant," repeated the Professor. "The question was 'how do we identify the gods when they walk among us? And the answer is: by diverse signs, such as the ability to control the elements. For example, fire and lightning." He turned to me.

"'Saint Elmo' is far too obvious an incognito for a storm god. Class, welcome to the Theodosia Seminary for the Pursuit of Divinity the ex-divinity 'Lord Typhon'."

At that point I made a dash for the door.

Just as I predicted.

Well you should have *said*. It might have saved me a fight. I have always been able to handle myself in dreams. Unfortunately this was reality, which meant I got knocked flat, bound with chains and put in a chair in the center of the amphitheater next to Ligeia. Cut-Throat and Tinker did better. She walloped Sobek with a chair while Cut-Throat grabbed the cudgel. But that excellent start ended

270

with a dozen guns to their heads. There wasn't any choice but to argue against being tied up while being tied up.

"You aren't our prisoners," the Professor assured his prisoners. "You are our fellow human beings. If this creature has deceived you, it is no fault of yours. It is in the nature of a god to lie. By fraud, by clever truth, by mere silence. The gods deceive us all." He pointed in my direction. I looked behind me to stare at the Belial under discussion. I just saw the wall. It was brick and seemed trustworthy enough.

"Typhon," said the Professor thoughtfully. "God of storms, lightning crowned, with dragons for legs. The god created to destroy the gods. Threw down Jove himself and sent all heaven into hiding."

The class stared at me impressed. Tinker blinked astonished. Even Cut-Throat gave me a thoughtful glance. I felt an idiot urge to admit it. *Yes. It is true. I am he, the one feared even by the gods.* On a safe street-corner of New Jersey with K watching or even my sisters I would have said something like 'Shhhhh. Don't tell.'

But this was Theodosia, the island of dead gods and living fools. I had blood dripping down into my eye. I ached with wounds and weariness that reminded me I was entirely mortal, not even ex-deity. I shivered at the racks of steel, brass and nickel instruments. They resembled shelves of books. Each tool promised a separate tale of agony in which a poet plays doomed protagonist. I considered the chess board and opened

271

with the sensible gambit of flat denial. "I really, really am not a god."

"It's true," said Thoth. "In all my immortal life I've never met a more ordinary example of plain clay mortality."

No doubt that was meant to help but somehow it rankled. It sounded like something Aunt Agatha would say. I felt an urge to qualify the god of wisdom's comment. "I mean, I *am* a person of unusual talents and rare poetic ability. Just in the usual human manner of unusual."

The Professor shook his head. "You call yourself by the storm fire, the storm that took the ship, the storm you announced. You survived the wreck though abandoned by the mortal crew. You danced with a night-haunt. In the cemetery a host of deities offered you homage. You commanded one by his secret name. In any case we have all witnessed you hiding the fire of heaven in your fist."

He turned to Cut-Throat and Tinker. "When he first came among you, did he seem familiar with the ways of ordinary life, of ships and sailing?"

Cut-Throat blinked. Don't think he hesitated to lie. It is just that some lies are of such shape and size that they require a moment's due consideration before lifting. To affirm I was a sailor of experience was a grand piano of a lie, and when my friend hefted it single-handedly with "This man showed everyone on Unicorn just what it took to be a master sailor," there was a fatal delay in the timing of his words. Tinker nodded so enthusiastically her glasses slipped down her nose. I felt put out.

The Professor turned to his racks of instruments, humming.

Ligeia turned her head and stared at me. She had a trickle of blood running down her face, same as I. Our glances crossed. I recalled that shy laugh we shared lying next to each other in the courtyard in the evening. She might have remembered the same, because she smiled, lips swollen with bruises. The sight made me suddenly furious. I considered the chessboard and decided to go on offense.

"Is this an establishment of science, or superstition?" I asked the class. They didn't answer. I had become an object not a guest. I spat at the students. "Anyone?"

"Science," replied the Professor. "We *study* deity here. We do not patronize its mythos."

"Then I propose a simple experiment to test your hypothesis," I said. I took a deep breath and shouted. "I summon Typhon Lord of fiery stormy angry burning loud conflagrations of flame and boom! With dragons for arms!"

"Legs," corrected Thoth.

"With dragons for legs!" I finished.

A long silence followed. The students looked more puzzled than impressed. Their object of study was not acting in standard angry ex-deity formula. There were a few glances at the windows but they might have been prompted by the usual classroom boredom. Then the Professor shook his head. "We really can't have the experiment proposing the methodology of the experimentation. It would affect the independence of our conclusions."

He took up a large wooden mallet. He approached me. I concluded he was going to hit me on the head. I experimented with a scream. Cut-Throat, Tinker, Ligeia and Coyote struggled to break their bonds. And then from the back of the class came a welcome interruption. From the door. A quiet *knock, knock, knock.*

Everyone turned to stare. In the silence Ligeia spoke. It was the first I'd heard her voice. It was a low sweet voice that incited shivers. "No," she whispered. I turned and saw another first on her face: fear.

The knocking repeated, a bit louder. *Knock. Knock. Knock.* This time it was accompanied by the faintest rumble of thunder from outside the windows, a distant drumroll to announce the approaching parade.

"Oh dear," said the god of wisdom.

My turn to say it: *just as I foresaw.*
Did you now. Then tell the class what happens next.

Typhon bursts down the door, casting lightning that slays the Professor and sets fire to the building. You and the others escape in the smoke and confusion.

274

Well, no. Actually we all just stared at the door until Typhon tired of knocking. Eventually he opened it himself, peeked in, cleared his throat apologetically, and edged in with the self-conscious quiet of a tardy student finding his seat after class has started, while teacher and class observe him take his place.

He sat in the front row, folded his hands in his lap and smiled at all.

Chapter 23

Excerpt, July 25th, 188?
Diary of K. King,
Archive of Rural Letters,
Maidenhead, New Jersey.

Today I watched a stone roll down a hill. Poetically speaking. Really it was just a wooden croquet ball. And not a hill, just our stairs. The Rectory has a steep wooden stairway just right for bouncing a croquet ball in the middle of the night. Not the grand sweep of ~~my Poet~~ the St. Elmo's house, but our greater incline gives the rolling object a quicker momentum. I am sure that could be reduced to a beautiful equation. Something like 'The momentum of decline increases with each step'. With each step. With each step.

I sat at the stair top and set the red ball rolling a thump and a bump and a jump to follow its fate. Each ump! came deeper, more satisfying for a soul in a mood for thunder. I considered placing a wine glass on the last step to make a satisfying finish. How the poor bride would tremble! But that would be cruel. We things of glass should be kind to things of glass.

Next I set the green ball rolling. Bump a bump! I considered how everything runs downhill. Shan't everything in the world someday be downhill? Won't that be a funny end to it all? Absolutely every rock and ball and soul and heart lying at the bottom of the last hill? In a big pile of broken things. But the green ball took an individualist bounce and cleared the railing, sending the vase on the hall table crashing. Poor vase! A victim of variables in the equation.

I selected the blue ball. It was the exact same blue as the dress I wore that day at tea. I felt a certain pity for it. I put my lips to its blue and asked "Do you want to roll downhill? Just say if you don't. But of course you want to, dear." The silly thing wouldn't give me an answer so I set it rolling off to marry the floor in the hall below.

I wanted to surrender the orange croquet ball to inevitability next but by then everyone was coming out of their rooms to see what the world was coming to. Gravity and decline were delayed for the night. But really I don't see how they can lose in the end.

Interviewer: describe the Libris Acherontia.

At her family's picnic K and I played croquet on the bank by the lake. Of course the balls kept rolling down the slope fast as we sent them up. We labeled the game 'Sisyphus'. It made K laugh till her hair escaped her bonnet, waving fronds of joy about her head. Her mother and brother refused to play, complaining there was no sense to work the ball uphill if it was fated to roll down again. As if a croquet game were a matter of sense and expense. I stood in the sunshine and watched K laugh, and I remember thinking I'd be happy to play Sisyphus with her for eternity.

It's only damnation when played alone.

Describe what occurred in the Asylum when Typhon appeared.

Our Professor of Pain was taken aback. He was no fool. One does not walk into the dissection laboratory cheerfully wearing the sign 'open here'.

Yet there Typhon sat, smiling mild as milk. Ligeia went still, pretending death. She was naturally pale and could pass for a pretty corpse if her breasts stopped trembling. I happened to notice. Thoth did an excellent impression of a stuffed bird in a shop window. Coyote showed more spirit; he gave a growl to match the distant thunder. Typhon looked about the room in curiosity. When he noticed me he spoke.

"Flame and boom? Dread nemesis? Dragons for arms?"

"Legs," I corrected.

"How exactly does one walk with dragons for legs?"

I thought about that, puzzled. While I did so the Professor approached him and inquired politely "Who *are* you?"

Typhon sat in shadow, I noticed. Bright sunlight shown through the windows and yet the being sat smiling from under his own personal shade of storm.

"Typhon, lord of, crowned with, dragon-appendaged, nemesis of, etcetera," he replied with a push of his hand to move the words forwards. "At your service, vaguely." He stared at Mr. Sobek. Mr. Sobek looked shocked. The patchwork man trembled. And yet I think it was not out of fear.

A proper Professor of theological pursuits is naturally suspicious of divine prey visiting the dissection lab. "If you are indeed that particular ex-deity, would you object to offering some *proof?*"

The stuffed-bird god of wisdom made a choking sound. Ligeia squeezed her eyes shut. Some of the more advanced students glanced towards the door.

"Incorrect on two counts," said Typhon, still studying Sobek.

"Then you are not Typhon?"

"Oh, I am him, he, it, as you wish. But as a confirmed atheist I reject the word *deity*. What you call 'gods' I call the Powers. Often evil, mostly corrupt, and infinitely self-involved. I am just Typhon."

"Nomenclature is secondary to a consistency of definition," said the Professor.

Typhon yawned. He was growing bored. That did not augur well. *Never bore the gods.*

The Professor glanced from Typhon to me, weighing the situation and the mallet. I could see he was quickly re-evaluating my divinity in the presence of the real thing.

"Satisfied I am humble clay?" I asked.

"Quite," he admitted, and struck Typhon a practiced blow to the side of the head that laid him flat on the floor.

Describe Mr. Coyote.

I boarded the train to California in Chicago. When the train passed through Arizona someone pointed out creatures of long legs and mournful howls. Some called them 'coyotes', with others arguing for the term 'prairie wolf'. By either name, no one expressed a high opinion of the creatures. Supposedly they were odorous, dishonest, and sly.

The 3rd class train car was so crowded we took turns sitting. It had been a long night and the place smelled like a crypt. I'd lost half my remaining funds in last-night's friendly game of faro and someone had stolen the hat I'd bought in Kansas. It was way past my turn to sit down, but no one sitting would meet my eye.

It was my personal belief that everyone in the train car was odorous, dishonest, and damned sly. *Mr. Coyote*, on the contrary, was as decent, elegant and eloquent a madman as ever walked on four legs.

What internal organs did Typhon reveal?

Now *those* entrails would have been a revelation for an augur to read, but we never had the chance to so much as browse. They stretched his unconscious form on another table and realized the Asylum was fresh out of chains. It had been a record week for bagging deity. I volunteered *my* chains and the Professor could think of no reason to refuse such charity. But he was put out by the business. Although he apologized for the misunderstanding you could see he felt something was not right. As I said, he was no fool. He was just in too much of a hurry to stop and ask the right questions.

After freeing me, Mr. Sobek untied Tinker and Cut-Throat. Two students then led us castaways at polite gun point from the chamber. I stopped to check the windows. Somehow I knew what I would see. I suppose that dream warned me. As senior augur present I considered sharing the fulfilled prophecy but the student prodded me on. So we were just out the door of the theater when we heard the first scream.

Who screamed?

It was one of the students. He'd caught sight of Tezcatlipoca at the window. Then another caught sight of Damnameneus peeking in, which merited another scream and received it. A third student realized that someone in a cloak blacker than night sat right beside him, leaking sea-water. I think it was Phorcys, father of the gorgons if you are interested. I never met a gorgon on Theodosia. I'm not complaining.

The operating theater seats were suddenly full of dark hooded figures, and the windows full of divine faces. It was the dead gods come to see their nemesis Typhon laid open for study.

Had the class kept its head, they could have continued quietly. Those ex-deities had no intention of *interrupting.* They were present to sit back and share cat-calls and roasted peanuts. No doubt shouting experienced tips on cutting and slicing.

But of course the students started firing.

Who is Damnameneus?

A decent sort, more or less. A kind of magic blacksmith from a Greek backwater. I talked to him some at the wedding, and he didn't have a word to say against Typhon. He insisted he was just there that day to see what everyone else was staring at.

Describe the burning of the Asylum.

Cut-Throat and I hesitated outside the operating theater. The room behind us filled with shots, shouts and screams, shattering glass and strange eruptions of light. We both wanted to have rushed back in and rescued the girl and the god and the bird. It would be satisfying to describe later how we'd been brave enough to dive head-first into such a pandemonium.

We just hadn't done it yet. Meanwhile the two students turned between the door and us, uncertain where to point their pistols. I recognized one; he was the student I rescued from Tezcatlipoca. I decided to remind him and he decided to shoot me.

"This is your fault!" he shouted, put his gun to my head and Tinker hit him with Sobek's cudgel. I never even saw her take it. Didn't I say Tinker was clever?

Cut-Throat had the man's gun before he hit the ground. The other student was the mechanical thought proponent. He looked ready to shoot something, anything. I pointed past him and shouted "The Mechanical Turk ' but he didn't turn to see if a chess-playing automaton was in the hall behind him. I maintain it was worth the try.

"We need to get around to the back of the theater," Cut-Throat told him. "Is there another way?"

The student looked through the door, down to the fallen student, then back at us. Finally he decided. "Down the hall, take the door on the right. It goes down to the basement. Follow past the containment rooms and it will lead to the back of the theatre."

He bent down, grabbed his friend and dragged him off. Smoke began flowing from the doorway. We ran.

Down the hall, through the door, down stairs and we stood in a long basement filled with shelves of bottles containing parts of gods carefully disassembled and labeled. I don't want to describe it overmuch. We hurried past doors of oak and steel. Containment cells, I guess. We unlocked them, pulled the doors open and hurried away before we could see what they contained.

At the end of the hall we came to the door through which Sobek had brought his carts. We burst past into a fireworks display during an opera recapitulating the battle of Armageddon as performed by lunatics and deities.

Cut-Throat rushed to Ligeia, who lay writhing in chains. I grabbed Thoth's bird cage and smashed it open. The god of wisdom flew free, squawking. The chamber was a smoke and scream-filled madhouse at war with a nightmare of lights and shadows. The students held the upper half of the theatre, saving their ammunition. The ex-gods surrounded them, hissing, cursing, throwing fire and chairs. Typhon lay on a table while Tezcatlipoca stood above him with a whole handful of bloody scalpels.

Cut-Throat hefted Ligeia over his shoulder, chains and all. Tinker worked to free Coyote. I stumbled towards Typhon. His chest was a preliminary excavation site already marked out in lines of blood. He glanced towards me. I knew he was about to wink. Then the Professor, bruised and bloody, staggered out of the smoke waving his mallet. He and Tezcatlipoca stood over the bound god of storms, rival surgeons surveying their most serious challenge.

"Ex-deity, we will make you a man," said the Professor. He was staggered but smiling, blood trickling from his mouth as though he'd drunk from his own bated offerings.

"I did say that was wrong on both counts," replied Typhon, calmly continuing the discussion. He considered Tezcatlipoca. "First, these creatures are not deities. Mere, dreary powers." Tezcatlipoca hissed furious.

"And?" asked the Professor, again a step behind. Whereas I was already stepping *away*.

"Second, I'm not *ex* anything. I'm one of the living ones."

And with that the real storm began.

Finish it.

We gathered outside the Asylum, watching it burn. Every so often flames would burst another window. The black pillar of smoke rose to the sky, a clearly stated thesis to all the island and half the sea. Cut-Throat sat with Ligeia under a tree, ignoring the fireworks. He had her chains off and her head in his lap, smoothing those red locks. Coyote and Thoth held a secret ex-deity confab under another tree. Every so often Coyote would turn to give me a red-tongued grin like he was hearing stories wherein I played village idiot. Granted, he could have just been happy to have escaped torment. Not everything is about me, I guess.

The living Typhon disappeared, merging with the fire and lighting he called upon the Asylum. Tezcatlipoca and several other ex-deities merged with the fire in a more final way. The Professor and Sobek were more humbly and mortally dead. The surviving students sorted piles of salvage. I was glad to see the remaining donkey, but it gave me a shiver how the rescued portrait of the Banker stared at me next to a pile of chairs and books.

We castaways had bravely helped the students escape the conflagration, leading them out the lower door, fighting past flames and angry ex-gods. They owed us their lives. But I wanted to be on my way before the student body felt some obligation to resume studies. The mechanical-thought proponent came over, showing his hands in sign he meant no threat. He was eyeing Ligeia. She did mean threat but just not then and there.

"We are going to camp for the night, see what else we can salvage in the morning," he said. "After that we'll make our way to the town on the other side of the island."

I tried to think of something to say. I wasn't going to apologize. They had come close to vivisecting me. Yet they seemed decent fellows when focused on mortal issues. I considered reminding him that the woods were now sprinkled with escapees from his basement. If I wore a black coat I wouldn't have stayed the night. I'd run.

"I didn't just see the Turk," I confessed. "I spent three dollars to play him. He used his knights weakly but then beat me with damned clever pawn moves."

The student smiled at that appreciative, as who wouldn't. Then Tinker explained how we wanted to find our missing ship mates. The Baker at least had to be wandering somewhere about. The student told us about a large, rich estate called The Green. It had a reputation for catching wanderers. He advised us to steer clear of it. But if we did go there, not to knock on the front door.

How did the Professor die?

Sobek grabbed him and hugged him tight as students and gods fled the theological discussion. Flames and lightning filled the room, wrapping them both. The professor struggled and protested. I wanted to do something but Tinker saved my life by calling me an idiot, shoving me hard towards the door and telling me to run.

I have no idea if Sobek clasped the Professor in fear, friendship or the desire to take a theologian with him on the path of pain that leads to higher being. Perhaps all three.

How did Tezcatlipoca die?

Typhon sat up, bored with his chains. He grabbed the ex-god of dark mirrors by the throat. They met each other's eyes in a long silent conversation that ended with Typhon ripping Tezcatlipoca's heart out his chest. Then he stuffed it into the beast-man's mouth. After that it got ugly.

Chapter 24

Easter Sermon, Reverend Obadiah King,
First Methodist Church,
Maidenhead, New Jersey
April 22, 1888

What is resurrection? Is it the mere resumption of life? The beat of a heart after silence? The return of breath to lungs, wind filling the sails of the ship becalmed? If resurrection is the resumption of life, must we not first define life?

But surely we know. For we live, do we not? Life is more than a drumbeat in the chest, a pulse in the wrist, a mist on the mirror held before the mouth. Life is the ten thousand daily acts of body married to spirit, moving in laughter, moving in astonishment, moving in thought and emotion.

Then what is Life's absence? Is it the silencing of the drumbeat? The body slowing like a stone rolling to a stop? How easy we understand that. Death is the coming of stillness; no more heat, no more energy; no more motion.

Surely that suffices. Life is motion. Death is to cease to move. To be resurrected then is just to return to movement, the windup toy rewound and set upon its tin feet to bounce and click its way further across the floor.

But no! That is not resurrection. That is mere continuation. We have made an error somewhere.

*What **use** is this churchyard word 'resurrection'? Perhaps it is for seeds in the ground. We bury seeds in rows like graves. We* *surrender them to the earth, balancing our hopes and fears of what may come. Perhaps they will rise again to our profit. But no man ever mourned a seed. No cynic ever scoffed at the spring. Reaping and sowing are not death and resurrection. They are mere repetition.*

Then what is this strange word, 'resurrection'?

For a man to die is to lose all that he has and all that he is. His house is now another's. His title, his job, his shoes and his name, no longer are his. He is no longer a reverend, she is no longer a wife. His body is no longer his. Rich, poor, gentile, Jew, wise man or poet, all are become pounds of unpleasant clay; property for heirs to label with some few words then store beneath the screening earth.

Death is oblivion. Death is erasure. Death is the entire and complete absence of you. You are ended. Death is the fire that consumes every last ash. Death! Death is the ocean into which every last ship shall founder. An ocean no sailor can cross.

And yet absurdly, we have a word for returning across that ocean: resurrection.

Impossible. Unthinkable. **Miraculous***.*

Interviewer: Describe being dead after the duel.

It was a state of stillness. Dark, but I had no words to define a world. I wasn't any more aware of darkness than a fish is of damp. I rested in peace. I was out of the storm, out of the fire, free from struggle. I awoke washed clean of the knowledge of such things as storms and fires, days and troubles. I shivered with contentment for the absence of the word *care*.

That time passed, as though awareness of a self required the creation of a world to hold the self, and the creation of a world required cares. I felt a cold surface beneath me. That implied a body, a location, a temperature, gravity. There was a smell of rot and dust, which told me I breathed. Two cold objects lay upon my eyes. I shook my head and they tumbled away clinking. A cloth covered my face, tangled my hands as I sought to brush it off.

I lay on a cold stone table in a cold stone dark, and realized I was alive.

Describe being alive after the duel.

A crowd shouting complaints from the body. Cold, hunger, thirst, bruises and cuts. A growing sense of panic. Where was I? For the longest time I couldn't remember anything past boarding the train to San Francisco. Perhaps the train had stopped in a mountain tunnel. I listened for the clatter and clank of the wheels, the shouts of the engineers, the grumbling passengers. There was nothing. Everyone had disembarked by tiptoe, leaving me lying in a baggage car under a mountain. I sat up, dislodging a thin sheet pulled over my face. I flailed at it, thinking it cobwebs.

I promptly tumbled through the dark onto a stone floor. That hurt. I sat up, feeling with my hands at the strange bed I tumbled from. It was a stone table, more like an altar.

"Where the blazes am I?" I whispered.

You appear to have been buried by mistake.

Yes, I confirm a mistake has been made. This is the last time I buy a 3rd class rail ticket. Henceforth its first class for me or I walk. However I do not wish at this time to tender a complaint to the rail authorities. No, direct me to the nearest exit and we will consider the matter settled. I'll buy you a beer. I'll buy me a beer. Several beers and I don't even drink beer.

Try feeling around you.

There is a plate on the floor. It holds what feels like bread. Hard and stale, two days old at least. I'm going to put it on the table. And here is a cup. Wine. Gone flat, of course. Here is a coin on the ground. It fell when I rose. Someone put pennies on my eyelids while I slept. I am pretending to wonder why.

Yes, and this place smells like a crypt. Not that I've ever been in a crypt. But I've read all about the dust and cold and stone and mold and dark and rats and pits and bones and the pendulum blades and flaming walls and absolute despair. Oh God, this is Edgar Alan Poe's fault. What did I ever do to him?

You are breathing. There must be a source of air. Feel for a current of wind.

In Poe the prisoner is locked in a dark cell where an open pit waits. He is supposed to explore the dark and then plunge into the pit. Poe declines to tell us what was in the pit, it's something too horrible to put into words, even for Poe. It might be safer to wait here.

Wait there for *what?*

Well, maybe the authorities will rescue us. Maybe I will wake up in bed. Maybe the train will pull out of the tunnel and sunlight will stream into a baggage car made of stone that just happens to smell like a crypt. I don't know! I don't know where I am or how I got here! Who am I talking to?

We are the project team for the interview... Oh, forget that. Look, I am trying to get what information I can concerning the lost last copy of an ancient religious book. You are the last person who may have read it. The problem is, you are a sailor from a century and a half ago and your ship sank.

Sank? I haven't even gotten to San Francisco yet! I've never *been* a sailor. And the damned ship is going to sink? How fair is that? To hell with fate. I'll decline to board. How do you know the future?

I don't know the future. I know the past. I have a machine I use to recreate the world as it was. Better said, the world as it possibly was. The past is as

indeterminate as the future. And not all the past, not all the world.

But the creation of a world builds on itself. A world must grow or it crashes. And the more a shadow defines itself as a reality, the more difficult it becomes to control. The algorithm of existence is too open-ended. A world always escapes its creator.

I used historical records, letters and pieces of my own life to reconstruct an old sailor who would tell me of the sinking of Unicorn in 1888. When I ask concerning some event, he constructs that world by recalling it. And by arguing it. He argues a lot.

Then things began to go strange.

'Then'? It wasn't strange already?

Don't interrupt. I agreed to send his letters to his antique girlfriend in exchange for parts of the lost Etruscan books. It shouldn't have mattered. If the real woman ever lived, she would have died almost a century ago. But I started finding old letters in archives and libraries, replying to what I sent. Words from her, from relatives and others that together seemed to continue a dialogue that never occurred. I won't say it is changing the past. But I feel that it is continuing the past, expanding it. At this point I suspect I am talking to a real sailor from a possible version of the late 1880s, as truly as that sailor is talking to a voice from a possible future.

I am buried alive with a lunatic. Definitely this is the fault of Mr. Poe. Say, let's build a model of the world to catch his ghost and tender our complaints to him.

Still sitting there?

Sitting? You think I am just sitting here huddled in fear? No, I am strategically contemplating the metaphoric battlefield, arms wrapped about my head the better to contain my thoughts. These books you seek. Where did they come from?

An archaeologist named Naville found a copy of the texts in an excavation along with an Egyptian translation that allowed him to produce a French version. An American collector of religious art named Banker stole it. It all disappeared when Unicorn sank off Theodosia.

Why not just re-create this Naville?

We did. It didn't work. Nor Banker. Nor any original Etruscans. You are the closest we have gotten. Perhaps it takes someone who isn't far away from us in time or culture, nor too defined as a person. We researched the roster of the vanished Unicorn and found C. S. Elmo, failed poet who went to sea. No record of death, no record of life; a blank of a man we could ask to create himself.

'A blank of a man'. Well. I am buried alive in a tomb talking to a ghost. And if that horror were not sufficient thereof for the day, the damned ghost talks like Aunt Agatha talking about me.

Sorry. Still sitting there?

I am eating the grave bread. I finished the burial wine. And I'm wearing the shroud as a cloak about my shoulders. Lo, I am become a poem by Lord Byron. I wish my girl could see. She likes Byron. Which is fine as the poetic womanizer is dead. Granted, so am I. Dead, I mean, not a womanizer. Now that I am deceased I'm tempted to have been a womanizer. Or a poet. Byron always struck me as being more a poem than a poet. I wonder which is better to be. Poet or poem? To be the words or the person speaking the words? I suppose you can't be both. And no I am not babbling because I am panicked at being buried alive. Ha, I always talk like this. Ask anyone. Granted perhaps I am just always panicked.

Think of something calming. Describe K that night at the lake.

I shall not. That's no concern of a prurient spirit of a lecher-voice from the future. No spying on my girl bathing or when I find your books I'll toss them to the sea. When I get to the sea, anyway.

Fine. Describe the contents of your pocket.

Just two coins. The first tumbled from my eyelid when I awoke. Size and weight of an American penny; my fingertips detect the braided hair of Miss Liberty. The second coin has a hole in the center, which means it's worthless. I don't remember it. Someone must have slipped it in my change as we went through Nevada. We played cards and I bought a boiled egg. I bet that egg on three jacks and lost. Lost! I've dreamt about that egg. It was already peeled and salted. Dammit.

You are going to keep the penny from now on, to remind you of a girl you haven't met yet. The one with a hole is a lucky coin given you by the Chinese goddess of sailors and lighthouse keepers, when you get to San Francisco. Later you are going to find a Spanish silver coin but I don't know when or what it means.

I don't know either. I lost the boiled egg and you say my ship will sink and I'm dead. Just how lucky is this Chinese coin?

Will you forget the boiled egg? You survive the shipwreck. Also the dance, the asylum, the labyrinth, and the duel. There was luck.

Do I want to ask? Why not, I am unoccupied at the moment. Describe the shipwreck.

Storm. Wind. Waves over the deck. People screaming. Avoid the lunatic with the axe.

Taken any way you wish, that's good advice for a man. 'Avoid the lunatic with the axe'. But if you know my future, oh Spirit, there is something I want to ask. But I am afraid to put the question into words.

I don't know if you make it back to her.

Oh. Say, what is your name?

Clarence. Same as yours. Not really a coincidence.

There is some of the stale bread left if you are hungry, Clarence.

Thanks. But I can't reach it from where I am. I'll get some snacks from the vending machines in the break room. They'll probably be just as stale. You finish off the bread yourself.

Thanks. I'm powerful hungry. Being dead takes it out of a man.

You aren't dead. If I had to guess, I'd say the Master of the Green didn't poison the wine. He drugged it with something to fake death.

Why would this Mister Green do such a fool thing?

I don't know. But there is an unpleasant possibility. You mentioned that he was a fan of Poe. Particularly

the gruesome stories. 'Cask of Amontillado', 'House of Usher', 'the Black Cat', etc.

Ah. I see. The light of understanding shines upon the dark truth, turning it yet darker. I have been buried alive in some act of revenge by a man I have not yet met?

Seems likely.

Likely? It seems unlikely as hell or an honest congress.

Well, yes. In terms of absolute probability it is unlikely. But in the context of being in a recapitulation of reality after a duel with a sadistic sociopath with a fondness for traps and tricks, it seems reasonably likely.

If you were to even try talking like that in Maidenhead we would knock you down. Then we'd lock you up. Then pray for you. Possibly not in that order.

Things have gotten out of order. Again. Your point of view from when you traveled to San Francisco jumped to the memory of when you awoke in a crypt after the duel. Or else the panic of waking up in the crypt jumped you back to when your train went through a tunnel in the mountains. Understandable. Things should reset if you can find a way out.

I prophecy the definition of the word 'understandable' shall have an amazing new meaning in the future.

Still sitting there?

Do I have somewhere to *go?*

You have to get *out* you total nimrod.

Let us recapitulate the present reality. I am in a crypt designed by sinister Mister Green, a man I have never met but is bent on my torment and is fond of tricks and traps. And you advise me to wander about in his dark imaginings, waving my hands and tapping my feet?

You have a point.

You're an honest spirit. And I'm a coward. I know I can't just sit here. Let's get it done. Here goes.

What can you feel?

Give me a minute, I'm still gathering up this courage stuff. I've read about it all my life but never actually felt the urge to indulge before. Wish I had a light.

Raise your right hand.

Why? Am I going to going to take an oath? Join a secret society? Testify to -

Shut up. Raise your right hand. Now think of something that makes you very, very angry.

Cats. Why must they sit on the still-wet inked pages of whatever you are writing? Why do they pester you soon as they see you sitting comfortable with a book? Are they at secret war with the written word? Or are they just the furry anti-intellectual nuisances they seem?

Do you see a light?

No. And yet, in the dark of my brain I see myself in a tomb with my hand solemnly raised, shroud across shoulders, complaining about cats to a bodiless voice from the future. Metaphorically I stand in a sudden blazing light of realization: I am completely out of my mind.

By a dead fountain, on a bed of stone,
In a hall of silence, I awoke alone.
In an empty courtyard,

Stop

In dust and morning light
I hurried from the ruin,
Where I had kept the night.

That son of a bitch.

What do you see, Poet?

My hand wrapped in blue fire. A square chamber. A cold bed of stone meant for a long cold sleep. An empty plate, an empty cup. And I am not alone. A cat sits in the corner, eyes aglow in the light. It poses tail curled prim round feet, surrounded by a pile of dead rats for battle field trophies. I wondered why nothing had eaten my toes. The beast gazes at me like it knows all my past and future and doesn't care to share a single secret. But all cats do that.

A few steps away is the black circle of a pit. No light returns from its depth. I am going to tiptoe close and peer within. Ha, the well is circled with steps. That's not in Poe. I suppose the steps could be trapped. I will walk carefully, they look slip

Poet?

Chapter 25

Dear K,

While this letter will seem written in an ancient undeciphered script, its mystery is simple. I write standing in a bumpy rail car. It is so crowded that I must scribble with elbows pressed to my sides. At least three individuals are sufficiently close that they feel it is no imposition to read along with my pen and contribute their thoughts.

A broom salesman from Atlanta asks to say hello to you. Very well: Hello to Miss King from Georgia Whisks! A land speculator from Florida says 'greetings' and advises you to flee the northern snow. The miner heading to Nevada who won my boiled egg in last night's faro game asks your permission to write you on his own but that isn't going to happen.

The city of Chicago smelled like a stock yard. Correction: the stockyard of Chicago looked like a city. Now we head west towards San Francisco. Next stop: ~~Albukerkie Albuquerky~~ *a town in New Mexico that no one in the car can spell. I am told there shall be mountains. I can't really picture a train climbing a mountain. Tilt this car by more than a few degrees and you will crush the people closest to the back. But don't, because I am against the back wall now. The broom salesman wishes to point out that if you are in the front you will be equally crushed when the train descends the mountain. The Florida speculator adds that if there is a train wreck, those in the center will be last to exit. The miner who won my boiled egg concludes there is no safety in trains, love, cross-shafts or cards. Wise words. That boiled egg was already salted.*

All last night I had horrible dreams of being buried alive. One can only speculate as to the cause. All the space in the car not occupied by a human body is filled with smoke. Pipes, cigars, cigarettes. I study the swirls and see your face, since I am not close enough to the windows to see your face in the clouds of heaven. The Florida speculator says that is beautiful and asks me if I am a poet. I inform him I am not. Just someone who sees one special face in the shape of things. The miner confides he hears the voice of his beloved from lantern flames in the mines. I consider that poetic but unsettling.

K, forgive me that I didn't say a proper good bye. I shall make up for it with a proper return. Something with trumpets and elephants, bacchanals in the street and fireworks from the roof while choirs of angels sing of a sailor's return. Failing that, a quiet walk by the lake under the light of our moon.

Hello? You there, spirit voice from the future?

Well. We appear to have lost the interviewing team. Perhaps the head nurse finally booted them for being a nuisance. Or some medication administered the old blind sailor has cleared them from his head. Then again, the well in the crypt was a boundary between worlds that even a spirit from the future might fear to cross. I shall continue the interview alone. But what to ask myself?

Self, describe K that night at the lake.

She confided how she harbored a spring-wind urge to sneak from house, hymns and aunts to swim in reflected stars. I told her strictly to do no such thing. She could drown, catch cold, be eaten by bears, or carried off by savage Indians and farmers who would force her to grind corn while listening to dismal rural dialogue.

But my voice lacks a defining strictness so when night fell I wandered worried to the lake. I went to the rock where she and her mother picnic. There wasn't a single slice of moon, but a feast of stars, owl eyes and fire flies sufficed. Frog song and a cooler wind told me I approached the shore. There I stood tree-shadowed, gazing at a figure of a girl standing knee-deep in liquid night. She bent and cupped black water in her hands, rose to pour it over her head letting it run down breasts and stomach and legs to the sea again. She stretched arms up to the happy stars as though waking from a deep sleep. I stood and watched, and no god could blame me.

She has better night eyes than I. Laughing, she held out those arms to me. I stumbled to her as if the distance were ten thousand miles, impossible distance never to be crossed with clumsy counted steps. But when at last I entered the water, shivering, she pulled me close in welcome. We held each other trembling and the ripples circled out across the lake. They must still be circling outwards. Those weren't the kind of ripples that can ever entirely fade.

Self, that was well said.
Why, thank you, self.

Now describe our descent to the underworld.

I followed the stone steps of the well, careful of their narrow width, their slippery surface. I spiraled down, round and down like a kite from the sky when the wind has stilled. I love flying kites. Remember, self, when we built one painted with a great golden sun? But it was heavy and needed a strong wind to lift. I finally flew it in a storm. It was like tossing the sun into a sea of angry clouds, a kind of argument played out in the sky. The storm won the first round by tearing the string knife-like through my hand. Then a thief wind made off with the kite.

But the sun came out afterwards, looking so like the image on the lost kite that I awarded sunlight the victory. Storms are drama; it is the daily sun that holds the true fire. For god's sake don't tell Typhon I said that. At the bottom of the steps was a large chamber. I raised my blue-burning hand for a lantern to shine on the figures awaiting me.

They were the dead gods, of course. The whispering cargo-passengers from Unicorn. Minus those slaughtered by Typhon in the Asylum. Also lacking those who'd decided to stay on Theodosia, content to fade into oblivion, raise gardens, watch the drifting shadow-clouds of Elysium. These wore those night-cloaks that hid their faces and the depths of their beings. I was disappointed, but glad too.

These remaining ex-gods hoped to travel the path to life again. They awaited their guide. *Me.* I stared at them and understood that here was the point of the whole journey. The book, the coin, the fire; all the fool events on the island had had their ceremonial purpose to prepare for this moment.

I nodded. I knew from the Libris Acherontia that it was a perilous journey. Their powers, their memories, the separate fires of their beings were all quenched here. They were mere lost shadows seeking the light again, knowing that light *eats* shadows. But it was their decision. So I walked among them solemn as a church usher at a funeral, burning hand raised for our light. They followed behind, a somber crowd keeping a guarded silence. They were frightened. But they were not the kind to seek comfort from others, any more than to give it.

This is where we get to things described in the Libris Acherontia that Thoth and Typhon told me to keep to myself. But there is no secret to most of it. We crossed a river. Not by ferry; there was a bridge. The water was black and hurried away to some underground sea. I looked down into the water and considered what Thoth said the day of the shipwreck, how water flows in a circle from cloud to river to sea and back to the sky again. So also, the gods.

Beyond the bridge we came to a village. Stone houses with peaked roofs, steps leading up to dark open doorways. The blue fire shown on piles of treasure lying heaped in front of the houses. Gold and glass and coins and crowns and diamonds sparkling with the tiny blue flames of a candle just barely burning. I felt a powerful urge to step inside one of those treasure houses. But the Acherontia had warned me. So I warned the others and we hurried on.

We left that village behind, following the same dark road. It was hard to say if we journeyed under some heavy sky or in some huge cavern. Probably meaningless to say. I turned and checked my charges. We had lost a few of our company. They had darted into those doorways, or tiptoed in, or boldly strode in. None had come out, nor would.

The road went down into a valley I recalled from the book. I instructed the ex-gods to stay close, to let no one wander from the path. Above all, not to reply to the voices they would hear. They nodded, solemn children warned of wolves. We descended into a mist-filled hollow where great dead trees held determined branches up, arms keeping a dreadful void at bay from the earth.

"Hallo, Poet," said K.

I choked but did not reply.

"I sent you an invitation to the wedding," said K's voice from the mist. "Your sister Alice is going to be a bridesmaid. She flirts with Henry dreadfully but I suppose that will pass once she sees us properly married."

I bit my tongue to stop my reply to *that*.

"I was so angry when you said you would not be coming back for me," chatted her voice. "What a child I was! Now I can hardly remember. Henry and father get along ever so well. Father says farming is the practical man's poetry. You should hear them laugh about the mismatched cow and horse. Father says -"

The ex-gods began shouting, arguing, moaning. I suppose they were hearing their own voices of despair. I don't know what words will take down the heart of a god. Probably the same that rip a sailor's heart. Like the Professor said, sift the gods and you find human clay.

I began to sing the official sailor's song Cut-Throat taught the fool's crew. "*So early, early in the spring, I shipped on board to serve my king, I left my dearest dear behind, she oft-times swore, her heart was mine.*"

Some of the ex-gods started singing as well. They sang better than I did. Be fair, they were gods, they had talent. We marched through the mist singing. "*And all the time, I sailed at sea, I could not find one moment's peace, in thinking of, my dearest dear, but never a word, from her did I hear.*"

At last the mist faded with the sigh 'Oh Poet,' and we were past the valley. I turned. There were fewer in the group. No point returning for the missing. They wouldn't be there anymore. There was only going forwards. In the underworld there is always only going forwards.

We crossed another bridge, came to another village. This one of great stone temples, church-doors open. The smell of burnt offerings, blood and incense wafted on the still air. A rhythm shook the ground like a heartbeat, as though a thousand feet stamped in ceremony just beyond the doors.

It held little temptation for me, but we lost a good many of our company to that village.

Past that village we journeyed through a wood, dark, lonely and yet beautiful. These trees were not dead branches pushing against the sky. They were living things watching as we passed. I pulled a black leaf and studied it. I saw writing etched on its surface, beautiful and mysterious. I almost pocketed it, then recalled the warnings of the Acherontia. I dropped the leaf and turned to the remaining gods. I opened my mouth to warn them not to take anything as we journeyed. No coin nor leaf nor smallest pebble. Then I hesitated.

There was a conversation I didn't reveal before. At the gate outside the cemetery, Typhon asked why I didn't order the dead gods to crew me a ship home. The reason was pretty simple. I was afraid of the creatures, and didn't have a clear idea of what they could do. But soon or late I would have summoned them by their names and said 'prepare to sail'.

But Typhon informed me they were confined to Theodosia. They couldn't take me home, though they might take my head off for bothering them. Instead he offered me a deal. Typhon wanted the dead gods to stay dead. He didn't care whether they rotted on Theodosia or sank to the bottom of Shipwreck Bay. Just no return to life. If I saw that no dead gods returned through the path of the Acherontia, he would get me a ship homeward.

So now in the dark wood I stared at the cloaked figures, deciding whether to guide them true or lead them wrong. If I could see their faces, fear and awe would move me to serve them honestly. But in their shadow forms they emanated no threat, no power; just a longing to return from a long journey. No different than any other band of lost sailors.

The dead gods were castaways, same as myself.

"Don't pick up anything," I warned. "Not coin nor leaf nor smallest pebble. And don't eat or drink a thing." They nodded. But when we passed under fruit trees, black and inviting, some pulled the heavy fruit down and savored the dark juice. The gods don't take our warnings any more than we take theirs. We exited the dark wood a smaller party.

The next village was populated with statues. Not of gods nor heroes, but of men and women standing in ordinary poses of daily life. A hatted lady statue bent down to pet a dog of marble. I recognized the dog at once. It was that mutt of K's brother. And the lady was K's mother. I whirled about astonished. This street was Main Street, Maidenhead, carved out in marble and grey stone. There was the granite dairy cart pulled by the stone mule, slyly munching into obsidian violets.

And there in front of the main street store stood K. She wore her bonnet loose, that one lock a delicate marble curl about her left ear. I rushed to wrap my arms around her for eternity. But something darted under my feet to send me rolling. Dizzy I stared up at a sky chiseled from black basalt. The ship's cat came over and put his face into mine, eyes terrifyingly bright in the blue flame. He batted out a paw to swipe my nose off but I dodged and he only got the tip.

I stood again, brushing grave dust away. I stared at the statue of K. Behind stood her father, a stooped figure of grey rock puffing a stone cigar. I read his dull pebble eyes; they said *'what poor gods chose you for a guide?'*

I took a breath and we went on. I don't think we lost anyone there. The ship's cat darted in and out, making the dead gods stumble.

We reached another river. This bridge had no railing. It grew narrower as we walked, till we went single-file. Then it grew narrower again. Some in the back retreated. We who continued began the child's game of walking a curb, heel to toe to heel. Someone fell. I was in front and couldn't see to help. They just cried out and were gone. A few in the line tried to back up, unable to turn. Someone else fell.

I began to unbalance towards the right, twisted to the left, then flailed with my arms and did what I learned to do as a child in such a game. I ran forwards, no longer trying to balance but only to reach the end. When I fell I rolled across cold solid ground. Those behind stepped on me in their hurry. Not many; there were now only five ex-gods and a ship's cat left. We went on.

It grew brighter, somber shadows that dared to hint of dawn. We came to fields that would have been green in the sunlit world. Poppies whispered in low quiet conversation with the grass-rustling breeze. Figures walked alone across the hills, or lay in the grass staring up at the clouds. I followed their gaze upwards and gasped. The clouds were explosions of fiery swirls across a sky wider than our mortal world's ceiling. I lost myself staring into whirls that turned into lands infinitely far, yet perfectly clear. I saw seas and mountains and forests, trains and ships and deserts and farms, I saw Maidenhead New Jersey and then my own house. My sisters were playing badminton in the front yard. Arguing furiously of course. They all cheat but so cheerfully you can't take offense. I searched in the clouds for K's house. And there was her window, so small against the sky's vast expanse, and yet so close.

I saw her face at the window as she reached out to touch palm to glass. I reached up to do the same, but the blue fire blocked the sight of her. I looked about me in surprise. All our company stood staring at the sky. Again I considered Typhon's offer. I glanced up at K's window. Those wondrous clouds were too bright, they made my eyes tear. She was so close but I couldn't reach her.

I shook the others out of their cloud gazing. "Keep your eyes down," I scolded the deities as if they should have known better. Four of them nodded respectfully. The fifth turned and walked off into the hills, gazing up at the clouds. I almost followed.

Instead I turned and walked on; the remaining gods following.

Let's finish it.

The path ended at a gate. Sunlight came through the gate, but it was locked. A house stood beside the path. In the house waited an old woman. She sat beside an old-fashioned balance-scale. In one scale was a feather. I had read about this in the French translation of the Acherontia. If our hearts were heavier than the feather then we were free to continue. Otherwise we stayed in the underworld.

One by one we gave the woman our hearts to be tested.

That sounds kind of strange now. It seemed perfectly sensible at the time. When it was my turn I found I was holding my heart in my hand. It was just a sheet of paper. I tended it to her, she smiled and placed it on the scale. I was upset to see that it wasn't any heavier than a damned feather. I would have thought it weighed plenty.

Only one of us made the scale move down. That shadow-cloaked ex-deity immediately turned and left the room. No doubt to pass through the gate and out into life again.

We four rejects exited the house. There the gate stood open. The heavy-hearted ex-deity was treading back into the shadows of the underworld. I considered the level of my ability to translate French and realized I had misread the translation. The test is to have a heart *light* as a feather. French is an art, not a science, you know.

We went through the gate. I could have closed it behind me but I left it open. We came out into morning sunlight on the top of Mount Theodosia.

Chapter 26

Excerpt, Aug 15th, 188?
Diary of K. King,
Archive of Rural Letters,
Maidenhead, New Jersey.

That is over. Here we are! That's done. This is it. Here I am. Finally! That is that. All finished! There it is. Done. Arrived. All over. That should do it. Here we are. No more now. That's an end. Journey's over. Finished. There you are. The end.

These are my new prayer words to be repeated at each catch of breath, at each thought of the impossibility of going on. They are just the words one says as one disembarks the train or awakes from the dream, or returns to consciousness in a hospital bed to gaze happily at the clean white space where a limb has been removed, the agony passed, the healing begun. All over! Finished! Done. No more now. Well, that's over. Nothing left. Done.

My love wrote me a wise and kind letter. "I see there is no place for me by your side." Well. Here we are. The end.

Oh but I do wish I could have seen him in his sailor clothes climbing ropes and staring out to sea. I'm sure he would have done it in a way to make me laugh. Clarence was always trying to make me laugh. He treated me as if he believed I was starved for laughter and he had to keep feeding me bits and pieces of comedy or I would fall to the floor a gray skeleton for lack of giggling.

It didn't seem true then. I was content before we met. And with him I was satiated on happiness. Yet it seems true now. I feel starved hollow and I can't breathe for lack of the least crumb of laughter, as if I had never feasted once. Can something work backwards in time and make the past different? So now all my life I've starved for what I only just lost? Oh well. That's enough. That's done. Here we are. The end.

Now there is only dresses and flowers and planning and teas and talk, talk, talk buzzing like bees to make a girl mad, if a girl had the energy to care to go mad. Done and done.

The new servant girl seems a bit mad. Irish I suppose though she scarcely speaks enough to catch a brogue. Maybe it is just that such pale skin and bright red hair makes one think of the mad and the Irish. All done.

I wonder how exactly one goes mad? Perhaps I shall ask her. Well, that's finished.

Interviewer: Poet?

Spirit?

What happened in the well in the crypt?

I led the dead gods through the pages of the Libris Acherontia. The gods that Typhon didn't slaughter in the Asylum, anyway. Those still in one piece who wanted to return to life. Not many survived the journey. Only three. Plus the ship's cat but I don't think he needed to come. He just tagged along to be a nuisance. We passed through the underworld and came out on the top of Mt. Theodosia.

Welcome back. Describe the view from Mount Theodosia.

It's a dead volcano. The top is a crater sheltering a grove of trees, centered with a pond so round and deep and blue it'd make a fine sky if you turned the world upside down. The wind flows constant as a river of air above the crater. Wind so steady you could lean over the cliff-edge arms spread without plunging into the void below. Not that you should do such a fool thing, but you could

But if you wander down into the crater the world becomes still and peaceful. A place of flower smells and bee buzzes, fruit tree branches rustling gentle invites. The sunlight comes brighter and warmer for its filtering through the leaves. Sun-gold light tinged with green shadow touches your face like you and he are old friends. Perhaps you are.

I stood in that place of peace staring about with no idea where it was or when I was. I was afraid to look behind me. I would see what I had led back into the living world. The cat rushed off to stalk birds. I told it to stop that predatory foolishness and it gave me a cat look. I glanced behind then, turning completely about. I was alone.

For about a second. When I completed the turn there was Typhon leaning against a large rock before me. That rock had a black and volcanic look for such a garden. A reminder of old fires. Typhon had a black and volcanic look as well. A threat of fires to come. Now he stretched as if he'd been waiting a good while.

"Not to be dramatic," he said and a lightning bolt sheared the air above my head like an axe. It knocked me flat.

He strode close to glare down with those dying-sun eyes. "You are a charming sort of fool, St. Elmo. I don't hold that against you. You stumble along from moment to moment no more concerned for your own well-being than a child in a tiger cage. But now you've opened the cage door and let three tigers out. More will follow. Tigers, devils and gods *eat* people, Mr. St. Elmo. Some with honest teeth, others with less pleasant tools."

He took a deep breath, fists and face clenched, restraining his outrage. It astonished me not to have understood him before now. Typhon wasn't an arcane aristocrat feuding with others of his class. He was a *believer.* He was a desperate revolutionary pitted against forces he hated and rejected.

He contained himself. "There is a truce that holds to this island. I advise you to take advantage of it. Keep to the shore. Because if a storm catches you at sea, Mr. St. Elmo, it will bear you umbrage. After that it will bear you to hell."

He turned and walked away.

What the blazes was that about?

It was what everything was about. The voyage, the books, the shipwreck, the names of the gods, being chased about the island. Thoth wanted the dead gods to be able to return to life. Typhon wanted them to stay dead. The two chose me as the coin to toss. Thoth gave me his books; Typhon gave me his fire. You see, Typhon counted on my angry side. I so wanted to go home and settle scores. That tilted me towards his way of thinking. But Thoth just wanted to give everyone a chance; lost sailors and lost gods together in the long journey home. In the end, I guess I saw it from Thoth's point of view.

And that was that. I'd made my decision. I supposed it might even be the right decision, from the point of view of someone resigned to never seeing home again.

I sat down under those beautiful trees and wept. It was over.

I suppose this is a bad time to ask about the books bound in green leather.

No, no it is fine. I'm alright. But what is left just makes one book, half Etruscan, half French. Thoth hid the remaining pages in the light house. I'll get to it eventually. It's a long path to that tower, winding around this damned island. Every time I head towards it I show up farther away.

Archives of the Maidenhead Weekly Chronicle, Sept 1, 188?

Together
-- C.S. Elmo, 1888
There is no time or space, except what we
share;
Alone I have no face; I need your eyes to
know my mind.
Solitude is a veil my smile cannot tear;
Mirroring myself to myself I see myself blind.

I do not flatter you to say, my heart is a
hollow shell,
Hold it to your ear; listen, do you hear, faint
as whispering,
The sounds of someone chattering, stalking
some lonesome shore
Self to himself as he kicks at the waves?
Then you laugh and, genie-like, I stand free
beside you;
The wind combs your hair in my eyes as we
laugh at the gulls.

No! The Chronicle finally printed one of my poems?
Is Blather in jail again? Because if he is dead I am not
going to raise the man. If editors were meant to return to
life they wouldn't put all those gates around hell.

Not dead, anyway. Edward Blather, literary editor of the Chronicle will die in 1899 while attempting to break into a Trenton hotel vault during a convention of police detectives. Describe what happened on Mt. Theodosia.

I lay in the grass staring at the sky. I decided I would never get up again. I would just lie in that peaceful place forever, watching clouds sail past, seeing home and K in their shapes. In the underworld you can do this but in real life you get hungry and thirsty and bugs tickle your ears, crawl up your nose. The ship's cat checked back every so often, sitting on my chest and staring into my eyes. It was a comfort to wind up his purr box and set it going.

Eventually I gave up and got up. The sun was setting. I stumbled to the pond, washed my face, scooped water and tasted to see if it was drinkable. It was fresh squeezed from clouds and flavored with flowers. I drank deep. When I finished a long-legged bird settled beside me, drank just as deep. The cat crouched down as though the murderous thing thought no one saw him.

Thoth stared uneasy at the cat.

"I'd like to get into that lighthouse," I told him.

Thoth nodded. "I figured you would. But it's a fort. Locked up and no one inside. You'd have to get the key from Theodosia."

"I thought we were on Theodosia?" I asked, puzzled.

Thoth maneuvered so that I stood between him and the cat. "I mean the lady the island is named for.

321

Governor Theodosia. She's old, old. She lives in the harbor town. You'll have to convince her to give you the key. That'd make you the light-keeper. No one's held the job in half a century. A shame. With the light showing more trade would come and that bay wouldn't eat up ships like, like a cat eating baby birds."

The ship's cat crept closer, froze, crept closer. Thoth stood on one leg then the other, nervous. He aimed at me the same one-sided look he'd used the day of the shipwreck. "Don't worry overmuch about Typhon. Storm gods like to make noise. Give him time and he'll forget all about it."

"You think so?" I asked surprised.

Thoth considered. "Well, no, not really. But maybe we can get him to come around. He's actually a decent sort. Just, you know, political."

"So what three tigers did I release on the world?" I asked.

Thoth turned from the cat back to me. Suddenly he wasn't a comic feathered creature. He was a great tall man, beaked and old, so wise as to make you shake. He leaned in close to whisper. "Nothing so terrible. Just a mad girl, a sly coyote and a comic bird," he replied. "Three lost creatures who trusted their guide."

The ship's cat leaped. Thoth vanished. The cat landed in the water with a splash and a yowling curse against the gods.

Chapter 27

Archives of the Maidenhead Weekly Chronicle, May 15, 188?

Letters to the Editors

Dear sirs of the literary contributions section. I write concerning the recent posting by a former local whose poetic enthusiasm did him credit for determination to transcend his limitations. His contribution was a clear measure of that determination, awing the reader with a view of the oceanic limitations awaiting further transcending.

The 'poem' was disturbing for its unmetered rhythm, its vapid rhyme scheme and a background insinuation of licentious ambiguity. The first line itself would warn all discerning minds and even your editorial staff that here was an injection of warped concepts into the community drinking-water of clean thought: 'There is no time or space'.

Well! So the Germans tell us. I however maintain there is Time; there is Space. There might not be a place and time for every dribble of poetic maundering; but as mathematical concepts and measures of reality, Space and Time remain constant as the tide and the requirements of true poetry.

Quite Sincerely,
Hildegarde King

Interviewer: Vicious old witch.

True. And yet she may have seen something I missed. *Licentious ambiguity.* How could I have overlooked something so obvious? The words of the poem positively drip with lust.

Where did you go after Mount Theodosia?

I stayed the night in the Grove, enjoying the fruit like an Adam granted full permission, staring at the stars, watching our moon rise over the sea. I still had that burial shroud for a cape. With it for a blanket, grass for a bed and leaves for a pillow I slept as well as I ever did in a ship's hammock, if not as well as that magical four-poster in the Asylum. It gave me a wrench to think of that wonderful bed burned up. Maybe it was in a better world now. I stared up at the stars and thought sadly how there ought to be a heaven for good beds. Perhaps we would meet again beyond the river, in the land of quilts and fluffy pillows.

I had a strange dream in the night.

This is where you tell us of the strange dream in the night.

A path crosses the mountain-top grove, connecting the north side of the island with the south. Around midnight I woke or dreamed that I woke. A party tramped down the path, pall-bearing a coffin. They marched slow and solemn. I couldn't see faces but their eyes gleamed bright. Green eyes mostly, with some yellow and blues. I lay in my makeshift bed and watched them approach.

They walked two legged but had tails that twitched behind like conductor's batons leading a requiem. They looked so solemn and mournful I felt obliged to stand and lower my head respectful. They nodded to me as they passed.

The last in the group turned to me and said "The old king is dead. Tell Grayfoot he is the new king of the cats." And with that they marched on into the night. I went back to sleep.

In the morning I told the ship's cat the old king was dead and he was now king. The feline was tormenting a bug at the time; catching it and letting it go, leaping on it just as almost reached freedom. He stopped to scratch and consider the news. Then he yawned and went back to tormenting the bug.

Yes. Well, anyway. About the Libris Acherontia.

You keep wanting to cut across country, Spirit. The trick to getting anywhere on Theodosia is to stay on the path. It winds about dreadfully but eventually arrives. I followed the path downhill all a bright day and arrived at the gate of the Green just at sundown. Without a single adventure, I point out. Think of that: an entire day narrated in one sentence. That comes from staying on the path.

The gate had no guard nor servant posted. I climbed over easy. My friends had last been here; perhaps still were. I followed a gravel path bordered with flowers. The gravel crunched under my feet so I switched to the soft grass. I desperately needed new boots, the soles flapped.

When we came as burglars looking for Cook and Tinker they caught us quick. This time I walked up to the front porch like a proper visitor. It was huge, with pillars like southern mansions or northern banks. Too early for lights, the windows presented a mournful look. The door was church-sized and had multiple parts and sub-doors. I put my ear against the wood and listened to vague sounds, distant and eerie as if from under the sea. Then, distinctly, the unmistakable laugh of a New York Cut-Throat.

Oh Spirit, that was a joy. I started to knock and then stopped. I pulled the shroud out from my pack and covered myself with it. *Then* I knocked. Eventually a wing of the door opened, squeaking slightly on bronze hinges.

Through the thin weave I spied a young girl staring back. She wore Tinker's wire rim glasses. She had a green dress on and a pencil behind her ear. I pulled the shroud off to see her face better 'cause it looked familiar. She screamed and I screamed back. She punched me hard and I went tumbling.

When I staggered to my feet she was gone. I peered inside the door to a wide empty hall. I tiptoed in, prepared to retreat. At the far end I met Cut-Throat holding a cavalry saber. Behind him was the Baker. Behind him came the white toothed grin of a Coyote.

"Tinker's wearing a dress!" I shouted. I was still mightily astounded. "I swear! It was green. There was a bosom."

Our New-York Cut-Throat stared at me, his wild horse's face pale as paper. "Poet?" he whispered. Then he decided he'd answered his own question and tossed the sword aside. There followed some ship-mate hugs and glad words. Ha, you don't know the meaning of the word 'tightly' until a Jamaican Baker has squeezed you in his arms. A boa-constrictor would take notes.

It wasn't home; yet it was a homely welcome. I even got a hug by a pretty thing in a green dress. Made me blush. Good lord.

Who took over the estate?

Our New-York Cut-Throat declared that as I had won the duel and he was my second the title devolved to him. As his argument was backed by two pistols, three ex-gods, a huge Jamaican Baker and a mysterious Tinker the surviving servants acquiesced with the sly patience of parasites waiting to measure the mettle of a potential host.

First thing after my funeral, Cut-Throat declared an end to the man-hunts and ordered the dismantling of the traps in the labyrinth. They took that as weakness. Then he ordered the Tree to be cut down and burned. They took that as blasphemy. Then Ligeia tossed the butler off the third floor balcony and Coyote ripped two of the twisted dogs to shreds. They took that as settled.

Strange to think I missed my own funeral. And Gypsy Cook's. I didn't get to say a proper goodbye. To Cook, I mean. I've plenty of time to talk to myself. Too much time.

Go ahead and describe the Gypsy Cook a last time.

While I scrub pots he sits peeling potatoes explaining how back home he has two girlfriends. Sisters. He isn't bragging. He'd doesn't want both. But when he smiles at the younger then the older bursts into tears. He gives the older a kiss and the younger scratches at his bedroom window. Eventually one takes a knife to the other. Neither are hurt but the business worries Cook. He decides to leave town until they grow up or find some other excuse for sisterly fratricide.

I stare now at Cook working away and realize I am in the presence of the most serious person I am scheduled to meet this life. He isn't a doctor saving lives nor a minister saving souls, not some energy-filled personage striding down the street to do great bothering things for the world. He's a young man still perfecting a shaving technique. He's still playing at who he will be. Last week he pretended not to know English. But he's the kind of character that would walk away if the play went ugly.

Imagine Hamlet grown up enough to just walk out of Elsinore, or a mature Othello taking a vacation from Venice.

Gypsy Cook is a grownup. But this world isn't for grownups. It's for fools and failed poets and dead gods and boring madmen and homicidal theologians and twisted dogs, all the incompetent crew who sail a proper ship straight onto the rocks. Our Gypsy Cook sits there peeling potatoes and thinking that when he understands the world's secrets he will see its wise purpose. Well, those secrets are planning to wash him onto an island of lunatics, chase him into a labyrinth then kill him to no purpose at all.

Spirit, I have no problem believing this world is a lesser copy. Gypsy Cook must have come from the real one. Probably in that world he stood with us at Cut-Throat's wedding.

Describe Cut-Throat's wedding.

I was best man. It made me proud. Tinker was Ligeia's bridesmaid, which made me snort. It was taking me time to adjust. We rehearsed and she said her part and the top of her dress jiggled and I blushed and she hit me. As a man Tinker was shy. But as a girl violent as any of my sisters, which is saying.

The Baker read the service holding the bible in his huge hands. I wished the ship's Preacher could have but it wasn't practical, porpoises being handless and confined to

329

the sea. Or freed to the sea, better said. And twixt you and me, Preacher would have made the service a ten-hour torment of holy yawns. The Baker kept it simple.

We opened up the house that day to any and all that came down the path. But we kept a weather eye for the wrong sort of guests, carrying pistols and swords just for luck. Several ex-deities wandered in, some pretending humanity and others just forgoing the charade. A party from town came over the mountain wanting to survey the new Master of the Green. They brought beer and wine and were welcomed proper for their good sense. Some of the former seminary students showed but kept to themselves. Really I don't know why people go to a party to just stand and stare. Eventually they always wander off looking for book shelves to talk to.

Yes. People like that are just sad.

Granted, extrovert that I am I escaped to the library soon as I'd danced with the bride. The former Master had book shelves that did justice to his pretensions, if not his reality. I slipped into the room to find Thoth in man-form leafing through titles.

"It's an actual first edition of The Hunting of the Snark," said the creator of writing, not turning about. "And it's *autographed*. Good lord."

What about the bride?

Since my return Ligeia avoided me, and I her. I still recalled her best as the ragged bleeding figure growling at dogs in the maze. Now she'd gone through the underworld to return a living goddess. Poetically speaking, she'd recovered a vast fortune after enduring a miserable time as a beggar. Why did she remain playing mortal girl to my shipmate? I worried whether to warn Cut-Throat.

But the wedding vows were said in the garden under bright morning sun. That light shone on a young girl standing proud beside her beau, trying not to twist her flower bouquet to pieces in nervous hands; checking braids and the train of her dress, checking Cut-Throat's face to see if he was happy. And being no fool, he was happy. She stood as fresh and pale a young thing as ever stepped from sea-foam or a father's door. She looked new.

And there I stood, listening to simple words more powerful than the names of gods. *Richer, Poorer, Sickness, Health. Better, Worse, Love, Honor, death-do-you-part.* No, this wasn't a situation requiring my advice. Ah, nor my envy. I couldn't prevent the second but I could swallow the first.

After 'pronounce you man and wife' there came the kiss, toasts, cheers, and various joyful noises. We went inside to share the cake. Then Cut-Throat produced his fiddle. I laughed, Ligeia laughed, and finally we allowed our eyes to meet. She held out her pale little hand to me. Cut-Throat began a tune and she and I began a slow rounding of steps careful for the train of her dress. Tinker paired off with the Baker good lord, and then several of the others joined.

It wasn't the mad moon dance in the ruined courtyard; and yet it was still a magic thing. Perhaps more magic. The candle flames jumped as we stepped, then twisted on their wicks to follow as we turned. Couples twirled about, pressing palm against palm, stepping together, retreating, approaching, laughing as they lost and recovered the rhythm of the dance, all while the fiddle told a long funny story about life and love and movement, a story whose meaning we could only catch by stepping in and out of time.

Eventually Cut-Throat wanted to dance with his new wife, the wretch. I sighed and allowed him this privilege. For a second, Ligeia turned her head to the side and considered me, weighing words. I bowed and backed quickly, quickly away. She smiled, turned to her new husband and forgot me completely. She devoured him whole using just her eyes, as he did her.

I did fine the whole day, spirit. I was as grownup as a Gypsy Cook. There are poets who would've made a sad face for their heart ache, dribbling tears on a friend's joy. But I kept it to myself. A grownup. Good lord, think of that.

Describe the economic basis of Theodosian culture.

The Green was a plantation run sensibly if you exclude the expenses of ritual homicide. It was the largest private holding on the island. It owned terraced fields extending all the way down to the shore, where fishing huts were set for sifting the surf with nets and lines. Groves of fruit trees, barns for storage, corrals for livestock, bees for honey, peacocks for show and dinner. There were some dozen workers with quarters in the main house, each with their own little world to run.

The Green traded produce for manufactured items brought around the mountain from the harbor town. Truthfully that was a slow long trade; not many ships came to Theodosia. But the growing season was year round, the island had a population base of semi-magical beings and long years of accumulating other people's wealth under Iskandar had made it an elegant yet working institution.

With Iskandar dead some of the servants took what they could and left. Others stayed, as the new Master proved a likable sort. Most of Theodosia followed that pattern. Holdings produced something to trade between them, the most prized items always coming through the harbor town. Arriving there from trade ships that wandered off course from Singapore and San Francisco and even New York, poor things.

Describe the harbor of Theodosia.

A week or three after the wedding, Cut-Throat, Tinker, the Baker and I made the journey over-mountain to visit the fabled harbor town. Yes, Tinker was in man clothes again. No, she didn't look like a boyish man now. She looked like a girl in boy's pants. It made me scratch my head.

No matter. As the surviving crew of Unicorn, we felt we had unfinished business with our former First Mate. He had murdered both captains outright and attempted to slaughter the ship's poet. We also assigned him a fair portion of blame for the shipwreck and the drowning of our friends. Then there was the business of him watching from a balcony while his shipmates were running for their lives. Sipping wine watching the Gypsy Cook die was not a light offense in our scales.

The Banker was holed up in town, worrying over what had escaped the containment cells of the Asylum. Whereas he probably hadn't given Unicorn's survivor's a thought, except to pencil us down to be murdered when he found the time. There is something annoying about a person who wrongs you without taking you seriously. The Banker was all the way across the island and he was annoying us. When we spotted the ship's cat trailing along, we understood our posse had gained official status.

While we walked, Baker and Tinker chatted of taking ship off the island, and where they'd want it to wander. I pretended the same ambition. I hadn't yet shared that if I stepped on a ship deck Typhon promised to sink it so fast it'd flatten the intervening fish against the ocean floor.

Cut-Throat argued for everyone to do their happily-ever-after's on Theodosia. He offered us equal shares of the Green. He declared it ours, not his, for all that one person had to hold the title. Which was fair and right. But while I was infinitely thankful of a room in his house to call my own, I had no interest in being the resident poet for a farm. And his convivial bliss was causing me to stutter and twitch. I wanted to train my mind not to think of K married to someone else. It just wasn't possible under that roof.

I'd begun dreaming of the light-house. I pictured myself in its top chamber, feeding the fire and watching dreadful storms rage outside. Wind and wave howled, and yet ships at sea steered true by the light, finding their way safe to harbor.

Say what you will, keeping the light for others is a worthwhile ambition for a man.

Go back. Describe the Library of the Mansion of the Green.

Wide dusty windows giving warm dusty light. Shelves high enough to require a ladder for the books peering curiously down, shy of coming in reach. No order to any of it that I ever saw, though the placement of different stories made you wonder if there wasn't a pattern hiding in the jumble. A lack of dust said the books were regularly cleaned. A lack of stained pages said no one ever read the things. Exactly the show library you'd expect from Iskandar.

The day of the wedding Thoth showed me different books he was excited about. 'The Mysterious Island', Jules Verne's sequel to 'Ten Thousand Leagues under the Sea'. A German edition of Gulliver's Travels with the Laputa episode deleted to prevent political offense. A "Robinson Crusoe" with an introduction by Johnathan Swift that devastatingly insulted the work it introduced. A copy of the Odyssey translated to Arabic. Or so Thoth said. I had to take his word for that.

"I can't help but noticing these are all about shipwrecks and castaways," I said, helpless not to notice.

Thoth shrugged. He wore a plain gray cloak and a scholarly look. "I tend to see things in terms of stories," he explained. "It goes with the job."

Two of the seminary students entered the library, staring about in innocent appreciation. I had a suspicion they'd followed me, so I stared unfriendly while checking under my coat for my pistol.

"Sorry we didn't have a vivisection for the wedding," I started to say and got as far as 'sorry," before the god of wisdom kicked my foot. I deliberately dropped the Arabic copy of "Ulysses" towards his foot but he caught it with his god-like reflexes. Then he handed it right back to me as though I had some use for the obtuse thing.

336

"We'd like to talk," said one of the students. It was the mechanical-thought student and I'd say his name but I didn't know it then. Wait till you are almost vivisected and check if you feel sociable afterwards.

"Talk," I said, leafing through the Arabic as if I could read it fine.

"We want to re-start the seminary," said the student. "But not on a basis of any, of any forced examinations. We just want to talk to them, ask them questions, set up discussions, maybe even publish some sort of manifesto,"

"That's political," said the other. "No manifestos. We agreed to keep it academic."

"An academic paper yearly just discussing things," said the first student patiently. "And you seem to be on special terms with the former deities. We were wondering if -"

I paged through the Arabic Ulysses, trying to remember if Arabic went left to right or versa-vice. The title page did seem to be at the end of the book. But maybe they just printed it with extra flourishes at the finale. I love when Ulysses finally, finally arrives home and gives the villains their payment due. Blazes, I'd print that whole glorious end in capital letters, assuming Arabic had capital letters.

I made the student force out a weak ending to his request. "If you could persuade some of them to cooperate?"

I turned to Thoth.

"They can't see or hear me," he explained. "I'm not 'ex' anymore."

"You really don't see this personage?" I asked, pointing.

They stared blankly.

Thoth sighed. "They also don't notice if you refer directly to me or stomp suddenly on my foot the way you are thinking so don't *even try it* St. Elmo. At best they will get an idea you talk to yourself, which this god knows, is no illusion."

Sort of like the interviewing team.

"Exactly," said Thoth.

I stared at him. "You can hear the spirit voice?"

The god of wisdom shook his head. "I meant 'an academic institution studying the unique ecology of divinity and humanity upon this island, is *exactly* what is needed.'" He blinked innocently.

He was lying, of course. The gods deceive us all. Maybe they have reason to. There always seems to be a good reason for us to deceive right back.

As for everyone else, sometimes, Spirit, I think others do hear you but they don't realize it. On ship the fool's crew worked hard to hide that we heard the whispering. Maybe it is no different now. Maybe every soul on Theodosia or the globe is being interviewed by invisible voices that follow along asking what they remember and what they see, what's happening now, what's in their pocket? The air of the island is so full of voices it's a wonder anyone can sleep.

"Clarence," I said, and offered a handshake to the mechanical-thought student.

"Steve," he replied.

"The Theodosia Institute for Theological Reconciliation?" I asked.

Steve made a face. "We want to move past theology. We want to identify what a mind is, whether animal, human or divine. We want to build a Babbage Engine and recapitulate the process."

"Oh do we?" asked the second student, sarcastic. It was news to him.

"That was three sentences beginning with 'We want'," I noted. "Is the Banker involved?"

The two exchanged worried glances.

"Headmaster Banker has retreated into his house in town," said Steve. "He says to hell with gods, students and all the devils between. He's upset about the escapees from the basement. He should be. Some bear him serious grudges. Also he's very, very angry at *you.*"

I thought about that and said "The Chess-Playing Automaton had a pipe he puffed on when he was considering the board."

The students blinked, wondering what that had to do with anything. Thoth blinked though he probably knew. Truth was I desperately needed a pipe. It would help me look thoughtful while I pondered things, just so people would know when I was considering what the hell my next move was.

Chapter 28

Excerpt, Aug 25th, 188?
Diary of K. King,
Archive of Rural Letters,
Maidenhead, New Jersey.

Aunt Hildegard hid the paper this morning. I suspect Greta wrote another letter advocating a common sense return to public whippings for debtors, adulterers and Frenchmen. How she dreams of throwing stones at some poor body with their head and feet in stocks! Alas, till the return to a Moral Basis gossip must suffice.

I have promised Mother I shall cease upsetting the household with night noises and lunacy. She is right. I am no longer a child. If I cannot have the choices I would, yet the duty of life is to make the choices I have. That sounds so wise, and yet it only means I cannot spend tonight stringing pots, pans and bells to every door as I next planned. I do wish I had stayed mad a bit longer. Think of how it would have sounded in the morning! Like a sudden storm had entered the house.

The new servant girl's right hand keeps going to the left to twist and fondle a wedding band. Nervous to see if it is still there, joyful to see it is. It can't have been there long. She sleeps in the servant's quarters so her man must live elsewhere. Perhaps hundreds of miles. You can see the ring makes her proud. I shall be the same. I am sure I shall.

Aunt Agatha has brought home a strange dog that quite resembles a wolf. Father says it is a yellow Alsatian and is

Valuable. It seems meek yet the other dogs are terrified of it. But it has the most knowing expression. Alice and the others came over to try out the bridesmaid gowns. It positively leered as they undressed. I finally sent the thing out.

Henry never leers. Really for all his chatter about barnyard scandal he seems shyer than a poet. Clarence didn't leer, exactly. But he would tremble in my arms, and his eyes would half-close while he grinned as the Wolf upon my Lamb-hood. I had no objection; not a bleat of protest.

Heavens that would make an Aunt think we acted as Savages in the forest. But really I mean only walking, and sitting, and talking, and the carefully counted embraces and kisses exchanged. So few to count. A walk in the snow-fall, a night-embrace at the lake. Scenes, times, feelings that will all fade. Must fade. They must.

Interviewer: Describe Theodosia.

Frail; ancient; the dusty remainders of a woman in a purple dress sitting in garden sunshine. Quite blind. A bit deaf; I had to repeat questions to get a proper answer. Unless she was being sly. Sometimes old people are sly, you know.

"When did you get to this island?" I asked. It was a dull question and she knew it. She yawned, eyes gray-white shells of sight turned inwards. She fished in a dress pocket and came out with a heavy iron key. The key to the light house, no doubt. It had more teeth than remained in her mouth. She clutched it in a hand scrawny as a bird-foot. She was being sly; warning me not to bore if I hoped to persuade her to give me that key. I considered just grabbing it and leaping over the garden fence. 'Course she knew I was thinking it. She grinned, waiting to see if I'd dare. The ship's cat sat at my feet grinning too. *He*'d have dared. I didn't. She sighed disappointed and put the key back in her pocket.

"A stormy Sunday," she said, answering my question. Now she waited for me to ask 'Which Sunday?' but that was too obvious a trap. What did I have to say to this personage? There is nothing you can tell the truly old. They've heard your latest news, your latest idea, your brilliant insight and your honest opinion, in all variations across the repeated seasons. You can't tell them things. You can only ask them. Ask about the old days, the good times, the terrible storms and the style of shoes, what loves they lost and who won the war. Ask a question and see some word trigger a conversation carried on since before you climbed out of the sea to breathe.

"I have a gal," I said. I might have been speaking to myself rather than those grey shell eyes. Maybe I spoke to the purple dress, or the ship's cat or the sunlight shining warm on us all. "She's far away. I don't suppose I'll see her again." That hurt to say. "Was there someone you left behind?"

The ancient face twisted at the question, an earlier face shifting in surprise beneath the scars and wrinkles. "Yes, a very stormy Sunday," she repeated, as if agreeing with herself. "We sailed south of the light and came here to harbor. If we'd gone into the bay that would have been an end. But here we cast anchor and lowered sail, tossed the cargo and rode out the storm. Then in the dawn light on a peaceful sea of a Monday morn, the powder store went up. Blew the entire ship to hell."

I blinked at that.

"That sounds bad luck," I said. Tedious observation. I sounded like Spirit. I bit my lip to hold back the demand: *describe the explosion.*

Well thanks.

Sorry. This woman scares me. She is so old I am afraid she is going to cough once, fall to pieces and nurses will shout *you broke her.* And yet she's not a bit absent. You can tell she is in there, considering you and the wind and the sea and all the years past. She's an old book of a woman, the pages falling apart but the printed words still making more sense of the world than anything being narrated in your own head.

"Oh, It was no accident," Theodosia said. "I blew it up. My shipmates were pirates. I didn't pity them a speck."

Well, they'd mentioned Theodosia had been a pirate. It happens. I considered asking about it and intuited she'd rather discuss the weather or oatmeal. I weighed asking why she went to sea and how she got to shore, what the town smelled like in ancient times and which estates were the dread of the island. I already knew what was in her pocket; the lighthouse key.

The ship's cat chose that moment to jump in her lap. I reached to grab the beast, not wanting it to dig claws into her parchment skin. Skin so translucent the blue veins showed like rivers on a map.

Governor Theodosia laughed. She reached out and stroked the feline as he settled gentle as a pillow. He set up a warm purr meant for insult to me. He blinked to say *'This* is conversation. See how it's done?"

"Why do you want to be the keeper of the light?" she asked, stroking under the cat's chin.

I considered answering 'I've nothing better to do.' It isn't a bad answer, if it sounds dull. A man has to do something. But the real answer was a bit different.

"I am not sure. I have a powerful urge to see that tower show a light. It's dark now, and that isn't right." I hesitated, the words getting confused in my head which doesn't happen often as you'd think. "You need light to see light," I finished. I knew it didn't make sense. But she was blind. Light was a thing to be caught in words since I couldn't just show it to her.

"My father," she whispered. "I miss him something dreadful."

I blinked. It took me a moment to realize she had jumped back to my question *was there someone you left behind?*

"I've been writing my girl," I said. "I know she won't get the letters. And I won't get any words back. But when I walked through town today I chatted to her in my head, telling her about the hike down the mountain and how pretty the brick houses looked from high up, and asking what she thought of the street lamps. And she told me she'd walked by the lake today and said the houses needed flower boxes, and we agreed your street lamps were a wonder. And maybe at home she's doing the same; chatting to me in her head, pointing at something and asking what I think about it, imagining my reply. So it's like we are together in a way because both of us are talking to the image of the other that we carry inside."

"Tom-fool nonsense," she sniffed. "Are you certain you are a sailor? You sound like a bad poet."

"Are you sure you're a governor?" I asked. "You sound like an old pirate."

"Hoity-toity," she countered sharp. "Careful of that tongue."

"Careful of that cat," I replied sharper. "He starts with purrs then goes for blood."

"They often do," she sighed. "Particularly the boys." She pulled the key out again and grasped it in her chicken-claw fist. "When he decides to remind me what a fierce beast he is, I'll thump him with this."

Unicorn's cat purred, unconcerned.

"I hear you've been dueling," she said. For some reason I assumed she addressed the cat. He probably *had* been dueling, he had more scars across his face than I've got lines on both palms. I waited to see what he would say. He purred smug. Theodosia continued, assuming I kept a proud silence. "Well, I don't hold with the practice. My father dueled. Worst thing that ever happened to him. Killed a friend."

I realized she was talking to me. I thought about apologizing but the affair hadn't been my idea. "It wasn't much of a duel. Iskandar and I clanked swords once. Then lightning crisped him flat."

She chuckled. "Welcome to Theodosia," she said.

She was first to say that to me. Really I think it was about time someone did.

Why is the light-house locked?

Thanks. "Why is the light-house locked?" I asked. "Seems important enough to the island."

"Politics," she replied. "From *that* side of things, you understand. The storm wants the ships to sink in the bay. The light would see them safely here to harbor. I'm of two minds myself. I'd like to see more ships come in. We could use the revenue, not to mention the lamp oil, powder, nails, cloth, rope, medicines and about a thousand other items wanted to keep a town from being eaten by its own dogs. But the storm has a point. Better for the world if some of the things that debark on this island sink to the bottom of the sea. Preferably deeper."

347

I think she means Typhon wants the light-house dark; Thoth wants it lit.

"Pretty much," said Theodosia. She sniffed again. "Politics." She turned her head as if trying to aim those grayed-away eyes into mine. "Why do you want to keep the light?"

She'd already asked me that. Either she was getting forgetful or my first answer hadn't satisfied.

"I've dreamed of doing so since I saw it," I admitted. "I keep finding myself up there at the top, feeding the fire, staring out at the storm and feeling a satisfaction that I'm helping ships get safe home." I weighed adding '*Since I can't go home myself*', but wasn't fool enough to do so. Pity is a trick that works on young minds. I know it; I'm young, I pity things. Particularly myself and old people, the poor creatures. But the truly old minds lose the faculty for easy pity. It's a necessary adaptation to pain, as the Professor would point out.

"Hmm," she said. "When you are having those conversations with your girl in your fool head. What does she say about your plan to sit alone in a light-house for the next fifty years?"

I stood up.

It's a fair question. You were going to have to answer it some time.

It *isn't* a fair question. It's an operating theatre question. Tell us, Clarence what happens when we cut

348

you open here and pull this out? God damn it to hell. God damn all the gods to hell and the sly old people too and all the miles and minutes between me and mine. Let the stupid seas just rise up and pull every light into the waves and drown the world in storm. Why not. Why not.

"What does she say?" I shouted at Theodosia. "She says 'come back'. That's all. She says 'come back to me, come back to me'." The cat skedaddled, alarmed. I wiped away tears with a blue-flaming hand.

"Well," said Theodosia. She tossed the key as if she saw exactly where I stood. I caught it in that idiot fist, and lightning wrapped the key to welcome an old friend. "Well," she repeated thoughtful, tasting the word. "Maybe you should stop *talking* to her, and start *listening* to her."

Describe Theodosia again.

Not a large town, but stretching all along the harbor rather than bunching up. A dock goes out into the bay. Not as big as Shipwreck to the north, but neither is it full of ship-killer rocks. They have a bit of a sea-wall so no one tumbles in the surf, and then the cobbled street with those wonderful lamps. The long street is lined with efficient brick buildings, shingled and orderly.

The town plan was laid out by Theodosia in her fierce authoritarian days. That pirate girl took over the village and rebuilt it in accordance with strict democratic principles, egalitarian ideals and a steel ruler she'd use to measure equal shares or slice the throats of counter-proposals, as circumstances dictated.

We arrived in town at sundown, weary and thirsty. The town watchman greeted us by name soon as we stepped foot to the cobblestones. Apparently they kept an eye on what came their way from inland. Sensible if you consider the things they shared an island with. He pointed his grandfather's musket towards the tavern and recommended the ale over the beer.

But they were just lighting the lamps. I stopped to watch. Each lighting was a separate little ceremony. I wondered if the lamp lighter gave each lamp a separate name. I would have. The non-poets of the party complained, their coarse souls hearing the siren call of ale. But my delay cleverly arranged us to collide with a man hurrying out the tavern as we prepared to enter. He wore a wide hat low over his face, and if he hadn't been seven feet tall we'd not have recognized him for the Banker.

Cut Throat stepped in his way, pistol out in greeting. Tinker stepped to one side, the Baker to the other. Tinker held a single-shot, light and slight as herself; the Baker favored a big walking stick with a weighted top. With that club and those arms he could have beat an anvil unconscious.

He settled for knocking the hat off. So we stared at the Banker, he at us. I was hoping to see some fear and remorse as he recognized the vengeful remainders of

Unicorn's crew. Naturally not. He just scowled annoyed at this interruption of his schedule.

"Out of my way," he snarled. "I'm in a hurry."

"Then slow down," countered our Officer Cut-Throat. "You being under arrest for murder."

"Whose?" asked the Banker sarcastic-like. "When? More important, *where?*"

"At sea, the first and second captains of Unicorn, two months ago thereabouts," I said. "I witnessed you shoot Captain Grocer."

"Not really in the jurisdiction of Theodosian court," grinned the man. "I haven't killed anyone in town. *Yet.*" He gave us his troll-grin but it didn't have the same shiver effect. I studied why.

He was hollow-eyed and older. He had a twitch to those hairy eyes. They weren't just covering us. They darted into shadows, up to roofs. He kept rearranging tongue, lips and jaw as though trying to chew a big bite of worries into submissive digestion. He was scared. I considered the things that ran out of the containment cells of the burning Asylum. Things no doubt anxious to deliver their side of the theological debate.

"In a hurry to get home, Headmaster?" I asked. "Anxious to get behind locks and bolts? Things been scratching at the windows by night?"

He snarled. "You accuse me of murder. I accuse you of theft. You stole my books and destroyed my seminary.

When I tender my charges against *you,* St. Elmo, it will be a long poem on the themes of agony and justice."

He moved to brush past, finished with us riffraff. The Baker shoved his cudgel hard into his stomach. The Banker bent double, struggling to aim the pistol he was suddenly holding.

"Well now," said the voice of the watchman behind us. "Let's all calm down before I hurt anyone." First thing he did, he had everyone put their guns onto the ground. The Banker grinned. No doubt he was a town alderman or some figure of respect.

There followed a long tangled accusation from the Baker, a short clear version from Cut-Throat, and an even shorter expletive-filled one from Tinker. We stared astonished, even the Banker. Not a crewman had ever heard her talk so before tonight. She must have been saving up every one of those sailor-words for a special occasion; and here was the occasion.

The Banker dismissed the accusations with a wave of a paw. He addressed the watchman by name and explained we had attempted to rob him.

The watchman nodded amiably, joined by another holding a cudgel and a lantern that shown in the twilight. I studied the lantern. It flickered for my attention and then it whispered. It whispered that for justice to be fulfilled upon the Banker required neither trial nor jurisdictional appeal, not a bullet not a length of hemp. It only required he be delayed in the street till full night fell.

I cleared my throat, gained the attention of all and began a description of the wreck of Unicorn. I *took my time*.

This is where I say, do not describe the shipwreck.

You wound me, Spirit. That was the best rendition I gave. I used words left out in earlier versions. I used 'eldritch', 'tempestuous', 'Götterdämmerung' and 'fulminous'. Wonderful words. I recreated the whole sinking right there in the middle of Long Street, Theodosia. How Typhon roared! Wind and wave raged like heathen hordes while sails ripped and doomed seamen shouted their separate lines on a stage that tipped and twisted in final agony. As I spoke you could smell the salt spray and hear the waves. Granted the shore was twenty feet off so perhaps it was not just my talent of painting a panorama with a pallet of words. I was approaching the climactic scene in the crow's nest, the best part. Naturally the Banker interrupted.

"Watchmen, I have changed my mind. I see now these men did not attempt to rob me. They are mere drunks and lunatics. I must be getting home. Now."

"What was that?" I screamed, pointing behind him. The Banker leaped, turning about.

"It's gone," I said, peering in the dark. "It, it scuttled. Like a spider."

The Banker's eyes widened till you'd fear they were going to roll out his face if you cared for his eyes. I didn't,

353

not a bit. He reached to reclaim his pistol but the watchmen stopped him. They collected the guns themselves and said we could retrieve them tomorrow at the City Hall.

"And now a goodnight to each," said the watchman. "The gentlemen from over-mountain can find rooms at the tavern. We will kindly accompany you so as you don't get lost."

The Banker started to hurry off down the street, then stopped to stare. *Every third lamp had gone out.* It left shadowed pools he was going to have to swim if he hoped to reach the shore of his door.

The Watchman shook his head. "Bad lamp oil again," he tsk'ed. But I thought there was something sly about his easy disconcern. He knew our names, he knew the Banker, and he knew the island. He knew what that dark street boded. All men are augurs, and most can read the clearer messages. That waiting dark was an easy portent, writ large.

He guided us with polite threats up the street while the shaking Banker went down the street alone. Spirit, I felt sorry for him. He hadn't gone five alley-ways before he screamed.

Describe Theodosia.

There is a path that will take you from one side of the island to the other in a quick two-day hike around the mountain. And there are places between the path that will

354

take you in a journey of years, from this side of life to the far side of dreams; to the shadows of death or wisdom or the back of your own mirror where you stare in fright and wonder at your own puzzled face. Theodosia is not a safe place. It is not a sensible place. It does not come into a describable whole that can ever be easily mapped and captured.

Not so different from anywhere else.

What ate the Banker?

We ran down the night street. The Banker lay on the pavement. Something dragged him toward an alley. Something else dragged him toward the street. Parts of the man went different directions in the tug-of-war.

The musket fired and one creature ran loping off. The Baker swung his cudgel and the second creature caught it its teeth and bit the end clean away. Cut-Throat gave it a kick and Tinker shouted 'Hi! Scat!' as though it were a stray dog. It snarled, backing away. Me and the second watchman grabbed the Banker's remaining foot and pulled him towards us.

Then the monster stood upright, revealing tatters of clothes. It made a gesture with a claw as though commanding us to cease this shouting and consider like men together. And it spoke. In a man's voice, strong and deep as the low note of a church organ.

"*When I reflected on his crimes and malice, my hatred and revenge burst all bounds of moderation.*" We stared. The

355

Banker moaned. It continued. "*I would have made a pilgrimage to the highest peak of the Andes, could I there have precipitated him to their base.*"

With that the beast turned its back to us, indifferent to our guns and opinions. It walked solemnly into the night and was gone.

I looked that up. It is from the novel "Frankenstein".

Oh, I know the book. Recognized it soon as I heard it. By Mary Shelley. Friend of Byron. Where ever I go, that man was already there.

Chapter 29

Excerpt, Aug 28th, 188?
Diary of K. King,
Archive of Rural Letters,
Maidenhead, New Jersey.

I have been lied to. I know this. I simply don't know what truth the lie betrays. Yesterday after the girl straightened I found a copy of the Weekly Chronicle upon the vanity. Inside was printed a poem. By my poet. Mine. My Poet's. My poem. For me. He wrote it. It was a short lonely thing describing how he missed me and imagined us together. I read the words aloud and for a moment we were together. We stood on a beach and gulls cried in the air around us. For a blessed second.

I confronted Mother and Father in the kitchen, demanding to know why it had been kept from me. Mother demanded to know who had revealed it. The girl Ligeia stood beside her, polishing silverware for the wedding. She paused, no doubt wondering if I would betray her. Of course I did not. I demanded again, why it was kept secret?

Father explained how they feared it would upset me to recall my old 'friend'. He said it so, as if Clarence were an acquaintance of years past. Then I think Father erred. He sighed and showed me the shipping news in a New York paper. Telegraphs reporting the U.S. cargo ship Unicorn out of San Francisco was long overdue in Singapore. The ship was presumed lost. Father explained how they did not wish my kindly heart darkened as my happy day approached.

At that the girl Ligeia laughed. She continued polishing, chuckling deep as a wolf growls. Father turned upon her his sad scowl. Mother turned furious and cuffed the girl across the ear. Ligeia paid no least mind, chuckling to the face she polished in the tray.

I felt bewildered. For a moment I recalled our Prayer for those at Sea. Had my poet perished in some dreadful storm? Why couldn't I have perished with him? But he had said there was no place for me by his side. Yes, but in the same letter that said he had arrived in Singapore!

I studied Father and Mother studying me. I doubted them. And then I doubted the kitchen and the house and then the town about me. The world was words and the words were false. The servants bustled about, pretending not to listen, pretending their work was real. At last the girl Ligeia looked up, pale face framed with braids of flowing red. And she smiled. It was a smile fierce and violent and happy. A mad and kindly smile. It was just for me, and it meant me well, but it made me tremble. I fled.

And in my room I sat staring at my own face. This girl in my mirror isn't a bit mad. Just frantic looking, sad looking, desperate looking. A sheep surrounded by shadows. Are the shadows wolves?

I took out Clarence's final letter and studied it. Had he written this? The words sounded dull and formal. But what use eloquence to say 'I no longer love'? I considered the words "My ship has reached Singapore." But if that was false, why not the rest? Who wrote these *words? Had Father or an Aunt? How could they? But then, how could Father have dared read my poem aloud at tea?*

It would seem I live simultaneously in two possible worlds. In one my poet is safe and does not care for me. In the other he loved me and is drowned.

I contemplated those two worlds, wondering which the girl in the mirror could bear and which I would choose. At last the mirror-girl began to show a bit of madness; some about the eyes and more about the mouth. It was a relief to see her do so, poor mousy thing.

Interviewer: Describe.

Do you have a girl, Spirit? A love?

Yes.

Describe.

She is smart. She is kind. Those alone are enough for satisfaction, but there are more words worth pinning to 'she is'. She is shy, but she loves people and laughter too much to hide in a corner. She has brown hair she's always fooling with. Her face changes expressions fast. She shows more expressions in a minute than the usual theater of a face performs in a day. She is creative. She likes cats. She laughs in her sleep.

You used to talk like a clock ticking. Now you talk like me?

You've been an influence. Also the project has gone to hell anyway so why not.

You can have all the Acherontia that remains, I promise. When I get to the light-house.

We the interviewing team no longer have any idea as to its value or validity. Everyone else on the project has gone home for the night. I'm hanging around the empty office just to see this through.

I am sorry. Are you sitting in the dark?

No. I sit under bright office lights that radiate a cold frosty pitiless shroud of illumination upon all. They hum. I can hear voices of the dead and unemployed in the humming.

That sounds awful.

It is. Let's discuss something more pleasant. Describe the death of the Banker.

We carried the torn body into an efficient brick box called the Infirmary. The town doctor/surgeon/barber/dentist lived within. He guided us to lay down the parts of the Banker that seemed worth patching. The tall man's remaining foot dangled over the edge of the table. Veteran of operating theaters that I was I got powerful sick and ran outside to talk to the flowers, bending low. The Baker and Tinker remained to be useful.

I didn't concern myself for Iskandar, Spirit. He didn't make enough of a man to pity as a corpse. But there was a good deal more to the Banker. He was arrogant and dishonest and proud and mean and crazy. Yet I remember on ship one night me and Gypsy Cook were washing pans after mess. He came into the galley and ordered us on deck. We wondered what he'd thought we'd done and how he'd known.

He just led us to the railing and pointed to the night sea. We gasped. The whole world of water was aglow beneath the ship, the ocean floor turned to fox fire. We two pretend-sailors stared amazed. The Banker explained the glow as a local phosphorescence produced by tiny plants in the water. Then he solemnly pointed at the stars, explaining them as a local phosphorescence as well. It was a joke, and we laughed appreciatively, he being the boss. I looked up at those lights and saw different constellations than from my roof at home. Then I looked to the Banker. He'd forgotten us, considering those stars. He reached up one of his hairy warty fists as though he intended to steal a few, stuff them inside one cheek like a monkey.

Then he recollected himself and ordered us back to washing pots.

I felt guilty not helping with the binding and the sewing and the bandaging and the mopping. Glad I missed it; but still guilty for my poetic stomach. So I volunteered to sit with the Banker when we carried him to a bed. The doctor-barber predicted he'd last the night, maybe the dawn.

The others headed off to the tavern to rent something flat to collapse onto. I sat in a chair wishing I had a book. I kept the candle lit. I wondered if Tinker would request a separate room. Or would married Mr. Cut-Throat demand separate quarters? Perhaps the Baker and Tinker would share a bed. That made me and the candle flame laugh together.

The Banker moaned and I felt guilty for the laugh. I felt pity, and then felt foolish for the pity. Blazes, we'd marched into town to see this man shot or hanged according to whether gun or rope were nearer to hand. I'd delayed him in the street just so creatures he'd wronged could have their say. And yet we'd fired shouts and shots to rescue his tatters. And now I sat by his side hoping to sooth his passing?

The candle flame shook its head at that, agreeing it was a mystery. I recollect it was a tall white angel of a candle, with a golden halo doing justice to the solemn office of distributing the light. We talked some about what it all meant, not making conclusions but pointing out the fearful symmetry. As the night passed he grew shorter and wiser, I just grew tired.

Before dawn the Banker woke. I had some potions I was supposed to pour down his throat but when I tried he shook his head *no*. He studied me some, face pale and worn. He was fifty years older now than when we'd caught him in the street. I wondered if he even recalled me from old times, but finally he grinned. "What the hand," he whispered.

"I put that poem to good use," I affirmed. "A lot of people don't see the practical utility in Blake."

He nodded, remembering. "Typhon betrayed me," he whispered.

I shrugged. "The Professor said it. The gods deceive us all."

The Banker nodded again. "He was an idiot."

"Typhon?" I asked surprised.

"No, the Professor," whispered Banker. "You can't remake the gods. And why the hellfire make them human? We've humans enough, and more than I like. No. The only ambition worth the pain of being a man is to *join* the gods. Catch them, beat them, dig into them and steal their secrets. Take their fire, take their names, grab their thunder! Then climb up there with them."

I hadn't anything to say to that. I still don't. It sounded a powerful statement, but it came from the bloody tatters of a cruel and selfish man. He'd have made a cruel and selfish god. But probably a respectable tiger. I exchanged looks with the candle but neither of us said so.

Banker and I talked till dawn. He asked if I intended to sail home. I explained how Typhon waited to drop a storm on my head soon as I stepped foot to the sea. He looked thoughtful at that. I could hear the sea-tide in his breath, drawing him farther from this shore.

Then he gave me a couple of secrets. He wouldn't take the pain potions in return so I gave him some memorized Carrol, The Hunting of the Snark.

"They sought it with thimbles, they sought it with care;
They pursued it with forks and hope;
They threatened its life with a railway-share;
They charmed it with smiles and soap.
And the Banker, inspired with a courage so new
It was matter for general remark,
Rushed madly ahead and was lost to their view
In his zeal to discover the Snark"

When I got to the part where the Bandersnatch attacks, the Banker chuckled and died.

What secrets did the Banker reveal?

A better question is *why reveal any?* He wasn't sorry; not for the murders nor chasing me with an axe nor all the pain he'd inflicted in his Asylum-Seminary nut-house. And he bore me considerable grudge. If he'd had a gun he'd have shot me, maybe with a quote from Swinburne. "In the end it is not well".

But he didn't have a gun. What he had was two secrets. Put together he hoped they'd serve for a last shot at someone he begrudged far more than me.

First secret: where I could find a ship to take me home. He had a cutter anchored in a cave on the west side of the island. A cave open to the water, leading deep into the mountain. He advised me not to crew it with poets or tinkers, which was sound advice.

Second secret: he told me how I could kill Typhon.

Describe how you could kill Typhon.

Spirit, you do keep wanting to cut across country.

Fine. Keep to the path. Describe leaving Governor Theodosia.

I held the iron key of the lighthouse, weighing it against my heart. Did I want it? I didn't see why Theodosia had given it, but suspected the sort of sly jest the old play upon the young. When I was ten I had a grand-uncle gift me his cigar. It filled me with blue smoke making me retch, no doubt teaching me a Valuable Lesson. This key looked to be meant the same.

But I said 'thank you, ma'am" to Theodosia, being so taught. She informed me the position received no salary but I'd get a share of whatever tariff they could squeeze from any visiting ship, which was once a year in a generous year. The town would provide a barrel of lamp-oil a month for the light, plus food-stuffs. Getting it over-mountain would be my problem. There were a few sloops in the harbor that could be contracted to bring supplies around the shore to Shipwreck Bay, providing the weather was sane.

With that she requested her nurse to wheel her chair away from the cooling wind. I stood till she was gone, then wandered to the front of City Hall where my friends loitered playing toss-penny. I showed them the key. Cut-Throat was glad I'd won myself a job; it meant I'd be staying on the island.

They could see I was distraught, stoic poet that I am. So we wandered to the tavern and tried both the preferred ale and the dubious beer. We labored to get Tinker to say all those swear words again. But being man-dressed turned him shy. We stayed the night in Theodosia. The Baker and the Tinker took a room to themselves and that was their business.

In the morning we had the body of the Banker to dispose of. We could haul him on our shoulders up the mountain to that cemetery. We voted no. Instead we wrapped him in his bloody sheets, weighed them down, rented a skiff to the edge of the harbor and pushed him over.

The Baker said some bits of 'The Prayer for those Lost at Sea' though privately we all considered the man not a bit lost so long as he continued in a downwards direction. While he spoke a porpoise leaped the sea sparkles. No doubt it was the ship's Preacher aching to add a few dozen hours to the ceremony.

We rowed back to shore and headed over-mountain.

We hiked uphill and slept the night in the mountain-top grove. I walked about smelling the blossoms as stars revealed themselves in hiding behind the fading blue. I felt restless. I kept taking out the key and weighing it.

366

That black rock where Typhon had leaned kept staring at me ominous. I tapped the key against it, making the *clink* of a tossed coin. Heads or tails, I needed to get to the lighthouse. I would have hiked on in the dark if my friends had not knocked me flat to the ground friendly-like. Night-travel in Theodosia is not wisdom, though if you survive you're wiser for the scars.

So instead we headed downhill to birds shouting the dawn, reaching the Green as they whispered twilight. It was a joy and a tooth-extraction to watch Cut-Throat and his bride embrace. She didn't wait at the door tapping a foot. No, she came flying down that long path and crashed into him at race-horse speed. Tinker and the Baker stood grinning and holding hands.

I studied the clouds awhile till the noise died down some, then went inside, skipping dinner.

Describe the journey to the lighthouse.

At sunrise I tried to sneak out of the Green by my lonesome. Course I found myself trailed first by a coyote and then by a tinker and then by a cut-throat. By the time I passed the gate Ligeia and the Baker and that cat had joined the parade. Which made me smile, stoic poet that I am.

So we made a picnic of it, keeping to the path. It was tempting to head straight downhill through the trees. What would we find in those quiet green tree-shadows between the paths? What would find us? We didn't want to find out.

Which wisdom meant that afternoon found us safe at the stone causeway connecting the shore to the base of the tower rock. The surf washed across, presenting a damp and slippery venture. Cut-Throat picked up Ligeia to carry her gentlemanly, bare feet kicking out from her green print dress. I suspect she could have carried him easier, but she looked pleased with the arrangement. I looked to see if the Baker would carry Tinker or versa-vice but they just splashed through together. I carried the cat, who looked put out. 'Course he bit me.

Steps carved in the stone led us up. At the top waited flat rock and that crazy tower. Five stories or more, depending on the meaning of the placement of the windows. The base was granite and looked to have been chewed by rats with steel teeth. I wouldn't have believed it then, but the storm sends waves up to the top of that rock and higher, knocking against the tower itself, making it shake.

I went up to the iron-plated door and put the key in the lock.

Describe the inside of the Lighthouse.

No one had kept the light in years, but Theodosia must have sent someone over-mountain occasionally to keep it standing. We walked in only choking a bit on the dust. Inside smelled like a ship. Not surprising as most of the floors and beams came from ship-timbers and storm-wrack. But there was a sea-tang of decks and bilge and dry rot, moldy canvas and salt spray and fresh wind. This tower was a thing of the sea.

The walls greeted us with hunting trophies, if you were a storm and you hunted ships. We stared at figureheads from ships whose crews and timbers must long ago have settled to sleep on the sea floor. Wood-carved figures of beasts and men, mermaids and gods, tritons and birds and a fat man holding a beer flagon. They were pretty to look at but gave a sailor a shiver.

All the tower was a treasure house of storm wrack collected across a century or three. We wandered about, splitting up, climbing the spiral stairs, shouting of some find, laughing or puzzling at the contents of some barrel or closet. I found a sea-chest of beautiful shells, each a unique creation of the sea, delicate as a porcelain orchid. The Baker discovered a cannon that could be pointed out to the bay or wheeled towards land, depending on whom you wanted to smite. He began cleaning and loading it fast as we talked to persuade him to leave it for god's sake alone.

Cut-Throat found a wall of sabers, cutlasses, knives, harpoons and various tools meant to do heroic harm to another. He and Ligeia began a careful duel that threatened fingers and eyes, so I bore my poetic stomach upstairs to find myself in the lantern room, the chamber of light.

Here I am now.

Describe the Libris Acherontia.

The scroll of surviving pages from the two books lay before the lamp where Thoth had placed it. I picked it up and unraveled them. Half were the original words of unknown meaning, their translation now lost. Half were the doubtful translation, of original words now lost.

You can have the real words, Spirit, just so long as you don't understand them. Or you can have a dubious translation of some piece of the whole. You will never have both at once.

What does that even *mean*?

You'd have to ask Thoth. He told it me. But when you ask, remember the rule of the Augurs: All things speak the words of the gods. Lightning, bird-song, the ripples of sand in the surf, steaming animal guts and the cloud-fires of dawn. All things speak for the gods.

And the gods only dare to speak clearly when they trust you will misunderstand.

Chapter 30

Excerpt, Aug 29th, 188?
Diary of K. King,
Archive of Rural Letters,
Maidenhead, New Jersey.

I was in the night. No, the dog was in the night. I was at the window. Yes, and the night was within the window. I pressed my palm against the dark glass, watching my reflection do the same. Then I dared to peer through. In the yard the wolfish dog stared up. He invited me to come out. I nodded and left my room, tiptoeing past the aunts' chambers. Agatha had pinned thread and a bell to my door so that she would know when I night-walked. But at the end of the hall the servant-girl Ligeia stood holding the thread, dangling the bell. She wore her nightdress same as I. She nodded respectful as I passed, swaying on white bare feet to music of her own.

Down the stairs in the dark, through the warm kitchen and out into cold night. Our moon shown bright, glad to see me. Its friendly beams guided to the oak where the wolf dog waited. He sat enjoying our moon, swallowing the light in great black eyes. He asked politely how I fared. I said poorly of late, but always better by moonlight. He said it cheered him too and asked if I would company him for a while and I said very well. Together we strolled through the Rectory garden, where the last summer blooms perished. I recall we held hands as we walked, which seems puzzling now. We chatted of moonlight and the destiny of flowers. Beyond the roses waited the compost pile, where old leaves and fireplace ashes, bits of trash and rot were heaped waiting to lose themselves to roses in the spring.

The wolf dog dug and tore into the side of the compost, as a dog will do. I suppose it smelled of treasures to a canine nose. I was indifferent, smelling only autumn rot. I started to shiver. Then he tugged with his teeth on a pile of trash and pulled it to the grass before me.

I bent down to find bits of paper, crumpled and smeared. The light was poor but it was kind. It gave my eyes the necessary light to read. You need light to see light.

"I have no use for wisdom that says we must part. I stand beneath our moon declaring I have no power to summon heart nor mind nor spirit and order them to forget you. I believe in your love for me. Believe in mine for you. Believe in my love."

I did not know these words, yet I knew their voice and meaning. I fell upon the grass holding these stolen letters tight, breathing the moon deep, deep into my lungs. And then I laughed, because I was loved; and I wept, because my love was drowned at sea.

Interviewer: Describe how to kill Typhon.

Oh, there are as many ways to kill a god as there are to destroy a man. Personally my favorite is to melt him down in confusion and despair.

Let's see. First you must catch him in a box. The box must be painted on the inside with clouds and suns and fires and volcanoes so that he imagines he is inside his own head. Naturally he will begin talking to himself. Now from outside the box you must ask questions he will mistake for his own thoughts. You must dangle before him in words all the things he loves and fears. Play messenger for him; play confidant; play voice of reason and kindly stranger and cruel mechanical antagonist. Confuse him; mislead him; hound him with shadows of reality. Construct boxes inside the box, and imaginary doors out of the box. Give him the words 'key', and 'light', and 'fire' and 'love', let him hold these things tight as though they were more than words.

Soon enough, soon enough, he will disintegrate into separate parts that vow to never again to form coherent mind nor body.

I am doubting that.

You doubt? You, who give me the yellowed pages of my love's diary from years past? Words telling me that beyond the box my love waits? Which is no hope, only torment. Theodosia is a box. Or the world is a box, or Theodosia is the world. I don't know. All I know is that *I cannot get out.* I keep the light, staring out the windows of the light house.

Be gone, Spirit. My world is this chamber of light, the walls are storm. You? The mere noise of the wind.

Reset. How did the Banker say to kill Typhon?

To goad him into manifesting as a man; and then hit him with something of his own being. The first requires merely making Typhon angry enough. The second merely requires making me angry enough.

A duel of lightning.

Describe the Lantern Room.

The lamp lenses focus the light into a bright beam sent far to sea. Beneath is clockwork gear to turn the lamp, once around a minute. I reset the clockwork pendulums every three hours, which is annoying but goes with the job. Tinker and Baker talk improvements. Tinker says we could make an electric fire if we had coal and a steam engine and copper wire and other things we don't.

It gets steamy up here by night. Placements of vents catch the sea wind for the lamp to burn the hotter. I feed it a supper of oil, and strike the light of the hollow wick, and then spend the night wiping the inner windows of the condensation so the light shines clearer. There is no knowing if any ship steers safer for this ritual of light. Alone in the lantern room it is hard to believe that past the windows there is a world of people and ships, of harbors and trains and houses and faces and parlors for tea. I could say 'you must trust', but there is no such rule. The light goes out into the dark, like a message in a bottle cast to the sea. There is no saying if it shall reach another.

I need more oil. A fellow from town named Heter is supposed to bring next month's supplies in his sloop. But the weather is playing games of late. Out of a blue sky the cat of a storm will pounce, looking for the bug of a boat.

Heter is a proper sailor but I worry he doesn't know how Captain Tempest bears me a grudge.

Cut-Throat comes by irregular, and we play chess and he tells me about the politics of the island. He's careful not to brag about married life; I'm cautious not to be a sour mope. Tinker and the Baker visit more often, having less to do. They still intend to sail back to noisier places but no ship has docked they trust to cross the seas. I told them about the Banker's sloop in the cave and they tracked it down.

It rested on a beach in a cave within the old volcano, just like something out of Captain Nemo. They've fitted it up and taken it out in the water a time or two. But they know they don't have the sail-craft to try and cross the ocean. Not yet. I'd like to see that cave, but I couldn't get there and back before sundown. I can't leave the light, you understand.

I am there now.

Describe a storm seen from the lighthouse.

I've picked up the knack for hearing the storm's footstep no matter how light it tiptoes. Sure, I have barometers to show the pressure is falling, and wind gauges announcing the wind is rising, and a view of the sea for miles about. But it's the color of the water, the color of the light, the static of the hair on my arms that sends me fastening window covers. Then-times the inside of the tower becomes a dark warm world of its own. Except for the lantern-room.

All last night I stared out at just such a sudden storm. The tower trembled, as did I. I heard voices in the wind, of laughing girls and crying men, howling beasts and growling machines. I stared into the dancing tempest that circled my tower, seeing faces and forms I could never dare to name, I, who knows the secret names of dead gods.

I looked down at the sea, white-foamed and mad, reaching up with waves to grab and pull at my tower. I thought *there is the original chaos*. Not darkness and light at war, not a random mix of cold and heat. Not a silence over a void awaiting a word. No, everything comes from this mindless rise and fall of waves upon the night-shore, and must return to it. I have come to rest upon the very edge of existence, shining a tiny light in a poetic foot-stamp of defiance.

Here I am now.

Describe a morning after a storm in the lighthouse.

Dawn pushes its way through clouds into the lantern room, an answer of light to light. I snuff the lamp wick, thinking of the mad fairy crowd I imagined whirling about the tower in the storm. I stare out now and see only gulls wheeling and shouting. But upon the outer side of the window seventy feet above the sea is a hand print, delicate and clear. I place my own rough hand against its smaller outline and shiver. Welcome to Theodosia.

I stretch, feeling the tension go out of the tower as it settles from its shaking. I consider making coffee but supplies are low. I should sleep. But it is part of my job to check the shore after a storm, to see what the tempest tossed. It's an augur's duty. Not to mention I need to get out of the tower or go mad.

I wind down the dark spiraling stairs, stopping to open the window shutters. Saves on candles, and lets a bit of breathable air into the tower. When I come to the great door I frown at dribbles of sea-water that made it past the iron frame. The waves washed high last night. I push and tug the door with a screech that says the hinges must be oiled again. Later, later.

I go walking the shore, watching the gulls, thinking how their wings resemble a girl's arched eyebrows staring down. I scan for colored shells. In all the time I have kept the light and searched the storm-drift I have yet to find a shell special enough to add to that box of perfect shells. Now I ask the gulls, why should I want to? Why hide a pretty shell in a box? Why not leave it to look pretty on the beach? I consider coming out here after a storm and scattering the whole box of shells. Why wait for the storm to do what I can do myself? I laugh and the gulls chuckle though they probably don't see the point.

I spot something gleaming out in the surf, splash idly towards it, careful of the little orange crabs. I scoop up something round and silver. An old Spanish coin, silver and scarred. For a second I am convinced I am holding our moon. I stare down surprised to see it in my hand instead of the sky.

Finally. Go home.
What?

Go home. To New Jersey. To your girl.
That was a long, long time ago. I can't leave. I am the keeper of Shipwreck Light in the Sea of Suns and Moons. She supposes me drowned, and who is to say I am not? And she's probably married now. Probably that is the last page of her diary. 'Happily ever after, a farmer's wife.' Read it aloud, spirit, and I will trade you a final piece of the Libris Fulminates.

No. No more trades. Not a page more. You can have the words of the girl or the girl herself. By the nature of the translation you will never hold them both. Go home and see what there is to hold.
Ha. But that'd be too long a voyage in too small a ship. Across the Sea of Time where the storm waits to balance accounts.

Don't give yourself airs. The storm is everyone's enemy. Gods, men, towers, ships, ants, the leaves of flowers. Dare it same as the rest of us; or else face a

**future staring out the light house window at ships
and sailors braver than you.**

It's a difficult proposition. Someone would have to
watch the light. Someone would have to crew the ship.
Who is to say what I would find when I arrived? Ah, and
I am old now.

Where are you?

In the Lantern Room, staring out the windows,
watching the sea and the clouds. Here I am now.

**Turn and look in the lantern mirror. Describe
yourself.**

Well, I see a skinny scarecrow of a young fellow, hair
floating about his head like a failed halo. He has green
eyes that look three-day fevered. He has a burn across an
arm, still a bit raw. He's shaking slightly like a tower in a
storm. He's holding a worn Spanish silver coin in his
hand as though afraid of it.

The coin. It's a gift of the tide, isn't it? And the moon
pulls the tide. Our moon. This is from K, telling me to
come home, come home, come home.

Chapter 31

Sermon #57, Upon a Marriage
Reverend Obadiah King, Maidenhead, New Jersey
October 15, 1888

Why are you good people here today? You'd be more comfortable abed, instead of sitting in stiff clothes in a cold church. Ah, but the flowers, the music, your happy faces are unmistakable signs. We must be here to celebrate a marriage.

Marriage? What is that? A legally binding paper signed by an ordained pomposity; a contractual agreement to combine properties and bodies for a sanitized and sanctified propagating of the species? Well enough, though better to perform the rite in a bank, with the joyful reception in a doctor's office.

Ah, but your scandalized faces remind me: Marriage is a thing for Church. Why? Because marriage is holy? So we are told. But what if we were not? What if we weighed the holiness of marriage in our own mortal scales?

Walk down a street in the world of your mind. Create a random couple; Mister and Missus So-and-so, married five days. So happy! If happiness were holiness, that would suffice. But now recreate them on the street five years married. Now ten years. Now twenty. Now thirty. Forty. Now fifty years, and that will do. Examine Mister and Missus So-and-so again. What do we see? Do those faded faces now glow with a sacred light? Do angels sing as they touch wrinkled hands? Does incense waft as they chat household expenses, argue over the dog?

I doubt it. You doubt it too. If your imagination is honest they look ordinary as dirt. You are now looking at the most inscrutable and least striking objects in the solar system: a couple grown old together.

But don't turn away. Look again! And realize they are dull to you because they are a mystery you are not invited to share. Those two old people communicate in a language spoken only between them. The clasp of their hands is a ceremony not for outsiders. Two people have combined lives to form their own culture, their own calendar and system of justice. And even their own secret church whose rites celebrate God by a name never to be revealed to you.

You observe the results of fifty years of marriage and your bored eye can gain no measure of its value or meaning except as mysterious lines across two faces. No bank balance, no registry of property, no diary nor neighbor's recollections shall translate those lines for you. They are a foreign script telling a tale not for you. A long-married couple are become a book writ in a language no outsider shall read.

Very well. Are we to conclude that mysterious book is somehow a holy text?

Yes!

The tale of two lives lived as one is the most sacred story that the Created shall ever narrate before Creation. All the rest of the tale of our lives we listen to as we live, wondering at our brief parts. Our birth and death and the daily travails of earning our bread, is a tale told us by another. But in the narrative of Marriage is it given us to be the tellers of the tale. A wondrous tale, a miraculous tale properly begun with choirs and flowers and great stone church walls echoing with song.

Marriage. A holy, comic story to make the angels stare astounded.

Interviewer: Describe arriving home.

Morning after a storm. Saturday. Cold. The blue sea of the sky showing white rips of cloud after the tempest. Branches down, strewn puddles reflecting shards of shattered sky. Gutter floods and dripping trees making a splashing fountain music. No a soul on the main street of Maidenhead, ominous to an augur's eye.

I hesitated, wondering whether to head to my family's house or straight to the Rectory. I longed for a sight of my loved ones and even my sisters. But then I saw the horses and carts at the Church. Saturday morning church meant a wedding. I headed there, my patient friends trailing behind.

I was ragged and wet, unshaven and no doubt the eyes in my face were fairly crazed. We had left the storm-damaged sloop in Trenton, rented a carriage to Maidenhead that rumbled and slid through the following storm. There had been no rest. Why drive myself and my friends and the poor horses so? Poet's instinct. My unraveling mind could only picture my return across the world as a minute too late. I foresaw I would rush through some door just in time to hear her pronounced dead or a farmer's wife if there's a difference.

We walked determinedly up the storm-wet steps of the church past astonished ushers.

Within was candle-light and the low bustle of a crowd attempting respectful silence. Rustling of starched clothes, coughs, children fidgeting and kicking the pews. Before the altar stood a bride in white next to a farmer in black. She wore a veil but I knew his pale face. *Smeed.* Before them stood K's father, looking grayer and more stooped, but slier for extra practice since I'd departed. He was playing low solemn notes on his holy voice, not yet delivering the final thunder of 'man and wife'.

Cut-Throat, Tinker and the Baker hesitated at the door, unsure. But I walked ahead down the aisle. Different faces turned towards me. The service stopped in its tracks.

Go back. Describe leaving the island of Theodosia.

Once decided, I had to stop myself from running out the tower and over the mountain to the harbor. I burned to be away before some change of weather becalmed my decision. But I'd grown journey-wise since I'd fled down the road from home and tea. First thing I did, I oiled the hinges of that iron door. Then I mopped the sea water out, cleaned all the tower best I could. I closed the shutters tight against the next storm to come. Lastly I cleaned the lantern room windows and filled the lamp to the brim with oil. I did not light it.

Then I got out my pack and wondered what to take. Clothes, razor, some provisions. I went to the box of seashells and selected one random example of beauty and purpose in Creation. Now I saw the point of putting pretty shells in a box. It was so you could take them out of the box. I went to the shelf of ship's logs and took down a tattered book that had puzzled me soon as I saw it. That went into the pack. Then I went down to the first floor to the ship's figurehead of an elephant. I tugged on a tusk. He swung open like a cabinet door, winking an eye at me and revealing a niche with a bag of coins. Sea-flotsam treasure, property of the Keeper of the Light. I took half, feeling guilty for that much.

There was a knock. I went up to the second floor and looked down to see who rapped, tapped at my chamber door, because Theodosia. But it was Heter come with the monthly supplies. I welcomed him and together we carried barrels of provisions into the tower. I chattered the whole time though I can't remember now a word I said. I was starting to feel dizzy.

"You alright?" he asked concerned.

I explained I had found a Spanish silver coin in the tide and had to leave immediately. That logic seemed clear at the time. Then I handed him the key and asked him to tell the sabbatical I was taking a Governor. I shook his hand several times and hurried away, then went back and retrieved my pack by the door, shook his hand again and walked away again, then considered and went back and asked him a favor. Being a sailor and a good sort, he promised to do it. I left his hand alone, said goodbye again and hurried off.

Describe the book you took with you from Shipwreck Light.

Remember Unicorn's ship log? It had pages written in a cypher of bird prints. Well this whole book was filled with the same writing. The prints of birds. That's good as a finger print telling you Thoth's committed another crime. If I make it home I'll put it someplace where you can find it when the clock reaches your stretch of years.

I don't... I don't think that would work. On the other hand, why not? I no longer have any clue where the boundaries are here. Mail it to the New Jersey Archive of Rural Letters, attention 'Clarence'. If the tide floats it my way I'll have a look at it.

Thanks. Consider it a souvenir of the trip, since the sea shell is for K.

Pity. I like shells. Describe leaving Theodosia.

My plan was to stop at the Green to say goodbye, then head on to the harbor. There I'd hire what crew I could to sail the Banker's sloop to San Francisco. There were some decent fishing sailors in the harbor. Between the coins from the light house and title to the ship when we arrived, I thought I could persuade a crew.

I didn't make it to the Green, though I got as far as the gate. There I found Cut-Throat already packed and waiting. He leaned against a tree playing a mournful tune on his fiddle. A storm-bird circled overhead, no doubt the source of the alert. Thoth's a helpful old busy-body.

I tried to persuade Cut-Throat to back out; he was a married man. And if he went adventuring the Green might return to its murderous ways. He clapped me on the back cheerful-like and told me to shut the hell up. I said what about his poor bride? At which fatuous words he laughed in my face. I had trouble not laughing too. Ligeia wasn't a workable subject for expressions of pity.

Cut-Throat had already told her sailor-like, how he was off with the tide. She'd just kissed him and promised to *meet us when we arrived.*

Which was cryptic. But we knew better than to question cryptic on Theodosia. So the New York Cut-Throat and I shook hands and went looking for the Tinker and the Baker to reform the fool's crew.

Describe sailing away from Theodosia.

First thing off I warned my friends: sailing with me invited Typhon's attention. Deity was forgetful. Perhaps he'd wander away to settle for smiting some unlucky descendent in a century. If he did show I had a hint of an idea how we could trip him up. But all said, my presence at sea equaled a cargo of lightning-rods, broken mirrors and black cats.

The crew looked unimpressed. They consulted privately. Finally Cut-Throat announced as spokesman for my shipmates how they felt a great and abiding weariness with my eternal sorrowful moping. Which was slander I'd been damned stoic. Tinker then stated that either we all went and got the girl now, or they'd fetch her kicking and screaming to Theodosia themselves and dump her on the lighthouse doorstep. Which wouldn't impress a girl much, Tinker pointed out.

At the time the easy courage of my friends cheered me. Later on ship in the final, dreadful storm, I wondered at my easy acceptance of their risk. Courage is a wonder, Spirit. So is selfishness, but for a different kind of wondering.

We hiked towards the shore cave, discussing the needs of the ship. The Baker announced that they had re-christened it the 'Annabelle'.

"Why 'Annabelle'?" I asked.

"Rhymes well," said the Baker. "Annabelle, ring the bell, what the hell." Tinker giggled. Baker informed us it was a two-masted Jamaican sloop. He being Jamaican I supposed he'd know. He thought a crew of five could handle it easy though he warned the sails wanted more tending than those of a schooner. It needed a proper sailing master, and that wasn't any of us. As we hiked to the cave we argued whether to sail it to the harbor and hire a fisherman or just learn as we went.

But when we reached the shore we spotted the Annabelle already floating peaceful at anchor a hundred yards out. The others feared she was being stolen, but the figure at the helm waved a bright red sleeve that told me otherwise. I explained happily as we maneuvered a rowboat unsteadily towards the ship. We the fool's crew now had the patron deity of sailors herself for our captain. Her presence made the venture a new proposition entirely.

"I've always wanted to steer one of these things," Matsu said by way of greeting. These words put the venture back on the dubious side.

"You're the patron goddess of sailors," I said, disbelieving. "What do you mean, 'always wanted to'?"

"I warn of storms," she said. "I am the keeper of the keepers of the lights. I aid the drowning and gather the drowned. This is the first I've been at the wheel of a ship still happily above water. But how difficult can it be?"

She took her place by the helm, tugging the wheel this way and that experimentally. Eventually my pondering silence annoyed her. She shook her divine hair, rolled her divine eyes.

"Go swab something," said Captain Matsu, dismissing me.

Describe leaving Theodosia.

Annabelle set sail with the tide's evening swell. Island and day slipped away together, replaced by sea and stars. I stood at the railing watching the northern shore turn to a purple line. Behind me the Baker and Matsu argued what a gaff rig did and if it was good to prevent jibbing by fooling with the bigger sail. I didn't find it in me to be pro-jibbing or anti-jibbing, as long as we kept moving. And we did, under a strong wind that headed us west and south.

I watched Theodosia disappear and found I no longer believed in it. Skeptical twilight became dogmatic night. Then, unbelieving but still desiring, I received my sign: the beam from Shipwreck Light. It swept across the sky clear and beautiful. I, the Keeper of the light, had not conceived how it scythed through the night, the sword of an angel warning storm and dark to keep their damned distance.

I'd asked Heter to stay and tend the lamp a few days just so as we could see it as we left. Now it made me feel I'd set something right, something that wished me a safe journey. A *quick* journey by the likes of it; the wind kept rising. The hairs on my arm stood, and from the corner of my eyes I saw flickers of blue fire in the waves and the clouds and across the back of my hand.

It was a storm wind hurrying us out to open sea.

Describe interrupting the wedding.

I'm not sure anyone recognized the ragged Byronic figure as he strode down the church aisle straight towards the bride. Smeed stepped between his fiancé and what must have seemed a dangerous lunatic. Which showed him more a gentleman than I'd have credited his rural soul. He was going to take a swing at me and I would duck as he did and then deck him fast. Then the groomsmen were scheduled to beat me to the floor.

The bride altered that entire history with a single scream. "Clarence!"

I held out my arms and she rushed forward, striking me hard across the head with her flower bouquet. "You idiot!" she swore. "You've ruined my wedding!"

I knew that killer left swing, despite the veil. The bride was my sister *Alice*.

"You're marrying *Smeed*?" I asked astounded.

"You're *alive*?" asked Smeed.

"You're marrying my *sister*?"

"Are you *insane*?" demanded Smeed.

"Me insane?" I asked outraged. "You're the one marrying her." So Alice hit me again then turned sentimental, worse than the weather. She hugged her resurrected brother tight not caring if his grimed sailor clothes stained her bridal uniform. I hugged back, knowing she'd pendulum over to violence soon enough. Smeed was in for a rough sail but that was his field to plow.

There followed a squall of hugs and tears. I have a large family, and they'd noticed my absence more than I expected. Blazes, I'd assumed they thought I was still in the attic. Meanwhile Reverend King stood there fizzing and fulminating. I watched him contort his soul to put a happy mask over an honest snarl. It made him twitch unpleasantly so I turned about, searching for the face and voice I wanted.

"Gracious," gasped Aunt Agatha. "What in Heaven's name is happening up there?"

I turned and looked up to the choir balcony. Five young ladies stood ready to sing hymns, white robes making them appear unlit candles. Four of the five. The fifth candle was alight. In blue fire that writhed about her pretty form like burning snakes bathed in brandy and sprinkled with gunpowder.

K held out a hand, staring astounded. She moved to the balcony and leaned down to stare at me even more astonished. I held a blazing hand up in return, matching her gesture.

"Now we're finally seeing a bit of St. Elmo's fire," I said. The words rang off the stone walls. I said them *loud*.

Describe rejoining K.

We sat in the balcony and watched Alice marry Smeed, Smeed marry Alice. As marriage is a dance its best said they did it together. He'd grown a thick mustache that anchored his pale face. Alice had grown a bigger bosom though I recall she'd stuff paper thereabouts when she was a kid last year. I didn't say so. I just sat next to K happy past mortal measure, while troops maneuvered about our position.

First offensive charge was K's mother who tried to sit between us; but our wall held. We clasped hands tight. So

391

K's mother led Aunts Hildegard, Plain and Greta to sniper positions in the pew behind Then Agatha and Jane took flank to our left and right. Not to attack; they were allies providing us cover. Not that a one of them belonged in the choir balcony being tone-deaf biddies.

K leaned her head close to my shoulder. "Father wrote a letter saying you no longer cared," she whispered. "He tossed your real letters without telling me. But our moonlight led me to them. Then I knew you loved me, though I supposed you drowned. I didn't feel like marrying Henry any more. I never much wanted to. It was just a thing to pass the days. So I ended the engagement and Alice swooped him up like something that, that swoops and grabs a thing for swooping."

"An eagle, a turtle," I suggested.

"A girl, a poet," suggested K.

"A poet, a girl," I countered, but I liked hers too. It was mutual swooping.

She smiled. "I don't understand how your letters even went through the post. They had such strange stamps. Were you actually shipwrecked on a mad island called Theodosia? Have you really been dueling and drowning and burning down asylums?"

"Would I make such things up?" I asked hurt.

She laughed in my face, sending her warm breath to mix with mine. "Of course," she said. "If you thought it would make me smile. Father insisted it was all poetic lunacy. I ceased listening." K looked suddenly alarmed.

She stared down at our clasped hands. "I, I'm not *dreaming*, am I?"

I looked into her eyes. "I believe in your love for me. Believe in my love for you." I advanced towards a kiss. A fusillade of hisses from behind forced strategic retreat. She took my hand and opened it palm up, feeling the callouses of a rigger. She traced a finger up the lightning-bite. "I do wish I could see your mad island."

"I'll show it to you," I affirmed, clasping her hand tight again. There came a fresh volley of hisses and nevers from behind. "Ssshhhh," an usher admonished the battle. I turned my gaze to the wedding to see Alice staring up powerful annoyed at the balcony. I clapped on a solemn face.

Not turning to her, I said something K didn't hear.

I said it louder.

"What?" she whispered.

"Marry me," I said louder. The aunt to the left fired "*Finally*," and the Aunt to the right shot off a "Ha!" but the troops behind rallied with cannonades of hisses that ricocheted off the walls. "Ssshhhh," pled the usher. The bride at the altar looked to be contemplating a charge up the stairs to beat both armies to peace with that bouquet. I did my best to keep a solemn quiet. K did the same but now she was shaking beside me. Fear, laughter, joy, I don't know. I do know she held my hand tight.

Eventually Alice and Henry were pronounced Man and Wife and told to go live happy. The best possible advice. K stood with her friends to sing a recessional hymn. Her mother fired me a glare, I returned a friendlyish smile. Agatha puffed her lips to blow at my frail form. I pretended to be knocked back by the blast and she laughed.

K and I filed out of the church sheltering in the crowd. We clapped, threw rice and waved, all while still holding hands. I don't say we did these things *well*. There were more troop maneuvers and I found Cut-Throat, Tinker and the Baker standing beside us plus three of my sisters hoping for a fight. We faced off against the very Reverend and his reserves. I felt confident enough of the tide of battle that I introduced my friends, ragged and wet as myself.

Reverend King had no choice but to nod polite. But he shook no hands. Cut-Throat bowed to K and said 'Is this the face that launched a poet?' which didn't make a lick of sense but her laugh allowed Cut-Throat to mistake her charity for his charm.

I turned to K. "Miss King, if I may have the pleasure of calling upon you *soon?*"

She smiled. "I shall look *forward* to it, Mr. St. Elmo."

We took our separate ways.

What happened after the wedding?

I led my friends to my parent's house, but of course the wedding reception filled it with a happy crowd. I wasn't a bit afraid Alice would thrash us but just in case we burgled through the back and barricaded the third floor. There we could do some bathing and cleaning and resting. I talked to my folks, introducing my shipmates.

Cut-Throat mistakenly thought it amusing to enact renditions of how I'd crossed a storm-tossed ocean to interrupt the wrong wedding. The man has a dull streak. But Tinker and the Baker praised K, saying she was clearly worth the long trip. Which was mere truth, and yet good to hear from sensible souls.

I weighed putting on my best clothes for a proper evening visit. The same clothes waited in the closet that I'd worn the day of the Tea of Catastrophe. I shook my head and made it a mix of a clean shirt and freshened sailor pants. Cleaned and shaved I stared at myself in the mirror. I looked a strange sort of person. That was alright, I was a poet, unconcerned with convention. A Lord Byron on a lighter key.

Byronic like, I set off at sunset to steal my girl.

You're going to *elope*?

I sure as blazes am not going back to courting K. at tea in her father's parlor. I've had enough of operating theaters, thank you.

We pulled the carriage up to the Rectory. Every window in the house was lit. Perhaps a bright omen, perhaps dark. My brave friends wished me well from the safety of the carriage. I walked up to the door, collected my courage and before I could knock Aunt Agatha opened and hissed. "Go round the side you idiot. Don't you know how to do these things proper?"

I felt relieved, glad an expert was on hand. I headed to the side of the house. Under K's window I found Aunt Jane holding a ladder.

"Can't we use the stairs?" I asked. She looked so downcast I sighed and climbed up the ladder. The rungs were slippery. I reached K's window and peered in worried that if she was dressing I would not be able to shield my eyes gentleman-like while holding on to the ladder safely. I would just have to look.

But she was already dressed and waiting, a bag packed. She opened the window. Being a poet on a ladder under my love's window, I recited the end of our poem.

"We laughed as our gazes met.
We rested while the moon set.
Then rose as the sun rose,
Then we went on together,
Hands clasped tight forever."

It's a strange thing. When K's father recited the same words it sounded awful. But it did fine now. She bent down to give me a kiss that went on until Aunt Jane began shaking the ladder. So I took the bag and descended. K followed while I stared firmly at the ground so as not to be peering up her skirt. Then I worried that if she fell I wouldn't know to catch her so I looked up and

Jane boxed my ear like I was a ten-year old. Damnable aunt.

Soon as K was on the ground she gave me a proper hug, romantic-souled Aunt Jane sighing happily. Naturally to complete the theater her father stalked on stage from around the house followed by two servants, K's embarrassed brother and a dog resembling a skinny wolf. The very Reverend held a shotgun that gleamed in the window lights.

"Past enough of your foolishness, boy."

"No," I said firmly. "You are the one here with the surplus of foolishness. I love your daughter. She loves me. Now's your chance to make peace with it."

He stared, honestly puzzled. It confounded the man's inner mirror when a body failed to be intimidated by his voice and prophetic aura. So he made the shotgun give a threatening 'click' and the servant-girl reached over and took it away. He tried to hold on but her pale little arm was entirely unimpressed. I knew that strength, those braids, particularly by night. I laughed. The wolf-dog laughed too, making K's brother jump in astonishment.

I took K's hand. "We have a tide to catch," I said. It's what sailors say. I didn't know tides from Tibet but the phrase communicated my desire to leave. She hesitated, looking at her father. She stepped to him and gave a quick hug. The fool didn't return it. He stared in outrage at the servant girl toying fascinated with his shotgun, which was just another reason to leave *now*.

397

K sighed, grabbed my hand and we hurried to the front. The servant girl and the wolf-dog followed. When we neared the carriage Cut-Throat jumped out and ran to her. Ligeia tossed the gun into the garden where it landed with a 'boom' clearing out the rectory rose-bushes and making most of the township jump.

K and I studied how a professional married couple re-unites, taking notes. At last we all climbed into the carriage and departed.

Go back. How did you sail past Typhon?

Porpoises leaped and dove along the sides of the sloop, pacing it across the sea. Perhaps they guided us, or else merely accompanied our Captain. Perhaps they were drowned sailors wishing for a chance to handle that ship proper. Also perhaps they were dolphins.

The wind blew so we did not sail; we flew, occasionally bumping waves with the hull. Annabelle was a smaller vessel than Unicorn, her deck closer to the water. Waves splashed across, spray blew into our faces. There was a tiny galley; I gave myself the job of ship's cook, making what meal I could for the others. My guilt and fear rose with each knot of wind. Why had I brought my friends into such danger?

I went back out and stared astonished. Behind the ship followed a wall of cloud reaching from sea to sky. Lightning-shot mountains of storm wherein roiled dragons and angels, eyes and volcanos twisting and turning in a mad-man's mind of unleashed wind and light.

The Baker tended the main sail under shouted directions from Captain Matsu, directions that sounded suspiciously like '*How about now? Anything?*' I took his place so he could get some supper. My feet were learning all over again how to shift and balance on a deck. Unicorn had never traveled this fast.

I staggered towards the wheel, where Matsu stood, long free hair standing out a black flag shifting with the wind.

"Him," I shouted. She nodded absently, then grinned. She leaned close to whisper. "I've always wanted to take that self-righteous bastard down to sea-level."

Whispers hid nothing from the storm. In flat reply a bolt shot over our heads. It was existence itself cracking open to reveal the background machinery of reality: an engine room of terrible light. Matsu tossed her hair defiantly but I cowered, recalling the slaughter of the ex-gods in the burning Asylum. I wondered if the ship could be spared by tossing the Jonah to the waves. I went to the rail and considered. A storm bird alighted beside me; long legs bending with the wind, feet holding tight.

"Don't even think it," said the god of wisdom.

"This is madness," I said, staring at the following storm. "What the hell was I thinking?"

Thoth shrugged winged shoulders. "Like the spirit voice said, the storm is everyone's foe. Gods, men, birds. No point in thinking you are special."

"Aha!" I cried. "Then you *can* hear him."

The bird gave me a weary look.

"Anyway he was flat wrong," I added bitterly. "This storm has me especially singled out. Chosen. Marked. Elected. Slated. Condemned. Cursed."

Ask Thoth about the Libris Acherontia.

Oh shut up about your damned book.

"Tell him I'll answer his questions later," Thoth said.

Thoth informed me sorrowfully that the secrets of the Libris were too deep to ever be revealed.

What? He didn't say that.

I could no longer hear clearly, the wind shouted so. I went back into the galley hoping if I hid there then the storm would leave off. It didn't, of course. It blew us south and east following the clipper winds at a rate to clear the Cape of Good Hope and reach New England faster than if we'd cut across Panama.

Will someone please describe the Libris Fulgurales?

This was pretty much the last page:

The holiness of lightning is in its purpose. Though it sets a dead tree ablaze, frights a dog or slays a king, what is struck is revealed by a light that makes no judgment, only resolution.

The purpose of lightning is to reveal that all things are holy because they stand against the storm. The thunder shouts that every existence is a creation of the gods. Existence itself is purpose; and so all things have holy purpose; the stones that roll, the ants that toil, even the gods who are mere wind and wave, scudding clouds and rolling stones, inevitable and impersonal as the stars that watch beyond and above the storm.

It sounded better in French.

Fine. Finish with the storm.

Typhon played cat and bug, catching us, releasing us, allowing the sloop to escape to clear skies then pouncing again from a different direction. Yet always storm winds rushed the Annabelle forwards. We stopped for supplies in Adelaide and rounded the Cape following dolphins and whales that knew the sea-road better than any sailor. Days passed in a fever of wind and sleep and repetition. As we turned north towards the equator the ice melted from the deck, the morning air grew warm.

Captain Matsu seldom left the wheel, though she expected me to bring her regular coffee. The gods drink plentiful coffee, explaining much. In off hours Cut-Throat played his fiddle for crew and porpoises. Tinker sat at the table designing a chess-playing automaton. Chatting with the ex-seminary students had exposed her to the fever to build a mechanical mind. The Baker sat beside her, his heart still dwelling in dreams of simple and practical death-machines. Currently he was designing a Typhon-gun.

The Annabelle had a harpoon cannon set to the stern, in case it bumped into a whale. When we stopped in Adelaide the Baker returned with a lightning rod he loaded in place of the harpoon. Inwardly I thought this was asking for trouble but it made him happy. He kept the Typhon-gun polished and loaded, an oil cloth covering the muzzle from the wet. I considered firing it at the tormenting storm. It would make a courageous poetic gesture; which is to say, a pointless 'pop' of defiance.

The east coast of the U.S. was to port. I began spending my time in the bow, peering in the distance for the first glimpse of New England. The storm-cat grinned and moved up closer behind, pacing along both sides. It intended to swallow us in sight of the lights of home.

There came a night of wind that ripped every last sail. We reefed the tatters. Captain Matsu ordered us to bring rope. In an ecstasy of dramatic gesture she tied herself to the wheel and told her crew to stay below deck till dawn. But around midnight I heard a voice calling me awake. I went out on deck, half-thinking I was back on Unicorn again. I stared at the sea in horror. The cat-play was over, all the world was storm. Behind, and to each side; and now ahead as well. We were caught in a closing circle of wind and wave meaning to break us and drown us.

The ropes at the helm hung empty. Matsu had vanished. The wheel spun in random turns of wave and wind. I wondered had she ever existed. Perhaps we'd hallucinated her. The gods deceive us all; unless we just do it ourselves.

I splashed across the deck to the bow, searching for a sign of her red dress, hoping for some glimpse of the lights of home. I watched dolphins leap into the storm and back to watery peace. I saw faces of drowned sailors float close to the surface to peer curiously up at me as though through green glass. Figures of unearthly beauty rode the waves, white arms waving, long hair wreathed in sea-weed garlands. I even spied the pale ogre face of the Banker, shouting something I did not care to hear. But these were mere audience. I dared myself to look up into the storm itself, higher than the sky, lightning-crowned, dragons for legs.

"Get the hell out of my way or you'll regret it," I told the storm. Which was decent bluster. In reply thunder rumbled an appreciative chuckle and a bolt blasted the top of the main mast. It shattered, bringing down ropes and fiery splinters. So that was that. Time to make Typhon angry. I'd figured the quickest way of doing *that* days ago. I took my clasp-knife and slashed my lightning-bit arm to drip the blood on the wave-washed deck. I did my best to snarl, though it came out more a gasp.

"I propitiate you, old god."

The thunder snarled, no longer amused. And Typhon appeared on deck before me, arms crossed in anger.

"*Not. A. God,*" he said. Each word spat a separate bolt of disgust.

"How humble," I spat back. "But you play with our lives. You stamp your divine foot on our offending mortal heads. So accept the title, wear the crown." I splashed some of the blood his way. "Drink up."

Typhon strode closer, furious. I backed towards the stern, terrified.

"I warned you," he said. "You made your choice."

"Liar," I replied. That stopped him. He stared surprised, eyebrows arched over those dying-sun eyes. The words poured out of me in a shout. "You led me at each turn while barking for me to go the other way. I chose *exactly* as you hoped. You allowed me the books. You rescued us in the Asylum, saved me in the duel. It was your fire that led through the Acherontia. It was even your threats that kept me on Theodosia to re-fire the lighthouse."

Typhon brushed these annoying truths away with a bolt that hit the deck, knocking me flat. He shook his head. "You think yourself angry at being used. You declare yourself filled with rage for a few months of confusion and despair. Carry it ten thousand years, poet, and I will accept your anger as peer to my own."

I struggled up, holding on to the harpoon cannon. A useless toy. I needed to hit Typhon with his own lightning. How had I struck Iskandar with lightning in the duel? By clasping something metal. I dug into my pocket, came up with the silver coin, held it tight in a hand dripping gouts of blood and blue fire.

Meanwhile Typhon studied the harpoon-cannon, lightning-rod poking from the muzzle. He was fascinated. The gods are easily distracted. "Are you going to shoot *me* with a *cannon*?" he asked. "That's so poetic." He moved directly in front, arms out wide. He grinned, and to give me a boost of anger began to recite.

By a dead fountain, on a bed of stone,
In a hall of silence, I awoke alone…

The silver coin in my fist blazed a bright ball of lightning. I threw it. He might have dodged but storm gods do not think defensively. It struck him and he burst into blue flame. With a roar he sent a bolt at me. It swerved to hit the cannon. There shouted a *boom* of entirely mechanical thunder. The cannon flew apart, Typhon went flying into the sea while I tumbled against the railing hard.

When I awoke the sea was calm, the ship drifting. A gull sat on the remains of the mast, holding wings open in celebration of the storm's end. Tinker stretched me out to apply bandages. I hurt, and was back to not hearing anything so don't bother asking. The Baker sighed and returned to carpentry, jury-rigging us a mast. He was put out with the loss of his cannon.

Our Captain was gone, but her dolphins continued to guide us as we made repairs and headed to port. Wind and wave were apologetically kind and helpful. You never saw a sea and sky more anxious to see a poor ship safely to harbor.

Well. That was a tale full of sound and thunder. So what did it all signify?

I don't know. I never saw Typhon again, not as man nor storm. I don't know if he died struck by his own lightning, or if he simply accepted thunder for thunder and called the debt even. I do know that when I threw the glowing ball of fire I saw one last conspiratorial wink. And that was enough. The gods put me in the story; but they were not telling the tale for me.

But I am certain Typhon, Matsu and Thoth conspired together to open the Acherontia for return and re-establish the Shipwreck Light. Perhaps the sly god of wisdom convinced the old revolutionary that such a return is no mere continuation. It is change; requiring destruction and re-creation.

Perhaps so convinced, he arranged to travel that path himself. After all, it'd be a poor storm-god who never dared his own lightning.

Chapter 32

Dearest Mama and Papa,

It is strange to think of you ice-bound in New England winter while here the world is so green and warm that we sigh happily with a cool wind off the sea. And yet I do miss skating upon the park lake, and the joy of hot chocolate by a fire, and speeding in a sleigh under thick quilts, and the sight of snowflakes falling in lamp-light. Almost as much as I miss the faces of those I left to the cold.

Do not be angry with us for eloping. Truly it was for the best. Your disapproval of my sailor-poet was such that there could be no reconciliation unless by years of patient visits he wore away your frowns. He loves me enough to have so endured; but truly I would have gone mad first. I almost did. Now I am whole, and happy, and as you only wished my best I believe that news shall sound sweet to you.

Clarence and I keep the light upon the island of Theodosia, in a great five-story tower upon the edge of the sea. Yet close enough to town and friends so that we do not startle to hear the bell rung at the door. Keeper of Shipwreck Light is no menial position. Indeed your son-in-law has the respect of all the island, as one holding an important and special office. Father always ironically admonished me not to marry a reverend, a minister or aught that gained employment through enactment of ceremony. But Providence has sent his daughter to keep a light for others, and she is the happier for the irony.

With that light and with these words, I send you my love. Though as my love is with you now, the light and the words shall cross the seas to find the love already there. Ha; that is how one learns to talk when one dwells in a tower with a poet.

I am happy. Therefore be happy for me; and happy for yourselves, as having raised a daughter who found her way home through storm.

Interviewer: describe your return to Theodosia.

Gracious, who is speaking?

Poet?

Oh! You are the spirit voice from the future he told me of. I don't think I really believed in you. Shame on me.

You are *K*? You can hear the interviewing team?

If that monstrosity is you, I hear well enough. But Clarence is sleeping. Ah, you can't *see* us, can you?

No; this is purely a matter of words.

Well, good. So then, my husband is asleep after a long night. Shall I get used to saying that? My husband? But he was showing me how he could carry a barrel of oil up the stairs without resting. Personally I would have rested and saved myself a bruised back; but isn't it sweet he wants to impress his bride?

Mr. St. Elmo is asleep?

Yes, and snoring. He had a busy night, poor thing.

Describe the busy night.

It stormed. We watched from the lantern room. Around midnight came a knocking at the door of the lighthouse, which was astonishing considering the tempest. Clarence took a lamp and I took a pistol, and we went down the stairs and opened to see who called.

Two figures stood in the dark and the rain. They wore heavy cloaks like old monks, and stood faceless and waiting till my husband bid them enter. They did; and then he led them down the stairs into the lower part of the tower he calls the dark chamber. He did not take the lantern, and you will understand why, Mr. Interviewing Team. The cat followed, as it does. I stayed to tend the light.

In the morning he was back. I asked him 'who'? and he said it was a good friend and a good enemy, who needed a guide through a dark part of the island. And that's all I'm going to say about it.

Now let him *rest,* Mr. Interviewing Team.

Absolutely. Let the man sleep. Say, while he snores, would you mind looking about for a scroll of pages, half in French and half in something that looks Greek but isn't? It's just something he promised to discuss with us when he had time. Hmm. Perhaps it would be best to awaken him…

No, no let's not do that. I'm sure I saw that very thing in the lantern room. I can't see it would do any harm if I fetch it and answer your questions, particularly if it means letting the poor boy sleep.

Oh yes. Definitely let him sleep. We'll wait here. No, wait we'll go along. Describe what you see. Describe the stairs. Describe something. Describe *anything*.

End

The poet's eye, in fine frenzy rolling,
Doth glance from heaven to earth, from earth to heaven;
And as imagination bodies forth
The forms of things unknown, the poet's pen
Turns them to shapes and gives to airy nothing
A local habitation and a name."

- A Midsummer Night's Dream, Act 5, Scene 1

About the Author:

Raymond St. Elmo wandered into a degree in Spanish Literature, which gave him no job but a love of Magic Realism. Moving on to a degree in programming gave him a job and an interest in virtual reality and artificial intelligence, which lead him back into the world of magic realism. Author of 4 books (all first-person literary fictions, possibly comic). He lives in Texas.

Made in United States
North Haven, CT
03 February 2024

48282082R00225